THE BATTLE FOR THE SKY

IN THE SHADOW OF A MONSTER

VOLUME I

DALILA CARYN

Evil Goddess
—— Press ——

Cover art and design by Yenthe Joline

(Hardcover) ISBN: 978-1-7338845-4-9
(Paperback) ISBN:978-1-7338845-8-7
(E-book) ISBN: 978-1-7338845-5-6
Library of Congress Control Number:
2022902544

Evil Goddess
—— Press ——

For Alethea Kontis whose characters I love, because trying to write in your style, helped me embrace my own! Thank you for the inspiration.

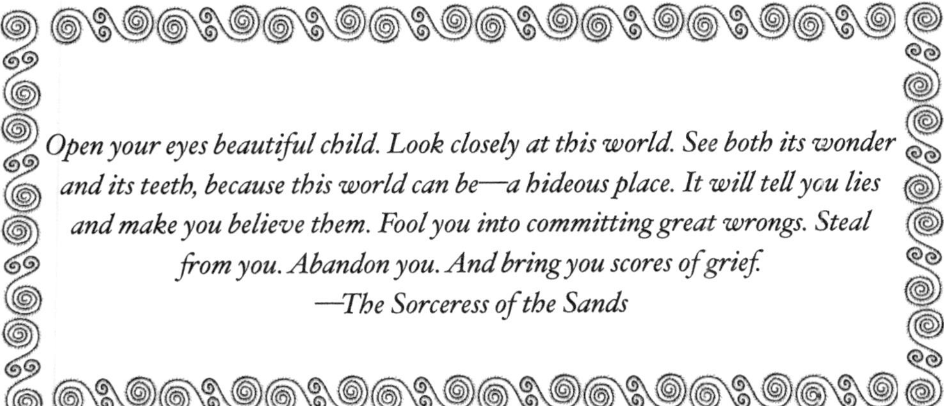

Open your eyes beautiful child. Look closely at this world. See both its wonder and its teeth, because this world can be—a hideous place. It will tell you lies and make you believe them. Fool you into committing great wrongs. Steal from you. Abandon you. And bring you scores of grief.
—The Sorceress of the Sands

THE MYSTERY

DRUM BEATS

Heavy drum beats sounded like a pulse, with a second and a half between the fall of the mallets. There was only one dancer on the floor as the music began, *the sun*. She began crouched, but with each beat of the drum she pulsed slowly higher, dawning over the floor, welcoming the other dancers. Nur, the great spirit of the sun was male in all the legends, but Isoke was one of the nations best dancers and had a commanding godlike presence that was well suited to Nur.

Hadhi watched the performance among her family: her mother, her sister, Nuru, and her baby brother Lin, in the arms of his mother, Sabra, Father's third wife. The Spirit Dancers were opening the ball before all the prominent citizens of Jaccada gathered to welcome home their prince after five years of absence.

As a rapid tingle of the tanno chimes reached over the air, the rest of the dancers raced out, each with their own form of motion to represent their character. There were seven traditional characters for any performance by the Spirit Dancers: The sun, the sand, the jungle, the animals—represented as predator and prey—and the nation—represented as its king and one dancer each for the five tribes that comprised its people.

Hadhi glanced sidelong at her younger sister, Nuru was stretching her arm out in an arc, unconsciously elongating her spine as the gazelle dancers were. Nuru would be among them one day. She deserved to be. No one surrendered so fully to the movement of life, happy, sad, angry, shy, Nuru embraced all with the same gusto. She should be a spirit dancer.

A dancer leapt out, just before Hadhi with his hands curled like claws and sharp teeth painted over his lips, the cheetah. Hadhi's pulse leapt, but in no other way did she react. She pretended not to hear the stifled laughter behind her family.

Would they laugh if it had happened to anyone but her? Yenge might be a false cheetah, but she had a right to be scared even of him, did she not? None of their children had ever been mauled. If she was her half-sister, Asha, no one would laugh. They would shame Yenge for even making the joke. Hadhi would never let anyone joke so with Nuru. So why was it acceptable as long as it was only done to her?

Ignoring her neighbors, Hadhi let her eyes be drawn across the room, to the ball's honored guests, Prince Azize had returned home with an odd collection of foreign men. Hadhi doubted very many of the men were even from the same nations as one another. As a group, they appeared to be older than the twenty-year-old prince, and most had the bearing of soldiers, unlike the timid boy who had collected them. They were his body guards, protecting him from his home. From his father. Hadhi supposed she couldn't blame him for wanting that, but sympathy aside, she didn't like the prince.

He was barely paying attention to the dance. Hadhi doubted he had even noticed that this one was designed especially for him. The dancers who represented the nation were throwing gifts at the king dancer's feet, bowing and leaping as he walked among them with hands raised to announce their prince's return. Azize was busy talking; he chewed on his lips and stood on the outsides of his feet, and from across the room Hadhi could see his pulse racing. He was embarrassed by the display. Embarrassed of his nation and his place in it. As he had always been. Hadhi ground her teeth, fighting hard to conceal her dislike for the boy she was here to trick into marriage, like every other unmarried woman present.

As her eyes were slipping away, Hadhi noticed one of Azize's friends was watching the dance enraptured. He stood closest to Azize and seemed to be the one Azize was speaking to, but unlike the prince, this man's entire attention was on the dance. His breath caught, and Hadhi's eyes chased after his direction to see what he saw. *The sand*: Faizah was indeed a lovely woman, but Hadhi did not think her beauty was what captured the man's attention. He was holding his breath. Did he notice the stillness falling over the other dancers as she came forward, approaching the bobbing dancers with their arms locked, to represent the boat bringing Azize home? Or had he only noticed that she was walking towards Azize, in slow whirling steps? Every few moments nearly turning back, as her being reached out for Azize. All at once the music took on a frantic rush of joy, the animal dancers leapt around Faizah, obscuring her from view, allowing the sun to adorn her with a crown and a thin golden shawl, to show that she was not just representing the desert, but a particular spirit who dwelled there: Queen Imara. Hadhi's heart went out to the dancer on the floor. Though she knew it was not Azize's mother, she couldn't help but feel for her pain, couldn't help but feel the pull to rush forward and wish her joy in the next life, to beg to know if she had found it. Imara had found so little joy in this life.

Hadhi watched Azize cringe and his friend nearly start forward in wrapt wonder, as Faizah stretched a hand out to Azize, beckoning him out among the dancers, welcoming him home as the spirit of his mother. For a moment, Azize's face displayed resentment and shame, then he blinked and painted on the sort of smile Hadhi was meant to be wearing. He stepped out, joining the dance.

Hadhi watched the young prince stumble through the dance, watched everyone pretend he was not exactly the same boy who ran away, and pretend that he had come home to protect them. Come home to stay. Every one of them pretending. Why was she the only one who could not manage it with any grace?

The cheetah dancer was moving her way again. Hadhi shot him a glare out of the side of her eye. He took the hint, stumbling away. One of them was a real predator, and it was not Yenge.

Noam was utterly fascinated by the dance. A performance taking no less than seventeen people, all moving differently but creating a story together. It was incredible. Every land he'd encountered while traveling with Azize had a different style of dance, and all were lovely, but this— He'd felt it in his gut when the drum beats sounded and the room slowly grew brighter and the music more complex and the dance so *alive*. So emotional. He felt the hope and the love pouring off the dancers as they welcomed Azize home. Noam loved it.

They had only been in Maltuba for a few hours, but already Noam had found so many things to fascinate him. Azize was a bit shy of his home as he gave his friends a tour of the capitol earlier today. Luckily the prince's *eoch*, a position that seemed most related to a secretary to Noam, had no such restraints. He'd happily stopped a number of times to point out aspects of different structures or describe the method for forming mud, branches, and reeds into these intricate conical homes, and the interwoven patterns on outer walls! It was exciting in both its ingenuity and its variation. Azize should have been boasting.

But Noam supposed he might have been equally shy if they were touring Glen Harrow, with its matched buildings and distrustful citizens wearing clothes so similar they seemed like uniforms.

They had yet to encounter anything worthy of embarrassment in Maltuba, but Noam knew enough of Azize's past to be certain this place had its own shames, like anywhere. So Noam hadn't joined the other men in teasing their friend over his embarrassment. He just watched and soaked in this vibrant new world.

In particular, he loved the colors. Every person wore some different brightly-hued and patterned clothing; no two were exactly the same. Shiraz should see this. All her life she'd railed against the constraints of their society, making everyone dress the same, and style their hair the same, and say the same words. She would love these people with their open smiles and booming laughter, so boldly embracing life.

Just as he was thinking it Noam spotted a quiet, serious girl across the room, so different from everyone around her. So different from everything that had been fascinating him, and yet she drew his eye. While other people smiled and laughed or openly gawked at their returned prince, she stood still among them, with a serious expression and an utterly compelling presence. Drawing in all the light and color and noise and silencing it into a soft, void-like halo around her.

There was a wild, exciting performance going on before Noam, and Azize was explaining different characters needlessly in his ear, but Noam was torn, part of him longing to watch the mysterious sentinel among the revelers.

But it wasn't until the performance was over and Noam was making his way around the room with his friend that Noam noticed the scars...*embossing* her cheek and chin. They neither marred nor embellished her skin; they simply raised it and drew the eye to her defiantly high head, amidst all the bending women.

Seeing the scars reminded Noam of the first moment he'd noticed her, when the cheetah dancer leapt out to frighten her and the people around her laughed. Noam felt the first uncomfortable shiver about this beautiful, compelling place. What ugliness were these bright colors and wide smiles concealing?

Nuru cheered wildly for longer and far louder than the people around her. Even Mzaa shot her a killing glare. How could anyone fail to be impressed? That performance was amazing by any standards and it had only been prepared for about three weeks, from the time the nation received word that Azize was coming home. Usually the Spirit Dancers prepared a piece like that for months at a time. They were incredible.

"Did you see the way Faizah uses every bit of her body to convey emotion? Even her fingers and toes would curl up in fear or stretch out towards Azize as she called him out among his people!" Nuru asked Hadhi, her pulse still racing from excitement. "Za mur *ingzall*!"

"In Fairy," Mzaa corrected habitually. She wasn't even looking over, busy whispering with Sabra.

Hadhi rolled her eyes at their mother and very nearly smiled, but the look faded away as she watched Azize making his way around the room.

Nuru repeated the words in the common Fairy tongue, as her mother wished. "She is spectacular." Fairy was being adopted by countries around the world as a language of trade. Maltuba was ahead of most of them, having made it a second language before Nuru was born. But though most other countries were only adopting it now, world travelers like the prince's companions would speak Fairy, so Mzaa insisted they speak nothing else.

"You will be even more spec..tacoo...tacular." Hadhi stumbled quietly over the word in Fairy, clenching her jaw in frustration. She hadn't taken to the language as well as the rest of them, and she didn't like doing things poorly. Which was fair enough. If Baba were alive, he would have mocked her pronunciation. He often used mockery to teach lessons. "Spectacular, when you are among them."

"Oh I don't know." Nuru shrugged. "She's only eighteen, and already she dances as great spirits. And she moves so smoothly, so captivating, like a willoomi floating through the air. I dance like the animal dancers."

Hadhi smiled softly. "You can dance anything. But I think you would make a...fierce Gitonga."

Nuru notched up her head with a bright smile. She would love to dance as the spirit of the jungle. His character was bold and quick, intricate steps and leaps and flips, sharp angles. She could feel her body wanting to slant into sharper poses. Nuru was so caught up imagining it that she didn't notice Hadhi getting quiet at first. Hadhi was frequently quiet, but now she was regulating her breathing as she watched Azize again. Calming herself.

She was nervous. Nuru should be too, but...the room was full of women nearer Azize's age, beautiful and talented, or of the strong supportive character one expected in a queen. He would never pick Nuru. Hadhi, on the other hand, was their family's best hope of improving their suddenly sunken fortunes.

It must be uncomfortable. Even before Baba died, Hadhi had not been the most outgoing woman. Now getting out of the hut their uncle thrust them into was all contingent on her attracting a prince three years younger than her with Mzaa breathing down her neck.

Maybe that was why she—maybe, possibly, if it was her who had done it at all—Maybe her fear was why she'd ruined Asha's gown and prevented her from coming tonight. Hadhi was always so much less of herself around their half-sister.

Nuru nudged Hadhi in the arm playfully. "Do you even think Mzaa knew the word in Fairy?"

Hadhi didn't smile. "Oh yes. If there was something Baba wanted of her, she always found a way to give it."

Nuru shuddered slightly at the tone, but there was no time to address it. Sabra was disappearing with their baby brother, and the prince was crossing directly to them.

TORTURE

Hadhi hated this. She held her head at the exact angle Mzaa liked, in towards her right, mostly obscuring her scars. She laughed at a high pitch, being sure to keep her lips open wide enough to be called a bright smile as the prince was making light of the celebration to honor him. Mocking his own people before his foreign friends. The man who had watched the dance so intently hadn't stopped smiling since the dances had ended. What could he possibly have to be so happy about? While he had watched the dance Hadhi was inclined to approve of him, but now his bright attitude reminded her of Asha and put her on edge.

She should be happier that her half-sister was not at the ball, but every time she saw this man smile, she thought of Asha's bright personality and she had to fight to keep from grinding her teeth. Asha would love this. Asha would shine here, but she was home, with her gown ruined and her hopes dashed, blaming Hadhi and hating her more with every minute, just like Baba wanted. And Hadhi felt uglier with every second that passed, for the pleasure she had taken earlier in the day, watching as Asha was brought low.

But she was not allowed to let any of that show. Not her rage, or her regret, not even her disappointment that his travels did not seem to have improved Azize. He continued making light of the ball for which the men and women of his nation had spent weeks learning foreign dances and preparing clothes and homes and daughters to please him. The ball for which the Spirit Dancers had given up all other performances to make something truly special to honor him. He laughed at all the sacrifice and work that went into welcoming him home, and his friends laughed with him. Her mother and sister laughed. And Hadhi must laugh as well. No matter how much she resented it. No matter how much they all knew, the farce of trying to win his attention was pointless.

She wished she could just be honest, look Azize in the eye and say, "I need a husband. If you mean to stay, you need a wife. Choose me. Help my family."

It would not work. But nor would this.

Noam tried not to stare at her outright. It was harder than it should be. She was absolutely riveting. *Hadhi*, he liked that name, it suited her. Or it had, before they came over, now he felt like she might need a more manic name.

Noam fought off a chuckle. Good lord, she needed to stop smiling. Noam could feel his friend growing uneasy under that relentlessly wide and toothy expression. Noam snickered softly, and her eyes cut to him for a moment. A delightful shiver raced down his spine. Her glaring eyes were a bit chilling when paired with that toothy, pained smile. She might just be the most interesting person in the whole nation.

She stood with her mother and sister, all of them had the baring of important people, but their clothes had clearly seen better days, thin and fraying in spots and covered over with beads or elaborately tied scarves.

Her mother was a lovely woman, sultry and blatantly flirtatious with men far younger than herself. And the younger sister was a bright, energetic child. Standing between them, Hadhi appeared like a shadow, quiet, doing nothing but smiling and agreeing with Azize. Yet Noam couldn't take his eyes off of her. Her hair was worn in two wide clouds of unwinding curls shoved forward on either side of her face, with the top flattened out and a little crown of painted wooden beads adorning it. It stood out. Other women wore theirs in bundles of braids like her sister or adorned with scarves or intricately styled, such vivid individual women were all around; comparatively, Noam supposed her hair looked quite simple, but with her intense eyes and vigilant posture it didn't seem simple. It had a goddess-like appearance, cool, distant, riveting.

Azize cleared his throat and faced the girls' mother, drawing himself up and bracing for a great chore. Hadhi gave him the briefest of sharp looks, seeming to grind her back teeth to hold onto that smile. Noam wondered if either of these two were aware of how nervous the other was.

Azize had hated being the center of attention for as long as Noam had known him. He pulled bolder, louder, more boisterous men near to draw the eye away from him, as much as he was pulling men near for protection. Walking around this ball with his friend Noam had begun to understand why Azize hated the attention so much. Everyone wanted something from him, and he was so afraid to fail them.

Noam wasn't certain why Azize had come home now. Until one month ago, they had planned to sail to the Blazing Sea and visit its many volcanic islands. Then suddenly, Azize announced he wanted to return to Maltuba. Azize loved nothing so well as being at sea and seeing new parts of the world, putting as much distance between himself and his father as he could. So Noam knew he was not the only one of Azize's friends confused by the sudden decision. Though Azize had never said it, all the men knew the prince was trying to build himself an army before he came home. And fifteen men did not an army make. But they were his men, so they followed where he led.

"Jauhar," Azize said gently, lifting the hand of the woman before him, Hadhi's mother. "Please allow me to express regret, on behalf of my father and myself, for the loss of Zuberi. He was my father's most valued emissary. Discovering and punishing his murderers remains one of my father's highest priorities." Azize bowed over the woman's hand; she and her daughters all cast their eyes down a moment silently with Azize.

Noam watched the exchange thinking over Azize's carefully chosen words. He spoke no actual words of sympathy, because he felt none, but if these women noticed, they drew no attention to that fact.

"Oxtia thioon szou," Azize had muttered as he'd caught sight of this family while they circled the room greeting his citizens.

Azize rarely spoke in the language of his childhood, but when he asked the gods to preserve him, as he just had, or when he cursed, that tended to be in Maltuban. So those were the words in the language with which Noam had the most familiarity.

"What catastrophe now?" Noam had asked with a laugh. When Azize nodded to Jauhar, Noam had followed the gaze and seen Hadhi watching them, her heavy presence like a whirlpool pulling them in. "You know her?"

"Yes, she's Zuberi's widow."

"The man you call gzufiga?" Noam had asked in shock. That girl was too...well he didn't know what, but she couldn't have been the wife of the monster *Azize spoke of with rage and fear.*

"Yes." Azize replied flatly. "She cannot be put off forever, and at least right now I don't see that infernal pest, Asha. Come on."

Noam had been pleased to discover Azize was speaking of Jauhar and not her daughter. He and his friend had looked at this family and been equally unaware of the woman the other saw. It was slightly amusing that. And surprising. Hadhi raised her head now, and despite the moment of silence for her father's memory, the bright, toothy smile was still on her face. How was it possible his friend could fail to see her?

"I see Maltuba has not changed at all in my absence," Azize teased. One moment he was failing to offer condolences for their dead father, and the next, he was back to insulting his home. Hadhi bit her tongue to keep from rolling her eyes. "I was never allowed to go anywhere without a thousand eyes on me."

Hadhi smiled, and a tiny moment of silence passed. Mzaa's foot connected with the back of Hadhi's leg. What was she meant to say to that? Her eyes had never followed Azize.

"I think the Spirit Dancers have gotten much better since you left," Nuru said brightly. The prince opened his mouth to respond, but Nuru spoke right over him. "Faizah is..." Nuru fumbled for the word in Fairy; she glanced at Hadhi, as if she would know any better. "Oon vonuri?" Nuru asked in Maltuban

"A vision," Azize laughed, providing the answer and thoroughly startling Nuru. Mzaa threw Hadhi a look as if to say she should follow Nuru's example.

"Yes," Azize agreed. "She is very talented. Do you dance, Nuru?"

"I..." Nuru swallowed, as though it had not occurred to her that the prince would speak to her. It had. Mzaa had made it quite clear that both her daughters would try their hardest to gain the prince's favor. Despite Nuru being thirteen, Mzaa was determined the prince would marry one of her daughters or no one. But now that the opportunity was upon her, Nuru looked frightened, and Hadhi found her tongue.

"Nuru is a beautiful dancer," Hadhi said proudly. "She will be better than Faizah one day."

"Ah, so my participation in the dance was as embarrassing for her to witness as it was for me to perform," Azize said self-deprecatingly. Hadhi had a thing or two to say about that but was not allowed.

"You have been gone many years. You did well!" Hadhi said, generously. "This is all a shock, is it not?"

"Very much so. I expected only to see my father on my first day home. The journey was so long I had thought to rest, but who could rest at a... welcome of this magnitude."

"It would be hard." Hadhi agreed with what she felt was a too bright smile, but from the corner of her eye, she could see her mother, and if this smile slipped, Hadhi would get far worse than a kicked ankle.

"Have you missed anything special from your home?" Mzaa prompted when a lull in the conversation suggested the prince and his three friends with him would walk away. The prince was making his rounds, as duty required and greeting every family in attendance. Eventually, he must walk away, but Mzaa wanted Hadhi to linger in his brain after he left.

Azize was struggling to find words, which did not speak well of his feelings for Maltuba.

His friend spoke up in his stead, smiling directly at Hadhi, which was... odd. "I am sure I would miss dances like that in his place," Azize's friend, Noam, as he had been introduced, spoke fervently. "It was quite moving. I remember you telling us about a phrase, Azize, that was used to begin your old legends—"

"No other nation could thrive between the claws of the jungle and the teeth of the desert!" Nuru chimed in immediately. It was her favorite part of the old tales.

"Exactly." Noam smiled. "The dance reminded me of that."

Azize nodded. "Yes. It is meant to. I have missed them, I suppose, and my mother telling the old stories."

Hadhi smiled and nodded, pretending to hang on his every word as Mzaa wanted.

"And I do love the quiet of the desert at night. Nowhere else in the world is there a sand desert like Ether."

"It is beautiful," Hadhi agreed without having to be forced. She, too, loved desert nights. "The music of the night bugs and birds and—"

Horns blasted outside of the capitol palace, cutting Hadhi off. Or perhaps it had been a bird's cry. A breeze shoved in the south doors, so they banged against the walls. As one, Azize and his guests turned that way. Several people shuddered and gasped.

"Azongma sifvao ooshooa," Oni whispered behind them. Hadhi glanced back to see the woman touch her daughter's foreheads with two fingers before bringing those fingers to her own lips. It was a superstitious response among the Maumai, to a sudden change in wind. *Curse bringer winds,* that tribe called them.

Hadhi had always admired the tradition; you touched the heads of those you loved and brought your fingers to your lips, in essence protecting their spirit inside yourself. Baba used to scoff at it. He scoffed at anything gentle, or sentimental, or based in faith. Scoffed at any power but oneself. Hadhi turned away.

When the wind cleared, a woman walked in—not a woman. *A vision.* She stood in the doorway, scanning the room, entirely unconcerned by the commotion she caused. And why should she be? She sparkled like the sun, in her gown made almost entirely of golden thread, it touched the ground like liquid, and there was a light music to it, like it was made of coins striking one another and singing together. The fabric had a rich, dramatic pattern of blue birds emerging from the centers of golden flowers. It was the loveliest thing Hadhi had ever seen. And the woman wearing it was no less lovely. Her hair was braided up off her face and neck, all braids leading to the apex of her head, where it exploded in a highly curled crown. Each braid was adorned with golden loops, connected with chains that drooped down on either side of her face. And she had such a lovely face, smooth, unmarred by life. She had full lips and a slightly crooked nose that somehow made her look sweeter. And her eyes were large and brilliant, nearly the color of emeralds.

Those eyes fell on Hadhi, and Hadhi felt her muscles tensing up and her pulse skidding with embarrassment. The woman looked her up and down critically and gave a little laugh, as if Hadhi were beneath her notice, then she turned away, walking towards a group of Azize's friends.

Hadhi had never seen the woman before, but she felt her entire being burning with shame, felt ugly and unlovable. She felt suddenly like crying.

Sour-faced-Hadhi, a voice taunted in her mind. Hadhi flinched. Her wooden beads bumped against one another, making a windy sound like branches tussling. Nothing like the music that woman's adornments made. The prince and his friends forced their gazes back, and Hadhi could feel their disappointment at having to pull their eyes from the mystery woman.

Azize opened his mouth, for half a moment, it seemed he might start their conversation where it had been interrupted. Then he laughed slightly.

Poor sour-face. Did you really think you could hold his attention?

"Please excuse me, ladies." Azize could not conceal his desire to be away. "It has been a pleasure, but I must...greet other guests."

Hadhi narrowed her eyes but said nothing.

"Perhaps we will see you later on this evening," Mzaa said sweetly.

Azize did not even pretend to agree; with a stiff jerk of his head, he walked away, taking his friends with him. Mzaa held her breath, waiting until he was far enough away not to hear before she began chastising Hadhi.

Nuru caught Hadhi's eye and shook her head at the retreating prince. "That wasn't very polite."

Mzaa sucked in a breath that made clear she would be yelling at any moment, Hadhi gave her sister a small nod, and Nuru slipped away while the prince was still near enough that Mzaa dare not shout after her.

Sabra had still not returned from changing her son, not that Mzaa would have chastised her, but perhaps if Azize's childhood love were here, he would have stayed. No one stayed for Hadhi.

"How long have we practiced?" Mzaa hissed quietly, but not quietly enough that their neighbors would not overhear. It made little difference, everyone knew Mzaa despaired of ever getting sour-faced-Hadhi married.

"Iooni?" Hadhi replied and got her arm pinched none too subtly.

"In Fairy," Mzaa instructed through her teeth, yet still managed to look lovely.

"Forever," Hadhi repeated in the common Fairy tongue. "It is not my fault the other woman came."

"If you were making any effort at all, he wouldn't even have noticed her," Mzaa insisted.

That was nonsense. Hadhi knew her mother did not believe it. She told Hadhi once a day how plain she looked without the scars and how ugly with them. Add to that, at twenty-three Hadhi was past the common age of marriage. Azize would no more want her than the other men in Maltuba did. Which would suit Hadhi fine, if it did not mean staying with Mzaa forever.

"Ma gitell nong bijum Maltuban ifiza. Ayzat pang vonuri kamko nong fupu mav ziva," Hadhi muttered in Maltuban: *He does not want Maltuban women. Even that vision will not make him stay.*

Mzaa did not move, did not shift her lovely smile, but her eyes dug into her daughter like claws. Hadhi felt them along the tracks of her scars and wondered, not for the first time, if her mother was not a witch. Her expressions alone held such painful power.

"You will not speak unless you speak Fairy, or I will devise tortures for you suitable to that sour expression you are wearing. You have no right to judge a prince. Your only purpose here is to smile, to make him feel heard, and welcome, and desirous of your company."

Hadhi caught sight of one of the men Azize had brought home with him nearby, smirking at the pair of them as though he had been listening to their entire conversation. He looked Maltuban. He wore a fine dress-silk like theirs but not in the pattern of any tribe she recognized. She wondered if he was from one of the tribes of the outer provinces, aligned with no one. He was one of those men who was beautiful to look at and knew it. The kind that used their beauty to trick and harm others. Like Hadhi's father had been. Hadhi's eyes slid across him in distaste and back to her mother.

"Since I am so terrible at it, shall I go home?" Hadhi asked.

"Get a drink to refresh yourself." Mzaa ignored the query. Of course Hadhi could not leave. "By Azize's friends. Welcome them to Maltuba. Ask about their travels. Ask about their friend. *Be lively,* and *engaging.* The night is far from over. *You* will make an impression on the prince, is that clear?"

Hadhi sucked in air through her nose and curtseyed to her mother like she were the queen she imagined herself. "Yes, *Mother.*" Hadhi bit out in Fairy, cutting through the crowd sharply to march away.

Hadhi noticed an unfamiliar bird flitting in through the open door to weave about between the lanterns decorating the ceiling and lighting the palace. It was tiny, but brightly colored with a long thin tail. She followed it with her eyes as she crossed the room, and...it did the same to Hadhi.

Hadhi shook herself; it was her imagination, her nerves. All day she had been noticing odd bird behavior. That ibis this morning, that just stood on the road from their hut to Jaccada staring at her family as they passed, staring at the extra camel tied to Hadhi's. It had made her uncomfortable. Made her feel like...prey, as this bird was now, but it was all in her head. She should have better control of herself. Animals were not out to get her; she was not being stalked.

They can change their shape to nearly anything when they hunt.

Hadhi shook off her father's voice. It had been a year and a half and no one had come for revenge. She was just jumping at shadows. She didn't fit here and she wanted to make it a threat and not her own lacking self. The bird darted down the hall, leaving Hadhi without even an imagined threat to focus on.

She longed to be home with this night's torture over. She hated crowds like these. Hated the dances she would have to participate in and smiling and pretending to be other than she was. Hadhi noticed that Azize had yet to approach the mystery woman. Still too timid. He was talking with Faizah, but his eyes constantly darted to the mystery woman. If Faizah could not hold his attention, Hadhi surely could not. But she had to try.

She might be fine spending the rest of her life in the hut Uncle Kafil shoved them into when Baba died, or she would be, if Mzaa were not there. But if she did not catch the prince's eye, Nuru might never join the Spirit Dancers. And Lin, her new baby brother, could be taken away by their uncle as soon as he was weaned. Hadhi needed the prince, whether she liked him or not. Whether *he* liked her or not. They both had duties to perform. That ought to be enough for him. But she doubted it would be. She could think of nothing more she had to offer that he could not get from anyone else, but she must find a way. She could not afford to give in to the rage inside. Something had to change.

DRESSED IN A SKIN OF MAGIC

Asha giggled, loud and long as the giant lokoki bird cried out like a squadron of trumpets, and because the bird was so loud no one heard her. Not that she cared. She had nothing to fear.

Tonight, she could do anything. Tonight she wasn't Asha. She was dressed in a skin of magic, made new with it! She was—*at last*—her freed self.

All her life, she'd lived on wishes and hopes, on imagined stories of worlds far away, but tonight she could truly live. She didn't need to worry about pleasing her family. She didn't have to scrub everyone's clothes and mend their rips; she didn't need to make meals and bring in bathing water. Tonight she could forget about holes that needed patching in the roof and the meats that needed to be cured and dried. She didn't have to worry about the fortunes of her family slipping every day closer to beggar women. Right now, she did not even have to keep her promise to Baba and look after his other girls.

Asha had done nothing but care for them for the past year and a half. She had not complained once as she went from favored child of a great man to servant of his widows. She'd cheerfully sewn clothes, cleaned, cooked, cleaned again. And not one of them appreciated her. Not one of them loved her. She'd always known Jauhar and her daughters did not love Asha the way they loved each other, but it was not until Baba died that she realized they did not love her at all.

Tomorrow she would be their servant again. Tomorrow her life would be merely work, and fantasy. Tomorrow she would be starved again for love. Tonight she would gorge herself on stories of the wide world, she would taste magic, and desire, she would be filled up—so that when midnight came, and she must hibernate again, she would have stores of adventure to sustain her.

"Daku uli, Baba," Asha whispered brightly. Sending her father's spirit her thanks for the magic he'd sent her way, even in death. "I will not waste one moment of this gift!"

Asha stepped through the door in her finery and her new skin and had every eye on her. She smiled, basking in the attention, in the hush that fell over the hall, in the eyes all drawn to her radiant power. This was so exciting! Baba would have loved this. He should have felt this. But there would be time for grieving later, he'd sent Zawadi to her with this magical gift, and she wouldn't squander it.

Asha felt a familiar chilling gaze and glanced over. Jauhar, Baba's first wife, was on the other side of the ballroom, still her eyes tried to peel away this magic skin and destroy Asha. But Asha wasn't known to her tonight. She wasn't her servant tonight. Asha slid her eyes slowly to Jauhar's right, where Hadhi always stood. And there she was, at her mother's side, trying to capture the attention of any man she could, believing that she'd kept Asha from the ball.

Asha wondered if her sister had realized yet, that Asha was not her problem. Hadhi could never capture a man's attention, not because she was the less attractive sister, nor because she was the less vibrant. She couldn't do it because she spent all her time worrying that everyone found her lacking. It wouldn't matter if Hadhi was the only woman in the room, she would still be the same pinch-faced, dull specter she always was.

Asha smirked at her half-sister, looking over Hadhi's fraying gown and simple adornments. Asha shook out her magic gown, so soft playful music escaped its layers, all but daring Hadhi to try and destroy this creation. Nothing she could do would stop Asha from being here, and if she thought her sister too much competition in the gown of silk she'd destroyed, then she would be helpless against this magical creation.

Asha flounced her gaze away; she wasn't here to think about her family. She was here to embrace the joy they wanted to deny her.

There was a group of oddly dressed and styled men, who must be foreigners; Asha walked right up to them and randomly selected a man to greet.

"Hello, tell me, where were you born? What does the air taste like there?"

The man with thick red hair and a fluffy beard laughed, as did his companions, but he nodded his head and complied with Asha's demand. "I was born in a tiny nation called Thlop. It is one of the southern most nations in the world, and our air tastes...cold." He finished with a grin.

Asha sidled up closer. "Tell me more. Tell me *everything*."

"Wait, what about me?" Another, younger man, with short dark hair as fine as the feathers at a vulture's neck spoke up.

Asha grinned. "Oh I'll be getting to you as well. We've all evening to travel the world together, and I mean to visit every land I'm able."

That garnered much enthusiasm, men talking over one another to answer her questions or ask her theirs. But they spoke so fast, and were all so eager to know her, or for her to know them, when what she wanted was to know the *world*. So within five minutes, she was full of what they had to offer and off to find more. More. More. She needed so much more than they gave.

The air in one land tasted cold, in another salty, in another it tasted like fire, and all were intriguing descriptions, but where was the man who could feed her imagination? Her favorite thing she'd learned among them was from the first man, who claimed that in the winters of Thlop there were full months with no sunlight. Night for all the hours. It had sounded thrilling and dangerous, until he spoke of families bundled up inside their homes around fires, riding out the majority of the darkness. That was essentially how Asha spent all of her days, trapped inside her same walls, with no new faces and no new tasks. The same chores and sights day in and out. What sort of adventure was that?

She didn't want to know that every land had some seemingly exciting element, but when you looked closely, all the excitement was mundane for those who lived it. She wanted magic! She wanted adventure! She wanted life, wild and open, and lived in every second. Who would give her that?

THE ANGRIEST WOMEN IN MALTUBA

Sabra had been trying to do better all evening; she hid with Lin in the mothers' room so as not to spoil Hadhi's chances with Azize...and a bit to protect herself, she supposed. But she'd emerged in time to watch Jauhar chastise Hadhi, her eyes tore into her daughter, so Hadhi looked smaller for every word she spoke. Sabra pressed her son softly to her shoulder and kissed his head, vowing silently to always show him her love. He would be so much happier than the rest of Zuberi's children. So much safer, and more loved.

Sabra wanted to allow Hadhi the pretense of privacy, she owed her that much after their less than friendly history, but she was sure Hadhi knew she was being observed. Oni, one of their neighbors, was whispering to her daughters in Maltuban about how lucky they were to have her for a mother; *imagine being Jauhar's daughters.* Sabra turned to face them fully and let Oni see her raised brow of challenge. At once, the woman rushed her daughters away.

Sabra made a point of not allowing anyone to speak ill of Jauhar or her daughters in front of her. She did not *like* Jauhar, but she understood her like no one else could. There was no joy to be had from being one of Zuberi's wives.

After Hadhi moved off stiffly through the crowd, Sabra shuddered and walked forward, poor girl. Sabra nearly laughed at herself: girl. Hadhi was three years older than Sabra, and she could not recall that she had ever seemed like a mere *girl.* But that didn't excuse the way Sabra and Asha had treated her.

Jauhar looked down her shoulder at Sabra, her brow went up and a small sly smile tilted her lips. "There was no need to hide from your boy love; despite his adventures, you are far worldlier."

Sabra felt her cheeks heating and looked away. She hadn't realized Jauhar knew Sabra had liked Azize before he ran away. She looked back on those light fluttery feelings and was embarrassed with herself for ever thinking it was something special. Yet still, when she knew she might see him in person, that she might speak to him, she had grown so shy and embarrassed that she hid with her son. How could she possibly face him? She had kissed him once, just once, but it was the sweetest memory her mind could conjure.

When Zuberi had claimed her as his wife, Sabra had hidden inside that memory until it was so worn and familiar that it seemed a fantasy of her mind's invention. She didn't want it spoiled.

"I was not hiding," Sabra said, with her eyes on the ground.

"Oooo. How is our sweet boy?" Jauhar said. Ignoring Sabra's words, she leaned in close and ran a gentle hand over Lin's head.

Sabra had worried when Lin was first born that Jauhar would resent him. As Zuberi's only male child, he could eventually inherit all of his father's possessions. But Jauhar had been nothing but gentle and loving with him. She was far kinder to Lin than she was to her own daughters. She was kinder to Sabra than she was to her own daughters. Jauhar should resent her husband's third wife. She should resent the child that would surely have been his favorite had he lived to meet him. But nothing could be further from the truth. She treated Sabra kindly, maternally. And she treated Lin as though he brought the sun to the sky.

"Would you like to hold him?" Sabra offered.

Jauhar's eyes lifted from Lin's soft head to meet Sabra's gaze. Jauhar smiled gently; it was an expression Sabra was near-certain her own daughters had never seen. It made Jauhar look like her true self, her aged beyond her years, broken and hungry, angry self. Sabra imagined most people, well familiar with Hadhi's dark expressions and quiet nature, would think she was the angriest woman in Maltuba. She never did seem to find anything but her sister Nuru to take joy in. But Sabra knew well the angriest woman in Maltuba: it was Jauhar. Hadhi was quickly catching up to her mother in inner rage, but she had a chance still to escape the fires of hatred that lived in Jauhar. The rage that ate away at her when she looked on anyone but Lin.

"You are a good girl, Sabra."

"He...enjoys being with his Mzaa Jauhar," Sabra said softly. "And I thought I might," she nodded across the room, "give Hadhi a bit of help."

"You might want to help yourself," Jauhar said, easily lifting Lin away and bouncing him across the air.

"No!" Sabra shook her head.

"It was not a criticism. I was never angry with you for how you were with Hadhi. I was a girl once. And Hadhi never has been easy to love," Jauhar said so casually, likely unaware that Nuru had been approaching from behind. At her mother's words, she stopped dead and glared fire into Sabra. Sabra never knew how to intervene in this family. But she knew she owed Hadhi a great debt of apology for the way she had treated her as a girl.

Sour face!

Sabra flinched at the sound of her own voice in her memory. She couldn't believe she'd ever been so cruel, but she had. And what was more, it hadn't felt cruel then. She'd seen Hadhi, watching with her dark glower, judging them, getting Sabra and Asha into trouble. She always found some way to spoil their adventures just when they were at their most exciting—and dangerous. But Sabra and Asha had never noticed the danger Hadhi kept them from. They only noticed the fun she prevented. Sabra had never understood why one as wealthy and important as Hadhi could possibly be so angry. Until Zuberi claimed her, a girl the age of his own children, for his bride, and Sabra saw inside the family she'd thought she knew for years. There had never been anything for Hadhi to smile about. Sabra realized now that Hadhi had been trying to reach out to them, in her own way, and had always been rebuffed.

She owed her a great deal. But...Jauhar was the only reason that Sabra had not killed herself in the first year of her marriage. So she did not know how to intervene. This whole family was tattered and scarred, even if only Hadhi wore those scars visibly.

Nuru, equally unable to speak to Jauhar's comments, spun about and stomped off through the crowd.

"What I meant is that this evening might be beneficial for all the young ladies of my house. Find a man."

"I...that is done for me." Sabra fumbled.

"Zuberi is gone," Jauhar said with a little soft hum between her words, as she rocked the baby back and forth. "I loved my husband, so to take another is abhorrent to me. But we both know you had no love for Zuberi, and he likewise had use for you, but no love. You owe nothing to him. Nor can any man fault you, for you were a dutiful wife and are an excellent mother."

Lin fell softly to sleep against Jauhar's shoulder and she led Sabra away from the crowd of the room towards the walls.

"You are a child still, my dear. Love and desire are far from over for you. Go, see for yourself."

Sabra was shaking her head still, and her cheeks were aflame with embarrassment, but she left her son in Jauhar's arms and crossed the room towards Hadhi all the same. Not that she intended to...flirt, or try to win Azize, or any man. She wanted to *help Hadhi*. So despite how angry and saddened Sabra had been when Jauhar prevented Asha from coming tonight, she was pleased for Hadhi. Hadhi could never see her value with Asha near, and she needed to see it tonight. Because this was Hadhi's chance to get away from all the pain her father had wrought. This was her chance to reach out to someone and have them pull her near.

As Asha was crossing the room, Sabra walked by. Asha's best friend but she barely saw her. Like always now.

Before she'd married Baba Sabra's eyes had lit up when she saw Asha. And her breath would hang on Asha's every story. Where had that girl gone? Asha's pulse raced as it used to when they ran laughing through the tall grasses, and magic bubbled up inside her. She didn't properly see the room before her, only her *ethus havio.*

Asha reached out and grabbed ahold of her greatest friend's arm. She stared into Sabra's eyes, willing her to see Asha as she would have in the past. Even in a skin of magic Sabra would have known her—before.

"Can I assist you somehow?" Sabra asked softly.

Asha didn't answer, waiting. Longing. They'd loved each other once, spent all their time together, Asha dragging Sabra on adventures. Sneaking into the capitol palace. Running away to the mountains, with sacks of clothes and food enough for a week. They would have made it too, if sour-face hadn't tattled on them. Hadhi hated anyone having fun. But Asha and Sabra used to have such marvelous adventures.

Maybe that would fill Asha up, an adventure with someone she loved. Asha ached from the absence of love in her life. It felt so empty. So pointless.

"Yes." Asha smiled provocatively, begging silently for Sabra to know her, to feel her reaching out. "You've been here longer than I, which of the foreigners seems the most...well-traveled?"

Sabra smiled genuinely, looking like her younger, lovelier self. Asha hadn't realized before now that her friend had been looking older. They were near the same age, had done everything together when they were young. But now Sabra was old before her time. Did marriage change one so much? Asha wasn't sure she wanted to be married if it stole one's youth and one's adventurous spirit and one's smile. The only time Sabra really smiled anymore was when she was holding her son.

"I've barely exchanged words with more than two of them. But...that gentleman has a pleasant spirit," Sabra suggested

Asha ignored her words and just watched her old friend. Was it marriage that had changed her? Or Baba's death? Because she seemed most days like an entirely foreign person.

"I'll try him out," Asha said vaguely, not even really knowing who they spoke of.

Too busy wondering what had changed in her friend. Sometimes she thought it was vanity. Sabra's pride at being married when Asha was not, for surely she had changed. The day Baba brought her home as his new bride, Asha had been thrilled! They would be family in truth; they would be together always. And with Sabra as Baba's new wife, even Hadhi wouldn't be able to spoil their fun. Except Sabra barely spoke to her after that. She spoke to Mzaa Jauhar more than she did anyone else. She'd completely changed. But Sabra could change back, couldn't she? Asha could reawaken her.

"But...save myself, you are the loveliest woman here." Asha said brightly, trying to rouse her friend. "Why are you not having an adventure to last a lifetime? You should be flirting and discovering worlds beyond our own. Come with me." Asha held out a hand. "We can see what he knows together. Let's have an adventure."

For only a moment, Asha thought she might accept. Sabra's eyes looked as hungry as Asha's insides. She looked deep into Asha's eyes, and there was a spark of adventure in her that was so familiar from their childhood days. Asha forgot to breathe. Then Sabra shook her head, looking at the ground like the dutiful wife she'd been for years now. She glanced off across the room. Following her gaze Asha saw her half-sister Hadhi, stiff and smiling like a demented woman as she talked to a pair of foreigners.

"I must return to my family," Sabra said. "But thank you."

The answer made Asha's blood boil with rage and magic, and a desire to bellow fire into the room. *Hadhi!* Hadhi was Sabra's family. And what was Asha, the girl she'd laughed with and sang with and shared adventures with, the girl she'd slept with under the stars and dreamed of far off lands with? Nothing? A servant, as she was to the rest of the *family*? Family. Asha hated that word. It was a lie. Just like her friendship with Sabra had apparently been a lie.

Asha nearly hated her friend in that moment, but more even she hated Hadhi, and Jauhar, two of the ugliest, angriest women in Maltuba, likely the whole world, who'd stolen everything that should be Asha's every joy, every memory perverted by their presence calling themselves family. Now they would pervert Sabra too. This wasn't the real Sabra. Asha missed that girl with all her heart.

"Are you always only obedient and respectful? Because...a *good* family would want adventure for you. You deserve to be joyful again!"

Asha didn't wait for an answer, her hours were dwindling. And Sabra's rejection threatened to leave Asha heartsore and lonesome. Again. Why was she always alone? She offered her love time and again. She used to bring Jauhar flowers and beg her to dress her or teach her to cook. Used to ask Hadhi to come on adventures. Yet time and again, her offers of love were met with coldness and rejection. She couldn't spend her magic this way. Couldn't waste one moment being that same desperate soul.

Asha had been remade with magic. All too soon the bells would toll for midnight and the magic Zawadi had given her would be gone. Her magic skin would be gone. And her adventure would be over.

She deserved an adventure, a joy. She deserved the one night—and she wasn't surrendering it.

Sabra felt electricity dancing under her skin from where the strange woman had touched her. Excitement like she hadn't felt in years. She walked away, having refused the woman's invitation with words, but inside she was...alive. Abuzz with that youthful tickled, hungry feeling she used to have whenever Asha was near. For a moment, that stranger had brought Sabra back to life as she hadn't been in years, made her feel and want in ways she'd thought were entirely destroyed by her husband. But Sabra tried to shake those feelings off as she crossed to Hadhi.

Hadhi had surely never felt such feelings at all, and Sabra needed to make amends to her. The goddess Ether demanded one acknowledge their mistakes and try to heal them. That should be Sabra's only focus tonight. Coming up alongside Hadhi, Sabra overheard bits of the conversation she was having with one of Azize's friends.

"I'd no idea Azize's kingdom was so small," a man with the neatly trimmed beard and kind face said. "We toured the whole thing today alone."

Hadhi raised a critical brow, which looked at odds with the smile she was forcing, making her appear just a bit unhinged. "Do you mean the capitol city? Jaccada. Where you are now?" She explained sharply.

The man gave an awkward little laugh. "Is this not the whole thing?"

Sabra slipped forward, taking up Hadhi's arm, though she stiffened and moved to yank it back.

"This is merely the capitol," Sabra said sweetly, smiling at the man. "One can follow the south road through to the outer provinces, and all the domains of the five tribes united under King Enzi's rule. Jaccada was originally home to the Ga'ogo alone, but it is peopled now by members of every tribe."

"Ahh, that...makes far more sense." The man laughed. "I am Daniel, your pardon ladies, if you thought I was slighting your home. It is lovely, and *very* welcoming." He said suggestively, lifting Sabra's hand to kiss it.

Zagok, Sabra hadn't meant to steal the man's attention, only to make sure Hadhi saw how to keep it.

"When shall we have some dancing?" Daniel asked. "The introduction was lovely, but you are allowed to dance with men, aren't you?"

"Ur uli?" Hadhi muttered under her breath in Maltuban: *are you?* Sabra snorted.

Another of Azize's traveling companions who had been passing by them to the drinks table stopped and chuckled as well.

"Kane," Daniel said in a slightly shy greeting. He glanced over at the man approaching. "What did that mean?"

"It meant she isn't interested in dancing with you," the new man said, throwing Hadhi a sharp smile.

He was *quite* lovely. Hadhi was not smiling back, and it took everything in Sabra not to do so for her. Could Hadhi not unbend at all? She looked on the man with rampant suspicion.

"That is not what it meant." Hadhi examined the man the way Sabra imagined she would her quarry while hunting.

"But, am I wrong?" He taunted.

Sabra stiffened. She'd thought he was flirting, but...he was not flirting, was he? His eyes were as sharp as Hadhi's. Sabra never used to be suspicious. She longed not to be so now, but being Zuberi's wife had taught her not to freely trust men. A lesson it seemed Hadhi had learned far more effectively.

"You are from Maltuba?" Hadhi asked.

He shook his head. "Reethurn. I pick up languages quite well, and Azize shared a bit."

Hadhi shook her head in slow disbelief. Sabra also doubted Azize had done enough speaking in Maltuban for his friends to learn it, but she seized on Daniel's earlier question to redirect the conversation before Hadhi could offend them by insulting their friend.

"There will be dancing after dinner," Sabra blurted out. "It is traditional for the Spirit Dancers to open any festivity so that each celebration begins by acknowledging the spirits that surround us. Then we greet one another, acknowledging the community. We dine, celebrating the bounty of our nation. And we dance, a celebration of life, under Gzifa's watchful light. Though, tonight we shall be inside, displaying King Enzi's impressive improvements to interior lighting. Azize must have wanted to...awe you with the process, if he did not tell you before you arrived." Sabra said the last in a playful way, casting Hadhi a quick look so she could see; one could easily insult the prince, so long as it was done in jest.

Hadhi looked away, cold and stiff. Sabra nearly sighed, but the men continued speaking, and she kept the conversation going. It was not Hadhi's fault that she mistrusted men, nor that she had never taken to the Fairy tongue the way her other siblings had. She'd been far older than the others were when it was first adopted as a language of Maltuba, and she had never had as much education as the others, always busy helping the adults. Cleaning the thread clouds left by swirrle when she was young and hunting when she was older. Even after their family moved into the mansion, she worked. It was only since Zuberi's death that she had stopped.

Daniel seemed to pick up on Sabra's attempts to draw Hadhi out, and though he didn't seem nearly as keen on the idea as Sabra, he made an effort.

"So, tell me, Hadhi, wasn't it?" She nodded once. He raised a brow but went on. "I am a stranger here. If you were to tell me the one thing that makes your nation the most special, what would it be?"

Hadhi paused, considering. Although— Perhaps it was not a pause. She was often quiet. Perhaps she had no intention of answering. The silence was stretching on—

"I have seen no other lands," she said at last.

Both the men laughed. Unaware that Hadhi was about to continue, they spoke right over her.

"Of course not," Kane said. "But there must be something here you love, that you think everyone else must love as well."

Hadhi's mouth was open, but Daniel spoke up first. "What about its history? Its architecture? Its industry?" The man suggested he waved at the ceiling to indicate the bows of painted stone oil lanterns that dipped, weaved, and lit the room with the help of small mirrors strung between them and along the walls. The palace was lit better than any indoor structure. "I've never seen the like of this."

"And I have never seen different," Hadhi snapped. Though of course she had, no home was so fantastically lit. This seemed magical, but Hadhi couldn't admit that, could she? She had been Zuberi's daughter and he'd never once let her challenge him, yet somehow Hadhi had failed to realize you couldn't challenge and glare and fight with men if you expected to gain their favor.

Sabra sighed and glanced away, was there no way to help her? Perhaps Hadhi was the angriest woman in Maltuba, but she didn't have to be forever, did she?

TALES OF BLOOD AND DEATH

Noam followed his friend around the room, greeting what was left of his citizens as Azize, not at all subtly, trailed the new woman in blue and gold. Noam wanted to tease him about it, tell him to go speak to her, but Noam hadn't a leg to stand on with that advice. After all, his own eyes had been trailing another woman, and he'd yet to approach her. His excuse was that he'd sworn to Azize that he would help him through this evening.

"No one has your ease with people," Azize had insisted earlier, after yanking his friend aside when his father announced that there would be a ball that night. "I need you with me, when things grow awkward and people want to know how long I am home or if I littered the world with bastard children."

Noam had laughed, though both the word and the concept annoyed him. Men who simply picked up and left women and children behind so they could have their own adventures had always been a sore spot of his.

"Brother, I don't know any of these people. How on earth will I know how to distract them?"

"You always know." Azize bit out, half frustration half shaking fear. Why had they come here when Azize was so far from ready? "Please. I need your word."

Noam smiled softly. "I am at your disposal, brother. If nothing else, I can always make a fool of myself."

The conversation had grown a bit awkward now, but Azize wasn't noticing, too busy watching the flitting bird of a woman go from one group of Azize's friends to the next and captivate them all.

"So..." Noam interjected, into the fifteen-second pause since this young lady informed Azize, with wide, uncomfortable eyes, that she was nearly engaged to another man. Really, did they think Azize was beating down doors to get a wife? "Felicitations! Who is this lucky man?"

The girl looked awkwardly from her parents to Azize, and finally to Noam. "His name is Kafil, he was brother of Zuberi, now he runs the port in his stead."

Zuberi. Noam's eyes shot briefly away to the man's eldest daughter, who was stiffly attempting to converse with Daniel. This girl looked younger than Hadhi; how old was the man she would marry? And why did Noam find himself suddenly nearly obsessively interested in information about that family?

"How wonderful," Noam said, glancing sidelong at his friend. Azize nodded as though he were paying attention to the conversation when anyone could tell he was not. "If it is not too...invasive, would you tell me, how did this, Zuberi, die? I have heard him mentioned several times tonight, but nothing specific is ever said."

"Oh." The girl brightened, but tried not to appear as though that were the case as she leaned in to whisper. "He was waylaid on the south road. It must have been *many* people, as he was a great warrior and hunter. Many have tried to kill him before. The king suspects sorcery, perhaps from Reethurn." She glanced around furtively. "Or the new leader of the Fazaat, a solitary tribe to the south. Zuberi had killed their leader."

"That is only a rumor," the girl's mother said, looking around uncomfortably. "He is said to also have been meeting with the Bor at the same time."

The girl shook her head. "The new leader of the Fazaat is a witch. And if it was not a group that slayed him, it would have to be one with power."

"Why would this, Zuberi, kill their prior leader?" Noam asked.

"They are not aligned with Maltuba," the girl said flatly, raising her head in a manner that seemed far older and wiser than he would first have attributed to her. "The king had made peaceful overtures for them to join our nation, and they refused. Zuberi had killed for less. I suppose all we know for certain is that he was found on the south road, ripped open with animals devouring his remains, and none but his family mourning the event"

"Sade," her mother hissed, though she too had been enjoying the ghoulish tale. The entire family before him began to bend, and Noam knew at once why the woman had chastised her daughter. He felt the heavy presence behind him and turned at a bow.

"Your Majesty," Noam greeted Azize's father.

Finally something other than that woman could capture Azize's attention; he jerked around and nodded at his father.

"It is nearly time for dinner to be called, and Sade is not an appropriate dinner partner for you," the king said with a soft, friendly voice. He winked at the girl. "Why she is practically married already."

Everyone laughed and played light, but there was a tension among them all that made the hairs on Noam's arm stand up.

"As she was just telling us," Azize said, displaying the fact that he had heard at least half of what was said around him. "I, however, am not here to court anyone, Father. I was merely greeting my nation, as tradition dictates."

"Good, good." The king laughed. "I don't want you to frighten the wits out of poor Sade."

They all laughed again.

"You," the king waved at Noam, he knew his name perfectly well, but he had taken an instant dislike to him and was making a point of letting Noam know it. "Do not be so shy. You've not left my son's side once. Are Maltuban's so frightening to you?"

"Your nation and your people are all things welcoming, Your Majesty." Noam said with the sort of calm polished friendliness Azize had come to rely on him for in their travels. The prince of Maltuba was not always welcome in the lands he most wanted to see because of King Enzi's reputation, and Noam did have a way of easing strained relationships for him. "I simply have been enjoying the chance to know them all through your son's introductions."

"Hmm. In Maltuba, men are raised to face the world alone." The king said, still with a bright, teasing smile, but the comments true target felt the strike.

Azize stiffened. "If you will excuse us, Father, honored guests. There are a few more families I need to greet before dinner."

They bowed and parted ways from the king, but Noam could feel his eyes on his back as they walked.

"Why did you ask about Zuberi?" Azize asked. Noam could hear the tension and anger still in him from the brush with his father. The fear. He looked ready to bolt back to the ship.

Noam shrugged. "Tales of blood and death tend to be decent distractions from men staring off at other women. Come on, brother, let's just go and greet her."

Azize laughed and shook his head. "Not yet. She's bound either to be someone entirely inappropriate or someone my father sent, and anyway...we aren't here for me to find a woman."

Noam said nothing more on the subject and followed his friend as they moved to another family, this one a little closer to the object of Noam's interest. Hadhi. Many people had tried to kill her father. Was that why she was so...withdrawn? It was hard to be happy knowing everyone around you hated someone you loved.

Asha noticed a man among the foreigners, whose eyes followed her everywhere. He was dressed more like the people of Maltuba, but she didn't recognize him. She had thought he might be the prince for a moment, but dismissed that. He was not wearing the honorary sash with stripes of pattern from all five tribes, for one thing. And she remembered Azize as a thin boy with a head too big for his body and a gaunt little face. This man had a nice face, sweet and engaged, with her at least. She enjoyed having him follow her. When she moved, he moved. He'd abandoned three groups of people already to be near to her. He'd been with Hadhi and Jauhar when Asha entered. But he never approached Asha. She toyed with the idea of walking right up to him, but...it was too fun being pursued. Asha cast him a coy look and flagged down the nearest foreigner she could find.

Wasting no time with greetings, she dove right in with questions, desperate to avoid the yawning pain in her chest after that encounter with Sabra. "Tell me the most dangerous thing you've ever done." She demanded.

"I..." the man fumbled, taken aback. He was a bit older than most of the prince's traveling companions, perhaps as old as forty. "I suppose fighting in the battle of Wyvern, hundreds of men died."

"That is a terrible shame. But...what did it feel like?" Asha prompted, her voice vibrating with restrained glee. She wasn't happy that men had died. Who would be? That was awful. But she needed to *feel* something other than this longing. She needed words, any words to pull her out of her world and into another. Was there no one who could do that?

"Terrifying. And exhilarating," the man admitted with a slight shrug. "It was...hot, and heavy. All around, men were dying, falling, crying out, but as long as you were still on your feet, you were still alive. And I...kept my feet. Every time someone else fell, and I stood, I felt stronger." Asha leaned in as he spoke, felt his intensity calling out to the hungriness inside her. Oh, he could carry her away.

"Until it was over," he said flatly. "I'd thought it all a grand adventure too. Then the battle was over, and the heaviness I felt wasn't from the exhaustion of fighting or the loss of energy. It was...their lives. The ground was scattered with dead and dying men. Carrion birds were circling above us and my skin was damp with the blood and sweat of other men. I had to hear them die."

Asha reached out, latched onto the man, offering him comfort as he continued to speak. "Their breaths fast, or so slow you could barely hear it, but on their last ones...you could always tell their last breaths. How their chests collapsed as their souls escaped their broken forms. The birds kept swooping with those last breaths as if they were devouring the souls as they floated into the sky." He shook his head. "I survived the battle, and until it was over, I had no idea how a terrible fate that was."

Asha shook her head, and a few stay tears spayed free, imagining Baba all alone on the road, stabbed and left for dead with carrion animals devouring his body and birds capturing his soul. She lifted this stranger's hand to her lips and infused the kiss with all the comfort she could.

"Please forgive my foolish tongue. I always thirst for adventure, but I forget they are not always just the stories I build in my mind."

"No, no. I am sorry." The man shook his head. "I knew that was not what you meant. But..."

"But your truth would not be silenced," Asha suggested, and the man nodded. "Well, you found the right ears to tell. For I shall carry those men with me now, as you do."

He smiled softly and lifted Asha's hand to his lips to kiss the back of it. "I find it hard to see why Azize resisted his home so long."

"Ha." Asha scoffed; she remembered the runaway prince; he was an idiot. "He never recognized the beauty before him. A desire to see the world is the last thing I would fault anyone for, but failing to see the beauty here is a crime. But come, forget the runaway prince, and now your sad truth is spoken, tell me your most exciting adventure, the one that brings you the greatest joy."

"I would love to, my dear, but I believe I need a moment. Please allow my friend Mikhail to entertain you," he waved over another foreigner, "and I shall speak to you again later."

Asha beamed at the new man; he was younger and brighter of face. In fact, he was quite lovely to look on. He would be perfect if he had any stories to tell.

GOLDEN THREADS

Jauhar bounced Lin from side to side, swaying as he giggled and tapped her chest with his tiny fist. He was so beautiful. His warmth against her skin and the little hum he was making vibrating across her chest were a soothing balm. Jauhar held him close and shut her eyes, whispering a prayer of thanks to the great spirits for preserving this precious life.

"One day," she whispered to him. "You will grow big and strong like your baba. You will carry on his legacy and be the most powerful man in all Maltuba."

Jauhar heard sniggering but paid it no mind. The jealous always mocked. She knew what they thought, that Jauhar only loved Lin because Zuberi was not alive to call him his favorite, but that wasn't so. This baby was as much Jauhar's as it was Zuberi's. Lin might not be alive, but for Jauhar.

Sabra had been wasting away under Zuberi's control. Even after his death, she hadn't wanted her child for the first months of her pregnancy, but Jauhar helped her through. She nursed her, brought Sabra's faith back into the house, gave her a reason to live. She brought Lin into this world. Just because she hadn't carried him in her own womb didn't make him any less her own.

He was a second chance. Her Gitonga reborn. She felt her heart burning and tears clawing their way towards freedom. But Lin giggled, and Jauhar couldn't help but smile. She could never hate this child. At last the spirits had allowed her to bring a son into this world.

Zuberi would have been so pleased. It would have banished forever the memory of their little boy, born without a breath in his body. The little boy she had not been allowed to name lest she offend the spirits. He was Gitonga in her heart, and always would be, though she could never speak it aloud. She rarely felt the need to say it clawing at her being now that Lin had been born. It would have been the same for Zuberi. Lin would have banished the memory of Jauhar's failure to protect her child. She wouldn't fail again.

"She'll hate him as much as she does Asha, if she lives to see him take over her home." Jauhar overheard Oni saying. "You notice Asha isn't here tonight."

There was a bit of laughing at that, and Jauhar felt herself smiling along. No, Asha was not here. Jauhar had seen to it.

Jauhar had Lin in her lap as she sat before the sand circle Sabra used for prayer. Zuberi never allowed Sabra to have this in the mansion. He was born Ga'ogo and did not worship the old spirits like Sabra's people, the Qi'on. He had not allowed Sabra to practice her religion, but it had little to do with his own beliefs and everything to do with controlling his new wife. Even when they had lived in the mansion, Jauhar had called the girl away from Zuberi when it was time for her prayers; she simply had to pray without an alter of sand to stir. Zuberi knew what Jauhar was doing; he'd smiled at her in that smugly fond way of his, enjoying that Jauhar exerted control in the home, so he let it be.

But after his funeral, after Jauhar realized that Sabra was pregnant and wasting away partly because she wasn't sure she wanted Zuberi's child...well then Jauhar made it her mission to help that girl and to preserve that baby. She'd sent Asha on foot twenty miles away to the grasslands where the stone for these alters were carved and traded her own gowns to get them. She'd made Asha build the alter and go three times to Ether for the sand. Just like today, she was making Asha walk to the village to request camels from her uncle to take them to the ball.

She could see that eager look in Asha's eyes as she raced out of the hut towards the city. She wanted to be at the ball; she would do anything to be at the ball. To meet strangers from all over the world. To outshine her sisters. To steal every bit of attention and devour every love. And just like when Jauhar sent Asha after the materials for this alter, and when she made her cook and clean for her sisters and mothers, it was nothing but what Asha owed them. All of them. All her life Asha had been Zuberi's favorite, escaped punishment and received every treasure that came into the house. Received nearly all of his smiles. For nothing. Not for raising his children. Or nursing his dying second wife. Or cleaning and cooking and weaving for him. Not for standing beside him and being a testament to him. Asha did nothing and earned everything, costing her sister's love, and attention, and punishment for not living up to her beauty or intelligence. Costing Sabra her freedom, her family, and her religion by loving her too much for Zuberi to bear. All of it was Asha's fault. And Jauhar would make her pay.

Jauhar watched until Asha was out of sight. She looked a fright already. Her face sweaty and dusted with dirt. Her fingernails torn and dirty from where Jauhar had made her beat out every rug that lined the floor of their hut and fix the crumbling wall of stone that protected their fires from the winds. She looked terrible, but there was something about that girl; she would find a way no matter what task Jauhar set before her. She was racing away faster now than Jauhar had ever seen her move; she was bound to be back quickly. Then she would bathe and look beautiful, and she would be rewarded again. She hadn't earned it yet. She hadn't even finished paying what she owed. A year and a half in no way made up for the sixteen years in which she'd been pampered and exalted over Jauhar's children.

Jauhar kissed Lin on the head and left him by the sand alter. Sabra and Hadhi were braiding Nuru's hair and adorning it with thread. Jauhar slipped quietly into the hut. She made her way through the main room that used to be the entire hut before Kafil made his improvements. She walked down the wide stairs into the coolest part of the house, the rooms below ground. She had to admit Kafil was clever in ways his brother was not. This home sat in the warmest part of Jaccada, but its mud walls and below-ground rooms kept it cooler than many of the homes in the city.

Jauhar slipped into the room the three girls shared and found the silk Asha had laid out to wear to the ball. It was a bright orange silk with golden threads making reflected lines like the outstretched arms of the jungle. Symbols of the women of the Tikoo. Her mother's silk, worn when she took Asha and presented her to the queen and king. Something that had never been offered to Jauhar, as if to say Asha was better than her daughter. As if she deserved more.

Jauhar sat quietly, humming to herself as her fingers played with the gown, her nail caught on one of the gold threads, tugging it up. That would never do. Jauhar tugged gently, twirling her finger to catch the thread around it as she unwound Asha's silk.

Jauhar wandered the grand room now, with Lin at her shoulder and a smile on her face, because she knew Asha was at home, sobbing over her ruined gown and her ruined adventure. Their neighbors were wrong about her feelings towards Lin, but they were right about Asha. Jauhar was nowhere near finished with that girl; every wish she ever had Jauhar would destroy.

Nuru was among her friends, smiling along as they talked and laughing, but her heart wasn't in it.

Hadhi never has been easy to love.

There were moments when she hated her mother. How could she speak of her own daughter so? And to someone who had made Hadhi's life miserable for years.

"Your hair looks lovely, Nuru," Arya said brightly. "My mother would never let me use golden silk that way."

Nuru's hair had been braided into what felt like a hundred tiny braids and gathered into a blooming bun at the apex of her head. She occasionally wore it in these sorts of braids; they could last for weeks and looked quite fetching on her. But today was special. Today there were golden threads of silk wound through all of the outside braids, rags of every color at the end of the inside braids, as well as rings and beads strung through at different spots. Hadhi had stood over her since near sun up, braiding her hair with Sabra's help when she put in the gold. Spending so much of the day getting Nuru ready that there was barely time to brush out her own dry hair into clouds around her face and place a headpiece of wooden beads atop it to adorn it.

How could it possibly be hard to love someone like that?

"Hadhi did it," Nuru said proudly. "We were at it all day, in the sun." Nuru sighed and shook her head. The others all nodded sympathetically. It was a very warm spring.

"Well, it was well worth the hours," Neema remarked. She was two years older than Nuru, and this was her third year among the Spirit Dancers; she'd danced as a vulture tonight. "Perhaps if she offered to do the same for the Spirit Dancers Eshe will allow you to dance with us."

"Do you think?" Nuru said excitably. "Many people do braids like this."

"Many people do the braids, but not like that. You look like a princess," Arya said brightly from her stool. One of Arya's legs was crooked from a troubled birth; she couldn't support her own weight without crutches, and just now she was taking a break.

"You look even prettier than Asha tonight. Where is she?" Neema looked around, her voice nearly bitter. "I thought the king wanted *all* the women of age to marry here to tempt his son. How did she get out of it?"

Nuru bit her tongue and hid her roiling stomach with a soft smile and a shrug. "She took ill earlier today. Ugh, Mzaa's glaring at me. I have to go talk to one of the foreigners."

"Me too," Arya agreed. "We'll talk at dinner," she promised and stood, slipping crutches under her arms and departing with a grin and an eye roll, off to find a man to satisfy her mother's hungry gaze, just as Nuru was.

Nuru walked away with a bright smile on her face, but a sick feeling under her skin. She tended to wear her hair with her tight curls peeking out from under a scarf. But she'd asked her mother again and again for a week to do something special. When Hadhi had woken her; she'd been at first a bit annoyed to have to rise so early, but then thrilled when Hadhi said she would prepare her hair like Nuru wanted. All day, they'd sat outside, braiding one tiny section after another, Hadhi dipping her fingers into a thick goo that softened the hair and held it together in the braids. They had all been sweating and tired. So it hadn't really struck Nuru at first that Asha had been working since dawn as well. She'd washed laundry at the river. Beat rugs. Repaired a hole in the wind wall. Prepared Mzaa's hair and Sabra's. Done sewing repairs to Sabra's and Nuru's gowns. She'd even prepared their meals. It was more work than Asha usually had in a day, but many of the chores were so much Asha's that none of it had seemed odd, until Asha came back with five camels borrowed from their uncle and Mzaa demanded Asha get mud from the river to patch a hole in the roof.

"What if the prince comes?" Mzaa said when Asha protested for the first time. "We cannot let him see our home in such shambles."

"I...I think it unlikely the prince will come here, Jauhar," Sabra had interjected. She was holding the gold threads high, as Hadhi braided around them. Even Hadhi had looked up in surprise. For a moment, she'd smiled, an angry, satisfied smile. Then her eyes had met Mzaa's and she'd raised a silent brow of reproof.

"It is a small hole," Hadhi said without inflection.

"Indeed," Mzaa agreed. "Small enough that it should be a very fast repair, if you stop protesting and get to it, Asha. But large enough to let in half the desert in a sand storm."

Hadhi looked back to Nuru's hair and set about her work.

"Of course, Mzaa Jauhar. It will be my honor." Asha smiled sharply and raced away to the river.

"She'll be an absolute sight if she even has time to dress." Sabra pressed once Asha was gone, forgetting her part in Nuru's hair until Hadhi nudged her.

"She has no desire to win the prince, only to see the strangers. And she can do that in any state." Mzaa said dismissively and turned back into the hut.

Asha was nearly done patching the roof when Nuru's hair was finished and she ran back in to dress. That was when Nuru had seen Asha's dress lying in shreds with all of its golden threads missing.

Nuru ran her fingers down the ends of on braid that hung near her neck, her stomach clenching. She could still hear Asha's cry when she'd seen it.

She'd fallen to the ground next to her bed and cried. Her gaze shooting to Hadhi in the doorway.

"Why won't you ever let me be happy?" She'd sobbed. "I had just as much right to go as you. Answer me!" She'd shouted, but Hadhi just stood in the doorway, looking on silent and impassive as usual.

"She didn't do that," Nuru rushed to defend her sister. "She wouldn't. Come, wear —"

"Of course she did it! Where do you think she got the threads for your hair? We have no gold silk. You're hateful and ugly and it won't make a difference if I'm there or not. Everyone will see how ugly you are!" Asha had screeched and took the remnants of the silk and run from the hut in tears.

Nuru had watched her go horrified. And hurt on both sister's behalves. She didn't believe Hadhi would do that. Not to that silk, it had belonged to Asha's mother. Hadhi wouldn't destroy something like that. Hadhi didn't like Asha, especially when she said such things to her, but Hadhi never went out of her way to hurt Asha. She was their sister.

Nuru let her hand fall to her side and tried to smile as she walked up to a stranger. But inside, she was churning with worry for her sisters.

Hadhi never has been easy to love.

Asha was speaking with a man named Tadeo, but his words kept drifting out of her ears. She watched Nuru out among her friends showing off Hadhi's handiwork. Who knew Hadhi had a talent beyond hunting and scowling? No one could scowl like sour-face. Asha bit her tongue to remind herself to stop being distracted by her family. This was her night; they didn't matter. She smiled up at the man before her, but as she moved, she heard the golden rings in her hair jangle against one another and had to glance at Nuru again.

She'd been scraping down old cracked mud to make room for the new stone she was fitting into the wind wall to repair it. This hole had needed patching for three months, and every day Mzaa Jauhar mentioned it. But it was never important enough for her to see to until today. Until she had a reason to make Asha do the work. Asha grumbled to herself as she did the work, but she was working hard and fast because tonight she would see the world.

Out of the corner of her eye, she could see Hadhi standing over Nuru in the little open area near the bathing hut. Nuru's hair had been combed out wide and long, so any curl to her hair was pulled straight. Hadhi held most of it out of her way with little ties as she worked a tiny section into a braid. She was working from the center of Nuru's head out, with a little stool nearby covered in beads to adorn the hair and colorful strips of old silks to braid into different bits.

Asha knew she wasn't Hadhi's favorite person, but they hadn't really fought since Baba died. Everyone was too grief-stricken to fight; they just lived together with their resentments simmering under their pain. But tonight was special. They were all going to a ball at the capitol palace. There wouldn't be time for Hadhi to do anything so intricate with Asha's hair, but maybe she would do a little something special, or maybe she would paint Asha's face for her.

Maybe tonight they could be like real sisters.

Asha shook off her earlier idiocy. Of course they couldn't be real sisters. None of them were a family. She focused on the man describing homes suspended between trees higher than buildings. She could barely picture trees that high, much less homes suspended between them. It should be the most fascinating, diverting thing in the world. But all she could do was see the golden threads dangling from Nuru's braids bursting between slightly thicker strips of purple and green and orange, and dangling with carved wooden beads.

Hadhi had taken, *found* golden threads, and by adding it to rags, made her real sister look like a princess. And Asha had marveled at it and fooled herself into thinking she could have even a fraction of anything similar. Until the very last moment. After she'd patched holes in the roof that could have waited another three months, made food, dusted, and done every other chore that was asked of her. Not as the hours passed and it became clear there wouldn't be time to do anything but change the scarf that hid her hair, so she wouldn't look special, and wouldn't be dressed by her sister, it wouldn't matter. She would still stand with them, they would present themselves to the world as a family, and she could hold her head up knowing all she did to provide for them. Nothing had shaken her hope and her tiny foolish fantasy.

Not until she'd stood over her bed, sweaty, hot, messy, and hopeful, and found her mother's silk in shreds—with every single golden thread unwound from the pattern.

She had never hated Hadhi so much. What sort of evil must live in her heart to destroy something so precious?

Asha was no one's sister. No one's daughter. No one's family. She felt like sobbing all over again. Like rushing to them and shouting out all her rage and hate and—longing. Asha's eyes tore across the room to her other sister and found Hadhi looking her way as well. Asha smiled superiorly at her *sister*. Asha leaned into the man with her, interrupting him.

"Do you know what's wrong with that sour-faced woman over there? She keeps glaring at me. Am I about to be eaten?"

The man laughed uproariously and offered to take her somewhere safer. Asha took his arm and happily let him lead her away.

She made her own way into this ball, and she wouldn't let *her father's family* ruin it for her.

Sabra had kept Hadhi's arm and followed her to a new collection of foreign men. Hadhi didn't know what she was playing at. Sabra was a beautiful woman; she didn't need to be on Hadhi's arm to look more lovely. And she kept trying to encourage Hadhi to speak. But this whole evening was setting Hadhi on edge.

They were nearer the mystery woman now, with her musically tinkling gown and her bright laugh. Hadhi was hard-pressed to look elsewhere. The woman was so compelling.

"Long before I met Prince Azize, I was intrigued by your nation." Mikhail was saying. "As a boy, I heard tell of your king Otutta and his daughter who could take gold and spin it so thin it became thread that she clothed herself in."

Hadhi rolled her eyes, looking away so they would not see. She used to love that story too, the trickster princess who swindled entire nations and was acclaimed for her brilliance. She was no longer fond of it. It reminded her too much of Baba.

"And look at so many of you clothed in gold like goddesses. I'd love to see the process."

"Of clothing them, or turning the gold into thread?" Kane slipped into another conversation Hadhi was involved in. She did not like that man. She'd felt him following her and Sabra around, and he had eavesdropped on Hadhi and her mother earlier. There was something wrong with him.

"It is not gold," Hadhi snapped unnecessarily loud. Around them, a tense sort of silence fell for a moment. "It is gold-colored silk. A bug makes it, not a princess," Hadhi finished, her skin prickling with embarrassment from all the stares.

Hadhi had learned from years of hunting to control her breathing and her pulse. She had learned to take light, almost imperceptible steps and hide her scent from her prey. And she had always been talented at holding her tongue. But there were two things she'd never learned to control: her sour expression, and when she spoke, her sharp tone. She saw people noticing the force with which she corrected the two men before her and felt uncomfortable for yet another reason.

Her gaze was pulled to the mystery woman, observing her as well. The mystery woman smiled smugly and leaned in to whisper some joke about Hadhi to her companions. Hadhi knew it was about her from the way the men looked her way before laughing. Hadhi tore her eyes away and found Azize's incessantly smiling friend, Noam, looking her way from another group. He gave her an odd...almost encouraging smile before he glanced away. Hadhi fought the urge to walk away. She should not need soothing from a complete stranger. She should not be calling enough attention to be mocked by one either. Mzaa would be furious. Hadhi had not meant for her words to come out so firmly, but Sabra kept touching her, and a stranger had been passing on her right, and Hadhi did not want to hear one more word about swirrle worms or their silk threads. Particularly not the gold.

Collecting it in secret and planning how she would decorate her sister's hair had been literally the first thing to make Hadhi feel like herself in over a year. It was the first thing that gave her hope that somewhere in the future, she might be...at ease, content even. But it was ruined now.

"Yes," Sabra rushed to soothe their uncomfortable male companions. Was she not tired yet of soothing men? Hadhi knew Sabra had hated Baba and everything he made her do. Why was she seeking another husband?

Perhaps it was for Lin's sake. Hadhi wondered if it would make any difference to her if Hadhi told her she would not let anyone take her son away. She doubted it. They were not close. Why would she believe Hadhi about that? No one believed her about anything else.

"The swirrle," Sabra went on. "Maltuban weever worms. I think one of our past kings made up the story about it being spun gold in order to," she giggled, "swindle another king into marrying his daughter."

Both of the men laughed.

"Now we..."Sabra searched for a word, glancing at Hadhi.

Hadhi looked away and pretended not to hear her. What were the chances she would know the word?

"It seems silly to say farm," Sabra said with a shy laugh. "But we intentionally raise the worms that produce the gold willoomi as it is the most popular for foreign trade."

"Cultivate, perhaps," Mikhail suggested.

That felt as good a word as any, Hadhi supposed. She ought to pay attention. But her mind was far away. She felt her hands unwinding the willoomi, as she had done in her free moments for the last week. It had to be a secret, so she could not take it home. She snuck to the cave when Nuru was in town with her friends, and Mzaa was off pestering Uncle Kafil to release her daughter's dowries. She felt the tiny hopes that had built up in her heart.

She had imagined herself and her sisters, all together sitting in the morning light, arranging one another's hair and laughing. She doubted any of them remembered, but the year Nuru was born just after Aunt Lolia married Uncle Kafil, she came to the mansion to prepare for the Festival of Ether. It was such a lovely day. Mzaa carried Nuru against her chest in a little wrap, and Aunt Lolia was so proud to have joined the family. They all sat together, with no men around. Mzaa prepared Lolia's hair, and Lolia prepared hers, and they both prepared Asha and Hadhi. *Everyone* was happy. Just for that little while.

It was Hadhi's favorite memory.

She thought of it all this week as she snuck up to the cave and unwound the thread. Thought to herself that maybe, with Baba no longer looming between them, they might have happy moments like that again. She had imagined laughter and sisterhood. And love. She wanted them to love each other again.

But it was not to be. Mzaa was maniacal in her quest to see that Hadhi married the prince. She had spent every moment breaking down Hadhi's flaws and pounding into her the need to smile, the need to be sweet, the need to be anything but herself. When they were discussing what she would wear, and Hadhi mentioned styling her hair up with a scarf that matched her gown and perhaps a single small braid to hold some beads to the side her mother had looked her over with somehow furious pity.

"We have been over this, Hadhi. Before you were scarred, you might have worn such a style, but you cannot have those hideous marks be the first thing a man sees about you. It is hard enough to combat your personality alone. If a man starts out seeing those scars the only things he will ever feel for you are pity or disgust."

Hadhi should be so used to such words from her mother. But somehow, she had let herself believe that they had more to do with the way Baba criticized Mzaa for every one of Hadhi's failings. Like she had convinced herself that Asha's teasing were brought on by Baba's prompts, until she watched her half-sister's hidden grin and amusement at Mzaa's rebuke. Every day of this week, more of Hadhi's fantasy died at her own hand. She kept grinding it up, wanting to lash out at her sister instead of pulling her close and trying to build a bond between them again.

But it was not until she stood over her sister as she sobbed; it was not until she saw the ruined gown and felt Asha's rage and her certainty that it was Hadhi who had destroyed it that Hadhi realized the truth. Her father might be dead, but his shadow loomed over all of them. They would never be free of his legacy.

There is no such thing as love, monster.

THE BLUE AND GOLDEN MACAW

Hadhi was certain her mother had something to do with where she was seated; Mzaa was skilled at arranging things. At the long table of the king, Mzaa sat at the king's right hand, before all the great women and men of the city. Uncle Kafil sat across from her, which was a shock to Hadhi; she had not seen him earlier in the evening. But her mother sitting beside the king was hardly the most impressive feat.

Hadhi was seated halfway down the table with only one man between her and Azize. Not that it would prove useful. Azize had looked Hadhi's way only once, and it was all to speak to the man seated just past her. On Hadhi's right were Noam, the man Azize wanted to speak to, and Daniel, the man who had flirted with Sabra, and Sabra was seated between them. On Hadhi's left was Kane, who had taunted her. Sabra had whispered that he must quite like Hadhi, when she saw the seating arrangement, but Hadhi ignored the foolish statement. The seating was Mzaa's work, and this man was her father's spy, Hadhi would bet her life on it.

Hadhi ate as inconspicuously as she could, not trying to draw anyone into a conversation though she could feel Mzaa's eyes on her. But for once, it was not Mzaa making Hadhi the most uncomfortable. Every time Hadhi would convince herself that she had something worthwhile to say to either of the men beside her or even to Azize; a high cheerful laugh, and an accompanying jangle of golden adornments would sound from the woman almost directly across from Hadhi. The mystery woman. Hadhi would look, as captivated as anyone by the exotic bird in their midst. Her hair was done quite similarly to Nuru's but with true gold, and likely false hair added to her own and such intricacy it made Hadhi's work look childish. It made Hadhi feel heavy, seeing in her mind's eye Nuru fingering one of the braids she had been so thrilled with a moment before, as she watched Asha sob over her ruined gown.

Nuru thought Hadhi had done it. Asha thought Hadhi had done it. It was likely even Sabra thought as much. But Hadhi had felt like crying when she saw it. That had been Rama's gown; she had worn it when she took Asha to meet the queen. Rama had even promised to take Hadhi, but Mzaa prevented it. When Rama returned home, she had wrapped the silk up and tied it with string. *"No one shall wear this until your sister is old enough. I am sure your Mzaa has such a gown of her own for you. You will wear them side by side and be the most beautiful women in Maltuba."*

Hadhi's eyes burned just thinking of it. She would never have done that to her sister. To destroy that would be like destroying Rama again. Hadhi had loved her father's second wife. For a time, she had even loved Asha.

Right now, as she watched this mystery woman, watched others gravitating towards her, heard her questions, and the eager responses, Hadhi —shrank.

Asha would have drawn such notice and had such questions. That was why everyone believed Hadhi had destroyed her gown, not just because she hated her, but because Hadhi could never live up to her. And it hurt Hadhi as much that Nuru would believe such things of her, as it hurt to know that they were right. Hadhi was no match for such a woman.

She listened as this girl asked men to describe the shape of buildings and the height of mountains. Heard as they described foreign animals to her and whispered magical tales. She drew out all the men around her with her curiosity and her intelligence. Even the men on this side of the table watched her in rapt wonder. Azize barely took his eyes off of her. Hadhi would never have thought of such questions. This woman was a shining macaw of blue and golden feathers, and Hadhi was...a scarred mole.

Beside Hadhi her father's spy leaned in and nudged her shoulder. "Do you know her?" Kane asked. "Is she from Jaccada?"

"I do not know her," Hadhi replied stiffly. She wanted to blurt out, *I know who you are*, but she couldn't. She was certain Azize did not know. Even if he suspected someone reported to his father, he wouldn't realize it would be one of her father's men, or he would never have felt safe. Zuberi had only trusted men after they murdered at his side, after they showed him there was nothing they loved. After they'd proven themselves monsters.

What if she was wrong? She knew Baba had a spy, or more likely several among Azize's traveling companions. And this man knowing Maltuban, and the way his gaze had just taunted Hadhi to say something about it reminded her of her father to the point where one of her hands was under the table clenched in a fist to keep from screaming. But perhaps he was just...smug.

"Even you would notice someone like her," he said through a laugh. "So she must be from one of the outer provinces."

"Ask her," Hadhi suggested coldly.

"Haven't you heard? She won't tell anyone a thing about herself. Not even her own name. She only wants to know about them."

Hadhi snorted derisively. No wonder all the men hung off of her.

"Hadhi, if you want men to show an interest in you, you must show an interest in them first," Mzaa snapped. "One doesn't have to be beautiful to attract a man, one only needs to stroke his vanity."

Hadhi had held her hands in fists then as well. Mzaa never could instruct Hadhi without insulting her. She had to tell her every fault she had, had to rip her up. Hadhi did not need her mother to tell her how ugly she was. She could see it. She watched her mother walk and sway, every movement designed to draw notice, but it was not practiced, at least not any longer. Her mother had been moving so, bending so, speaking so for such a long time that all were simply part of her. She was alluring and beautiful —with men. And among women, she was all the other traits of a viper—vicious, deadly, and cold.

"Treat them the way you want someone to treat you. See the best in them and speak only to that. Listen to them, feed them with your attention."

"And then they will give it back?" Hadhi had asked doubtfully.

Mzaa shifted her head aside dismissively, and Hadhi saw the vast chill Mzaa carried within, deadening her to both pain and love. "If you do it right."

Hadhi looked away from the stunning woman across from her. She should be able to do what her mother asked. But it seemed worse to Hadhi, to have to beg for a man's attention by giving him hers. She was bound to do it wrong, and then it would be a wasted effort as she would never get the love she wanted back. But—

Hadhi looked down the long table to where her mother sat, and across the table to her uncle, who she used to think loved her and Nuru, and Asha. Maybe it would be better just to get out of her mother's house. Maybe Hadhi had no need of love, as long as she got away. Hadhi ran her eyes in the opposite direction, down the table to where Nuru sat among the younger women and men of Jaccada. If Hadhi did it right, she could get Nuru away as well, before Mzaa pulled her apart the way she had Hadhi, before their mother made her feel small, and ugly and unlovable. Before she made it true. Like it was for Hadhi.

Hadhi glanced at Kane. He had scars on his hand. Long since healed burns from the look of it. Even that made her think he had worked for Baba. He loved seeing other people's trauma rendered visible. His power proclaimed across their hands, or legs. Or faces.

Hadhi hated this man and the way he taunted her. Hated the man he reminded her of, but she felt a stirring of sympathy for him too. Had Baba done this man's scarring himself? Or just tricked him into it with offers of love and approval he would never give? She let herself feel so for one moment. Then like she did with her friends and neighbors, she shut this man out of her dwindling supply of gentler feelings. If he was Baba's man, then he was another monster.

Hadhi could not do things Mzaa's way, and flatter and play, and bend for him. But...if she could expose him, right here next to Azize, maybe she could gain Azize's attention that way.

Hadhi smiled the way Mzaa told her to, showing nearly all of her teeth, and tilting her neck so her scars were not so obvious.

"What is Reethurn like?" Hadhi asked.

He smirked like he knew her game. "It is far more temperate than here, cooler. Our settlements are smaller, but far closer together. All of the old tribes are called families now and are united under our general, Naveed."

Hadhi's clenched fist flexed under the table, bunching around the worn silk gown so tight it was likely wrinkled. But she held onto her angry grin. "Yes. I have heard the basic information about our neighboring nation," Hadhi said, trying for light and friendly, but based on the stifled laughter from her right, she had not succeeded. She pressed on. "I meant...why did you leave?"

"I wanted to see the world." Kane took a bite of his meat after that bland comment.

Hadhi fought the desire to chew up her tongue. "So you joined Azize's company when he went through Reethurn?"

Kane shook his head with a smug brow in the air. "No. I had been traveling already. I was in Jaccada when Azize left; I took the same passage."

"Passage?" Hadhi narrowed her eyes. "Did the king sell..." But Hadhi fumbled, searching her mind for the proper word. She knew she could say it in Maltuban, the man next to her would know it. But if he was indeed her father's spy, he would not be so sloppy as to say it here, in front of Azize.

Hadhi hated this. She felt exposed. Vulnerable among all of these people. She had never liked celebrations, too many people, too much laughter, too much touching, and lies. She never fit. And that was before you brought foreigners and exotic birds who ate up confidence and light and attention.

What would Mzaa do?

Men love to know more than you do, Hadhi. Let them know you need them. Even if you don't.

Hadhi drew in a deep breath, pasted on her brightest smile, and leaned around Kane, tapping the table next to Azize to get his attention. Mzaa would probably have laid her hand gently on his sleeve and cooed the words, but Hadhi *could* not.

"Azize, excuse me," Hadhi said as softly as she could, but it still came across as forceful. He glanced over. "What is the Fairy word for *oon kaapar?*" She asked the last bit in Maltuban.

"A room?" Azize said as though not understanding how she could be so foolish.

"No, on a ship? Is is still called a room on a ship?" She asked, but barely got the words out, her chest felt so tight.

"A berth, perhaps," Kane suggested, leaning into the space between Hadhi and Azize's heads.

"Oh, yes, exactly." Azize looked away. Straight back to the girl across from them.

Hadhi faced away. He would not notice even if she did trip up her father's spy, would he?

"Enzi's boy is a fool. I have my spy with him, and he doesn't even know it." Baba had boasted at dinner one evening. "You could lead him on a merry chase, Asha."

"What could Hadhi do to him?" Nuru chirped, she was always trying to trick one of their parents into complementing Hadhi, and it had not once worked.

"Ohh," Baba laughed. "Hadhi is too obvious. If she were hunting to kill, she could handle the boy. But...you never do see a cheetah playing nicely with its dinner, do you?"

"I didn't put my request to the king," Kane said, pretending to be unaware that Hadhi had lost interest. "But to the man who ran the *docks*," he said meaningfully.

Baba.

"And to the prince himself."

"Of course," Hadhi agreed vaguely. She pushed the food around her plate. People were beginning to finish their meals and Hadhi had accomplished nothing. She had not eaten, she had not exposed her father's spy, and she had not caught Azize's attention. She could feel the smiling man on her right watching her and felt even smaller. Surely he, like Kane on Hadhi's left side was just watching for something to mock.

Sour-faced-Hadhi.

Hadhi tried to remember what she knew of Azize as a child. Determined to do her duty despite all the mocking eyes around her. Azize was...timid. He hated his home. He adored his mother. He was intimidated by his father. Or perhaps worse—Hadhi glanced down the table at the king. She tore her eyes away before he could notice her attention. Notice her. She needed to keep focused on Azize. She needed to win Azize, so she could be trapped forever in the same home as the king. Hadhi clenched her fists.

She heard laughing on her right and glanced over. Noam was smiling and laughing at something his companion was saying to Sabra. He looked so bright, like the mystery woman. Like Asha. What must it be like to have such light inside of you? To be loved. To have the world adore you.

It made Hadhi so angry. So envious. She felt sick and ugly and small. But also just a little bit...sad. Asha would have fit in so well here. She would have sparkled, and Hadhi would have felt jealous, but she would have been happy for the sister she had loved—long ago.

Hadhi heard her name spoken off past Azize. She did not turn, no one was calling to her. But she trained her ears in that direction, shutting out everything else, letting the distant voice reverberate in her ears like ripples on the water, until she could feel the tone and follow it.

"What can she do to you anymore? Zuberi isn't here for her to tattle to."

"Ugh," Yenge's voice shuddered. "Have you ever seen her glares? She reminds one exactly of her father. If you want to scare her, you do it."

The man beside her spoke again, his voice crackling over Yenge's voice in the distance, but Hadhi heard both men.

"You didn't have the scars when we sailed. How did you get them?" Kane asked.

As Yenge hissed to his friends. "I'm not going to be beaten in the dark as I walk home."

Hadhi tore her attention off the people mocking her and focused on her father's spy. Narrowing her eyes sharply. Not about to answer the question, but unnerved that he remembered her. She did not remember him. "You remember me from then?"

"Yes. I was a bit surprised you didn't recognize me. You nearly knocked me into the harbor as you raced to tattle on your stowaway sister and... your...friend?" He nodded in Sabra's direction.

Hadhi shook her head at that question at the end of his odd statement. That alone was no reason to remember her. "Sabra was Asha's friend then, and my father's widow now. I do not remember you. And I was not *tattling*."

Two girls locked alone on a ship full of the king's men, Hadhi shuddered at just the thought. It was not safe. Asha never did anything that was safe. And Sabra had always followed wherever she led. They would have gotten themselves killed, or worse.

"You didn't want them to have any fun you couldn't have." Kane shook his head.

"They were not safe." Hadhi had heard plenty of times that she spoiled all of Asha's fun. That she was just jealous. That she was too scared to do anything and spoiled anyone else's joy. Even Nuru said such things sometimes.

"Zuberi's favorite daughter and her best friend?" Kane laughed. "There isn't a man in Maltuba that would touch either one without his permission," he said with a twisted grin. Hadhi wasn't sure she believed that. But even if it were true, she would not have risked her sister so. Not that it made any difference.

"All you saved them from was a trip around the harbor playing stowaways, before the captain noticed them and took them back to shore. You just didn't want them to be happy without you." His voice dropped to a whisper. "And no one wanted you along."

Hadhi bit down hard on her tongue. Curled both her hands into fists and fought off the burning in her eyes. This was definitely her father's man. It was precisely the sort of thing he would say.

Monster, you know you're not needed here.

Hadhi wished she could prove any of them wrong. But—she *was* ugly and angry and jealous. Right now, though she did not know the woman, though she had done nor said a thing to Hadhi, Hadhi was staring across the table at that mystery woman and wanting to strangle that captivating laugh right out of her. How dare she be so bright and joyful when the world was so ugly?

"Excuse me." Hadhi rose, heading out of the dining hall to wait for the dancing.

"Hadhi," Sabra called out as she was passing. "Hadhi, do you need anything?"

Hadhi did not stop walking, did not look back, even as she felt her mother's gaze, even as she heard snickering from women along the table. She did not belong here; no one wanted her here.

OTHER FAMILIES

Sabra watched Hadhi walk away with that same stiff posture she wore whenever someone had taken a bite out of her. She should go after her. But Sabra had no idea how to help. Hadhi wouldn't trust a thing that came from her.

"What was that about?" Noam asked Kane.

Noam and Daniel were two of Azize's closest friends and had been entertaining her with stories of all his firsts. The first time Azize tried to swim and nearly drowned. The first time he tried the dances, everyone in Maltuba had been forced to learn for tonight. The first time he saw the whales of the deep ocean. Sabra had been loving every minute. She could imagine him, so sweet and shy, exploring a world so much bigger than he. She had been so thoroughly enjoying herself that she hadn't worried about Lin or Hadhi. Nuru would be fine on her own, there was no need to worry about her. But Hadhi worried Sabra, and she'd forgotten her again. And something Kane said had sent her off in tears.

Kane laughed. "She couldn't get Azize's attention. It seems to have upset her."

"Who wants my attention?" Azize said and looked over.

Sabra's breath caught. She couldn't explain why. She didn't love him the way she'd thought she did as a child. And even then, he had not been her strongest love. She just...he was a memory of a time before the world showed her its true, ugly face. She desperately needed for him to stay sweet and gentle.

But her breathlessness was all for naught. He didn't even see her, looking at his friends instead. To be fair to him, there were two men between them, and he hadn't seen her in five years.

"Did you know her before?" Noam asked.

"Know who?" Azize asked.

Sabra wanted to blurt out Hadhi's name and see if she could get Azize's attention that way, but she rather thought she should be chasing after Hadhi instead.

"Not you, Kane? The girl who was sitting here, the pretty one with the scars."

"Pretty?" Kane and Azize said in disbelieving unison.

Sabra opened her mouth to shout something in Hadhi's defense, but before she could, the king stood. Silence fell as he took to his feet; he made no announcements, just wiped off his face, held a hand out to Jauhar, and walked from the room. Dinner, it seemed, was at an end. Azize left behind his father, most everyone was watching in silent deference, but across the table, the mystery woman still spoke in hushed enthusiasm to the man next to her. She looked...voracious. Too desperate for the knowledge she sought to notice the world moving around her.

It was really quite lovely, her enthusiasm. It reminded Sabra of her childhood and Asha's bright face insisting Sabra join her on some quest. She missed feeling that alive. She missed seeing Asha so bright. Asha should have been here. Sabra should know by now how to speak. She was a woman grown. A mother. A widow. But she still waited for Zuberi's permission to breathe. She waited for the back of his hand to strike or his fist to fall. She waited to be told who she was. Shouldn't that have ended when he died?

A hand slid down before her, and Sabra glanced up; Daniel wore a bright smile as he offered to lead her from the table. But Sabra shook her head.

"I should really go check on my son," she said softly and watched his eyes withdraw just a bit.

"Oh, are you married? I hadn't realized."

"Widowed," Sabra said with a half-smile, knowing for this man it made no difference as it would not for Azize. It was the word son that had made him uncomfortable. Jauhar was wrong. Zuberi had left his mark, and no man would want her now.

He was very polite, offering to escort her, but Sabra let him go. She walked out of the room in the same direction Hadhi had taken, then turned down the first hall on her right, leading to the room where the other mothers had taken their little ones so they would not disturb the meal. She should have stayed here too. She should not have listened to Jauhar.

Across the room, she spotted her son on the ground, lifting and stirring the sand in one of the alters used for prayer. He looked so happy. Sabra felt a burning sun of peace in her heart. Lin was safe. He would never be beaten by his father for failing to be what he wanted, he would never be picked apart for his tiniest flaw. It didn't matter that Sabra would never have the sweet romantic style of love she'd imagined as a girl, the sort of love she had was so much better.

Nuru sighed as her sister marched from the room. She'd hoped tonight would be the thing that made Hadhi better. She'd been so sad since Baba died, entirely changed. Not that she had been bright and cheerful before, but she didn't hunt anymore; she didn't really go anywhere unless it was to follow Nuru or Mzaa.

But tonight had seemed like the perfect chance to give her something to excite her. None of the men Azize brought home knew anything about her. But it seemed even the new men didn't see in Hadhi what Nuru saw. Hadhi wasn't stunningly beautiful like Mzaa, nor bright and alluring like Asha, nor even as quietly lovely as Sabra. But Hadhi was pretty, and the scars were much less pronounced now. But those weren't the best things about her, Hadhi always tried to protect other people. Sometimes a little too much. She would take the brunt of their mother's or their father's criticism, so Nuru didn't have to. She was always worried something was too dangerous for the smaller children. She protected their cousins hunting for them without telling Baba or anyone else and leaving it for them to sell, when Uncle Kafil was ill and could not provide for them. She was kind. But no one ever saw it because she was not friendly or bright or very social.

Nuru saw their uncle watching Hadhi as she left, he looked uncomfortable, but he didn't say anything to stop her or to help her. Before Nuru could chase after her sister, the king stood, and everything else stopped. He held out a hand for Mzaa and led her from the table. After he was gone, Azize stood and escorted Faizah, who he'd been seated beside, but had not spoken to much. Nuru waited, watched as all of the prince's friends escorted different women from the room. Watched Mzaa Sabra get up to go after Hadhi. Nuru was never sure how she felt about Sabra. She'd hated her when she first came to live with them. She and Asha had spent years teasing Hadhi, so Nuru hated her on principal. But Hadhi always forced Nuru to be polite to her. Always.

"Why are you defending her?" Nuru had shouted at Hadhi. Nuru had captured a snake to put in Sabra's bed to scare her. Just to scare her, it wasn't venomous. But Hadhi caught her at it and wouldn't let her. "Now that they're in the house together, they'll taunt you all the time."

"She has done nothing in the hours she's been here." Hadhi pointed out softly.

"She will!"

Hadhi shook her head. "That is not protecting me, Nuru. It is hurting her. Nuru... There was no celebration, no negotiation, no choice for her." Hadhi had said so tight and quiet Nuru had to strain to hear. She looked so angry, the words had to squeeze out between her teeth.

Nuru felt Hadhi's intensity inside herself, everything balling up tight. And Hadhi saw, she released a breath and softened her words, laying a hand on Nuru's shoulder as she said her piece.

"Baba took her for his wife, without giving her a chance to say no. And her family went along with it. She is younger than I am. I heard Baba tell her she cannot see her family or Asha without him present. Sabra is not here to hurt me. Be kind to her. We are her only family now."

Nuru hadn't liked hearing any of it. It scared her, made her angry at Sabra's family, at Baba, and unreasonably angry at Sabra. She didn't even know why; she just knew somehow it must be her fault. There must have been something she'd done because other girls were married with vibrant celebrations. Other girls had choices, didn't they?

Nuru hated it, but she did what Hadhi said. And in at least one way, Hadhi was right. Sabra had not once taunted her since she was married. Sometimes Nuru let herself believe that Baba had married her to stop her hurting Hadhi. Sometimes it even made sense.

Nuru watched Sabra walking out of the room after her sister now and felt Azize passing by, and she realized something she had not in the past. Nuru *wanted* being forced to marry Baba to be Sabra's fault, because Nuru was terrified of being forced to marry someone she didn't want. If it was because of something bad Sabra had done, then all Nuru needed to do to avoid such a fate was do as she was told. But if it wasn't, if it was not a punishment, then it could happen to anyone. And Nuru didn't want that someone to be her.

The room was clearing. Only a few people remained, besides Nuru, her friends urged her out to go and dance. Nuru loved to dance, but her uncle was still in the room, and Nuru's anger on her sister's behalf and on her own only grew.

Nuru marched over to the king's vacated seat and took it boldly. It was not the throne after all, but she doubted anyone else would do this. Uncle Kafil raised a brow at the action, and a small smile played at the corners of his lips.

"You were always the boldest of my brother's girls. Did he ever tell you that?" Kafil asked, nodding for Sade, the young woman he was courting, to leave them alone. Sade was only about Hadhi's age, but Uncle Kafil needed a new wife now Aunt Lolia was gone. All his children were still younger than Nuru; he could not care for them all alone.

"No, but Hadhi tells me."

He smiled genuinely for a moment, then looked away.

"Why will you not release our dowries?" Nuru demanded boldly.

"No one has been worthy of you, and your mourning time has barely ended. Do not take after your mother and imagine a plot. I will release your dowries when an appropriate match comes along."

"Will you ask us?" Nuru pressed.

"Ask you what?" He looked genuinely confused.

"If we think the man is worthy. If we want to wed." Nuru explained.

Kafil wouldn't look at her. "Your father would not have."

Nuru didn't know what to say to that. Surely Baba would have given his own daughters the chance to refuse husbands. Wouldn't he? Nuru wasn't prepared to examine that question, so she pressed on with others.

"Why do we live in the hut? We could be helping care for our cousins if we all lived together. The mansion has room enough."

"Then why did I live in the hut with my wife and three children, Nuru?"

"You are punishing us for things Baba did!" Nuru shouted in his face. "Hadhi is the one who fed your family when you were ill, did you know that?

She would hunt in secret and leave the meat or the money at your door. She made me collect willoomi and bring them to Aunt Lolia so she would not have to leave you to do her work. You and Baba were always like Asha and Hadhi, you hated each other and I could never see a real reason why, but...we aren't Baba. I thought you loved us."

Nuru shoved back the seat and marched away. She wondered if things were really different in other families, or if they were all like this, but you couldn't see through walls, so you didn't know. She couldn't honestly say which she hoped for because Nuru loved her family, all of them, even Asha, even Mzaa though she could be so cruel it tore into you. Nuru loved them all, and she didn't want them to be the bad family, but nor did she want to know that all families housed such pain.

Hadhi was hiding on the shadowed walk of the veranda that ran the perimeter of the capitol palace.

You just didn't want them to be happy without you, and no one wanted you along.

She did not like that man. Perhaps if she hid here all night, Mzaa would not find her and she could just be—

"Oh! Hadhi!" Sade exclaimed in shock. Hadhi turned in time to see the young woman's eyes widen as if she expected to be eaten.

They had never been as close friends as Asha and Sabra were, or even Nuru and Arya, but Hadhi and Sade had been friends as young girls. So why Sade would be afraid she could not say.

"Sade," Hadhi nodded her head softly after a moment. "Paax pzaam vay kamko io qidjiva ini." Hadhi spoke the words in her own tongue, enjoying the familiarity of the tones and textures. And something of that comfort made her mind quicker to provide her the words in Fairy: *it seems we will be family soon.*

Sade nodded softly, looking away. " Yes, evis ini."

Hadhi heard the nerves in Sade's voice: *very soon.* Hadhi stepped forward softly, smoothly trying not to startle her as Sade looked away shyly or in fear. Hadhi knew there was quite a large age difference between her uncle and the girl before her, perhaps as much as nineteen years, but she actually thought them well suited in temperament. Kafil was a gentle man, and Sade was sweet and playful, beloved by children she would be a good mother to Hadhi's cousins.

Still, if *Sade* was unhappy with the match, it should not take place. Hadhi felt her heartbeat slowing as her hunting skills took over. In the back of her mind, Baba was taunting her. *You know better than to worry about things you can't change, monster. You can't protect her.* But—Baba was gone. Perhaps there was a way. Perhaps this neighbor, this frightened girl Hadhi could help.

"Ur uli nong lala ava kup aq'alltic," *Are you not happy with the joining,* Hadhi queried in a whisper, only to be greeted with peals of laughter.

"I am most pleased and honored to join with your uncle," Sade said with a bright smile. Her eyes seeming to ask if Hadhi was insane.

Hadhi settled back, shoving away her concern. "Ta qidjiva kamko io bona vihotell." Hadhi said easily. *Our family will be those honored.* It was true, and easy to say without much thought, for her mind was far from her mouth.

Was she truly so different from everyone? Was she the only one who did not long for a husband? Was she the only one wary of even a man's touch? Hadhi glanced away. She should return to the ballroom before Mzaa came to find her.

"Szii ashuri uli ethee vozala." Hadhi inclined her head, giving the girl the traditional felicitation for an engaged woman: *I wish you great joy.*

Sade shot out a hand to stop Hadhi before she could escape. "I..." Sade fumbled. "I should have tried before now to comfort you. I know you are most grieved by your father's passing."

Hadhi ground her teeth across one another and fought off the urge to vehemently deny any such thing. Apparently the years of only greeting one another in passing had made both women equally incapable of understanding the other. Hadhi opened her mouth to reply with the expected thanks, but Sade's eyes teared up, and she spoke on.

"I will not lie as some do and say I cared for your father, but when you ran from the alter in sobs—my friend—Szii mbiditell paax akil szo qio."

I felt it in my heart. Sade's teary eyes spilled over at the words, and Hadhi could not help but be caught as well, breathless, nearly pulled into the anguish of that moment.

Hadhi could not deny that the funeral had undone her. It was forbidden to cry at funerals, whether one was born Ga'ogo, Maumai, Qi'on, Tikoo, or

Bor. All five tribes believed funerals should be moments of joyous surrendering, offering souls to the hands of Ether. Crying was said to rouse unhappy spirits but— As much as she had expected to be joyful as her father departed her life forever, there had been no joy in Hadhi that day. Just anguish. But not so now. And Hadhi had no idea how to express that without revealing the entire ugly truth. There might not be joy in Hadhi still, but there was no grief either. Only hate.

"Let me offer you, szo centok gzaijivi kif ulin bao." Sade finished, taking Hadhi's hand and squeezing as fervently as she spoke: *my deep sympathy for your pain*. Hadhi couldn't think what to do but to squeeze the girl back. Offering a small smile of gratitude. What else was there to do?

Despite her own inner struggles, Hadhi was pleased to have her earlier feelings affirmed. Her uncle had made a most excellent selection for his new bride. Sade had a good heart. Hadhi was saved having to lie about her father, spotting her mother's approach from the corner of her eye. She nodded that way and let it be an excuse not to speak. No one expected the monster to speak anyway.

Sabra looked up from her son's head; Jauhar had found her, and apparently Hadhi as well. Hadhi stood in the doorway as Jauhar marched across the room. When she was towering above Sabra Jauhar launched into a quiet lecture.

"You are all of twenty, you cannot spend the rest of your life at my side, wasting away. You will enter that great room and attempt to catch a man's attention, if not for yourself, then for your son. Lin needs a father, and if you don't provide him one, Kafil will do it."

Sabra stiffened. She much preferred Kafil to his brother, but since his brother's death, Kafil had seemed harder. And Sabra had no interest in being forced to wed—again. She pulled Lin nearer her chest; she didn't want him exposed to anyone who was not kind.

Another young mother, Bayo, had overheard the entire conversation and moved nearer.

"Sabra, you should do as Jauhar says," Bayo said softly.

Sabra was nodding; she knew they were right. Past Jauhar, she watched Hadhi, so angry, so hurt, tattered by her parents. She could not allow the same to happen to Lin.

"I do not like leaving him alone so long," Sabra said, even as she was preparing to lay her son back on the ground beside the sand circles to play.

"Then do not," Bayo suggested. "I will bring Wema and we shall play in one of the alcoves along the balcony. When you want to dance or talk he will stay with us."

"Or leave his with his Mzaa Jauhar," Jauhar said coolly, casting Bayo a dirty look. She had allowed the interference because the woman agreed with her, but she liked control.

"Alright," Sabra agreed and followed them from the room. As she fell into step beside Hadhi Sabra whispered softly. "Are you alright, Hadhi? What did that man say to upset you?"

"Hadhi is fine," Jauhar snapped. "She is going to stand with us, wearing a smile and attempt to entertain Azize's friends, and Azize himself if the opportunity presents itself. As she should have been at dinner."

"I tried," Hadhi said flatly. "He was only interested in that stranger in blue and gold."

"Oh yes!" Bayo said like she was part of the conversation when Sabra was certain most everyone had forgotten her presence. "I haven't seen her yet, but all the other mothers are agog. No one knows who she is, but they say she is the most beautiful, most vivacious woman here."

Jauhar made a hum like she was about to speak, but Bayo being not as familiar with Jauhar as other women, didn't pay it any mind and kept right on speaking, with her daughter gumming at one of her fingers and her eyes alight for all the attention she was being afforded.

"I said it must be Asha in disguise. Everyone knows she is the most desirable woman in Maltuba."

"Clearly that is not the case." Jauhar snapped. "That woman is not my husband's daughter."

"Oh, no. Clearly not; it was a jest."

"You had bet—

"It is lucky for the woman that she is not Asha, or the prince would have thrown her out." Hadhi interrupted her mother loudly. Hadhi seemed to be trying to save the woman from a severe tongue lashing.

"Oh, is...that why she didn't come?" Bayo asked Hadhi hesitantly.

Hadhi didn't respond. They had reached the ballroom. Hadhi scanned the room before starting forward. Sabra hadn't spent much time with Hadhi at celebrations of this nature. Hadhi tended to keep to the perimeter when she was able. Sabra watched her move now and was a bit jealous. Hadhi moved with such grace. Her feet were silent and her movements smooth. Not once, despite the crowd, did she falter or brush another being. She could move through the crowd entirely untouched. She was lovely, like a large cat prowling through the grasses or across tree branches.

"Speaking of that woman," Jauhar said in a low whisper. "I saw her speak to you, Sabra. What did she say?"

A good family would want adventure for you.

"She wanted to know about the men. So I...pointed her away from Prince Azize." Sabra said because Jauhar would want to hear it.

Bayo tittered, and Jauhar nodded pleased, but it was Hadhi's graceful back that drew Sabra's eye. Hadhi was so aware, so much herself, in all situations.

"Good," Jauhar remarked. "She can have all the men she wishes, but not Azize."

Hadhi rolled her shoulders. A casual move to the unaware observer, but Sabra was near enough to feel her tension. Hadhi was preparing herself to try again to attract attention she knew she could not get.

It really was silly to be jealous of Hadhi. Sabra knew that. After all the person with the least understanding of Hadhi's value, of her talents, her appeal, and her beauty, was Hadhi herself.

Jauhar stopped suddenly, and though she was walking before them, Hadhi stopped as well, and her body swayed slightly. She was listening to the room around them with her whole being. Sabra wondered if she could convince Hadhi to teach her to hunt. Hadhi was a great hunter. She hadn't really done any since her father died, and Jauhar allowed it, because it was a sign of grief, honoring what Hadhi had once done at her father's side. But it was over a year since his death now. Perhaps she was ready to start hunting again. Perhaps she would teach Sabra, so that Sabra and Lin could care for themselves. So that she need not find another man and tie herself to him. So she could make it the forty miles south on her own and go live with the Bor, where a woman and child alone was accepted.

"There is a fine place for you to play with the children, Bayo," Jauhar said, and without so much as a brow raised in question, reached out for Lin.

Sabra allowed her to take her son, mostly to avoid a scene, and watched as he was handed into the arms of this woman that Sabra saw as a little girl despite their mere one year of age difference. Bayo was allowed to be a little girl still. She was the second wife of a kind man. He was a tanner, and she spun silk from the swirrle worms, and her husband's other wife kept the house. They were a quiet, happy family. Bayo knew nothing of the darker side of marriage. She wouldn't understand how another wife could be both your greatest ally and at times your enemy. She couldn't understand what it was to be owned by your husband, rather than treasured. And she most certainly couldn't understand what a threat an unloving world was to her child. For surely, at some time Hadhi must have been as happy and soft, and innocent as these babes, but not so now.

Sabra's eyes were drawn once more to Hadhi standing vigilant before them, stiff and scarred, and far from innocent now. Sabra needed to get her son away from this family. She needed to get him a family like Bayo had, a family where he could remain sweet.

FOOD TO SATE THE SOUL

Asha had made it through most of the foreigners and she was beginning to feel she'd made the wrong wish. Some had stories worth the hearing, but none fed her. When the stories were done, she was left starving again. How was she to prepare herself for the hibernation that was her life if she couldn't even consume enough wonder to be full for more than a minute. Was there no one like her in the whole world? Was there no one who understood that a story couldn't just be told, it needed to be experienced. A body needed to sing from excitement that was too far away to grasp. Breath needed to be stolen by threats that could never harm you. Pulses needed to race, muscles needed to coil, you needed to *shout!*—just because the moment called for it. You needed to be overcome by laughter that tumbled through you like thunder.

"I haven't spoken with you yet." Asha grabbed the wrist of a man as he was set to pass her. She should probably let him go; he was headed towards Sabra and the rest of Asha's *family*. But Asha needed to be fed. She could still feel her stalker. He was pretending to talk to another man. Asha eyed him for a moment as she pulled this man nearer.

"You have not spoken with me yet," the man whose arm she claimed agreed with a smile. "And who do I have the pleasure of speaking with?"

"My name is unimportant, but my questions are vital. Tell me, what was the most beautiful, most unique, most...exotic place you visited in your travels?"

"Well." He hesitated, possibly thinking. "All of the different lands had their own charms. There is a nation, at the opposite end of the world, so frozen it seems nothing can live there, but people do. It is astonishing."

"What about it astonished you?"

"The resilience. In my home nation, we are quiet people. We have mild summers and cold winters, but our winters are not very long, and we are prepared for them by months of cultivating the land and storing up for the winters ahead."

"You were awed by the fact that they remain alive?" Asha asked, annoyed. "What were their buildings like? What did they worship? Was there magic? Did you not travel to any of the islands near Great Island, where fairies roam freely, or to Mount Willcut where the elves dwell?"

The man looked briefly offended by her tone, but he did not leave, and he smiled as he responded. "We visited the isle of Feather, where the temple of the nymphs once stood."

The Temple of the Nymphs! Asha held her breath in anticipation of the story. Wouldn't it be delightful if they'd met the same nymph, worlds apart?

"But we saw no fairies there. The temple is a ruin now. It is quite lovely in fact, the trees and flowers have overtaken the walls."

"You are a terrible storyteller; where is the wonder, the intrigue?" Asha demanded impatiently. The man laughed loud and bright. "Did you get any sense of the beings who once lived there? Why do you think they abandoned it?" Asha pressed fervently, feeling the desperation building under her skin. He'd seemed amused at first, but by the time Asha finished her passionate speech, her companion took a step away.

He fumbled for words, but behind him, Asha's stalker was finally made bold enough to step forward.

"Surely they saw how lovely it is as a ruin and left it so on purpose. Perhaps it was never a great building at all." The young man stepped forward and spoke over the other.

The man Asha had been speaking to gave his compatriot a look like he might want to reconsider talking to Asha.

"It's a mirage, brother," he muttered quietly.

But her stalker paid him no heed. He might not have even heard him.

Asha grinned, basking in the undivided attention and the desire to please her falling off the man before her. The other man shook his head and slowly backed away, leaving Asha and her pursuer alone.

"The light as it falls through the trees creates such patterns on the ground, and on the remains of the walls, it is artistry." Her pursuer spoke passionately. "And when the wind stirs through the grasses, the leaves jingle, and the flowers release sweet fragrances, and the bugs sing! If they wished a temple to celebrate all that is wonderful and unique in Feather they have achieved that, without a ceiling or any hand guiding the growth into a particular path."

Mmmm. Asha sighed internally. Yes, this was the food she'd been after. A like mind, an equally curious and hungry explorer.

"How long were you there?"

"We stayed only a few days. I wanted to find fairies, but none emerged while we were there."

"Ohh, scared of you, do you think?" Asha teased.

He laughed. "I doubt it. I imagine we simply weren't exciting enough to wake their notice. Or they liked to observe us in secret. Do you ever wonder about that?" He asked, then eagerly spoke right over himself to explain his question. "Do you think fairies and other magical beings find us...exotic and magical in a different way? Or do you think they see us as lesser creatures like animals?"

Asha giggled. "Ohhh, I think magical creatures see our value." She said coyly, thinking of Zawadi and the gift she'd given Asha for this one night. "I think they want to know and understand us as much as we do them. I think there are sprites and nymphs and elves out in the night right now, wondering what happens in Maltuba."

The man scoffed, looking around the room in distaste. "They ought not to waste that journey."

"How can you say that? There is nowhere in the world but here where the moon touches the ground. There is nowhere as uniquely situated. We live between the claws of the jungle and the teeth of the desert. Nowhere else in the world are their bugs who can make gold. Or deserts that lead the way to the next life."

The man smiled wide and disbelieving. "If Maltuba is so wonderful, why have you spent the whole evening asking about every place but here?"

"I live here, I do not need to know it better. Maltuba is a jewel in the crown of the world. I simply want to know all of the jewels. One can love a thing, but...be interested in loving others as well. Why limit myself?"

"Why indeed," he agreed, and Asha saw a spark in his eyes. She couldn't tell for certain if he was agreeing just to remain near her. Or if he truly agreed. But she also wasn't sure she cared.

"Would...you care to dance with me?"

Asha tilted her head down slightly, looking at him through her lashes coyly. "I suppose I might be tempted if you will tell me about the land where they dance that last twirling piece."

Her pursuer smiled wide. "It would be my pleasure. You've never seen a thing like it! It is called Gods Parted, and there, they worship mermaids."

Noam watched Azize and the whirlwind of a girl for a moment. She seemed frantic, abuzz with something unnatural. She was funny, and bold, and utterly demanding, and had he not already been captivated by her opposite, Noam might have enjoyed talking and dancing with this woman. But she had no patience. That sort of energy burned so bright it obscured everything around it, until it burned out, and you took in the wreckage.

Noam wasn't sure Azize was ready for that sort of woman. Every woman he'd taken to in his travels was...well, like most of the other women here tonight, hanging on his every word, willing to entertain him. The woman Azize was with now would demand that he entertain her. She might be good for him, or her impatience combined with Azize's shyness might make Azize even more hesitant.

When Azize led the girl towards the dancers, Noam decided to leave his friend to it and go satisfy his own curiosity and speak to Hadhi without Azize along to make her nervous. He wondered what her smiles looked like when her mother wasn't pinching them onto her cheeks. But before he made it across the room, he noticed Mikhail leading Hadhi out to dance. Hadhi didn't look very happy about it, nor did Mikhail, but Sabra was all but cheering. Noam smiled; he liked that woman. Noam considered crossing to ask Sabra to dance, but he noticed a younger girl he'd met earlier, sitting in the corner bobbing her head along to the music.

Noam walked over and bowed gallantly as men did to pretty young ladies in his hometown.

"Hello," she greeted him cheerfully. Before Noam could ask her to remind him of her name, she leaned up in a conspiratorial fashion. "Did Azize teach all his friends Maltuban, because I have heard no less than three of his friends exclaim in our language?"

Noam chuckled. He had a feeling this girl with her crutches was unused to being asked to dance because she showed no signs of any such expectations, and even disinterested women usually knew what a man wanted when he bowed before them.

"If by exclaimed, you mean spewed foul epithets, then yes, Azize taught us that. But I confess he taught us little else."

She giggled. "I don't know any curses in Fairy; do you think perhaps they have none?"

"Oh, they have some. They just conceal them from foreigners, so we will think them higher beings."

"And so they can curse right to our faces without us knowing." She grinned pertly.

"A worthwhile reason to keep them secret," Noam agreed gamely. "Would you, do me the honor of a dance, though, to my shame I have forgotten your name?"

She looked utterly shocked for a moment and didn't speak. Then she blinked several times and laughed, but this one was forced unlike the others he'd been treated to. "My name is Arya, but I would only trod on you with my crutches. You should ask someone else."

"If you prefer not to dance I would enjoy a bit of conversation at your side. But if you dance with me, and I think you will do quite well with the cozy, it is essentially a slow walk forward and a slow walk back, but should you crunch one of my toes I promise to curse for you in Fairy."

She grinned big and bright and held out her hand. "What girl could resist such an offer? But now I may have to stomp your toes by design."

Noam chuckled. He quite enjoyed Azize's people, for the most part. Such open friendliness and welcome were not universal, as surely Azize had seen. Despite their playful exchange, the girl was very careful of her steps as Noam led her to the back of the dancers. Noam tried his best to set her at ease.

"Now I know I am a stranger, but if you allow me to put my arm about your waist, and you grip my left arm with your own, as the other ladies are doing, I will hold your second crutch here should you need it, but you can lean into me for balance."

"I should have asked before I let you lead me out here, are you familiar with this dance? Will you tread on my toes?" She asked quite seriously.

Noam chuckled. "I am quite familiar with it. It is a wedding parade dance from my nation and can take a full fifteen minutes. An odd choice to bring here if you ask me." Noam said as he led her forward. As he'd said, it was nothing more than a slow walk forward to a stilted beat. Very stiff and formal compared to most of the dances he'd heard played so far, from all over the world. "We men are only allowed this near to women at weddings in my nation," Noam said to amuse her.

The girl looked up playfully. "No wonder you were so shy with me." She looked away, and Noam thought she was focusing back on the steps, but her gaze drifted forward to where Azize and his partner were leaning into one another and whispering.

Noam watched them too and realized he was being a bit hard on the dance of his own home. They looked very intimate together as if there were none but them in the room. After his travels, Noam looked on the nation of his birth as too stifling, but it had its beauties like anywhere. Although some people didn't appear to appreciate the intimacy of the dance. Hadhi looked stiffer with Mik, than Arya on her crutches was with Noam.

Noam wondered what it would feel like to slide his arm around Hadhi's waist, and press her into his side. Would the world disappear? Would she stop smiling and go back to being the quiet whirlpool who dragged his attention away from one of the most vibrant displays he'd ever witnessed? Would she soften against him, forgetting her nerves as they moved together? He wished suddenly that he'd made it to her before Mik.

"Do you think she is a fairy?" Arya asked, startling Noam. "With her rich clothes and her bright, captivating light. I know I have never seen her before. She just draws one in like magic."

"Hm?" Noam followed Arya's gaze to the mystery woman and tilted his head aside. "Well, she certainly thinks she's a higher being."

Arya laughed loud and mocking. "Aww, were you hurt when she wanted better stories? You poor calf."

Noam smiled broadly at this giggly girl who gave one the false impression of being childish. She overheard plenty, and she had a sharp wit that she was using to defend a perfect stranger who'd been the talk of the ball while this girl sat in corners. She was no child. This was a woman who knew her own worth. He liked the woman of Maltuba, bold bright, and supportive of one another. He'd seen it earlier with Sabra before he'd even met her, when she tried to champion Hadhi through an uncomfortable conversation. And even Hadhi had grown brighter and found her tongue when defending her sister. These women were something special.

"She was very mean," Noam said, trying to make his voice sound tearful.

They laughed together. And she told him all sorts of gossip in exchange for curse words in languages her parents would not know. Shiraz would have gotten along with such a girl. He truly enjoyed himself with her, but a tiny part of his mind kept wandering to the stiff-backed girl three rows ahead of them. Longing to hold her in his arms for this dance from his home that he'd never much appreciated before today.

Asha was captivated, but no longer just by his stories; it was his excitement in them that fed her now. As they danced, he told stories of one nation after another, one adventure after another. They laughed and they spoke and Asha gorged herself on his adventures. But the more she knew, the more she needed to know, and not just of the world.

"Were you never satisfied? Did you never find a land and say to yourself, here is where I am meant to be?" Asha asked hungrily during their second dance. Her pulse raced and she pressed herself closer to him. There was an intimacy to these dances that she quite liked. In Maltuba, there were courtship dances. Your eyes would be locked with your partner, you might sway towards them and pull away, or reach out and be pulled back by other dancers, there was always a push and a pull, always a distance separating you as your bodies found the rhythm of your partner. It was all anticipation, build, the pounding drum beat growing louder and stronger with every sway. But this...you were in your partner's arms from the moment the dance began. This could create intimacy where none existed. This wasn't about build and anticipation, this was about creating a world of only two, even when surrounded by a thousand eyes.

And they were surrounded by a thousand eyes. Every eye in the ball was on them. Asha had meant it to be so, but she wondered vaguely why no one was watching the king or his son. Asha scanned the crowd for a scrawny, sickly young man of about her age. As Azize had surely returned home the same timid reed he'd left. He was probably the man Hadhi had spoken with at dinner. Mzaa Jauhar could certainly see it arranged, just like she could force Asha to work all day and take all the camels to keep Asha away. Clearly Jauhar meant to make the most of this opportunity, so that man must be Azize. Not that it mattered, Azize had sent Hadhi off in an angry pout.

"I never found a *place* where I belonged." Her dance partner said, at last, drawing her eyes back to him, and only him. He'd invested such meaning in the word, and Asha tingled from the loveliness of it. He meant her. He felt like he belonged with her.

Something delightfully bright and ticklish tripped along beneath her skin, making her shoulder roll and her hand tighten on his. This was what she'd been missing. She almost opened her mouth to demand his name and give him hers. To make this...real. But she heard the bell clanging the hour and knew she had only one left before the magic left her, and she was the rag girl she'd been at the beginning of the evening. She would go back to the hut she'd lived in since Baba died and be loved by no one. The woman in front of him would be gone.

What if he only wanted her as she was? What if the magic coating her skin and sizzling inside her was as tempting to him as it was to her and he just didn't know it?

She needed to store his words up. She needed to store up these experiences. She had an hour left and she wasn't about to fill it with reality.

"No, me neither." Asha released a little laugh.

He smiled softly. "Where do you most want to go?"

Asha thought long and hard, then grinning looked into his eyes. "Everywhere." He chuckled, but she kept right on talking. "I want to climb the highest mountain, swim in the clearest lake. I want to meet fairies and dragons and mermaids. I want to find out what they worship and how they spend their days and what inspires them. I want to feel the frozen wastelands and taste the ash as it drifts off a volcano. I want to live. Everywhere, every minute. I want adventure, even if it costs my whole heart to have it."

"Your whole heart?" The man seemed shocked, possibly appalled.

"Oh, yes! I would give anything to travel as you did and see the world." She leaned in close to whisper as they moved around the room. "And the price would have to be high. I love it too much for it to be anything less. Baba always said if I loved and wanted something with my whole heart, I must be prepared to give my entire heart to have it—for only a moment."

The man gave a small chuckle, watching her incredulously as if he found that not to be very good advice. Asha supposed to the untrained listener it might sound like Baba was cautioning against setting your hopes too high, least they be dashed. But it just wasn't so. Baba wanted the world for Asha. He'd promised the world to her. And tonight, he had delivered, sending her a magical being with a gift, on the exact night when half the world was crammed into the capitol palace.

Baba's advice wasn't a warning. It was a promise that if she wanted something with all her heart, she could have it. She just...had to be sure it was worth her whole heart.

"What would you give your whole heart for?" She challenged, her being burning with intensity. This man had trailed her all night, first with his eyes, then with his being, missing out on every other part of the ball, barely marking it when others spoke to him, not eating a single bite. Surely he was feeling at least an inkling of the sort of desire Asha spoke of, the sort of desire that consumed everything in its path. Surely this man understood. It was why no land had called out to him. No mystery held him to one place. He was as hungry as her. As hungry as Ether devouring every soul that marched through her sands. Surely he would tell her so.

Asha waited, though she began to grow hungry again, though she began to wonder if he would ever open his mouth and prove to her that they truly did understand each other the way she felt they did.

"To be completely my own man," he blurted out at last. "To never be forced to answer to my father or anything but my own desire."

"Exactly!" Asha's hands tightened on his, and her eyes raced over him excitedly. She stood on her toes, and whispered in his ear what she felt like shouting: "*adventure*. It must cost your whole heart, or you'll never know it was worth it."

They smiled into each other's eyes, and for a moment, it seemed the whole of Maltuba vanished. There were only the two of them.

AFTER MIDNIGHT

TWELVE BELLS

Bong.

The mystery woman slammed hard into Hadhi, her breathing labored with delight and her eyes bright with amusement and desire. Hadhi fell into the wall with a thud that went entirely unmarked. The woman ran past, giggling, leading the prince into the night as the first bell of midnight tolled.

Hadhi leaned against the wall and watched Azize run past, not even noticing her presence. Like Hadhi was nothing. She could not stop her eyes from following the couple, just as every other pair of eyes in the room were. Mzaa would be so disappointed, Azize was captivated, just not with Hadhi. Azize was reaching out for the woman; his hand just missed her elbow as she yanked up her gown, revealing a lovely pair of beaded slippers of matched blue and gold to her dress that shaped into wings around her heels. Everything about her was *so* beautiful, so free— *desirable*.

Hadhi turned away. Half the ball's guests were pressed up to the windows and doors along the veranda to watch, as if it were a performance by the Spirit Dancers. Even the strange bird that had been circling the ceiling followed the couple into the night. Hadhi moved through the crowd unnoticed. Let the others stare. Hadhi felt nothing curious, nor even envious.

Not of Azize's interest anyway.

Bong.

How many bells was that?

"Stop," he shouted, panting. "Please, tell me your name."

Asha smiled to herself. She would be so much faster barefooted. Her grassy-eyed, buttoned-up, pampered pursuer, would have no chance of catching her then.

But where was the fun in that?

"Only if you catch me," she called back.

This was life. This was *adventure!* She hadn't felt this good in so long. Her heart pounded with delight, her breath tickled and her spirit flew! She was alive!

Baba always promised her adventure. When she followed him to the docks and counted the sails on every ship, watched the passengers, and the cargo, and the commotion. Felt the cool breeze slip across her face, smelling of salt and sun and far off worlds.

They would stare together, or he would nudge her shoulder, asking, "where is that one going, Asha? What do you think they'll find?"

She was likely an infant the first time he took her, and for years after, he would carry her in his arms and tell her all the things he thought waited for him in the world beyond their own. But the first time he asked Asha, she was just seven; she looked up at him with wide, honored eyes and couldn't utter a word for the longest time.

Bong.

Zawadi flapped outside with her bright plumage and settled on the lip of a column to watch. Asha stood frozen, poised before a plunge into darkness. All that separated her from the night was a flight of ten stairs. The moon was partially hidden behind thin clouds. Not a herald of rain, just a layer of mist separating Maltuba from the heavens.

Azize had caught up, but stopped, his eyes devouring the bright star before the darkness. Zawadi would not have predicted these two coming together. Enzi's frightened son and Zuberi's fearless daughter. It didn't quite fit in her mind. But humans would do things their own way.

She noticed soldiers were hidden, watching, as were some of Azize's traveling companions and both Zuberi's wives. But neither of his other daughters.

When Zawadi looked on his youngest girl, all she could think was how young she was and of all the other lost children: *Sylph, Honeycreeper, Babbler— Kiwi.* The list went on. It wasn't right. So Zawadi could not approach her.

His eldest, however, Zawadi would approach without qualm. But with her every thought one of anger and resentment, Zawadi wondered what form her gift could possibly take.

She ought to go inside and find her answers. But she couldn't move. She must see the moment Zuberi's *beloved* finally understood.

Bong

////

"Well, Asha?" Baba prodded her that first day. Nodded at the dark wooden ship, bobbing as the waves bumped against it. He prompted her once and never had to again. "What's it to be?"

"A monster," she said in a voice quiet with twisted glee. Baba would understand, and indeed he crouched beside her, a desert-wide grin growing slowly from his lips. He only smiled so for her. "It will have a furry face, with pointed ears like a hyaena, but ten times as big."

"Oh my!"

"And it will have a hundred sharp teeth!"

"A hundred?" He sounded appalled, but Asha knew it was only for show, letting her words impress him. Baba loved her words.

"And a body of giant glistening scales that turn color with everything they pass," Asha's voice grew in volume, rising to match her enthusiasm. "And it will have wings, Baba! Wider than the whole ship."

"My goodness, how will they fit it on board?"

"They won't. They'll give it a harness and make it fly behind. And when it gets tired of flying, it will just lay down on the ocean and swim, with tiny little duck legs."

"HA! Ha. Ha. Ha." Baba's laughter, when it truly came, when Asha called it forth, was a booming thing, like thunder or a stampede.

Bong.

Darkness cloaked the city with its empty, unlit homes awaiting their occupants, and the full ones dark with families long abed. It appeared as though the dark void stretched out before Asha, painted in varying hues of shadow. But Asha was light! Asha was awake. And though she knew a few moments would bring an end to her adventure, there was one more thing she wanted before the mystery woman died, and she was everyday Asha again. She tried to look behind her and run, but stumbled down the steps.

She hit the fifth step with a thud that vibrated across her bones and tumbled down the rest of them into the dirt. Dust flew everywhere, clouding her vision and choking her throat.

"Ethee Oxtia! Are you injured?" There was no playful hesitance to his steps as he rushed to her side.

He cursed in Maltuban? Asha tried to stand and dust herself off. Wasn't it just like the real her to be lying in the dust at the feet of this fine, pampered boy. Before she reached her knees, he was there. His arms slipped between hers and around her back, so swiftly and gently she barely had time to catch her breath. He cradled her against his chest and lifted her from the ground, like so much laundry.

Bong.

"Are you well?" His voice was quiet, against her ear, like they were back in an alcove in the palace again, not alone in the night.

Asha loved the desert at night. The quiet expanse full of possibility. It was a different sort of magic, the way the darkness folded in around you until you felt like a star in the heavens. So far from every other being like you—reaching out.

"Fine," she lied. How could she be anything but wonderful, and alive, and beautifully, chaotically lost, when his arms were around her and his breath was a warm breeze against her ear?

She might never feel so again. She was so lucky. So special. Tonight—at last—when she reached out, she'd finally been touched.

"You know," his voice was slow in coming, one of his hands rubbed a circle into her lower back. "If you wanted me alone, all you had to do was ask."

"No," Asha sighed, and leaned closer to this near-perfect stranger. "I could never ask."

"No," he chuckled. "You could only whisper 'catch me if you can' and run away, so I chased you like a child."

Asha smiled up at him as he slowly inched nearer. There was no time to waste, but this incremental pull between them was so lovely.

Bong.

///

Jauhar watched the couple out in the night like everyone else, captivated. She felt her heart beat, *softening* in her chest. Remembering.

When Zuberi first wooed her, he would hide in the tall grass along the river to wait for her to come to wash laundry, then grab her wrist and drag her laughing away. Or after they were married, when he would walk to her so slowly, his eyes intent on her own, and a pulse building between them, their hearts joining before their skin ever touched. She could feel it still, in her quiet moments, that pulse, that pull towards him. She felt it now.

Jauhar watched the young couple and felt grief burning through her.

That is done for me. Sabra had said it about herself, but it resonated inside Jauhar. She felt it and shoved it far away from her conscious mind. But she couldn't shove it away now.

That powerful, all-consuming *passion*. That bliss— was done for her. She would never feel so again.

Jauhar turned away, her eyes falling on her sour-faced daughter across the room. Hadhi. *How?* How did someone so dour, so different from both her parents, come out of something as lovely as the display outside?

Rage ate away at what had been bittersweet nostalgia only a moment ago.

Bong.

///

Eight bells. Asha must be gone when it struck twelve.

His hand traveled up her back to play with her bare neck. Asha didn't suppose this was what Baba wanted for her when he promised her adventure. But she rather thought there wasn't any real adventure without a bit of danger.

And what Asha wanted was dangerous beyond any monster she could imagine.

She wanted a taste of this world she could never enter. These lips. She wanted one moment, where he was hers.

To keep the magic living—after she woke up.

"What is your name?" He pulled his head away from hers, just far enough to peer into her eyes.

"It doesn't matter," Asha smiled at him, though she wanted to cry. It couldn't matter. This magic, this wonder, this adventure, was only a moment stolen. A treasure to carry with her for the rest of her days.

While she was with him, she had truly forgotten the...*vengeance* she wanted against her family. She'd forgotten the heartache and the loneliness. She'd lived as though she was someone wholly new. Someone who belonged only to herself. But that wasn't reality.

She glanced back at the lokoki bird she'd arrived on. What if she was flying on its back when the bell tolled? Would she fall from the sky?

Bong.

Asha shuddered slightly, something like desperation licking across her skin as her fear of losing the magic grew.

"I want to know," he pressed. Asha did not know his name either, only that he was among the court of the returned prince. Whatever his name, he was far and away outside of her life without this magic.

And she had barely moments of it left to bask in.

"I am midnight and laughter, and adventure," she said through a sad smile.

He chuckled, setting her just a bit further away. His hands grasped both her shoulders, but left her standing completely on her own. She didn't realize until he set her down that he had been holding her above the ground.

"I've heard that song. Are you a nymph? Come to grant my wildest dream, but only for the night."

"Not even that long." Asha stepped back, off-kilter. She glanced to the ground; one of her lovely beaded slippers lay in the dust. Beads of gold and deep blue fit neatly together to make a winged shape around the foot. It looked as magical as it was. All she needed to do was stretch out her foot and slip back into it, but she stared at it in the dirt and her lips curved. "Do you believe in magic?"

Bong.

"With you," he whispered playfully. "How could I not?"

"Do you know how you cheat a nymph's clock?" Asha asked.

"Very carefully, or they'll cheat yours, stealing all the years you have left." His eyes were smiling, but his right hand tightened on her shoulder. He *did* believe.

"You do not cheat their clock at all. You take what is given," Asha stood on the toes of her barefoot, and the pad of her beaded slipper, stretching up towards the one bit of magic she had yet to taste. "Then you hold onto it forever."

"Tell me your name," he whispered. His breath rushed out to tickle her lips, *so* close.

"Why? This moment is perfect without it?"

"No, it isn't. Because it's only one moment."

Asha was suddenly panting, and her heart ached with excitement and fear.

Because it is only one moment.

It couldn't be anything else. But oh how it sang inside her that he longed as she did—for more.

"I will find you, I promise. Just give me one clue, and I will trace you to the ends of the earth."

Asha laughed at such a pronouncement. They had only just met. Was it the magic, calling the words forth? Was it this other Asha, this wild, free woman she was allowed to be tonight?

Bong

Or did he mean it? Could something of her words have so impacted him, something of the feel of her in his arms, so touched him, that this was... love? Already?

"You cannot cheat a nymph's clock." Asha felt the power beneath her skin preparing to flee and was desperate to hold onto it. "But..." she led his eyes to the shoe. "You can leave a bit of magic behind."

She wouldn't be getting that last taste of magic she hungered for. Asha stepped lopsidedly away.

This was madness. The sort of madness Zawadi warned her of when she granted her wish. The kind that, rather than leaving you with a treasure to keep, left you with a great longing that could never be filled. The madness of hope.

She could have had anything from Zawadi. She could be across the sea or never have to work another day in her life; she could have become an animal, or a star.

But not Asha.

"Never long for the ordinary, Asha. You were meant for wonder and adventure. Like your Baba. You are untamable."

Asha could not have made a simple wish. Did not even wish to go to the ball. She wished for only one thing: to feel, for as long as the spell lasted, a true taste— of *magic*.

Bong.

THE STRIKE OF MIDNIGHT

The night exploded with bright white light, yanked out of Asha by nothing but the last bell tolling the hour. Thunder threatened the air, wild winds shook up the sands and sloshed them glistening into the air, and leaves deserted their branches. In that moment no part of the world was still, as the magic was dragged out of Asha and into the night.

Asha felt the loss like death. Every pore, and sinew, and organ bled magic, leaving her more tired and empty than she had ever felt before. Her young man looked away for only a moment. But it was long enough.

She stumbled into the bushes as the magic she had coated herself in fled, and she was clothed once more in a torn, dirty rag of a dress. A beetle flew by shivering and shaking, and Asha understood its discombobulation well, her poor magical lokoki chariot, the world must look so different to it as well. Asha lay in the bush with her arms wrapped around herself and her tongue clamped between her teeth to fight off her shivering body. She felt chilled inside and out, and so...empty. Everything was different now. The stars looked further away, the air was dull, and the world seemed to move slower.

It took Asha a moment to notice that while her right foot was bare, her left foot still had a slipper of blue and golden wings wrapped around it...did that mean it had worked?

Asha drew her foot carefully out, afraid the slipper would vanish the second her foot left its warm beads. But when both her feet were bare, and she stretched out a desperate hand for it, the slipper was still there. Asha snatched it up with both her hands and cradled it close. She didn't move a moment. The earth felt oddly dry and bumpy beneath her. This ground that she had run across beneath rain and beating sun was alien now. All because of five hours of magic.

Her body felt heavy and slow, and ill.

It wasn't. She was perhaps a little tired for the loss of power. But she was well.

She had just been so much more a moment ago.

When the light was fully gone from the clearing and the winds were silent, she peeked out and saw him again. He stood just where she left him, searching the night for her. He did not speak, but a smile of awe and disbelief emerged. He had such a lovely face, even more so when he smiled. He had a smile that could steal the heavens to darkness for the shame of never matching it.

All of a sudden, he jerked aside, stooping to the ground. The other slipper! It worked, it was still there. The one piece he had asked for. His hands closed gently around the shoe and Asha's heart jerked, it wanted to run to him, but she daren't move. They were both still, cradling their slippers, and for each moment of contact, the connection between them grew. Asha nearly cried it felt so lovely.

She may never have the magic again, might never feel so completely alive again. But she saw in his eyes what she felt in her own soul; he wanted this magic again.

She shouldn't hope. Hope led Baba to die, never having wandered more than sixty miles from his home. Hope meant being dashed to pieces when reality woke you in the morning.

Still, Asha's lips curled, and her mind raced through the brush to whisper in his ear—

Come find me.

Hadhi slipped to the side of the ballroom, where Bayo had taken Lin and stood in the shadows watching him play. He was such a sweet child. He loved sharing, passing the little ball with Bayo's daughter. His eyes so much brighter when he had a friend.

As the last bell tolled, the hour light split the night wide, and winds shook the palace. Hadhi looked towards the light, but almost at once, her eyes were drawn back to Lin, who clapped and laughed at the show, and across the ballroom to Nuru, laughing with her friends. They were both oblivious, contented as all around them the world shook. These were curse bringer winds, and Hadhi longed to reach out and touch her sibling's foreheads, longed to bring their fragile spirits into herself and guard them. But her hands stayed stiffly at her sides. With her eyes alone did she guard them.

People were moving off the walls, flooding back into the ballroom before the prince could catch them spying. Hadhi moved further into the room as well, to a spot where she could watch both her siblings at once and see the world around them, watching for the threats they were too innocent to see. Ethee Uvaasha, she prayed silently, as she watched over her siblings. Borikan bon utik ongmaa. Holin szou bozou emnok fa qiftic. *Great Spirits, shelter them from evil. Give me their share of suffering.*

Hadhi saw her mother crossing to her with a look one could only call distaste in her eyes, her eyes that took in only Hadhi. Hadhi drew in a breath and shoved down any feeling that might long to rise up at the sight of her mother's hatred. She had offered to eat the suffering for her siblings, she could not balk so quickly.

Zawadi stayed on the veranda for several minutes after the light cleared, after the magic fled, after Zuberi's beloved was separated from her deepest desire—Waiting to find some understanding of what she felt.

She had been drawn outside with the rest of the balls occupants, magnetically pulled to the mystery woman in blue and gold, though she was no mystery to Zawadi. Asha had been...*alight* with the magic. Chaotic with it. It wanted to be used, to be out from under her skin. Zawadi didn't know how the girl had failed to feel it. She was supposed to *feel it!*

That magic didn't belong in her form. In the fey, magic was calmer, natural. A mere extension of the self. But in humans, fey magic turned voracious, unpredictable—*poisonous.*

It grew brighter and louder, drawing every eye, burning with an intense desire to be seen for its true self. Like a dying star, casting off its last deadly bloom of power. It was a sight of irresistible beauty and *horror.* One should not be able to look away. Zawadi certainly had not been able to. But Zuberi's eldest daughter had. She had looked right at that dying star, seen its power, and walked away.

How? Was she so lacking in any curiosity? Was she truly her sister's opposite?

More interesting to Zawadi; would she have stayed to watch if she'd known the mystery woman's true face? If she'd known the suffering to come, would she have watched her sister in delight? Or turned away as she had with the stranger?

Zawadi didn't know. All she knew was that as she hesitated, watching Asha crouch in the bushes to gaze at the boy prince, she felt a sour mixture of...delight and rage! She had followed her out, wanting to see the moment the magic was ripped away, wanting to see that girl realize she had not been making wishes of a benevolent stranger.

The wish was meant to have taken more than it gave! It was meant to have ripped through her and made her feel small and broken inside—but it hadn't. And Zawadi was almost—*pleased*. For that girl.

With the magic or without Asha was so bright and dauntless. So open. Zawadi had watched those bright eyes gazing at the prince, watched her cradle the shoe that should have vanished with the hour of new day, and she felt almost...mistaken. Felt that, perhaps, she had come only to gift. She felt like a benevolent stranger. But it just wasn't so.

Zawadi cast apart Sylph's feathers, that sweet bird had taken Zawadi as far as she could. Getting her into the ball to watch her trickier prey more closely. She wasn't just here for Asha. Everyone who benefited from Zuberi needed to pay. But even in Sylphs body, she had not been able to approach the king. For a man intent on destroying magic, he seemed not at all shy of using it to guard himself. Zawadi needed to know how, so she could shatter that protection and sink her talons into the man. So she slipped into the skin of another sister. Grackle.

Grackle's fey form would serve as a decent enough disguise here. The flock didn't hold with that popular fey practice of spending magic to maintain a youthful appearance. They embraced sagging skin and creaking bones with pride. So Grackle's form of one-hundred-and-six years, when she died, would command far too much respect in such a land to ever be questioned. Zawadi hid her pointy ears beneath a black and grey scarf patterned not with the markings of these nations, but with feathers and claws. The markings of a predator. Leaning heavily on a gnarled cane, she made her way into the ball. She was no more certain of what the feeling swirling around inside of her was now, but she had prey to study.

Zawadi was no benevolent stranger. She was a hunter. A vengeance seeker.

She was doom.

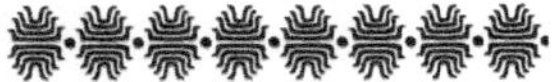

FREE

Sabra hadn't caught her breath yet. *Asha!* The mystery woman was Asha.

Sabra had been furtively watching Azize flirt with the mystery woman clothed in a golden and blue gown and a face Sabra had not recognized. She'd been around the edge of the veranda checking on her son when she'd heard them run by, and she had followed out of an overpowering sense of adventure. It had felt like in the past. All night that woman made Sabra feel like she was in the past again, and now she knew why. She was Asha, dressed up in a different face so that Sabra could see her without the mixture of love and resentment that so defined their relationship now.

As the light distracted others, Sabra watched her friend run out of the space where a stranger had been and into the brush along the walk to the palace. The gold and blue gown was gone, the golden hoops and disks that had adorned her hair were gone, along with the intricately braided hair, even the *giant lokoki bird* that had waited wearing a golden saddle was gone.

Asha was back in the worn, dirty gown she'd been wearing when the family left for the ball, with no jewels adorning her, and her hair wrapped with a scarf to protect it as she cleaned. She was a totally different person, but though Sabra had not truly believed in magic until this moment, no part of her doubted that it had been her friend driving them all mad with curiosity tonight. But how? Asha had been seeking magic all her life. How had she found it tonight of all nights? How had it changed her so thoroughly?

It felt quite strange that Sabra had not realized it was Asha sooner. Who but Asha could so stand the world on end? Who but Asha had that charmingly insatiable curiosity? Who but Asha could see so much and so little at the same time?

Asha. Sabra felt a laugh, or a sob, bubbling up in her throat and didn't know which would emerge, but before she could make a sound, she heard someone coming and ducked into the shadow of the large column she'd been leaning around. Azize's friend Noam walked by. The sweet man who'd called Hadhi pretty. Before Asha had demanded his attention.

Sabra shouldn't feel resentful of that. She hadn't when they were children. Even when Asha stole Azize's attention from Sabra, she had not minded. Asha wasn't trying to steal the boy Sabra was interested in; she just hated to be ignored. But since her marriage, Sabra had been resenting a great many things about the girl she would once have called her closest friend. Right now, she resented her for coming at least as much as she was thrilled that Asha had bested Jauhar and had a chance to see the world. It was such a twisted place Sabra held in this family. Resentment and love tangled up around her feelings for all of them.

"There you are," Noam called out to his friend, coming up behind him and slapping him lightly on the back.

Sabra could still see Asha staring longingly out of the brush after Azize. It was…unbearably hilarious. Asha—and Azize!

Azize hadn't noticed his friend coming, and he jumped at the contact. He was cradling a beaded slipper in his hand. Asha must have left it, but Sabra hadn't even noticed that bit of her attire, with all the other beautiful adornments to draw her eye.

"A shoe is an odd trophy," Noam commented when he had Azize's attention.

"Trophy?" Azize looked at the slipper as though his mind was far away. Sabra smiled to herself because she completely understood. There was the boy she'd liked caught up in the whirlwind that was Sabra's best friend. He had no idea what he was in for if he chased after her.

This was oddly pleasing, maybe better than it would have been to talk with him. Seeing him like this, knowing what he was feeling so well, reminded Sabra of the past like nothing else could. He was exactly the same boy who'd run away, wasn't he?

"Please, brother. Everyone knew what you were doing when you chased that woman out here. You weren't at all subtle." Noam laughed.

"Nothing happened." Azize made to throw the shoe away, but stopped running his fingers along it gently. "She said she was 'midnight and laughter, and adventure.' Do you believe that?"

"Came right out and called herself a nymph did she?" Noam made a sound like a laugh, but Sabra didn't think it was a true one. He glanced around the palace, looking for Asha perhaps. Or a nymph. Was that what had given Asha magic? Such beings had never felt real before.

Noam shook himself. "Finding her should be a fun way to pass the time. By the by, how much time are we planning on here? Not that I'm anxious to leave," he walked around Azize and seemed to breathe in the night. His chest expanding and his head tilted up towards the moon. "You were right about the evenings. Why isn't this party outside?"

Sabra watched Azize furtively slip the shoe into the pocket of his dress silk. "My father is showing off his improvements to the palace, his lighting system, and how much more he knows of other nations than they knew of us," he said bitterly.

Noam smiled and allowed his friend to vent. "Well, it is certainly a special place. I've never met so many funny, intelligent and interesting women."

"All the better to tempt me with," Azize muttered.

"Oh, there seem to be plenty worthy of tempting you, but I wouldn't say many expect to. They just all have parents and a king *making* them try." It was lightly said, but Sabra thought she heard a touch of reproach in Noam's tone. He was trying to remind his friend to respect the women of his nation.

It hadn't occurred to Sabra before, but Azize and Asha were quite similar. Neither one ever saw beyond surfaces to understand other people's struggles.

It was odd they had not gotten along better.

"I've never seen so many nervous faces and eager mothers. There was that one family." Noam spoke a bit slower, his tone and expression remained the same, but watching in this furtive way—out of the light, into the shadowed world where the men were lit by nothing but moonlight and the after cast of light from within the palace—Here Sabra saw more. Noam had gone from being light to playing at it. He was more connected to these words. "Zuberi's widow and her daughters, the dancer and the one who smiles with all her teeth."

A little smile played over Noam's lips when he said that, a bit of delight that his friend must not have noticed, as Azize began to snigger unkindly.

"Yes. Sour-faced-Hadhi, even with all her teeth showing, she doesn't look anything pleasant."

"You call her that because of the scars?" Noam demanded, sounding utterly appalled. Sabra liked him even better than she had before. She should introduce him to Hadhi. Hadhi could do with some pleasant company. Even if it was only for the remains of the night.

"No." Azize excused himself. "She was scarred after I left. Everyone has called her sour-face for as long as I can remember. She's just...never approved of anything or anyone. She was endlessly suspicious, always suspecting people were up to no good."

Ugh, funs over, here comes sour-faced-Hadhi. Sabra heard the giggled taunt in her mind and tensed up. She had been a part of teasing Hadhi, but she'd always assumed Azize was not. Learning differently was disappointing. A feeling clearly shared by his tense friend. How did Azize not see it?

"She'll sacrifice herself on the family alter and marry me if her mother asks though," Azize said with an expression of distaste, like it should be shameful that Hadhi was a dutiful daughter. "And Nuru is ten years too young to be here."

"Ohhh, not quite that young. But I'll just bet she agrees with you. What is so terrifying about marrying a prince?" Noam asked casually. He still wasn't happy with how his friend spoke of Hadhi.

"Well, she can't be more than thirteen."

"No." Noam laughed. "For H—the other one."

Smiling, Sabra leaned on the railing to watch. It could be he'd hesitated because he could not remember Hadhi's name, but Sabra thought he was trying to pretend less interest than he had. He liked her! Or was attracted to her at least. Sabra doubted Hadhi would believe it, or her mother—Jauhar was so used to seeing only her daughter's faults—but Sabra had always thought Hadhi was rather lovely, even with her less than friendly expressions. She was compelling. Even when Sabra had teased her in the past, she'd always thought there was something special about her.

"Oh." Azize shrugged. "I suppose Hadhi wouldn't mind. Not like her other sister."

"You mean Sabra?" Noam asked, in shock. "I didn't realize until dinner that she was even connected with the family."

"No, she isn't their sister. She is another of Zuberi's widows." Azize paused a moment, looking wistful. "I'd heard she married him the same time I learned my mother was sick."

"The girl you used to love? The perfect, sweet paragon of a woman, that was *Sabra*?" Noam asked with a smile on his face, but nothing mocking or derisive in his tone.

Sabra's heart raced again, and a slight flutter in her stomach made it hard to breathe. This was lovely. She didn't need, she wasn't even sure she wanted, another man's attention. She would try her hardest to find someone kind to marry, to give her son a good father. But for her, just this, just listening to someone who'd loved her once was lovely. It was…innocent.

"Yes. I sometimes think she was half the reason I didn't come home then." Azize shook his head. "I couldn't face her knowing I'd failed her. Even if she hadn't married me, the fact that that monster had forced her to marry him…I couldn't face her and my dying mother at the same time."

Another man might have walked away from Azize, as he spoke so fervently. But Noam was sweet. He moved in nearer his friend and lay a hand at his shoulder. "I am sure your mother knew how much you loved her."

"She did. But—I'd sworn to myself I would free her, and I wasn't fast enough." Azize nodded. "I should have helped her. I should have been here." Azize slipped his hand into his pocket, where the shoe was. "All my life, she stood between me and my father's cruelty. Between him and *anyone* she could protect. When I left, I swore to myself I would return with an army to overthrow him. But…once I got away, once I could breathe," Azize confessed in a tearful voice. "I felt so safe that I stopped thinking of her and her people and what they deserved. I just lived. I embraced everything with this terrible fear that if I looked back, I would be dragged back, and I would never be free again. I ran further and further so I wouldn't have to hear the screaming, so I wouldn't have to know what he did. He always wanted me to know." Azize shuddered.

"I ran. And she died. She was always so strong. I pretended to believe she would be stronger without me to defend. That she might defeat him herself. I built my army so slowly, I never really even asked other nations for support. And there were some that would have supported me. I'd barely done anything but made friends of a few soldiers, and then she died, and Sabra was forced to wed that monster, and I just could not face all that failure at once.

Noam lay a hand on his friend's shoulder. "You were only seventeen. There was not much you could have done. Then."

"Yes," Azize agreed easily. "And anyway, my mother is free now. Sabra is free now."

The words struck a chord in Sabra. Startled her so much, she leaned against the column, turning away from the men as she absorbed the words. She was free. Zuberi was dead. And she—was—*free*. It hadn't truly struck her before. She'd celebrated that her son was free of that man and that she wouldn't be subject to Zuberi's control any longer, but she hadn't behaved like a free woman. Part of her still waited for him to come back, waited to discover that that body on the road south was some trick of Zuberi's and that he would return just when they were all comfortable. But...he was gone, wasn't he? Sabra could breathe.

And she did, in and out so slowly, so gently. As she hadn't done in years, her lungs always too tense to pull slowly of the air, to breathe deeply.

"And now you are here," Noam said quietly. "Do you know why?"

Sabra held her breath. Felt that old tension catch her. Was it hope? Or fear?

Built his army, he'd said, and she had barely marked it, still thinking of him as that shy boy. But...had he come back to *overthrow* his father? To protect them as his mother had always tried? Zuberi was dead. There would be no chance like now. Was that why he had come home?

Azize didn't seem to have an answer, staring down at the shoe in his hand.

There was a quiet stretch then Noam's playfully goading voice emerged, breaking the tension. "If Sabra is the woman you loved, why did I not see you speak to her once?"

Azize shook his head. "At first, I was worried that seeing her again would ruin the memory." Noam huffed out a small laugh. "Then, my nymph arrived. Do you know she wouldn't even tell me her name? She did not want to know mine, she just...wanted to know the world through me. I've never felt anything like that before. Everything else disappeared."

Sabra's heart didn't precisely sink. She hadn't really believed he was here to free his people. She'd just wondered. So she let her ears pull her along to the lighter subjects where these men were at home.

Noam laughed. "I noticed. That girl, Hadhi was trying to speak to you at dinner, and you ignored her."

"I did not. She just didn't know a word in Fairy."

"She was trying to flirt with you."

Azize shook his head. "Hadhi doesn't have those sorts of feelings."

Noam looked at his friend despairingly.

"Truly, she doesn't! Her half-sister flirted with me more, and we've never once liked each other. I'm surprised she wasn't here tonight. Asha always wanted to know about any place but Maltuba. But that little pest hated me as much as I hated her, so she must have found some way to avoid coming tonight."

"I didn't realize that was allowed?" Noam asked in quiet curiosity.

"She was her father's girl, had his penchant for danger, as well as his manipulative ability. I can't tell you the number of times she caused some catastrophe, and my mother made *me* apologize to her for trying to reprimand her."

Noam's laughter filled the night like a cluster of stars. "A girl who can so thoroughly annoy you is a shame to have missed."

"Trust me, she was not," Azize said sharply, and Sabra had to cover her mouth to resist laughing.

Oh, he deserved it. And so did Asha. They'd always treated each other terribly, and half the time, they'd thrown Sabra right in the middle of their bickering. Now Azize was obsessed with the last woman he would ever want, and Asha...well Sabra couldn't be sure. She'd seen her watching the prince from the bushes, and that had looked like interest, but it could be she was just trying to have the same old fun and trick him. But if that was the case, why not reveal herself?

Sabra wasn't certain, but she had a feeling that Asha too was intrigued by the last man in the world she would want.

Sabra shoved herself deeper into the shadows as Azize and his friend went inside, still talking about Asha and the sorts of trouble she'd gotten Azize into over the years. Sabra watched them go and felt a quiet sort of peace settle inside of her. Azize had thought of her all these years, had loved her.

She supposed knowing that he now only felt guilty when he thought of her should bother her. But it did not. She had never blamed him. And looking back now, Sabra didn't know that her life would have been so much more her choice if she had married Azize. If he had asked, she would have said yes. She would not have known how to do anything else. But Sabra wasn't sure it would have been because she loved Azize.

She'd liked him. She'd adored his attention. And she thought him sweet and so safe. She would have said yes, but part of it would always have been duty.

She wasn't duty-bound any longer.

She had no desire to be a wife again, to be subject to a man's rule again. Perhaps...she could find a way not to be. Kafil was not like his brother. Sabra could convince him to leave them be. She was free. Azize was right, she was free now. *Free.*

Sabra wouldn't give that up without a fight.

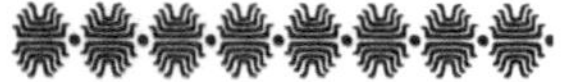

SOUR FACE AND THE SMILING MAN

As soon as Prince Azize walked back into the hall Mzaa smacked Hadhi on the shoulder, Hadhi carved on an overly bright smile. Honestly, she could not think of a thing she hated more than forcing a smile. Except perhaps talking about her dead father, as she had been forced to several times tonight. Having to pretend that he loved her. It had been over a year since he died yet all anyone wanted to speak to her about was her terrible grief. She did not think she could stand to hear it one more time without blurting out the truth. She hated herself so much sometimes, as much as everyone else seemed to hate her. But she could not think about that right now. Prince Azize's constantly smiling friend, Noam, was walking towards her. She could not afford to offend the prince's closest friend.

When he reached them, Hadhi sunk a bit at the knees, bowing her head.

"Oh, please do not bother with that for me," Noam laughed. Always laughed. Who carried such light feelings with them all the time? "The only special thing about me is my friend."

"Nonsense," Mzaa patted his arm, tilting her head to the side in a way she knew was lovely. "You would not be so fortunate in friend were there not something very special about you."

Hadhi felt her shoulders tightening and resisted the feeling. It had always struck her as odd that her mother got along so poorly with Asha when the two had so much in common. Both so lovely, both so adept at using that beauty to manipulate men. Hadhi had to work even to hold their attention.

"Don't you agree, Hadhi?" Mzaa's voice was sweet as it slipped dart-like from the corner of her lips to stab Hadhi back to attention. "The prince would never befriend an unremarkable man."

"Of course." Was all Hadhi could manage.

Noam chuckled; he tilted his head only slightly in Hadhi's direction so Mzaa could not see and winked one eye. It was a tiny motion, but combined with his smile, it struck Hadhi in the stomach like a swift kick, stealing her breath.

As quickly as he had managed it, he turned back to Mzaa smiling and covering her hand with his own. "How unfortunate for all those unremarkable souls out there."

They laughed together, her mother and this man who was perhaps only a little older than Hadhi, and Hadhi felt slighted. That was the sort of thing her father used to say about her, that she was *unremarkable.*

Their laughter made her bitter. This man was no more remarkable than she was. Why was he so light? Just because he was beautiful? Did he think that made him special? It did not. Beauty was bestowed on terrible people as often as good. Perhaps more. Baba had been beautiful.

"Where is your friend?" Hadhi asked. Her tone was perhaps a bit sharp, but all her teeth were showing, so they could not fault her for lack of a smile.

Noam turned slowly. Beyond him, Mzaa was glaring at her, but he, as always, was smiling. This time the look was so big, and so...amused Hadhi felt herself heating with embarrassment.

"His dance partner fled without giving a name." He spoke slowly, and his eyes traveled over Hadhi so carefully she was sure he must know everything about her: from the anger she felt inside to the way her blush and his eyes were leaving her with a bit of a chill. "You know men love a *mystery.*"

Perhaps it was just her imagination again, but she felt like she had been slapped by the comment, as though he meant her to be.

"Prince Azize is off to discover her identity. He thought he knew every woman here."

"Yes," Mzaa drew his attention away again, setting Hadhi free. She wanted to sink into the floor. "It is quite odd. She is a stranger to us as well."

"Perhaps she is precisely what she claimed to be then, a nymph stealing into the party for a bit of fun."

"A nymph!" Hadhi's heart raced as she searched the wide room for her sister. Nuru was dancing with a local boy, Ayinde, in the middle of the floor, bright and happy and free, because she knew the prince would not want her. Hadhi's gaze tore to Sabra chatting with other mothers and holding Lin in her arms. They were safe, thank the spirits. If the nymph had come for them, it left without getting its prey. Perhaps it would go in search of Asha, she was Baba's favorite after all.

Hadhi felt her heart pounding against her ribs and forced her breathing to slow and her pulse to steady. She had felt suspicious earlier, stalked, but not by the woman. Even when the light and the curse winds came, she hadn't connected it to that woman. Why had she not even considered her?

When that woman had stood in the doorway, her eyes had scanned the room, locking in on Hadhi. That alone should have made her suspicious. But she had looked Hadhi over like a carcass and smirked, filling Hadhi with all those old familiar feelings, ugly and unloved. She had felt *worthless* from the way Azize left without giving Hadhi another thought.

She did not want Azize, but—*Why* did she always have to be the last person anyone wanted to be near?

It had all felt too familiar to be magical. But what if that was the nymph? What if she had come not yet for vengeance, but to play with them?

"It was a joke, I am sure." For once the prince's friend did not sound amused, only curious. Was she a mystery now? How flattering. Hadhi thought she might spit at the man were this any other day. What did she care if she had attracted him? She was not here because she desired a husband. She needed to wed the prince for her family. "Actually I came here about another mystery. I understand not all the ladies of your family are in attendance." Hadhi looked up to find him still regarding her, and he was not even looking at her scars. She had felt him do so earlier, when he was with Azize, but now his gaze studied her eyes and expression and he even seemed a bit pleased to have her attention back.

"Yes, my daughter Asha."

"Oh, is she your daughter?" Noam glanced back at Mzaa. "I thought she was a child of a different marriage?"

"Any child of my husband's is a child of mine," Mzaa said with genteel grace. "So believe all Zuberi's wives."

Hadhi's eyes found the ground, and her teeth rubbed hard across one another. It was such a blatant lie. It should show on her mother's face the way lies always showed on Hadhi. *All lies show but one.* Why had no one seen her biggest lie?

But Mzaa had a talent, as did the *daughter* she would never but now claim. Lies never showed on them.

"Of course," Noam said pleasantly. It seemed sincere, but Hadhi doubted he was.

"She took ill just before the ball, poor girl. The truth is she made herself ill, insisted on patching a hole in the roof, right in the midday heat." Mzaa leaned in conspiratorially, even going so far as to dart a look around the room before continuing her little invention. "I think she was unnerved by the idea of seeing the prince again. They were well known to each other, but not in a friendly way."

"Ah," Noam nodded his understanding. He would leave now. Hadhi could just stand here, with her mother and her sour face, and watch over her siblings from a distance. Hadhi felt his gaze on her again and looked over, forcing a bright smile, she would not contradict her mother, but that did not mean she must speak and agree with her.

It should make Hadhi happier to see her father's favorite missing this ball. Asha would put her sisters to shame with her bright smile, and her easy conversation, and her knowledge. All Zuberi's daughters and wives spoke enough of the common Fairy tongue to get by; they had once been wealthy and well educated after all. But Asha was fluent. More than that, she'd spent her formative years studying other lands and talking with every foreign ship captain who came to the port their father had controlled. Asha knew enough and was lovely enough even to have outshone the nymph.

Hadhi felt oddly torn over the whole thing. She knew why Asha was Baba's favorite, even she felt the pull to smile when Asha did, or to laugh at her jokes. It felt wrong to hate her as much as she did, but she doubted Asha ever gave much thought to her. And now Hadhi couldn't tell if her heart was racing in fear for Asha, all alone and unprotected—or in anticipation, for what she might suffer. She was hateful. Just like Baba wanted.

"Well," Noam broke the silence, he would be nice to have around dinner, the only ones who ever broke that silence were Mzaa or Asha, and usually with a fight. "Lady Jauhar, would you allow me the honor of dancing with your lovely daughter?"

Both Mzaa and Hadhi were a bit shocked by this. Surely he would prefer to dance with Jauhar herself. Two of his friends had come to dance with Mzaa and wound up tricked into dancing with Hadhi first. Not that it had helped Mzaa at all.

"By all means," Mzaa beamed. "But you must call me only Jauhar. We have no titles here."

He lifted Mzaa's hand and lowered his lips to the back of it, smiling into her eyes up to the very last second before his lips touched. "It will be my very great pleasure, Jauhar."

Hadhi ground her teeth. Really he need not pretend. He should just court Mzaa. They would look beautiful together, even if he was no less than ten years her junior. Mzaa's dark, intense beauty would complement his lovely open smile and strong build. Hadhi was not lovely, even without the scars. But...she had noticed Noam dance with Arya earlier. Perhaps he liked dancing with women other men rejected. He dropped her mother's hand carefully and took up Hadhi's with the same bright smile he had been wearing all night. So Hadhi had no choice but to do the same.

ZAWADI

Asha made her way home slowly. One hand treasuring her slipper against her chest. The other swinging at her side as she danced her way heavily forward. Her body was exhausted. Starved. It moved not with energy, but with the force of her delight alone.

Was this love?

She wasn't sure. But it was definitely adventure. And she hungered to taste it again. For that, she would need Zawadi. She had tried calling, but the woman had not come. How had she come to Asha at just the right moment earlier this evening? Why? How could Asha find her again if she didn't understand how she came to find her at all?

Was it her heartbreak and devastation that brought her? Or was it only coincidence that her presence had so altered Asha that she barely felt that pain now?

It seemed such a small thing to have been hurt by, with the power and wonder and excitement of this night still coursing through her. She'd never known her mother after all. Asha wouldn't even have known her dress existed had not Aunt Lolia told her about it. It should be such a small loss. But earlier this evening, with its threads unwound and her every hope dashed, losing that dress had felt like the most devastating thing since Baba died.

Asha had come in to find the beautiful gown her mother had left for her utterly destroyed and she'd felt that same destruction in her own heart. Felt the hopes that had carried her through the day, of standing beside her sisters, beside her father's wives like a real member of the family, of truly belonging among her family *at last*. She felt all of that curl up and split apart within her. So she collapsed on the ground sobbing.

She had cried over pains she should be long-past feeling, over a sister's love she would never have, and a mother she barely remembered, over a ball that had felt like the fulfillment of all her father's promises. And that was where Zawadi found her, outside in the dirt by the stove, sobbing with her ruined gown turning slowly to embers, and devastation weighing down her heart. She found her, just when Asha needed something to bring hope and light into her life.

"I am not sure this is the right home." The cool, disinterested female voice startled Asha right out of her tears with a hiccup. She sat up quickly, wiping her face with a dirty hand, so it was streaked with dirt as well as tears.

"Who are you?" Asha demanded. The woman was drowning in lovely black fabrics, every piece was of a slightly different shade, and all had intricately woven patterns in silvery-grey thread. Only her eyes were visible, and so striking, they seemed to be made of a liquid form of the same silvery-grey as the thread. Asha could not take her eyes off them.

The woman jerked her head at Asha critically. "Not terribly polite, are you?"

"You're the one who barged in without permission." Asha pointed out, slowly coming to her feet to stare the woman down, her anger and pain leaving her short on patience.

"I wouldn't think the daughter of Zuberi would care overly that someone had barged in unannounced. But then," her tone took on a contemptuous snarl, and she walked to a low stool near Asha to sit, "it is a different matter entirely when someone barges in on you, isn't it?"

Asha held her tongue. Baba always said it was best to be silent when you weren't sure what was going on. Be quiet. Watch. People will give you clues to defeating them if you wait long enough. *She was a lovely woman, for all Asha could see of her, her vaguely foreign voice was smooth and rich. And she knew Baba's name; perhaps she had been one of his women. He never traveled far from home, but she could have been someone he met. Baba loved foreign women. Foreign anything, really.*

Of course when she spoke of him, her voice was not kind. It was different when someone barged in on you, *implying Baba or even Asha had barged in on her at some point. Asha was certain she would have remembered such a woman, so it must have been Baba.*

"Who are you?" Asha repeated at length when the woman only stared. She seemed to know this game as well as Asha, perhaps better.

"You may call me Zawadi."

"But that is not your name?" Asha pressed.

The woman merely raised a brow.

"What do you want here?" Asha drew her shoulders back and raised her head as unease grew in her stomach, making it swirl. The question sounded too weak to her own ears. But she was here all alone, defenseless and exhausted.

"It is best that a woman sound weak with a man and strong among other women," Baba insisted as he led her up the steps of the palace. "Trust me on this, my best beloved."

"But what if there is a woman and a man present?"

Baba smiled, long and wide, so all his teeth showed and his eyes nearly disappeared into his cheekbones. "Now I know you know the answer to that. What do you do, Asha?"

Asha grinned. She loved it when Baba expressed pride in her skill, loved it when he smiled only for her. "I perform for whoever has the most power."

"Thats my girl."

The woman, Zawadi, leaned back a bit and looked Asha up and down. Her gaze was at once warm and cool, seeming to leave a shiver wherever it touched. "Your father performed a great service for his king. A service that touched my people. I am here to return the favor. I only wish I had found him alive. So he might have seen me do this."

"What favor?" Asha felt a rush of pride. Baba had been a great man! But she felt a bit cheated, not knowing all his great deeds?

"I did not travel all this way to answer questions. Are you Asha? He spoke of his best beloved." Was it Asha's imagination, or did the woman sound angry when he said that? "Of his own self reborn. His legacy. Is that you?"

Asha felt the glow of her father's praise lighting her from within. She felt his love wrapped around her again. How she'd missed being loved. Asha raised her head to the air and let it dip once.

"Good." An unnatural silvery light settled around the woman.

Asha caught her breath, and excitement such as she had never known filled her. The woman was fey. Baba had promised to give Asha adventures, to find her the magic and wonder! Now his promise would be fulfilled!

"I will grant you a wish. Any one thing you desire, be it within my power." The woman offered in a deep soothing voice that swirled around Asha like softly beating wings.

Anything. Asha's skin tingled, and her mind ran away in a thousand different directions. She could travel the world. She could go beyond it, into the fabric of the universe. She could take her entire family and make them wealthy once more, always cared for. She could make herself queen.

"Ha. Ha." Asha all but forgot the woman before her, giggling at the course of her own mind. She could do anything, be— "anything?"

"I cannot wake the dead, if that is what you are thinking." The woman's eyes gave nothing away, but her tone was judgmental, as if she knew Asha had not been thinking this. Asha's heart plummeted. She should have been thinking that.

But...Baba would not be angry that she hadn't thought of him. He sent her this gift to make her happy, to give her adventure. And she had to assume her mother had been an equally selfless being; they would want Asha happy.

"Have you seen the world?" Asha demanded of the woman, most likely a nymph. She wanted to change the topic, but also, she simply had to know.

"Much of it. It is impossible to see the entire thing."

"Why?" Asha demanded, it was perhaps her only goal, to see the entire world. It had been Baba's goal as well, and if Asha could do it, his own self reborn, *it would be as though he was doing it.*

"The world keeps changing." The nymph leaned her hands on her knees and pushed off the low stool. She rolled her neck and the silvery glow began to pulse with impatience. "In the time it took you just to greet me, the world around you has already changed. But you never do look at what is before you, do you, daughter of Zuberi? You look to the horizon and beyond, look to what you cannot see and cannot have. You will always want more."

"Not if you give me my wish," Asha whispered eagerly.

In the silvery light, Asha could see the barest hint of the woman's lips beneath her scarf; they were curved at one end and her eyes crinkled. "Out with it then, what is it?"

"I wish to be like you."

Zawadi's eyes settled into quiet pools of silvery calm. "By that, I suppose you mean beautiful, intelligent, and sought after?"

Asha ignored the woman's sarcasm. "By that, I mean magical. *Answering to no one, able to do what you want, when you want. Powerful!"*

"*Ah, yes. You would be Zuberi's daughter.*" It was a though she could not make up her mind if she was angry or pleased; the light around her grew so powerful it fluttered her clothes like a raging, silent wind. Her eyes were so full and sparkling that they gave Asha her first real sense of the danger such a creature could pose to a young girl all alone.

Asha took an involuntary step back and struck the stone wall she'd repaired earlier. She stumbled, her hand reaching out for purchase fell straight into the flames. Asha cried out and jerked forward to get away from the pain cradling her hand.

"*You want to be all things. All powerful.*" The woman advanced on Asha, uncaring of her injury. "*To be maker of your own fate, as you think magic beings are,*" She wasn't questioning, but nor did the words sound like a spell. It felt a bit like being read a lecture. She spoke in the voice of many women, and all of them unimpressed.

It was the most horrifying thing Asha had ever seen. The wind of her power shook Zawadi, and Zawadi alone. The light surrounding her at once pulsed and swam like the surface of a boiling hot spring. She was *power*.

"*It is beyond you,* human, *to be as midnight and laughter and adventure,*" Zawadi said, her voice not falling on the air but taking it over. There was no air in the world but her words. "*Your mind is too small, and your body too limited. Were I to give you all you desire, you might have a few short hours to marvel in the vastness of the world. Then you would explode. Ceasing upon the course of your life so selfishly that not even your body is left for the earth to devour.*"

Asha gasped. Zawadi could split her apart with a thought. Asha could die simply for saying the wrong thing to such a woman. But the more Asha saw or heard, the more her body shivered with fear, and the more desire chased after it. What must it feel like to be so powerful? Asha entirely forgot the searing pain in her hand as her being hungered for the true danger.

"*How many hours?*" The question slipped out of Asha's lips on a whisper.

"*Um, ha, ha, ha, ha, ha!*" Zawadi threw her head back, and the folds of her voluminous dress shook out like the branches of a tree, swaying with a happy breeze. With a suddenness that stole Asha's breath Zawadi's every motion and amusement halted. Her eyes pierced Asha with their flickering silver intensity. "*Fifteen, at most. But one moment more and you will surely cease to be.*"

"*Alright,*" *Asha could not seem to touch her own mind, words simply fell out of her, and she stood, unaware that her right hand was blistering from being in the flames. "So give me only five hours.*"

Slowly Zawadi lifted her hand to the scarf. Hiding half her face, she pulled it free of some fastening Asha could not see. It fell to the side of her face, revealing the brightly curved lips rounded cheekbones, and wide nose of the nymph. With her face revealed, she looked to be older than Jauhar, perhaps as old as sixty and very kind, even mischievous. Completely gone was all sense of danger about her. She only looked like a tickled aunt, come to bestow a great gift.

Zawadi stepped forward and took Asha's face between her palms. "Have a care with that hunger dear." She kissed Asha's left cheek, and magic darted from the patch of skin, dancing through her veins. "It will consume all that is human within you." She kissed Asha's other cheek, as before the feeling raced through her body. When the two bits of magic met lights of every color imaginable exploded before Asha's eyes.

She felt buoyant, as though her feet were not touching the ground. She felt every tingle and brush and breath of the air around her. She saw lights from across the world. And the music, of night, and the animals, and the earth itself, all pulsed within her.

"I am daybreak and music and wonder." *Asha could not stop smiling, could not banish the joy within.*

"Well, you've only five hours," The nymph raised the scarf to hide her lips again, but Asha was not so easily intimidated now. "What will you do?"

Asha looked down at her blistering, stinging hand, all she did was think of it as it should be, soft and smooth, like Jauhar's, and at once, it was healed. It was perfect. No burn, no soot beneath her nails, no scratches from patching the roof, or calluses from where she carried the water each day. She could be beyond beauty with this power, could put Jauhar and her daughters to shame with her beauty and perfection and finery. Make them regret not appreciating her.

No sooner had Asha thought it than colorful light slid down her in waves, transforming her. She wore a gown of deep blues and shining golden threads, as hungry as nature itself. And her hair bloomed atop her head like a crown, surrounded in golden hoops and chains and tiny blue gems. And her feet were clothed in the loveliest winged shoes, made of blue and gold beads. She might as well be a queen as finely as she was garbed. A goddess.

"A ball. Truly?" The nymph seemed genuinely puzzled. She stepped away from Asha raising a quizzical brow. "I give you all the magic your body can hold, and you will take it to a party?"

"Half the world will be there." Asha effervesced. "I can see the world in five hours."

"Ummm. And showing up your sisters, your mothers, this has nothing to do with it?" Zawadi inquired blandly.

Asha shrugged. "Only a little."

"Then I suggest you take a look here." She waved her hand and produced a looking glass that looked like it was held in the death grip of a vulture's claw.

Asha bent before the low mirror and stared in absolute shock. Someone else's face was gazing back at her. It was a lovely face, large green eyes, plump smooth lips, and just a hint of dimples. But it was not her own.

"Where has my face gone?"

"Nowhere," Zawadi's tone smiled at Asha's ignorance. "Magic skins do not show what is, they show what..." She shrugged as if she did not know how to complete the thought. "What is seen."

Asha wanted to ask more questions and pick the magic apart, but she could feel time passing. Soon she would be Asha again. No magic, no longer anyone's best beloved. A servant. And since her family had taken all the camels, it would take half Asha's time just to get to the ball.

Asha grinned, remembering the story of Nur descending from his home in the heavens to announce himself as ruler of all humankind, riding on the back of an eagle with a golden saddle. Colorful lights filled the night, latching onto a beetle flying by. It caught in the web of light and began to grow. It grew until it had been transformed into a colorful green and purple lokoki parrot. And it continued growing— until it was as big as an elephant. Asha walked right up to the bird and lay a hand on his beak. He knelt low, so Asha could climb on, and a golden saddle sparkled into existence on its back. Asha climbed on with a broad grin. She only wished Baba could have seen this. The bird took off and Asha giggled in delight and exhilaration as it carried her into the night, to the ball where half the world waited—for her.

In that moment, she had been so consumed, so awestruck by the power within her Asha had completely forgotten the nymph. Forgotten her questions about the woman and her curiosity about the magic. She was so certain that this adventure would fill her up that tomorrow and yesterday had seemed unreal and those five hours had felt like a whole lifetime.

Now she felt hungry, and tired, and more than a little foolish for not having asked more. For not having taken a moment even to see if the nymph would come again. Or to consider her point. She should have, as it seemed Zawadi was right—

Asha wanted more!

Surely there was a way to find the woman. A way to have the magic again. Asha cradled the shoe close and begged the universe to send the woman her way once more!

SURRENDER

Hadhi felt oddly like a camel, with her bridle handed off from one person to the next. She simply took the hand of this new master, without thought to her own tastes or desires, and walked to the floor wearing an over-bright smile as inside she cringed, hating her constant impotence.

They walked hand over hand, for rather a long way, to opposite side of the room, before they stepped out with the other dancers. It occurred to her as she walked and saw various other foreigners on the floor that she could remember where this man had been all night, but the same could not be said of the others. Though many were quiet pleasant looking he—

"She cannot see you now. No reason to smile quite so brightly." Noam spoke like they were old friends and Hadhi was in on his joke.

But Hadhi startled so badly she nearly stepped into a dancer behind her. Noam laughed. Hadhi clenched her free hand into a fist and fought the urge to snarl. She hated this. She had barely learned the steps to this infernal dance, and now he would make her stumble and laugh at her misfortune. An old woman Hadhi did not recognize was watching her and laughing in delight. Her bright, nearly silver eyes gave Hadhi a shiver.

"Do you often dance the Vantoom here?" Noam asked. His amusement was still apparent, but he was slowly easing her into the steps. "Azize seemed quite...surprised by the style when we encountered it on Gods Parted."

No, they had nothing like this sort of dance here before Azize returned. And Hadhi hated it. They turned and Hadhi searched for the woman again, but she was already moving away.

"My father's man reported it was one of Azize's favorites, so we were made to learn," Hadhi said without inflection, focusing back on the steps.

In Maltuba, dance was not...constrained this way. A woman was never forced into the command of a man who led her about as though he owned her. A man and a woman might dance together, though far more often one kept to one's own sex or danced entirely alone. And while there were particular steps or motions one might learn, they were not forced into a pattern unless it was a performance. One danced to the movement of the music, to the movement one felt inside.

Noam allowed her a quiet moment to settle into the movement of this dance. He was...easier to follow than Hadhi would have expected. She hated being controlled. As a rule, Hadhi did not like to be touched, but that was inescapable tonight. What was surprising to Hadhi was that she was, in fact, relaxing into the movement. She had learned the steps with Sabra; it was a thoroughly uncomfortable experience being directed and criticized while holding onto one of her old tormenters. Hadhi had been wretched at it. But now...this did not feel like being controlled. Noam moved to a rhythm that was well known to him, and Hadhi followed him because it was less familiar to her. Like being guided into a new land.

"Tell me the real reason your other sister is not here," Noam said when it was clear Hadhi was more comfortable. "You know you want to."

As soon as he said the words, Hadhi's back went up, tension shooting through her. She wanted to walk away, leave him to stew, but he was the best friend of the prince. Even if he did not mind, which Hadhi imagined would be the case, it would disturb Mzaa, and might offend the prince. He had her trapped.

"I know no such thing," Hadhi replied sharply.

"Yes you do," he countered in a whisper, leaning closer. "I saw it when she was speaking. You don't lie very well. And you don't like it when others do either."

"Ah yes, disapproving Hadhi. Sour-faced-Hadhi. I have heard this all my life," Hadhi snapped, but made certain to continue smiling; Mzaa would not catch her failing to do her duty. "Why should it bother you?"

"It doesn't." He leaned away, and his smile was so easy, so full, so unconcerned that Hadhi hated him a tiny bit. What she would not give to find the entire world a joke. "I just want to know why the 'pest' escaped the ball. Azize seemed to think his father would insist she be here."

Hadhi sighed and looked beyond the man. Why was lying so much easier for everyone else? She could keep her mouth shut, not tell him a thing. She was very good at that.

"I won't tell a soul. I promise." Hadhi looked into his suddenly serious face and she believed him. He just wanted to solve his mystery, and she was his key. Of course that was why he would dance with her. She was not lovely, she was not sweet, she was not a mystery, nothing that would tempt a man. Hadhi looked away before answering, pretending to focus on her feet and the steps, though she was not feeling a need any longer.

"She is beautiful," Hadhi said honestly and bitterly. "She is clever, and she is much known by the royal family. Loved even."

"Azize hasn't much love for her."

"Not when she was a girl. But she is grown now, all remark of her beauty. And his mother adored her. She would just smile for hours listening to Asha's stories when she was dying. Mzaa could not risk the prince forgiving her past and choosing her."

"What did she do?"

"Made her work all day. Then ruined her gown," Hadhi said flatly, seeing the curly piles of unwound thread.

He was so quiet that Hadhi had to look up. He watched her as though he was trying to read her soul, and she felt insulted again. Clearly he thought she should have stopped Mzaa. That's what it was about him. He looked at things, looked beyond the surface. His eyes saw too much. Hadhi disliked having that pointed at her. It made her feel even uglier.

Maybe she should have stopped Mzaa, but she had no way of knowing what Mzaa intended to do to that silk. And Asha would never protect Hadhi so! And they *could not* risk it. If the prince married Asha, Asha who had no love for the rest of her family, she might leave them all to the control of Uncle Kafil. Hadhi's mind fought against Noam's judgement and her body stiffened, fighting his control in the dance as well. She stepped forward, when she was meant to step back, and trod on his foot—hard.

He jumped slightly, but did not release her, or get angry as another man would have. Baba would have slapped her. Noam's eyes crinkled and the corners, and he bit down on his own grin. "What is dancing like in Maltuba?" He asked with a quiet, groaning chuckle. "Are you better at that?"

She should be insulted, that was clearly an insult. But she felt bad. She had not meant to pound on his feet, but she had been angry, and he certainly felt it. Yet he was not raging or calling her a clod. Hadhi hated being bad at this. She should be better; it was nothing but careful movement. And she was a great hunter. You could not be a clod and be a great hunter. Her body was tuned to quiet, gentle movement, and when needed, deadly speed. Her muscles were toned from it, though perhaps not as firmly as they had been when she hunted often. This should be easy. But...there was an intimacy and a vulnerability to this sort of dancing that set her on edge. So many things set her on edge. He should be dancing with someone pleasant and pretty, someone graceful. But he seemed not to mind Hadhi's wealth of flaws.

So Hadhi found herself relaxing the tiniest bit and just talking with him. He was easy to talk to.

"You saw the Spirit Dancers, before dinner." It was not a question. "There are movements one learns, and certain music calls certain movements forth, but the dance is ..." Hadhi struggled to find the right words in Fairy. Her answer came out slow and stumbling though she felt the words deeply. "Catching-hold of—the divine. You let go of yourself. Feel what the world offers. And answer with motion. In pairs. Or groups. Or alone. All are important. Nuru should be a spirit dancer." Hadhi's words began to come out easier. "She surrenders fully to life. When she dances, I see the light of the next world shine through her."

Hadhi let the words hold the air a moment. She glanced to his face and found Noam watching her in a quiet, intent way that had a shiver rolling through her. She wanted to stretch out in the feeling, but could not explain why. And she knew she should not. She glanced over his shoulder and answered the rest of the question.

"It is not possible to be bad at dancing here, unless you refuse to surrender. But I am not talented like Nuru, nor mysterious like Asha, so I suppose I am not much better at it than this."

"You are not so terrible at this," Noam said with a softer smile. "Only unfamiliar, I think. I was not very good when I first tried these dances either. Too stiff. Dance, where I come from, is far more constrained. You danced one of ours earlier, with Mikhail, the cozy."

The comment startled Hadhi, internally. She followed the steps smoothly enough despite the surprise of knowing he had noticed her tonight, perhaps as much as she had him.

"Perhaps it isn't the dances you are poor at, only the surrender," he mused. "There is a large element of surrender to these dances as well."

"I have noticed," Hadhi replied stiffly, again growing uneasy with his strange perceptiveness, and with this unfamiliar desire for...it not to end yet.

"Tell me, Hadhi," he said curiously, surprising her again. She would not have expected that he would remember her name. They had been introduced only once. He must have been introduced to hundreds of women tonight. "You said *your sister* is well known by the royal family; why aren't you?"

Hadhi shook her head. "She was our father's shadow from the time she was a babe, and he was much in the company of the king."

"While you were at home, gathering cobwebs." He smiled at his own quip. But Hadhi was unfamiliar with the word, and looked away. Asha would know it.

"He loved us differently," Hadhi replied, well used to saying this, but she had not once believed it. He loved Asha. He tolerated his other children. Though Hadhi supposed he would have been quite pleased with his son, Lin, had been allowed to see him born.

"My father loved my siblings and I differently as well."

Hadhi was startled again; she had never heard Noam use such a bitter tone.

Never? She nearly laughed aloud at herself, but his tone required quiet. She had only met him a few hours ago. Strange, she felt like she knew him so much better than a few hours would allow. He seemed so open, easy to know. Perhaps she had misjudged.

"He loved my older brother for his strength, and his looks and the legacy that would be carried on through him." Noam spoke with a wry smile on his lips as though he was amused by his own resentment of his father's love. "And my sister he loved for her beauty, and how well she loved him. And me...he loved only from a *great* distance."

How could Noam not have been the favorite? Such pain should have left him with a shattered, ugly soul, like Hadhi's.

"I am sorry." Hadhi's hand tightened on his. Her soul reached out, offering comfort. She only ever felt so with Nuru. And like Nuru, it seemed this man required none of her comfort.

He smiled at her softly, amused and touched by her offer of comfort, then he shrugged. "There is no reason to be sorry, it simply is."

"Do...do you miss your home?" Hadhi often wondered about that, when Asha would go on about all the places she wanted to see. Hadhi loved their home, the land, the air, the nights when all the heavens opened and revealed the distant light of their promises. But she did not think she would miss it if she left. None of it would miss her. Nor have any chance to. She would die in the hut where she was born, if she were lucky. Or in the home of some man Uncle Kafil forced her to marry if she were not. That was why she needed the prince, for Mzaa, yes, but also for herself. He was the only option that could truly be called her choice. She *needed* it to be *her* choice.

"Sometimes," Noam replied after a quiet, thoughtful moment. "More than the places I miss my siblings, even my father."

"Why?" It came out as a snarl, and Hadhi knew her smile had vanished, but could not retrieve it. Every time she was offered sympathy over her father or asked how she was, she felt such anger fill her being. They hated him as much as her. Everyone did! Yet they wanted her to pretend he loved her, to pretend he was a great man. To pretend she was sad.

Hadhi did not miss her father. How could she, when he never loved her? She did not need sympathy. She only needed space to celebrate within herself and to feel like the monster he had shaped her into.

Her dance partner was silent so long Hadhi had time to feel the dark emptiness within suck away even more of her joy, twist her a little further into an ugly thing. She wanted to curl up and sob, but not for her father. For herself. While he lived, she felt ugly and unlovable through his eyes, but comfortable within herself. Now he was dead, and she was only the ugliness, and the hatred.

"I miss my father," Noam spoke gently. "For the days when he was so happy that he forgot he didn't love me and laughed at my jokes or patted me on the head. I miss the looks on my sibling's faces when they had pleased him, as though the world in that moment was perfect."

Hadhi felt tears sting the corners of her eyes and tensed up with the need to run off to a corner to shed them. But, as if he knew exactly how she felt, Noam led them off to the corner of the room, and then, so suddenly it felt like magic, whirled them out of the still heat of too many bodies and onto the terrace. The air was cool against her face. She did not cry as expected. She smiled softly into the night, on the arm of this strange man she should not like, but began to think she might.

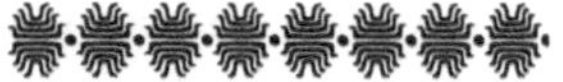

THE GREAT SPIRITS

Ayinde led Nuru back to the side of the room with her friends after their dance.

"You're so good at those dances already, I'm sorry," Ayinde said shyly. "It was my fault we hit Oni."

Nuru notched up her head with a satisfied smile. "Oni insulted Hadhi earlier, she deserves it."

Ayinde laughed. He was always good fun. He and his twin Arya were just two years older than Nuru and lived near the mansion where Nuru had grown up, until Baba died. They used to play together, run to the docks, or dance together. Ayinde and Nuru taking turns having Arya on their backs so she could truly enjoy the dancing. They were some of her closest friends.

He walked Nuru back to join Arya and Neema who seemed to have gathered a pair of Azize's friends. Arya was bearing up on the crutches with a smile though Nuru knew it was harder just standing on them than it would be walking or even dancing.

Nuru didn't want to try to flirt with strange men from strange places like Mzaa wanted. But if she went back to her mother, Mzaa would force her to try and find Azize to flirt with, and she wanted that even less. At least this way she could be with her friends.

"Nuru!" Neema shouted when Nuru joined them, as though they had not seen each other earlier. She reached out and pulled Nuru to her side, beaming wide as she introduced her to the men.

"This is my dearest friend, Nuru. She will join the Spirit Dancers one day and put us all to shame. Nuru, these are some friends of the prince, Masahiro, of Uukio, and Tareek, of Reethurn."

Nuru smiled at the men. "Welcome to Maltuba," *may the spirits preserve you*, she said the last bit in her head. Mzaa had told her the traditional

Maltuban greeting would make strangers uncomfortable, but Nuru's mind couldn't seem to greet people without it.

"It is our pleasure," Tareek said with a grin. "How will you put the other dancers to shame?"

"I shall not." Nuru laughed, shaking her head. "Neema was being kind."

"Ha." Arya scoffed aloud and, at once, looked at her feet to stifle her embarrassed laughter.

Ayinde smiled calmly. "Neema is a talented dancer, so it should be no insult to her to say that Nuru is a great one."

"And it isn't," Neema said sharply, her eyes boring into Arya, who could not stop laughing. "I was the one who said it."

Azize's friends looked distinctly uncomfortable. The man named Masahiro opened his mouth to change the subject. "I have never seen a building of such an intricate design as this palace. Six sides and six towers with the open central courtyard...it's lovely! Even the outer walls have such lovely reliefs carved into them. I did not get a chance to see it as closely as I wanted today; hopefully tomorrow will afford us more time."

Nuru appreciated the change of subject; she couldn't very well say that she was a better dancer than Neema, it would be rude. But nor could she say honestly that she didn't know that there was a difference in *passion* between them. Neema liked to dance, she knew the motions and she loved being a part of things. But Nuru felt the dance even when there was no music; she felt the dance though she was not among the Spirit Dancers. She felt the passion with Arya on her back or standing alone beneath the moon. There was a difference, but she did not want to hurt her friend by agreeing that it was so.

"I hope you get the chance to see the walls closely. Each side of the building has an hour of the day when the sun hits it and makes the design shine," Nuru said. "But make sure you look closely, they aren't carved, they are formed out of mud and clay, and sometimes wood or rocks and gems." Nuru said helpfully. "They depict two stories each for the three great spirits that surround Maltuba: Ether, the spirit of the desert, Gitonga, the spirit of the jungle, and Nur, the spirit of the sun."

The two strangers smiled broadly at Nuru. "Is it the art, the architecture, or the subject you enjoy?" Tareek asked.

"Oh, all of it!" Nuru said brightly. "I suppose my least interest would be the architecture."

The men laughed.

"Nuru was named for Nur," Arya announced, trying, Nuru thought, to latch onto the change in subject as well. "The god of the sun. Ruler of all other gods."

"Were you indeed?" Masahiro asked asked, he was clearly just being polite, but Nuru found herself talking about it as though he were truly interested.

"Yes. My mother loves the old stories. She had dreamed of naming all of her children for the spirits. But my sister Hadhi was born early and ill, and my grandmother thought it would insult the great spirits to name her after them. When I was born, she was determined to have at least one great spirit among her children." Nuru rolled her eyes. "A shame it has not worked out."

Everyone chuckled, and Nuru was relieved to find this not the chore she'd expected.

"Forgive me my curiosity," Masahiro said shyly and leaned nearer. "All evening, I have heard the same beings referred to as both gods and as great spirits; is there a difference?"

Neema smiled softly and lay a hand on Masahiro's arm in a flirtatious way Nuru would have expected of her own mother. Neema was only a year older than Arya, but she was a far bolder flirt.

"Many tribes make up our nation, and they all believe in different ways. The Ga'ogo, and the Maumai were the first two tribes to comprise Maltuba, so you hear those beliefs most. The Ga'ogo, like Nuru's family and mine, believe the great spirits are part of nature voices that emerge to guide, but not gods to rule us. The Maumai," she waved at Arya and Ayinde, "believe that these same beings are gods and must be worshiped."

"And this causes no strife?" Tareek queried.

"It did in the past," Neema remarked. "As recently as eighty years you could say."

Nuru was surprised that Neema would bring up the war that neither of them had been alive to see. She knew some Ga'ogo families still greatly resented King Enzi's father for taking the throne. Proclaiming it as his right bestowed by Nur. Nuru never really thought about it. It was the past. Ga'ogo had ruled, now Maumai did. Perhaps one day the Bor or the Tikoo would take the throne. As long as they were all one nation, did it really matter?

"There was infighting between the Maumai and the Ga'ogo, but that was over the right to be the ruling tribe, not over religion." Ayinde argued.

"Ruling tribe gets to, among other things, decide which religion is most honored. If the Ga'ogo ruled, the vaashta would not hold such high positions in our society."

"Perhaps," Ayinde conceded. "But now we are one nation of many nations. The vaashta are important, yes, but they do not dictate to those who do not believe as they do. We are a nation that respects and honors many beliefs. If Nuru believes only that Ether is a spirit, it does not diminish my faith that Ether is a goddess. Nor does my faith challenge her belief, all are valid and our own. Provided we respect each other."

"Well said," Nuru beamed at her friend for the lovely peaceful sentiments, but in the back of her mind, she wondered why Neema was so vehement. It felt personal.

Nuru knew it was the vaashta who had made an offering on her friend's behalf so she might join the Spirit Dancers. Neema's family had always been poor, almost as poor as Nuru's family were now. The vaashta took pity on her and offered gifts to Eshe so she could join the Spirit Dancers. Why do that, when Neema did not believe as they did? And why did Neema seem so greatly to resent them?

"Indeed, very wise," Masahiro remarked.

"Maumai and Ga'ogo," Tareek said thoughtfully. "I believe Azize said he was part of two tribes."

"Yes," Nuru said, quickly latching onto a simpler subject. "But not Ga'ogo. He is Maumai and Tikoo. His mother was the leader of the Tikoo."

"The people with the head wrappings?" Masahiro asked.

Arya giggled. "No. They are Qi'on, worshippers of Ether exclusively. And then there are the Bor, who worship no one and think we are all fools."

"They do not think we are fools." Ayinde sighed put-upon. "They think the old stories are lessons, but not about real beings."

"Exactly," Nuru smiled and tried to help Arya out. Every time she spoke, the men looked to someone else, treating her like a child or an ill creature to be ignored. "The story of Sekou and Gitonga teaches us that everyone is valuable no matter how different." Nuru notched her head up sharply.

"Yes." Arya giggled high pitched and shy. "While Nur and the travelers from the sea teaches us not to trust foreign men."

Nuru giggled at her friend, subtly telling her she didn't need help with these men.

"There are stories to teach you not to trust foreign men?" Tareek laughed.

"Oh yes," Neema said with a grin. "Many."

"Do any teach you not to trust the men of your nation?" Tareek returned Neema's flirtatious look.

"Only life teaches one that," Neema said, and everyone laughed. But Nuru noticed an oddly serious expression in her friend's eyes and a sharp stiffening of her spine. "Anyway! The Tikoo, Queen Imara's tribe, are worshippers of all, but followers of Gitonga. A warrior tribe." Neema said with exaggerated intrigue.

"I see," Tareek said, nodding slowly

Nuru laughed. "A lot to keep track of, no?"

The two men laughed again. Nuru liked that she could amuse them. "Do not worry, we will not be offended if you ask again and again what we believe. We like to share. Tell us something about your homes that we will have trouble remembering."

Masahiro smirked. "I could confound you just by listing the names of my seven brothers and four sisters."

"Twelve children in one family!" Ayinde exclaimed.

"The spirits have great faith in you." Both Nuru and Ayinde said in unison, though Ayinde had said *gods*. They looked at one another and began to laugh. Nuru lost her breath a moment as Ayinde's eyes flared wide and he looked at her so intently she couldn't think.

But the strangers laughed, breaking the spell.

"Is that a kind way of saying my family is cursed?" Masahiro asked, seeming to grasp the humor himself as his smile was wide and his voice was warm.

"No! It is a blessing." Arya shook her head wildly. "Many people want large families, but to have more than ten, and to have all the children survive to maturity is so rare, even in homes where men take many wives, that we say only those parents that the gods, or spirits, have great faith in are so blessed."

Nuru was finding it easier to breathe now, she glanced at Ayinde from the corner of her eye, but he was not looking at her. She felt an odd sort of tingle running over her skin. It wasn't bad, it wasn't good, it was just new. He'd never looked at her that way before. She didn't think anyone had.

It was easier to focus on Azize's friends. They were bright and friendly and safe in an otherworldly sort of way.

"Well," Masahiro said lightheartedly. "I'd say it is a bit of a blessing, and a curse. I nearly starved. I was the youngest child and everyone got to the food before me. It's why I left home."

Nuru laughed hard, though everyone else was looking at him in pity. Nuru didn't mind being the only one to laugh. She was certain it was a joke. And indeed, the man winked at her. And the oddest thing happened. Nuru felt her mother's voice leaving her mind and Hadhi's entering it.

Do not let Mzaa's rules intimidate you. The foreigners are just people. They will come, we will meet them and they will leave. You need never be anyone but yourself.

"May the spirits preserve you," Nuru said with a little wink of her own.

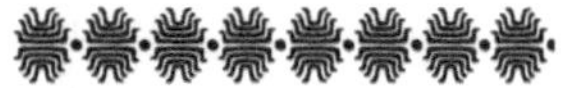

FOREIGN TONGUES

Zawadi intentionally stumbled into the boy prince as he made his way around the room, seeking information about his mystery woman. It was as intentional as it had been when Zawadi let Zuberi's eldest trip over her on the dance floor, but that was more of a pleasure than anything else. Watching her eyes widen and her body tense. Smelling her fear as it coated the air. All day long, in whatever bird form Zawadi had taken when she looked on that girl, she found her looking back. The relentless hunter always seeking a way to kill. So Zawadi wanted something special for her. As she would have for her father. She wanted that girl, for once, to feel what it was to be hunted. She wanted her tense and waiting. Wanted her fear, long before she faced her death.

But with the boy prince, she wanted only a means to reaching his father. It was the same reason she had nudged him home with dreams, so she could reach his well protected father. Now she would use him to see what that protection was.

The prince reached out to steady Zawadi, smiling gently like an adult to a child.

"Ur uli gibo, zhavaa mzaa?" The prince asked gently. *Are you well, good mother?*

Zawadi nearly rolled her eyes. She did not speak Maltuban, but she understood his meaning the way all fey could; she felt it in his mind. It was a large source of amusement to the fey that so many nations were adopting their language for common communication when the fey had no need of translations. There were entire groups of fey that did not speak at all, merely communicating with their minds.

Just now though, Zawadi was imagining Grackle's response if she were greeted so by one so young. *Just because I am old doesn't mean I was a mother, boy.*

There are other things to be. It would have been said with a laugh, but it would have been serious; she hadn't much patience for men or women who assumed a woman's only function was to give birth. Zawadi missed that humor, that spirit, that fight she had that gave her such empathy for all the exceptionally unique beings of the world. Zawadi felt tears building up and her contained pain colored her response.

"Have you no pride in your people, prince?" She challenged coldly.

"I..."

"Where are the colors of your nation?" She struck him lightly in the chest. "You do not wear the colors of *any* tribe, nor the sash of succession. What are your people to believe but that you want no part of them?"

"I..." The prince fumbled, and the man next to him, Elof, hid a grin in his bushy beard.

"You assume because I am old I cannot learn Fairy for our guests because you have no pride in your people."

"No. No, good mother, please hear me. I meant no disrespect. I have great pride in the *united* tribes; that is why I do not wear the colors of any one specifically. As for the sash, it has not been fitted to me in five years, and I have grown. I am humbled by the greatness of my nation and its people. I was simply...unprepared for this event."

Zawadi nodded slowly. She couldn't say she liked the prince, but there was nothing in him so powerful it could rouse her anger or her pain. He was a peaceful little cloud to float through. But she doubted he found her the same, and that...felt good. Just unsettling this boy was a relief for the anguish that had been rising in her as she watched one after another of Zuberi's women enjoying their lives. Laughing, flirting, moving through the world with ease. Ease that had been provided to them through the suffering and the deaths of others!

It enraged her. Depressed her. Shook her from her well-laid plans of letting each woman decide her own fate with their wishes and made her want to simply destroy them all. Simply kill.

So goading and prodding this boy of fluff was a mighty relief. And she reveled in it.

"So you mean to stay? And select a bride? And prepare to rule?" From anyone else, this would be pushing the boundaries so far there might be a threat of jail or punishment. One did not speak so to a prince, but Grackle's age granted her a level of respect and freedom that not even the prince could question.

"It would be hard to pick a woman to marry the same night as I arrived home. But I intend to do my best to honor my people," Azize said uncomfortably. Look at the boy sweat.

"Madam," Elof said, bowing before her. "My friend is a bit shy," he winked, "already he has found a woman to turn his head. We have been asking everyone, do you know the name of the woman who was clothed in gold and blue?"

"Ha! If she left you without a name, you would do better not to pursue her," Zawadi said with Grackle's knowing brows raised. "Temptresses always hide agendas, or," she nodded towards the king, "associates."

She watched Azize's muscles jump with rage and tension and slipped her arm through his. "Come, take me with you. Shy boys always need their *zhavaa mzaa* to protect them."

Elof snorted and covered his mouth. Beneath his beard, his cheeks were turning as red as his hair. Zawadi might enjoy this man. She nudged the prince towards his father, and he walked forward stiffly, with his heart pounding. But Zawadi wasn't certain if it pounded in fear, or anticipation or anger, or shame. He was at sea without a rudder, this boy, just following the strongest current. What sort of leader would he make for his people when Zawadi had finished with her vengeance?

The closer they grew to Enzi, the more Zawadi felt the magic pushing her back. She clung onto the prince's arm, leaned into the strength of his young form, but every step was more difficult than the last. When they were nearly upon him, only five people separating her from her quarry, Zawadi noticed that the man's hand was— as it had often been tonight—on the hilt of his sword. Every time he ran his fingers across its jewels, she felt pushed back.

Zawadi blinked, changed her eyes alone to a more useful pair, Caracara's bird eyes. She focused in on the jewels from this distance. Green gems with runes etched into them. *Fey bleeder*s. The magical repellants used to protect the dwarf temple in Mount Riddle from the old Fairy King, Raglan. The Unnamed King, as Queen Meave deemed him after he was unseated. Those stones stole fairy powers, pulling the magic away from its rightful home within a fairy and giving it to whoever held the stone.

Zawadi stopped. She could not go any nearer, or the king would feel her power and be able to steal it. There were ways around the stones, but it would take...time. Or perhaps if he were distracted. Or if he approached her instead of the other way around. Zawadi glanced around the room. All her quarries dancing, gossiping, laughing, enjoying their lives safely, surrounded by neighbors and friends. She had waited a year and nine months for this revenge. Zawadi could wait a while longer.

Zawadi looked up to see the prince regarding her with concern, but unsure how to speak to her. She patted him on the back of the hand and smiled up at him.

"We think of you as the son of Enzi," she said gently. "Such a boy would need a mother's protection in all things. But you are also a son of *Imara*. Even facing death, she knew her voice. Be that son." She slipped her arm free of his and nudged the boy. Zawadi took Elof's arm, holding him back as his friend started forward, his eyes wide and wondering. Full of fear, and shock, that anyone thought him strong enough to face the world alone.

"Daja fa Imara," Zawadi said, taking the words right out of his mind, *son of Imara.*

Azize's shoulders straightened as he was gifted with a tiny bit of faith. Zawadi nearly laughed as she watched the boy walk away more confidently. Who knew, perhaps, he could be a decent leader, given the chance.

Elof leaned near to Zawadi's ear. "Thank you, I believe he needed to hear that."

Zawadi looked up at the stranger and winked. "This is what a zhavaa mzaa does. Gives confidence to little boys who need it and adventures to little girls. And tells grown men to get her a drink already."

Elof laughed hard. Releasing her arm, he bowed. "It would be my honor."

Zawadi waited until the man was well away to slip off through the crowd. She would not be getting any vengeance tonight, but this was far from over.

Zuberi had done his king a *great* favor. Removed from his path any power he did not understand, any power he could not control. Any power he feared he was unequal to. Beings that had not even cared to learn his name before Zuberi came along. Enzi had had no reason to fear her before. But he did now. Zawadi was his superior in every way. They just should have done a better job of destroying her.

Noam snatched Hadhi out of the bright lights and crowded room into the dim quiet where she belonged. He could tell she was on the point of tears from things he'd said. Any moment now, he expected her to draw away from him and dart off ahead. But she left her arm in the crook of his as they walked, passing other couples and a few laughing groups. He led her further around the south side of the palace veranda where there were fewer and fewer people until they were all but alone and could see the moon boldly escaping a strand of clouds.

"Were you raised speaking Fairy? You do not seem young enough. It was...made the...common language in...all lands only ten years ago." Hadhi's voice sounded teary as she stumbled through the words.

Noam knew an attempt to fill silence and avoid pain when he heard one. He happily took up the lighter topic to give her the space she needed.

"Glen Harrow, where I was born, is very near Great Island. We've had trade with fairies for generations. So Fairy is the only language I know. Although I have learned a few words in others here and there."

"What need have fairies to trade with humans?" She asked suspiciously.

Noam laughed, ever so slightly offended on behalf of the home of his youth, though no longer his home. "Fairies are like anyone, they have need of things that do not exist where they live."

Hadhi was not looking his way, but he could see her profile in the moonlight cast in stoic lines like a statue looking with disdain on the world below her. Her face would make a magnificent masthead. Bold, imposing, compelling...sad. She had such a sad face. For the life of him, he could not explain why it was compelling, but any man who wasted moments alone in the moonlight with a woman he desired, trying to explain away that desire was a fool. So he just enjoyed the novelty of her and her sorrowful face that could lead men across worlds.

"Maybe they wanted to know how great a threat you are. My father said that is the true purpose of trade." Her words fell heavily through the air.

Noam snorted. Her father had been a friendly man, hadn't he?

"That is why he and the king let Azize leave when he was fifteen. He promised reports on other nations, military strengths and weaknesses..." her mouth was open a moment as she searched for another word. "Number of people," she said with a sharp tension. Those weren't the words she wanted, he'd bet.

"Were your father and the king bent on world domination?" Noam teased to put her at ease.

"Yes." She replied flatly. "They keep reports on every nation Azize visited. They were...displeased that he could not explore Great Island."

Noam was a bit aghast. He was fairly certain his friend had not sent any such information. For one thing, they had never examined any military armaments. For another, Azize had, in fact, been invited to visit Great Island by an emissary of their queen Nolwyn. An invitation Azize had turned down. But surely not because he didn't want to send reports on the Fairy.

"Did they have reports on Glen Harrow?" Noam asked lightly enough, but he was a bit uncomfortable with the idea.

Hadhi nodded.

He shouldn't be worried for Glen Harrow. There was no one there for him any longer. Both of his siblings had left the island. His mother was dead, and his father...His father, who was not his father, who Noam should have given up on loving long ago, as the woman beside him surely seemed to think. Noam should not worry about that man. But he thought his father might be the cause of his concern. Because he knew enough of King Enzi to take the threat of world dominion seriously.

"What did it say?" Noam pressed.

Hadhi's arm on his flinched slightly, and her eyes drifted slowly away. He found this woman the oddest combination of rage and sadness. Nothing about her expressed any expectation of joy. In fact, whenever she seemed even pleased, she immediately shut down and pushed her rage forth. Yet. When he expressed the tiniest pain, she opened up and gently offered comforts that such an angry *wounded* woman should not have. Right now, he wanted desperately to know what was going on in her mind.

"I never read it." She removed her arm from his walking toward the railing.

Noam stopped where he was a moment, riveted. He'd never felt a thing like it before. She was...devastatingly compelling.

Noam crossed to her and nudged her shoulder playfully. "You must have heard something if you know it existed." There was something bothering her, and as much as he was asking to look after his old home, he was also asking because...he wanted to know what had disturbed her.

"It was not a threat. My father marked it as a good place to...watch the Fairy nation."

Noam smiled. "Not an unfair estimation. We keep no standing army. But all our male citizens must learn to defend the nation. We would not be easily subdued."

Hadhi's eyes gentled in a nearly pitying manner. "You never did battle with my father." She notched up her head and her eyes narrowed slightly, as if expecting a rebuke. "I saw you, before Azize greeted us, you asked him something. You said, gzufiga. *Monster.* You were talking about my father. Did Azize tell you why he calls him that? Why everyone did?"

Noam shook his head. Unable to disrupt the intensity around her with words. She was on fire with tension and pain and rage. Noam stepped closer, wanting to take up her hand and offer comfort, but he couldn't presume to tell her Azize hadn't meant words that he clearly had. And she looked so entirely forbidding.

"The Tikoo, whose colors you wear," she said and very nearly fingered his long tunic. Her fingers hovered near the mirrored arching lines of golden thread that decorated the purple silk. To Noam they looked like flames, but Azize had said they were meant to evoke the limbs of the jungle outstretched to draw one in.

Many people had remarked on his wearing Maltuban clothes, but none had come out and asked what they wanted to know. Why? Why would a foreigner wear their clothing? And Noam had not offered the information. He wondered if Hadhi would finally be the person bold enough to ask. But her eyes darkened and her hand dropped.

"They are the tribe of Azize's mother. They were the largest free tribe in the area before my father conquered them for Enzi. First, he stole Imara, *their queen,* before she was ours. He trapped her with Enzi, but her warriors were not broken. So he stole fifty children and...chose...five to take to the battlefield. He killed them before their mothers and fathers. And the Tikoo fought harder. So he...bound the other children near the fighting and burned them alive." She was silent a long frozen moment, her eyes boring into Noam with rage and desperation, begging him for something, but he had no idea what. To take the truth away? To stop her speaking?

"Rama, my sister Asha's mother. She was one of the warriors. My father...*selected* her as a trophy of battle. She used to wake in tears. When she was dying, she told me it was the screams of those children that defeated the Tikoo." Hadhi's eyes burned into Noam's with certainty and pain her calm recitation had concealed. "That is only some of his evil. So many of our neighbors have reasons to hate him, but were too...defeated already to challenge him." An expression came and went on her face, like a stomach turning, like sadness, or regret.

"The Bor used to have a friendship with a group of...*fey?*" Her tone implied a question, but she did not wait for an answer. "They did not eat flesh, and when the Bor agreed to do the same, the fey doubled their crop. It was a friendship of no threat. But they had magic. My father, and *Enzi,*" she snarled the name, "fear any power not their own. They trapped a child fairy —" Her voice just stopped a moment.

A stillness came over her entire being, so it looked like she wasn't breathing at all. When she spoke again, he could see she'd been breathing the entire time, just so shallowly she'd looked...absent.

"When adults came to rescue it, my father had sent his *best hunter* to follow them. They were tiny, no bigger than mice. Very hard to track. But once he knew where their stronghold was, he went with other monsters and slaughtered them. They always use children," her voice broke over the words. "Always use the things you love to destroy you. Your people would have given in to him had they any love in them. It is why he always won. It would take one with—*no love in their heart* to defeat him."

Noam was devastated. Her tales were so flatly related, and her posture so sure someone else might mistake the anguish within her. Might think her last pronouncement was one of pride. It was not. And it stopped his heart a moment. No wonder she was so grim. To know someone you loved had committed such atrocities must eat her up inside. It explained things that Azize had only ever hinted at. Such wounded children these two powerful men had raised. It was heartbreaking. Before his heart started back up Hadhi had recovered herself enough to walk away further. So quiet and calm, were it not for the magnetic force of her Noam might have lost her in the shadows she meandered through.

He needed to change the subject. He'd brought her out here to give her a moment of levity, not drag her further into the well of sorrow that surrounded her. But he had, in fact, made it worse. How was he to possibly clear that story from the air?

"Kuffik!" Noam expelled Azize's favorite expletive with a little shake to release the tension. Hadhi spun around in shock. Noam was gratified to see the tiniest hint of a smile on her face. "That's one of those few words I picked up in other languages. It seemed appropriate after your story."

She bit her lip, very nearly grinning. He rather missed seeing all of her teeth.

"Gzufiga, and kuffik? Did Azize teach you only ugly words?" She asked.

"Ugly? Oh dear, am I about to meet the disapproving Hadhi you were telling me about?"

She snorted, swallowing her laugh. Noam grinned.

"What words would you teach me in his place?" Noam asked softly, slowly moving nearer to this quiet magnet. She looked away shyly. "You called the desert beautiful earlier. How would you say that?" Noam pressed. "What is your word for beautiful?"

"Ethuri," she answered so softly the wind might have carried it away had not his ears been tugging near even the slightest sound she might make.

"Ethuri," Noam repeated. Looking at the back of her head, as she'd turned fully away from him now. "I like that. It's a good word. Though I still think kuffik has its uses."

She giggled softly with her teeth, fighting to trap the sound inside her. They drifted into silence together. Noam rarely spent much time in silence, but he found he rather liked the quiet, with the right sort of companion.

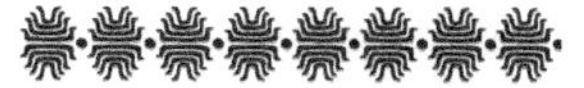

THE LAST EMBERS

Asha was nearly home when a cheetah, as dark as the shadows it slipped out of, blocked her path. It had silvery eyes that held Asha frozen. Her heart caught in fear, but also in excitement. What a night! Magic, adventure, and now, to stand face to face with a cheetah. And not just any cheetah either, Gitonga was said to have visited Sekou in the body of a black cheetah when he rescued the outcast babe.

Asha ought to be terrified. It was either one of the great spirits who protected Maltuba, or a very hungry hunting animal. Hadhi had been mauled by a cheetah when she was eighteen, already a hunter and had a weapon. Asha should fear death, but all she could do was marvel at its beauty.

She should have wished to be a cheetah! Although... She tilted her head to the side, smiling as the animal did the same. Maybe she had been a cheetah, playing with her prey. The man she led around all night had been fine prey. Perhaps that was why the animal was here. Perhaps she sensed another such as itself and came to make friends.

"Are you here to devour me, cheetah?" Asha bent forward, stretching towards the beautiful animal before her. The nearer she grew, the better she could make out the vague spots, of a black just a touch lighter than the rest of her pelt. "Or do you recognize some of your power in me?"

Humans, the voice chuckled in Asha's mind, and the cheetah shook its head. It walked forward and rubbed against Asha's legs, circling her. *Give you magic for all of five hours, and you grow so self-important you do not even fear death. I did warn you: the* magic *will devour you.*

"Zawadi?" Asha laughed despite herself. She couldn't believe it. This was the nymph who blessed her hours ago.

Magic skins never appear the same way twice. The cheetah that was Zawadi circled Asha's legs again before walking on ahead. *Was it all you dreamed?*

"Ohhhh. So much more!" Asha spun around as she followed the creature. "It was incredible! I want to feel so forever."

The cheetah made a low, scratchy mewling sound that might have been a laugh. Asha cringed a little at the less than pleasant sound.

Asha's insides were dancing and bouncing with such wonder and excitement. She opened her mouth to ask, to demand, to beg if she must—to have the power again. It was everything she wanted, she must have it again.

"There is so much more to the world than I have ever seen. So many questions," Asha giggled, thinking of the things she and her stalker had discussed in corners.

Beside her, Zawadi was an animal. Or so she seemed. It filled Asha with a curious hunger.

"Zawadi, have you any shape of your own? Is there a shape you cannot take? Do you know the woman whose form you wore when you blessed me?" Asha would have gone on asking questions, but the nymph began to answer.

Yes, we have our own forms, and we can assume them at any time. Magic skins are simply another way of encountering the world. I've yet to find a shape I cannot inhabit. And—yes. I knew Wren very well. She was quiet a moment, making Asha's mind run away with questions. She wanted to ask about this Wren, but almost as though Zawadi knew the direction of her thoughts, she spoke again. *Your turn. Tell me about your home. Does your king have a royal magician? Had your father met many magical beings? Did he know much of magic?*

"Oh no. To all your questions." Asha laughed. "There is no magic in Maltuba. Only humans. Baba and I always dreamed of traveling the world and meeting magical beings. What great service did he do for the king the brought you here?"

The cheetah seemed to growl low inside its mouth. Her steps slowed. *That is…too long a tale for this night.* She answered slowly, her voice stretched tight with some emotion.

"Wait!" Asha exclaimed, sure the nymph meant to leave but wanting to know so much more. She hadn't asked for the power again yet. She longed to, but it seemed equal to her desire for power was her desire for answers. "Please, won't you tell me more about your kind? Do nymphs have children, or do you just appear?"

Nymphs? The voice filled Asha's mind as the cheetah growled in a way that sounded distinctly like yawning.

"Is that not what you are?"

What I am is not defined by one name. The cheetah rolled its shoulders and padded on a bit faster ahead of Asha. *But I have been called that name. I am called a great many things by a great many people. That word will do as well as any other. And yes, my kind can have children.*

"Do you?"

There was a long silent stretch as Asha awaited her answer. Then it came like a pained mewl in her mind.

They were taken from me.

"I did not think nymphs could die."

All— Things— Die— in their time. And all things can be killed— before it. The cheetah stopped a few feet before Asha, turning its head back to bare its teeth. *We live longer, so humans are desirous of our power or our deaths. At times both.*

"I am so sorry. Who would—"

That is enough questions, daughter of Zuberi. Your body is worn from my magic, and your mind is a storm of wonder and excitement. I will send you home. Sleep.

Before Asha could say a thing, she found herself on the ground before the fire, with a blanket on her back and a rug beneath her. She was so tired, rung out like a rag. She closed her nearly limp fingers around her slipper, the last embers of the flame of power that had lived inside her tonight. With all her might, she wished it safe, preserved. As her eyes drifted closed, she could see the slipper in her mind, tucking itself into Jauhar's box of treasures that even she never opened. It lay beside Baba's knife, safe and treasured. Asha felt a small smile on her sleepy lips, felt the tingle of power on her finger tips; it wasn't quite gone was it? She curled up in the warmth before the fire and fell asleep with visions of the night dancing within her. One image prevailed over all the rest. Her pursuer with a smile like life and magic, reaching out for her, his lips only a breath away.

Come find me.

IN THE COOL OF EVENING

Hadhi leaned on the railing, feeling very nearly *relieved*. They were such terrible truths to share and such an angry reason she had chosen to do so. Only because she felt him preparing to offer sympathy, and she wanted none. She far preferred disgust to sympathy. But Noam had offered neither.

He let her speak her ugliness then offered levity in exchange. How did such a man cross her path? It seemed...impossible. Hadhi let herself pretend, only for a moment, that he had asked to know her word for beautiful so he could say it to her. So he could call her beautiful. It was beyond silly. She was not beautiful. But his quiet acceptance of her hideous stories made her feel incredibly safe beside him. She never felt safe.

All evening she'd been on edge, maybe longer. For a year and a half, she'd been watching vigilantly over her family, waiting for any of her father's victims to come seeking vengeance. It felt like she hadn't breathed in so long. But even knowing the mystery woman might have been a nymph, even knowing she would have to face her now and defend her family however she could. Still, when she walked with Noam she felt safe. Even before she spoke, she felt...different with him. When they had walked the veranda silently looking for more privacy. Hadhi liked knowing what they were doing, though she had not asked. She rarely experienced that sort of affinity with anyone but Nuru. It was strange that she felt in tune with him when he was so different from her. Strange and lovely. But it was not attraction like she was letting herself pretend. It could not be. He was so bright, and happy, and just—different from her.

He seemed only to love his siblings when he spoke of them. She heard no resentments in his tone. He would not understand what it was to be thrilled and vindicated that Asha was not here, but also to feel sad for her.

The silk he wore reminded her so much of the one Mzaa had destroyed, with the golden outstretched arms of Tikoo. Hadhi felt ragged inside from her failure to protect it.

"We are family now, Hadhi, that means we protect each other." Rama's strong voice commanded.

Over the years without her, Hadhi had forgotten all the lessons Rama tried to teach her and become the monster her father wanted from her instead. It was shameful.

Noam was nothing like Hadhi. Nothing that was ugly and resentful. And yet, he seemed to understand her. Who was he? How did one become so lovely?

"How long has your father been gone?" Hadhi asked, wondering at Noam's ease with his father's memory. Perhaps one day she would look back on her father and smile. Perhaps one day she and Asha might be comfortable with one another again.

Noam laughed at the question, so thoroughly surprising Hadhi that she jerked aside to face him.

"My father is not gone. I am." Noam grinned.

"Ha, ha." Hadhi threw up a hand to cover her lips, startled by her ability to be truly amused despite the monster within. "That would make a difference."

Oh, what a difference it might have made if she had escaped her father. Hadhi began imagining herself so, but her mind stopped working. Noam was walking forward, his eyes so intent she felt trapped by—anticipation. She wanted to speak, but could not think of words in any language.

He reached out when he was just before her and pulled Hadhi's hand gently from her lips. "Now there is a smile you should not hide." He stared at her lips as he had stared at the dancers: *entranced*. "It is very becoming."

Hadhi could not tell if she was still smiling or not; with his eyes on her lips, her entire face tingled. Even her heartbeat felt skittish, tickling her from within her chest. They lingered, so still that she could not say how long it lasted, but the cool of the evening brushed across her face, and his gaze so captivated her that she forgot everything but him.

All at once, he dropped her hand and turned away. He leaned over the railing into the night and spoke lightly, as though he had never held her hand, never stared into her eyes, as though she was not ugly, as though she might just be—

Hadhi stopped her mind right there. Every bit of her felt tingly and alive and free of ugliness. But she could not let her mind wonder and *want* what it clearly could not have.

"Why can't you risk your sister catching Azize's attention?"

Hadhi rubbed her hands down the sides of her gown and forced on her bright smile even with his back to her. Very carefully, she walked to the terrace a few feet from him and stared into the night as well.

"After our father was murdered, our uncle took over his home, work, and family." Hadhi could feel Noam startle at her calm words about Baba's demise, but he said nothing, so Hadhi just answered the rest of his question. "He has made a point of refusing all men who ask for us." Hadhi did not mind that fact; it was what it spoke to of his feelings that concerned her. Uncle Kafil left the ball after dinner. He had not said a word to any of them. He did not even treat them like family anymore. "If a prince were to ask, he could not refuse, and the prince would be responsible for the family."

"So why not bring her and have one more chance at catching his favor?" Noam did not look her way. Hadhi tried not to feel hurt. It had all been her imagination. She was sour-faced-Hadhi still, an unremarkable.

"Because she has no love for us," Hadhi repeated her mother's explanation. Most times, it made sense. It was certainly true Asha had no love for them. But she did work hard without complaint. She could make much more of a fuss or stop working altogether. Hadhi shook off her questions. "She might convince the prince to leave us to Uncle Kafil."

"And you'd die all alone in your cobwebs." His voice did not quite smile, but it sounded unconvinced. "Don't you think eventually your uncle will allow you to marry some boy you love?"

Hadhi stared into the night. Loved? What was that anyway? Mzaa loved Baba and he had treated her as coldly as he did anyone.

"One day we would marry." Hadhi spoke quietly. She felt a shudder shake her spine and clenched her teeth against the feeling. "To someone useful to Uncle Kafil. Or someone he owed. And we would be good, do our duty, and strive never to bring any negative notice to ourselves."

"But it would be different with Azize?" Noam asked, startling Hadhi.

She had almost forgotten he was there, so caught up in the realization that nothing had really changed with Baba's death. She had just been voicing fears she'd needed to say to someone, but never could in her home. Noam was *so* easy to talk to. Hadhi did not talk like this with...anyone.

"How can you be sure Azize will be any better? He only came back into your lives tonight."

"Azize...loved his mother." It was the best compliment she could find for the boy she had seen as a child, but never really known. "And he's never *wanted* power over others. Perhaps if I marry him, I will still be nothing but duty-bound, and useful to my family, but it would be *my choice*. My use would be to the part of my family that I chose. My sister Nuru would never be offered up to satisfy someone's debt or to coddle their ego. Mzaa Sabra and Lin would be free to remain together without her having to remarry. Asha... would be free to choose her fate as well. And I would get away from Mzaa." Hadhi snarled the last bit without meaning to.

Noam's gaze soothed her like moonlight after a punishing day, so gentle.

"What of love?" He asked, with a smiling whisper.

"Love is the luxury of men," Hadhi snapped. And felt immediately bad for it as she watched him flinch. He was worrying about his friend. Worrying about what Hadhi's plan would cost Azize, the way Hadhi worried for Nuru. "But..." Hadhi said more gently, wanting to soothe him, but needing to do so only with the truth. "If he cared for Nuru, saw to her safety and happiness, I could love a man for that."

Noam's eyes crinkled like he might smile, but it was a sad expression. Hadhi leaned closer, pulled towards him with her breath trapped in her chest, so it ached.

Noam straightened and clapped his hands together, looking away. Hadhi felt oddly bereft for a moment, then his eyes met hers again, with his playful smile returned. "Then we'd best get you back in."

"Yes." Hadhi held tight to her bright smile as she took up his arm again. She wanted to cry. It had been so peaceful simply being with him. Forgetting the night, and her duty, and...herself, for a while. She'd been someone else for a moment or two, someone who was not so ugly.

"Don't smile so much," he instructed as they walked back the way they had come. When Hadhi opened her mouth to protest, he smiled and spoke once more. "Trust me. You are much lovelier when you don't force a smile. It also wouldn't hurt to be less than receptive to his attention."

Hadhi glared. Why was he trying to ruin her chances? And what made him think she was so foolish she would surrender to his commands?

"The woman he danced with all evening, Azize liked her because she did not care a bit that he was the prince."

Hadhi stopped near an open arch to the ballroom and her eyes cut across the floor and found the prince, talking intently to his father. Hadhi smiled wryly.

"Then, as usual, Mzaa knew best. Asha never cared that he was prince."

Noam's hand tightened briefly around hers, and his thumb rubbed the inside of her wrist. When she looked up to meet his eyes, he wore his usual easy smile.

"Why doesn't she care?" he asked.

Hadhi shrugged. "She was the daughter of Zuberi, his best beloved. What care had she for princes? She was the child of a *great man*."

Noam snorted. "You may not have been your father's 'best beloved' but you were his child. Perhaps you should try thinking as she does."

Hadhi nodded, for no reason other than she suddenly felt like agreeing to whatever he asked, anything to keep him looking at her as though she was the only person who existed.

"What is a mzaa?" he asked suddenly, a sheepish smile dancing across his features and making him look truly beautiful.

Hadhi sighed and smiled at once. "Mother."

"Oh." Noam blushed. "That was what I thought. Then you used it for your father's other wife and..." He trailed off.

Hadhi grinned. "It is an honorary title, for Sabra." Hadhi bit her lip, about to resist the urge to ask her question. She hated looking foolish.

"Fairy is a simple language, Hadhi. Even your insignificant mind should be able to master it." Baba swatted Hadhi's head, enraged and embarrassed, when she stumbled over her words before his friends. *"Be silent if you can't wrap your tripping tongue around it. Or make yourself useful and go hunt. No man wants a fool around."*

Hadhi shook off her father's voice. Noam was nothing like him. But her father's memory was half the reason she had not admitted to Noam that she did not know what the report on his home said. She could not read or write in Fairy. She was so foolish she could barely speak it. But...with Noam, she did not feel foolish.

Just unfamiliar. It felt innocent and fun sharing anything with him, even if only failing to entirely know the other's language. "What is a cobweb?" she asked softly.

He beamed at her, as if her question charmed him. "A spider's trap."

"Oh." She bit the inside of her lip to fight her spreading smile. Learning had never felt fun before, only threatening and embarrassing. Like dancing had never felt comfortable. And letting a stranger touch her had never felt safe. Everything was different with him.

"Come along," he spoke quietly. "Let's go try to trap you a prince."

Hadhi yanked his arm back, suddenly stopping him. "You are like my mother!" Hadhi said in shock. "You smile, and you laugh—and you lie. So people will like you. So they will not send you away."

Noam made no response, just smiled and tugged Hadhi back into the room. He led her to the prince without speaking another word. But Hadhi felt certain she was right and wondered, in absolute horror, if she had perhaps been unfair to her mother all these years, resenting her easy smile and conversation. If someone like Noam could worry about being cast aside, surely her mother had a right to fight as hard as she could to be wanted.

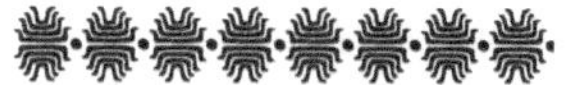

SOMETHING OF A SHOCK

Jauhar grabbed Nuru by the arm and led her away from her group of friends to a corner for the lecture she deserved.

"You are not here to talk with the same children you see every day. Nor to entertain yourself. You are meant to be ingratiating yourself to Azize."

"Mzaa." Nuru sighed, allowing her arm to lay limply in her mother's hold, but showing no remorse. "I've talked with his friends. I've even danced with some. But it doesn't matter; Azize does not want me. He's only interested in the mystery woman, and he thinks I'm a child. Sabra overheard him say I was *ten* years too young to be here."

Jauhar bit back the words on the tip of her tongue, *show him he's wrong!* He wasn't wrong. Nuru was too young. But something had to change. Hadhi was content to sulk in that hut forever growing older and less appealing by the day. Nuru saw the world as a game for her to play. Even Asha and Sabra were listless. Zuberi had fully commanded their world, now they were all adrift. It was up to Jauhar to set things right.

Hadhi would marry Azize. She would move into this palace and take her family with her. Sabra could marry one of Azize's friends and Nuru...well she was just here in case none of Jauhar's other plans worked. She did not want this daughter married yet. But she'd been told to talk to the prince and his friends, she'd been told to make herself memorable and she was barely even trying. And now Sabra had disappeared again into the room with the mothers.

At least Hadhi was with Azize's closest friend; that would help. He'd taken her for a dance before Jauhar had even manipulated him into it. But the dance had ended, and they weren't back yet. This evening was not going well. When Jauhar found out who that mystery woman was, she was going to wring her pretty little neck. That flash of light that had blinded them all didn't fool Jauhar; that was just a girl, not a magical creature. The girl was trickier than most, but Jauhar would still best her. Jauhar would not live one more year in that cursed hut but a mile from Ether. Half the day was spent sweeping the sands from the house, and every time they rushed back in, she heard Rama's wheezing lungs as she died. Jauhar hated that hut. She'd been overjoyed when Zuberi built them a mansion in the heart of Jaccada, but not, as he suspected, just because it showed off their importance.

She'd loved it because it was free of all the painful memories from the beginning of her marriage. Free of little reminders of how Zuberi's second and favorite wife had birthed his favorite daughter, and their whole world had grown angrier and darker. And how her sweet Hadhi had been warped into an angry little girl so young. The mansion was Jauhar's domain. Rama had never set foot in its walls, and when Sabra did, she was young enough and desperate enough to turn to Jauhar for guidance. But though Jauhar had ruled the hut first, it would always belong to Rama in her mind.

Jauhar looked at her youngest now with sharp eyes and a seething desperation to escape building up inside her. "You were told to leave an impression in his mind and you will do so. Endear yourself to him; prepare him to be your *brother*. You are here to do your duty, and if it is done right, by this time next year, you can be performing with the Spirit Dancers."

Nuru sighed, but nodded. "I have met a few of his friends. I will go find them."

"And see that they bring you back to Azize."

Nuru rolled her eyes and walked away. Jauhar was about to go to the room of mothers and drag Sabra out, again! But she saw King Enzi and Prince Azize arguing. She edged closer, being sure to stay behind other groups of people until she was near enough to duck behind a statue of Ether with her arms wide to welcome the spirits of the dead.

"Do you honestly expect me to believe you do not know every woman in attendance?" Azize demanded of his father.

Interesting. It was a fair point; such a woman was the sort of thing Zuberi would have organized to trick the prince into staying. Maybe Enzi had learned a thing or two from his closest advisor.

"I know every woman invited, and she was not." King Enzi snapped, gripping his sword in a manner that implied fear to Jauhar. Apparently, the women she'd overheard were right, and he was *afraid* of the mystery woman. Zuberi never would have been. "I assumed one of your friends sent her to disrupt my plans for you."

Foolish of the man to come right out and say he was trying to force his son to stay with a wealth of women to marry. But Jauhar supposed there was little chance the boy had missed that.

"Who could she possibly be? If neither you nor I, nor apparently anyone present, knows her," Azize said, and his hand slipped into his pocket.

"I do not know, but I know how to find out," His father glared briefly over Azize's shoulder, cutting himself off. Jauhar followed the motion and was momentarily overjoyed! That overly cheerful boy was serving his purpose and bringing Hadhi to his friend.

But Hadhi was not smiling! Jauhar would have something to say to her about that—later. She couldn't very well berate her in front of all these men.

"Your Majesty." Noam bowed to the king, with Hadhi curtseying on his arm. "Prince Azize, I hope we did not interrupt you."

"Of course not, Noam," Azize said brightly, though his father looked ready to contradict him. "My father and I were just discussing the mystery woman."

Hadhi looked away disinterestedly. Her eyes catching on Nuru in the crowd. Jauhar could have slapped her. Noam raised a brow at his friend and jerked his head in her direction as a mild reproach. Jauhar was surprised to find him quite useful. She couldn't imagine what had inspired it. Surely not Hadhi.

"You are certain she was not a game of your friend's?" King Enzi's gaze bit into Noam.

"I cannot claim the credit." Noam smiled unfazed. "It did not occur to me to prepare a mysterious woman, for the ball I was surprised by."

Hadhi snickered, her eyes on the ground. Jauhar wanted to burst out and shout at her daughter for mocking her king, but Azize looked at her in amused shock. For the moment, she had his attention. Jauhar looked not at her daughter but the man on whose arm she stood. He *was* useful. But she would have to watch him, because he too was watching Hadhi, and his eyes showed all the intensity of a man's desire, while Azize's gaze thus far held only curiosity. Noam could get in the way.

"Of course it had occurred to me she might be an agent of Your Majesty's invention," Noam remarked.

"What use would I have for trying to trick my son?"

"Everyone knows he means to leave again almost as soon as he came," Hadhi said, and her eyes rose to the king fearlessly. Right now, Hadhi looked like the sort of child her father always wanted her to be, bold, fearless, powerful. She met the eyes of her king, as her father would have.

Jauhar shuddered. She hadn't thought Hadhi had it in her. She had expected to need to do all the work for her daughter. But there she was speaking boldly and shocking all of the men to silence. This could work.

"Prince Azize has never loved his home. But if you provide him with an attractive mystery...he might just stay to solve it," Hadhi looked up at Noam searchingly. "Men do love a mystery."

Oh yes, Jauhar would have to do something about that man. He held her daughter's eyes too long before looking away without saying a word. And Hadhi looked disappointed.

"My son loves his home," The king said tightly, drawing everyone's attention. "He has returned home to stay."

Hadhi looked from one man to the next, then nodded sharply. "Just as you say, Your Majesty." Her tone was almost a snarl. "I must be wrong."

Jauhar clenched her fists at that tone. What was she playing at? Enzi was capricious and vicious if ever he thought someone was less than terrified of his power. Hadhi knew that.

"You are wrong. And to prove it to you, I will find this mystery woman," the king snapped. He was baring down on Hadhi, but she did not cower. Like her father's daughter, Hadhi returned his gaze, unsmiling. For the first time in years, Jauhar felt a twinge of fear for her.

She never feared for Hadhi. She had not even felt afraid when Hadhi stood in their kitchen dripping with her own blood after the cheetah mauled her. Hadhi had looked so scared then. There were tears on her face, she was shaking, and her eyes looked so wide and terrified, but Jauhar hadn't worried or coddled her. She'd ordered servants about and sent for a doctor to clean her wounds. She'd been fetching someone to clean the blood off the floor when Kafil's wife, Lolia, had rushed in and pulled Hadhi into her arms and let her cry.

Jauhar remembered hearing her whimper as she marched out of the kitchen, angry. But never afraid. There was no need to worry for Hadhi. But she worried now. Hadhi could not bend. People Enzi couldn't bend—he broke. Hadhi knew that! What had possessed her to challenge such a man?

"We shall have another ball tomorrow," the king announced coldly, his eyes still boring into Hadhi. "The mystery woman will come. I will order all women in Maltuba, old, young, married, ill, all women will attend or face death," Enzi announced.

"Really, Father, that is too far." Azize was appalled, Noam looked shocked, but Hadhi's calm expression implied she had expected nothing else from her king.

"You want to find her. You blame me for her leaving behind enticements and mysteries, but no name," Enzi snarled.

"Enticements?" Hadhi interrupted. It was a quiet interruption, but this time at least, she had the sense to look just a bit startled by her own gall.

And they liked that too. Enzi's eyes flashed, enjoying the power, and Azize took pity; he swooped in sweetly to save her.

He pulled a slipper from his pocket and cradled it before her. Jauhar narrowed her eyes. That tricky little manipulator. Oh she was going to find that woman and rip her head off. She was far too clever a competitor for Hadhi to best alone.

"Her slipper," Azize said. "She dropped it, and...well she left it quite purposefully."

Hadhi laughed. Opened her mouth in a broad smile that Jauhar fully approved of for once. She looked from one man to the next and truly laughed. It might be the first time Jauhar had heard her laugh in years. For just a moment, she was beautiful.

"She just took it off? And left it? With you there to see?" Hadhi asked, and Azize nodded. "Asha would do that."

Why would she bring her up? How Hadhi could go from tempting men one moment to alienating them, the next Jauhar would never understand.

Hadhi shook her head her resentment showing through and bit her lip. With apparent difficulty Hadhi pulled her hand from Noam's arm. "If you will excuse me, Your Majesties, *Noam*, I see my Mzaa Sabra with Lin; he needs to get home to rest."

"Wait." The king ordered. Hadhi flinched but obediently remained where she was. "Where is Asha? You are right; it would be very like her," Enzi asked.

"She is home, Your Majesty." Hadhi shook her head dismissively, wisely not sharing the whole of the tale. Enzi adored Asha. If he knew what Jauhar had done, he might strike out, or he might laugh. It all depended on his mood. "She was not here. Goodnight."

Hadhi did not even bow before walking away. Just spun on her heel with her head high and marched across the room towards Sabra. Azize couldn't keep his eyes off her, staring after her in open-mouthed wonder. Jauhar beamed, even as she noticed Noam was watching Hadhi just a bit too fondly as well.

"Finally showing a bit of her father," Enzi remarked in an overly warm voice. Jauhar shuddered involuntarily at the tone, but her eyes trailed her daughter with pride. It was working. Jauhar could have everything she wanted. "A shame Zuberi is not here to see it."

"So, we're to kill all the women?" Noam interrupted in a falsely bright tone. Was he trying to distract Enzi?

"We will not need to. They will all come." The king said boldly. It sent a tingle down Jauhar's spine that tone. That certainty. She felt an answering certainty in herself.

All the women would come. But it was Hadhi who would leave with a crown. Jauhar would see to that.

UGLY LEGACY

THE MONSTER WITHIN

Mzaa rushed out ahead of her daughters and Sabra, leading them into the night. Hadhi could not help a glance back at the lights of the palace. She rather thought somewhere in there Noam was looking out, watching her go. It should not be such a pleasant suspicion, but the feeling that drifted through her was something akin to joy.

"A receiving line before noon, with every woman in Jaccada and the nearest villages! He must be mad! When you win the prince, Hadhi, you can cause such a stir yourself." Mzaa was not looking Hadhi's way, nor were her words a compliment. Mzaa believed in visualizing the future you wanted.

To her left, Sabra caught Hadhi's eye and rolled her own sympathetically as she rubbed a hand over her sleeping son's back. They had ridden to the palace on camels, but their uncle took them back when he left the ball, now they were practically running home, on foot. Lin was unlikely to stay asleep long. He was such a sweet babe, calm and happy. Sometimes Hadhi looked at him and wondered if she had been like that as a child. Was evil something one was born with? Or did it grow over the years? She longed to reach out, take her brother into her arms and wrap him up in a magic blanket so he would never change.

"I still can't believe you were so bold," Mzaa's voice cut into Hadhi's consciousness, startling her. Had she been talking all this time? "What possessed you to walk away from the prince without him dismissing you first?"

"I..." *a handsome man, who told me not to smile and to be a mystery.* "I am sorry Mzaa..."

"Sorry?" Mzaa stopped so suddenly Nuru bumped into her. When Mzaa was facing Hadhi, she reached out with a soft hand and raised her daughter's chin, smiling beautifully. "It was *brilliant!* I knew one day you would come into your own. You should have seen them staring after you."

"Especially Azize's *handsome* friend, Noam." Sabra's voice held a playful smile, the kind she used to carry when she and Asha were friends. Back in the days when they would whisper *sour-faced-Hadhi* at her back and run away. Despite their past, Hadhi could not stop her hungry eyes from seeking affirmation that Noam had watched her.

She should not want to please a man she could never have, but she did. More than anyone, she wanted to please him. It was lively, chaotic, exci—

"He is nothing!" Mzaa yanked Hadhi's chin her way. "The prince watched you, and the king. Your father would have been so proud. Do not spoil this as you do everything else."

Hadhi felt all her excitement shrinking away under a wave of resentment and rage. With a jerking nod, she agreed so Mzaa would release her chin. Nuru was looking between her mother and Hadhi, her eyes tight and angry.

"Good." Mzaa spun away and rushed forward. "Now we must hurry; there isn't time. We must be the first people the prince sees tomorrow."

"Would it not be better to be the last?" Sabra suggested. "So we are the most prominent in his mind when the ball begins?"

Oshid, ethee uvaasha, Hadhi silently begged. *Kinnu zav py io ngzaatell: Please, great spirits, allow her to be swayed.* Hadhi didn't want to spend midday standing in the heat. If they went last, they could line up later. Such a line would take all day. There were at least five hundred women living near the capitol city it could take until well into the night to try a shoe on all of them.

"Ordinarily yes, but we cannot risk it." Mzaa's voice took on a low growl. "If I knew who that girl was, I would cast her into Ether and let the desert take care of her."

No one spoke as Mzaa ranted about the girl spoiling Hadhi's chance with the prince, all with a shoe. Hadhi sighed and looked beyond her mother towards the desert.

Maltuba sat at the edge of two worlds. Behind the capitol city, there was a lush jungle, so dense that while it provided two-thirds of Maltuba's food, and water; it was completely uninhabitable. The animals were too many and too vicious, and the trees too old and intertwined. So Maltuba sat at its very edge, hunters went in regularly and the occasional adventurer, but none stayed long. Beyond Maltuba a road led to the southernmost edge of the continent, passing by many tribes unconnected with any nation on its way to the kingdom of Reethurn, and from there to the eastern side of the continent with its mountains and several other nations. The road was the only way out but by sea, because stretched out before Maltuba was the desert the continent was named for, Ether.

Vast dry dunes of sand took up one-third of the continent and were completely impassable. No one had crossed her and lived to tell. The ancient kings of Maltuba used the desert as the ultimate punishment, reserved for the lowest of their citizens. Criminals were dragged to the edge of the desert given one skin of water and ordered to walk. Entire tribes came to watch on the first day, and sentries were posted to be sure the criminals did not attempt to return for weeks after, though by that time, it was understood, the criminals were dead.

Those absorbed into Ether could never return. She was a hungry desert.

Though Hadhi was unremarkable and had not her father's thirst for adventure, she gazed into the desert, searching for some sign. If it truly did lead to the next life, a place one was freed of their sins and burdens, was that not the kindest punishment a criminal could ever receive?

At night, it looked quite welcoming.

"But, Mzaa," Nuru's whine pulled Hadhi from her reverie. What was wrong with her? She could not focus. She did not even know what her sister was complaining about. "I'm so tired."

"Blame that intruder. And be prepared for her tomorrow. You will not sleep; everything must be ready."

"Can't Asha do it?"

Hadhi was surprised to hear her little sister throw Asha to their viper mother. Nuru seemed to like Asha well enough.

"She must prepare as well," Mzaa snarled. "And you Hadhi must put extra effort into being vivacious and catching the prince's eye. Your half-sister will always outshine you in beauty and wit, but she need not surpass you in all ways. No man wants a sour-faced wife."

Hadhi did not respond. The crawling, snarling beast of her anger could not be released now. It could not be released ever. It was a predator and

Hadhi held her back by will alone, letting her consume anything inside herself so she would not strike out and destroy Hadhi's entire family.

Their hut was just ahead. Before her father died, they lived in a large mansion, a short walk from the capitol palace. Uncle Kafil lived there now and had sent them to their father's childhood home, and even Hadhi's and Asha's for a time. Hadhi did not care where they lived, the other house was lovely, but whether she was rich or poor, in a castle or the desert, she was only ever sour-faced-Hadhi. Except for a few moments, on the capitol terrace, with her hand cradled in Noam's.

Hadhi was only disappointed that they had not spoken earlier in the evening. They could have had hours together. It was entirely unlike her to want such a thing. What could she even come up with to say, for hours? But she wanted it; she wanted to have enough interesting things in her head to fill hours with him or to learn the things he knew. Just to be with him. It would have been so peaceful. So new. Nothing like reality.

Asha was curled up before the fire outside the hut when they arrived. Lovely despite the smattering of ash across her face and laying on the ground. Until this moment, part of Hadhi had been worried for her. But Hadhi saw her sister, and Mzaa's voice taunted her, devouring any caring. *Your half-sister will always outshine you in beauty and wit.* The monster within lunged, trying to lift Hadhi's leg and kick Asha for being beautiful, and beloved, and oh so easy and happy.

"You will be my monster one day, Hadhi." Baba chuckled. He'd watched silently as Asha and Sabra teased his eldest daughter, called her names, threw sour berries at her. Watched it all with a smile, but when they'd gone, then he turned to his eldest, saw the rage and resentment in her eyes and beamed. "You will decimate all before you, as your Baba does. This rage will feed you, and make you strong."

Hadhi's foot remained on the ground, and she swept around her sister towards the hut. Hating Asha, and Baba, and herself more every moment. She wished she were different. Wished she were like Noam.

"Where do you think you're going?" Mzaa shouted, halting Hadhi. Mzaa ripped the blanket off her *other daughter*, startling Asha awake. "Every one of you will listen to me and listen well."

Asha cowered against the stone hearth wide-eyed. Hadhi watched her falseness and wanted to kick her even more. Baba would kick a younger sibling who had the gall to sleep before him. So Hadhi's foot remained on the floor.

"The prince is bewitched of some little invader," Mzaa said for Asha's benefit.

"The prince?" Asha asked, her wide eyes searching. Mzaa ignored.

"He has ordered a second ball, which every woman, regardless of age, station, or illness, *will* attend. I can do nothing about this woman." Hadhi caught a small tickled smile, curving Asha's lips, but it was gone before Mzaa glanced her way again. "But the king ordered every woman to try on her slipper, and all who fit it will compete for the prince. You," her talon nailed Hadhi in place, "*will* fit that slipper. If it is too large, you will claw your toes into it. If it is too small, you will break your bones to fit them in. Am I understood?"

"Yes, Mzaa," Hadhi said flatly, her resentment settling heavily around her, covering everything but her desire for sleep.

"You," Mzaa turned her wrath on Asha, "will attend. You will be polite to the prince and not shame your father, is that understood?"

"Yes, Mzaa Jauhar." Asha nodded once. But her eyes were still far and away, too active for Hadhi to ignore. She knew something.

"Sabra, you know your duty and have always performed it well. I trust if the opportunity arises, you will serve this family and your son once more." Sabra nodded, with her hand over her son's head as if Mzaa would devour the baby. Mzaa did seem particularly volatile tonight, but... Lin had Zuberi's eyes. Mzaa would never harm him.

"As for you, Nuru." Mzaa rolled her eyes, looking on her youngest daughter, now crouched next to the fire, with her head against the wall, half asleep. "The prince will never marry you, even if you fit the slipper."

"So I may sleep!"

"No."

"He will not think any of us lovely if we do not sleep." Nuru pouted.

"Which is why it was so kind of you to volunteer to prepare your sister's and your Mzaa Sabra's gowns, so they may sleep."

"But," she stomped her foot, waving her arms about, "that isn't fair. I did everything you asked me to."

"And you will continue to do so. Sabra is a mother; she needs her rest. Asha, as you have been sleeping already, you will help Nuru. If you hurry, you may get a few hour's rest. Sleep Hadhi," Mzaa tossed off with a dissatisfied scowl. "Your looks need all the help they can get."

Hadhi swept into the hut, enraged. Usually, she would offer to help Nuru. Not Asha, but it was nothing she did not deserve, was it? But just now, she was so angry she could not speak without her words killing someone. She raced down the stairs to her shared room and threw herself onto the bed in the dark. The beads at her throat dug into her like angry pebbles, but she was too frustrated to move. If only she were someone other than herself. Someone beautiful and lovable. It was probably for the best that she spent so little time with Noam. If they had more time he would have found reason to revile her as the rest of the world did.

"Hadhi?" Nuru came into the room with a lantern, her voice petulant. Hadhi did not respond. "Mzaa said I must help you change, so you do not spoil the fabric."

"Why does that matter? No fabric can make me beautiful."

"She doesn't mean it, Hadhi," Nuru said sympathetically and sat on the edge of her sister's bed. "She is only anxious. If Uncle Kafil never releases our dowries, we will be stuck here forever."

"There are worse places."

"Everyone loved what you did with my hair." Nuru coaxed, breaking the silence that had followed Hadhi's remark, trying to soothe her.

Hadhi opened her mouth to reply, but nothing came out, and she felt tears building.

"Neema suggested that Eshe might accept such a service in place of an offering," Nuru went on hopefully.

I will offer. Hadhi thought, but could not force words past the burning fist of tears in her throat.

When Hadhi continued to lay silent Nuru nudged her. "Sit up, she'll yell at me if you tear it."

Rolling her eyes, Hadhi sat up.

"Why are you so angry?" Nuru asked quietly as she began untying the beads that held up the dress. "Mzaa always says such, and it never bothers you."

There was only anger inside her. How did Nuru not see that? How was Hadhi meant to sort through why tonight was different in such a way that her sister would understand? She could not tell her about Noam, about that brief time when she felt like someone other than sour-faced-Hadhi. She could not explain how that smile on Asha's lips had reminded her, of all the differences between them, of how the world would always love Asha and hate Hadhi. Of how Asha would surely be loved by Noam, exposing his moments of kindness with Hadhi for what they surely were: pity. That smile reminded Hadhi of how Asha could hide, or lie, or get away with anything. But Hadhi— If she revealed her secret, she would be despised.

The dress slid away, and Nuru handed her sister a thin slip to pull on. Nuru left the room without her answer, pouting and glaring.

"You will be my monster, Hadhi. My legacy."

"But, you love Asha best."

He laughed so loud then, as though the idea that being his legacy meant loving Hadhi was ludicrous. She felt desperate and lonely inside. Ugly. "Hadhi, you are my own image. A monster of rage and destruction. Asha is my joy, my best beloved. She could never be my monster; she has no darkness in her. No, Hadhi, you will be my monster, and the world will never forget my power."

Hadhi rolled onto her side and cried silently into the pillow. She would not be his monster. She refused, now or ever, to do anything that would bring him joy.

HEAD IN THE CLOUDS

Asha leaned towards Nuru to whisper as soon as Hadhi stomped away. "So...there was a strange woman dancing with the prince?"

"She is of no consequence to you," Jauhar snapped. "Nuru fetch your sister's gown before she ruins it! You can adjust it and wear it yourself tomorrow."

"Is Prince Azize much matured?" Asha snuck her question in as Nuru, rolling her eyes and grumbling, moved to obey her mother.

"What does it matter to you? You never liked him." Nuru trudged away like it were the most strenuous chore in the world. Hadhi had seemed a bit more sour than usual, but hardly worth all her sister's grumblings. Nuru would be just like Hadhi one day if she kept on like this, content to have everything done for her.

"Listen well," Jauhar's tight voice pulled Asha's gaze away from her half-sister. Asha caught sight of Sabra watching her with an odd searching expression. "If you shame this family, if you insult the prince or the king, you will have no home here."

"I have known King Enzi since—"

Jauhar cut Asha off with a snap. "You know what your father wanted you to know."

Asha wondered what Jauhar meant by that, but hadn't a chance to ask as Jauhar jerked her head towards the house. Asha followed Sabra through into the main room. Only one lamp was lit. Of course, neither Nuru nor Hadhi had lit them. Sabra walked about the room, lighting the oil lanterns set high on outcroppings built into the walls.

Jauhar walked to a covered basket in the corner and selected a trio of silks that would do. None of their clothes were particularly fine any longer, so Asha was required to embellish older worn and dull silks.

"Hurry up, Nuru," Jauhar cut herself off to yell at her youngest. "And take off your own gown, see what can be salvaged from it to make something for Hadhi."

Jauhar didn't finish her earlier lecture, just snapped out her orders, threw silks in Asha's face, and walked away. "Pull your head out of your fantasies, Asha. See what is before you, it's all you will ever have."

"I want to sleep," Nuru whined the second her mother was gone. She flounced onto a stool, dropping Hadhi's dress on her legs, and stared with a scrunched-up face into the fire.

"Then we had better get working," Asha pointed out cheerfully, yanking the dress from Nuru. "Altering this for you should be no trouble. Take off your own so we can work on one for Hadhi."

Nuru left the room again. Asha hadn't realized Sabra was still there until she approached, pulling the bands of beads from her arm and laying them in Asha's pile of possible embellishments.

"You seem much recovered, Asha," she said with seemingly great meaning. "I am glad. I was sorry to see you hurt. As were your sisters."

Asha laughed. "I am sure," she said dismissively, ignoring Sabra as she took sides against Asha, just like she had been since she joined this family.

Sabra nodded several times, rubbing a hand over her son's back. She spoke low and heavy. "We can miss out on a great many beautiful things when we aren't willing to look beyond the surface." She left quietly without another word.

Her cryptic words like Jauhar's about the king held the air for a moment, but quickly enough, Asha's mind carried her away. Her fingers found the threads of the gown from memory, knowing instinctually which places to rip, so the seams fell apart in her hands without harming the silk.

Azize. Her childhood enemy. How could he possibly be the man she danced with? But he had her slipper and was enchanted enough by her to use another ball to seek her out. It had to be him, but she couldn't quite believe it. *Azize* was the man who spoke and drew her into another land with him. Only Baba had ever been able to do that. Even Asha didn't have the talent. She could wear a person down with the force of her enthusiasm. Or overcome their opinions with her adorable innocence, but she had never been able to completely drag someone else into her wonder, except for Baba. But Azize, the man she'd danced with, he could do it. He could bring a fantasy alive.

Nuru came back, grinding her teeth. Asha watched her sit and begin ripping the seams of her own gown without a word. That wasn't like Nuru. She didn't look pouty any longer or tired even, just sad.

"What's wrong?" Asha asked, absently searching for the thread she had put away earlier.

"Nothing to bother you," Nuru muttered under her breath.

Asha shrugged, ignoring Nuru's tone. This was the sister Sabra thought was upset by Asha's pain. Asha made a bit of a mess tearing through baskets until, at last, she found the purple thread she'd been seeking. Seeing as the work had been all her own, she should have known where it was, as she did with the stitches. But tidying was different. Jauhar was *a bit* right, Asha's mind was rarely on the work. It was one reason she didn't mind her chores. Her mind carried her anywhere. Everywhere imaginable. Everywhere but here.

"Do you think wanting to see the world must mean you hate your home?" Asha asked, thinking of all she and Azize had argued about, whispered about, fantasized about.

Azize. It was still too radical an idea for her mind to accept.

"Everything has to be special for you," Nuru hissed, tugging too hard on the seams and tearing a bit of her fabric in the process. "You were never satisfied with your home or your family."

Asha rolled her eyes, "I didn't mean—"

"She cried herself to sleep again," Nuru choked the words out, over what sounded like tears of her own.

"Oh," Asha didn't know what to say. Hadhi had been prone to sudden bouts of tears in her sleep since Baba died. No one spoke about it with her. But Nuru grew angry whenever it happened. "I am sorry. I'm sure it wasn't what Jauhar said. She just misses Baba."

Nuru sniffled still, but she did not cry.

Asha still grew overwhelmed and sobbed at odd moments. She would see something Baba would have loved and want to rush home to tell him, realizing she could not. She would have to sit down and sob. Or sometimes...

she'd just be working, or walking, not really thinking of him at all, and tears would come slipping down her cheeks before she even felt the burning sorrow fill her chest.

Nuru wasn't like that. She cried every day for two months straight after Baba died. Then one day, she got up, saw the sun rise and went about her life again. She was still sad; she just didn't cry any longer.

It was strangely comforting that Hadhi still suffered. She must have really loved him, and Asha hadn't been sure of Hadhi's feelings.

Asha let Nuru be for the moment, settling in to sew. Her fingers had calluses again, scrapes and old scars, and the tips of her fingers were dry and thin from too much time in the water. He would have to believe she knew how to work now, her prince. He hadn't earlier.

After they danced the first time, they slipped off to a corner to speak more. They got to discussing the oddest things; it was mostly Asha's doing.

"Do you suppose fairies ever wash laundry?" Asha asked with a smirk. If she had magic all the time, she would never do laundry again. Not because it was too hard, or because she was lazy, but magic as she felt racing up her spine and teasing the hairs on her skin, it was too powerful, too lively to be stuffed down long enough to wring and score and wring again. It was too frantic a power to be held still long enough to thread a needle and pull it through a tattered gown.

Azize had laughed. "I'm sure they have servants to do it."

"Yes, but are the servant's fairies?" She demanded excitably. "Wouldn't that be awful? To have such power flooding your being, but to have to wait on others."

"Maybe they like it," Azize said. "I've been around servants my whole life. Most are much happier than the people they serve. Maybe the work makes them happy."

She smiled, all the broader for her incredulity. "You have never worked a day in your life, have you?" His mouth fell slightly open. He was so cute. Azize was cute. "Work is frequently fulfilling and occasionally clarifying, but it doesn't make you happy," Asha informed him lightly.

"I won't stand here and be insulted," he said with mock outrage, because of course he would. "Particularly not by a lady with such pampered skin." He lifted her hand in one of his own, running his other over it, seeking a flaw so gently. "These hands have never done laundry."

"I've done my fair share of work. More sometimes," she defended, with her heart racing from the contact.

He shook his head in playful disbelief, but refused to release her hand. He opened his mouth slowly, as if he would speak, but he said nothing, his gaze shifting to Asha's lips, his thumb rubbing across her hand in a steady rhythm.

Asha was breathless with anticipation and the tiniest bit of nerves. She'd been kissed before, but this was different; this stole her breath before his lips were even near her own. This held her trapped on nothing but the possibility. She was so caught up in his eyes she couldn't move. His eyes were so...lush.

Asha giggled now, in spite of her audience. Lush was a lovely word. It didn't have an exact match in Maltuban. The closest word meant bountiful, and that wasn't at all the same. Lush. Asha was tempted to open her lips and press her tongue against her teeth to speak it, *lush.*

But Nuru's gaze was suddenly critical. Some moments she looked so like Jauhar and others, she reminded Asha of their father, his energy, his wildness.

"Do you think Azize is handsome?" Nuru rolled her eyes at the question, but Asha was undeterred. "I never thought he was handsome before."

"He's a prince. No one cares if he's handsome. Ssss!" Nuru hissed, stabbing herself with a needle. The gown she was altering for Hadhi was not what Asha would call beautiful. Its adornments were barely held together; Nuru had no patience. And the gold that ran all throughout it, while a lovely color on Nuru, would do nothing for Hadhi's eyes. On their own Hadhi's eyes looked nearly gold, but by comparison to the real color, they looked pale and lackluster, sandy.

When Baba was alive, they could have any fabric they chose, as many gowns as they wished. Asha had been too busy working since his death to miss that, but she thought Hadhi might. She needed all the help she could get to offset her constant scowl.

"Is the entire ball tomorrow meant only to find one woman?" Asha demanded, tickled by the idea. "Here." She yanked a large, vibrant green scarf out of her overturned basket. It was fraying at the end, and wasn't nearly enough to improve the whole gown, but it might help. "Add it to the shoulder." She tossed it to Nuru. "Yes, make a bow just there. No leave the fraying bit hanging off the shoulder and string some green beads to it. Hadhi looks much better in green. And if it's on her right, it will help hide her scars."

Nuru softened after the help. She yawned, taking Asha's suggestions somewhat sloppily, but it looked better.

"Azize stole her shoe when she ran away from him." Nuru spoke in a lethargically amused tone. "He's vowed to find her and marry her on the spot."

"On the spot?" Asha could barely breathe. It was one thing entirely to accept that her stranger was truly Azize, to realize she wanted to kiss Azize, her old enemy. But to marry him—

"His friend Masahiro says Azize is bewitched, that he was never this passionate before." Nuru went on, nodding a bit, fighting off sleep. "But the king told Mzaa he doesn't trust any woman he doesn't know, so he made Azize promise to have the second ball first and give every woman who fits the shoe a chance to be his bride."

Asha paused with her needle poking through the fabric; she saw him in her mind again, as he'd been when he chased after her.

Come find me.

He was, wasn't he? He'd known her only a few hours and already he loved her.

Marry her on the spot.

She could be someone's most beloved again. Asha's eyes leaked, and her skin shivered from a sudden wave of grief. She had been trying so hard not to miss Baba, not to miss being so well-loved.

"Asha." Nuru lay aside the gown she was altering and watched her half-sister with evident concern. "I...am glad you will be at the ball tomorrow. You will like Azize's friends. I am sorry..."

Asha cut Nuru off, though it was nice to see that at least one sister cared about Asha's feelings. "I was thinking what fun Baba would have had teasing him."

Nuru accepted this with a nod and settled back into her work. "Baba did love teasing."

"Tell me more about Azize; did you talk to him? Did he seem intelligent to you?"

Asha asked her questions until Nuru fell asleep with her needle in hand. But Asha couldn't sleep. She felt truly alive, truly herself for the first time since Baba died. She wasn't only pretending to smile, in hopes of feeling joyful again.

She could be someone's best beloved.

"Thank you, Zawadi." Asha smiled into the night despite her silent trickle of tears. Somehow she just knew she had found her fate tonight, and tomorrow she would go claim him.

MZAA

Jauhar paused outside the room the girls shared; she should go in and give Hadhi more pointers for tomorrow. Remind her not to clench her jaw when she smiled and not to roll her eyes even when men were not looking at her. But before she could walk through the arch, she heard her daughter's sobs.

They weren't loud, muffled against her blankets and pillow, but they shook the bed with tiny gut-twisting gasps. Jauhar hadn't really heard Hadhi cry much since she was a small girl, not until Zuberi died. Honestly, Jauhar had begun to believe Hadhi was no longer able to cry. She'd thought the mauling had cured her of such...mortal, womanly displays. But perhaps the mansion had just been large enough to conceal a few sniffles.

Jauhar marched away. Hadhi would be fine. A few moments of wounded pride would be nothing once she was a princess, in line to be *queen*. She would have nothing to cry about once they moved into the palace. None of them would. And even if they did, in a building with six wings who would ever know? They could be at peace.

Jauhar entered her own room with a half snarl on her lips. They would escape this hovel for good. She hated this place. Though Kafil had greatly improved it in his years living here, with Hadhi's help! Not that he showed any signs of remembering. When Zuberi injured him, to teach Kafil to respect his king, Hadhi had fed his family behind her father's back, risking a beating at the very least. Yet now that he had a chance to return the care, he treated his nieces like burdens.

Jauhar sat on her bed, releasing a pinched breath. She couldn't hear Hadhi crying, but she could feel it still. Her body ached to cuddle her like she would when Hadhi was small. Like she had when it had only been the three of them. Jauhar, Hadhi and Zuberi, this had been their home once, only theirs.

When it was only them, Jauhar had loved this hut. It was only one room which they all shared. At night Jauhar would lay in Zuberi's arms with Hadhi on a bed of blankets nearby and he would tell them his plans: power, wealth, status, jewels and silks, and servants for Jauhar, the pick of any man she wanted for Hadhi. They would be the most respected, most important people in all Maltuba.

Jauhar clenched her hands together until she heard them begin to creak, until the pain of being crushed so tightly snapped her out of the past. That was long ago. So long that it seemed like she had invented it. Jauhar doubted Hadhi even remembered that her father had loved her once. He never loved her as he did Asha, but he had loved her. And Jauhar had as well.

She had adored her—when she was young. Had devoted her every moment to that tiny, sickly baby, willing her to continue living. Before she grew older and stronger and every year more of a disappointment to her father. Hadhi didn't take to languages, couldn't sew or keep a pattern with beads, and she was far too shy to ever be a source of pride for a man as bold as Zuberi. A new wave of blame fell over Jauhar for her daughter's every failing.

That little fool is no child of mine.

Can't you teach your daughter anything useful.

Jauhar still felt the parts of herself that wanted to walk back to her daughter's bed and close Hadhi in her arms. The part of her that wanted to tell her how truly proud she'd been of her tonight. But since Hadhi was ten, she'd not trusted her mother. She never turned to her with her fears, never came to her for comfort. It simply wasn't who they were.

Zuberi had wanted more strength from his child, and he'd gotten it. Jauhar kept her distance, and Hadhi became the greatest hunter in the nation. She left her alone tonight, and Hadhi finally captured a man's notice, captured the *prince's* notice. Hadhi thrived alone now, as Zuberi wanted.

A shudder ran through Jauhar, imagining her sweet little child Hadhi thrust into that vibrant world where she was ugly. Every woman was more gregarious, more beautiful, more accomplished and knowledgeable. Hadhi just didn't fit. She never had. And tomorrow would be so much worse. She would have to compete not only with the mystery woman, but with her half-sister as well.

Hadhi would never prevail alone.

That was why she was crying herself to sleep. She knew that tomorrow would show all her failings. Hadhi would fade into the walls without her mother's help.

Jauhar leapt up. She crossed to the heavy chest where she kept what few treasures she'd managed to hold onto. She would give Hadhi something truly special to wear. Something to make her feel powerful.

There was a silk wrap with a vibrant pattern, sewn by her aunt in all of Hadhi's favorite green threads with a cheetah fur trim. It was made with a bit of the pelt from the cheetah that had mauled Hadhi. One full pelt went to *Asha's* dowry. And the second pelt was sold. Hadhi's aunt had bought a section to make the gown during the months of Hadhi's recovery when she could barely speak for the pain in her jaw and ate only liquids. She'd looked ill and weak, but Zuberi had not let her stop hunting, and Lolia wanted to comfort her. She'd made the silk for Hadhi's dowry, but Zuberi refused to use it so. He said it was too fine to be worn by Hadhi and gave the silk to Jauhar instead.

Jauhar had only worn it once; when Zuberi insisted, as they were dining with the king. She'd never felt right wearing it. Hadhi could have it now. She should have it. Zuberi would approve. Tonight Hadhi had finally shown the sort of confidence Zuberi wanted from her.

That silk would set her apart. Mark her status and her skill. Hunting was a useful skill and a fierce one. Dressed in the fur of the predator she'd bested, Hadhi would look regal.

Jauhar threw back the lid. She would take it to Hadhi, wake her to give her something truly pleasant to dre—

Jauhar utterly lost her thoughts. She reached into her box of treasures with shaking hands. Atop the silks, right next to the knife that had killed her husband, was a beaded slipper that Jauhar had most certainly not placed among her treasures. It was sewn with blue and golden beads to resemble wings or—teeth.

The second slipper. The mystery woman's slipper. She had come here somehow and hidden this among Jauhar's things to taunt her. She was a fey creature come to torture—

No!

Before Jauhar's fingers even reached the shoe, she saw the smirk on Asha's face again as Jauhar spoke of the mystery woman. She remembered the way Hadhi had faded into the shadows as that woman stole the attention of every being in the room. Like Asha always had. The mystery woman was *Asha.*

Jauhar crushed the slipper. The beads grinding against one another like angry stones. She wanted to bellow. She wanted to lift Zuberi's knife and hack this slipper to pieces.

Of course it was Asha. Zuberi's *most beloved* would always steal her sister's place.

It was always that girl!

Jauhar twisted and ground and crushed the slipper, but it wouldn't be harmed. Not even a single bead was scratched. She felt the hungry power holding the shoe together and nearly shouted.

What need had Asha for magic? She could best Hadhi easily without it. She'd stolen all the love Zuberi had to give without magic. Now she had found magic too.

Well she wouldn't have this tomorrow. Jauhar stood, taking the shoe with her. She might not be able to destroy it, but she could make sure Asha didn't have it. Asha must be plotting how she would steal this back tomorrow and show it to Azize to prove herself and win his hand.

But Zuberi wasn't here to make the world suit his beloved girl. It was Jauhar's turn to have her plans made real. Jauhar would never let her win.

Rama would never win again.

IN THE MANSION OF THE PAST

Hadhi approached the tall gate of her father's mansion with the blood from her kill still smattering her gown and a wrapped and properly cut haunch in a bit of paper under her arm. Her hands were mostly clean. There were still flecks of blood beneath her nails, but by the time those flecks faded, she would be out making more, she knew from experience. Baba was wealthy enough that they had no need of Hadhi's skill as a hunter to provide for them, but Baba wanted the world to know that just because he'd had all daughters did not make his heirs any less fierce.

"You're Hadhi is a proper predator, Zuberi!" The butcher, Amal, had laughed the day Hadhi presented the man with both a gazelle and a cheetah. Baba laughed as well, as Hadhi stood there bearing up under the weight of her kills, and dripping with her own blood, in so much pain she could barely see, but not allowed even to make a noise. The world had to see her skill, his progeny.

"You've taught her well."

"That I have. A proper monster she is. Though she needed a bit of her Baba's help today, didn't she?" He'd thrown the second cheetah over the butcher's table, so he could slide his hand under Hadhi's chin and lift it. The movement sliced across her injuries anew and tears slid from Hadhi's eyes, but she gritted her teeth across the scream that wanted to slip from her lips. She exhaled through her nose. Baba was waiting for her response, for her to lie and agree to his story.

"A bit," Hadhi repeated though moving her jaw was excruciating and made her blood flow again when it had stopped, and made her shiver inside her face like a thousand beetles were racing through her jaw bone. Beyond the pain, all she felt was the ugly sloshing of self-disgust. She hadn't needed his help. She wouldn't have been injured if she were alone.

"Only to be expected when hunting hunters." The man said, still no less impressed with Hadhi. "Shall I clean the pelts and send them to the mansion. They would make fine pieces for your dowry."

Baba laughed and nodded to the man to say he should. "And she'll need an impressive one to win men over after the mess she's made of her face."

Hadhi hesitated outside of the gate now. She could hear Mzaa inside ordering the servants around. Baba was due home soon. He was expected earlier, while the family was at the funeral for Aunt Lolia. It had seemed to offend Mzaa that a mere funeral should disrupt her plans to have the house cleaned for his arrival. Hadhi had been left home to wait for Baba earlier, and to do a bit of the cleaning, she should still be at it with the servants. But she had brought home a dinner worthy of his return, so Mzaa would not be too angry. Hadhi could hunt, or she could clean, but Mzaa was fond of saying Hadhi was good for nothing else. Especially after the cheetah.

Hadhi did not want to go in. She did not want to clean. She did not want to hunt. She wanted her hands to be still and her mind to be silent. She wanted to lay down and wait to be consumed by the angry spirits and sands of Ether.

"Avoiding your Mzaa, sour-face?" Asha said, walking by Hadhi towards the house. She had some new purchases wrapped up in her arms. She must have been in the market while Hadhi was selling the gazelle, but she had not seen her. How could she be out shopping after Aunt Lolia's funeral? Hadhi had adored her aunt; she was the only person Hadhi could talk to. Now she was gone, and Hadhi had not been allowed to properly send off her spirit. Her desires and loves meant nothing.

Hadhi said not a word to her sister, as was generally her practice. But inside, she was a bellowing ugly beast who wanted to rip Asha apart. It was all Asha's fault this ugly, this deadness inside of Hadhi. But Asha could just saunter through life, smiling and laughing and destroying without a single consequence. Hadhi looked at her sister with all the hatred roiling through her and wondered what had ever made her think she might love Asha. There was nothing about her to love. Not for Hadhi at least. Even as a child, the world found Asha so much more lovable. Hadhi had not worn a sour face all her life, and the scars on her neck and face, now much less unsightly, had only been with her a few years. But it seemed the world had always hated

Hadhi and loved Asha. Anything she wanted was hers to have. All she need do was smile and ask.

Even pelts that Hadhi had bled to earn. There was never even a question. Their father's love, joys, treasures, adventures. Now—look at her smile as her family suffered.

Hadhi ignored her half-sister, walking forward with her head high. The moment she cleared the fifteen-foot-high wall, her mother spotted her.

"Hadhi, you look disgusting. Leave the meat in the kitchens and get yourself clean." Mzaa's voice ripped into Hadhi. At the moment, the sting was dull and familiar, but there were times, when she turned the full brunt of her hatred on her daughter, there were times when her tongue took more out of Hadhi's flesh than the cheetah's claw had.

So Hadhi walked silently forward, doing as her mother instructed without complaint. She left the meat in the kitchen, bathed, and dressed anew. As soon as she was clothed in a bloodless gown, she noticed how boldly the blood beneath her nails stood out against the yellow silk she wore. Mzaa came up behind her and grabbed Hadhi by the shoulder so she could examine her.

"I suppose that will have to do," Mzaa said with a small shudder as her eyes slid quickly by Hadhi's scars. "Sabra has been ill all day and has not had a chance to clean your father's room. He will not have the servants in it; take care of it," Mzaa ordered and stomped around her.

Hadhi watched her walk away and wondered if Mzaa even knew what Hadhi's voice sounded like. She never waited to hear what Hadhi would say. She wanted to call her mother back and make her listen, but before she could say a thing, Nuru ran in, dripping in sweat and covered in dust. Mzaa caught her around the shoulders and pulled her near. "There is my little one. What have you been up to?" She asked almost sweetly. Not sweet like other mothers were, but when she spoke to Nuru, her voice softened and her features relaxed, she was lovelier.

Hadhi looked away, walking quietly down the halls and out of the wing where the women lived together, to her father's half of the house. Sometimes when Hadhi was hunting, she would see mother and child animals, she would see the care they took of their cubs, she would see their love. And she would wonder why humans were so different, why they failed to love their children. Then she would remember her mother, hugging Nuru, and the joy Rama had taken in Asha before she died. Or Lolia's adoration of her children.

It was not *all* children that human parents failed to love. It was just her. There was something wrong with her.

Asha watched her sister trudge into the house. For the life of her she couldn't think why Hadhi didn't fight harder to get their father's attention or her mother's love. The only things Hadhi fought for were Nuru and...well maybe it was just Nuru. Hadhi was the only child Baba had ever taught to hunt. Asha had always been jealous of that, but Baba told her it wasn't for her, that she was too fine. Still, when he spoke of Hadhi and her skill as a hunter, you could see his eyes sparkle with pride. He'd said she was better even than him.

Hadhi could get his love if she really wanted it, but she preferred to sulk. Just like she sulked when their tutors said she had no skill for languages and no mind for figures. Nuru was a proper genius with figures, and she could pick up any language she heard spoken. But she had no real interest in studying the rest of the world; she only wanted to hear the stories of Maltuba. So, by and large, Asha directed their lessons. Their tutor Okal was thrilled with her curiosity; he loved to feed it. Every time he brought up a subject, she challenged him to explore it more thoroughly. He'd told Baba that Asha had a brighter mind than any woman he'd ever met, brighter than most men even. And Baba hadn't even been surprised.

"Of course she does. My girl is the brightest mind in all Maltuba save her Baba's." He'd beamed at her.

Asha grinned to herself as she made her way into the house. She ran through the women's wing of the mansion and banged on Sabra's door. Sabra was not the same since marrying; she fancied herself too adult now to do things with Asha. But she was more fun when Baba was away, and he would be home in a few hours. Asha wanted to tell her friend about Okal.

He'd met her in secret again. He'd kissed her once, and he'd wanted more, but she'd danced around him, giggling that he didn't want to know what her father did to men who toyed with his favorite daughter. She'd just meant it as a jest, or maybe a prod to see how much he liked her. But he'd backed right off at those words, with his body anyway. His words were positively scandalous; Asha would bet he'd ask for her hand soon.

But she wouldn't marry him. He knew a great deal of the world, but he hadn't *been* anywhere. She wanted to see the world. Maybe she would never marry, but one day she would find a man brave enough to kiss her, even with the threat of Baba's wrath.

"Sabra," Asha hissed through the door. She'd banged on it a number of times already. Servants were beginning to give her disapproving looks, but Asha could tell she was inside.

"Asha, not now," Sabra groaned. "I'm very ill."

"I only want to talk. Let me in. I'll bring you a cool cloth."

"I only want to be alone. What do I have to do to make you leave me alone?" Sabra shouted. Asha wanted to shout something foul back, but a hand descended on her shoulder. She jumped.

Jauhar could be very stealthy when she wanted.

"Good evening, Mzaa Jauhar," Asha said sweetly. "Is everything ready for Baba's return?"

"No. Good of you to offer." She said with her viper hiss. Her hands had left Asha's person, but Asha still felt her restrained rage. Mzaa Jauhar did not speak sweetly to anyone of a feminine persuasion, not even her daughters. But there was a special tone she reserved just for Asha, the angry bite of a woman denied her teeth.

They both knew Jauhar hated her, but there was nothing, not a single thing she could do about it because Asha was Baba's favorite. He loved her more than any of his children, more than any of his wives. More than anything. If Jauhar harmed Asha, she would have hell to pay with him, and she wouldn't risk doing anything that might cost her Baba's love.

"Hadhi is cleaning his room, as your Mzaa Sabra is too ill. You may help her."

"It would be my pleasure," Asha said brightly. "Just as soon as I've prepared this gift I got for Baba's return."

Jauhar looked down on the little bundle with a sharp brow in the air. "What is it?"

Asha didn't like her Mzaa Jauhar any more than Jauhar liked her. She used to, but once too often, she'd offered this woman love, and friendship, and mere kindness and never received even consideration in return. Now all was cold and formal between them, but for one subject. One subject they could speak on that made Asha almost feel loved by this woman. So as much as she hated Jauhar's treatment, Asha couldn't help indulging in their shared love, and pretending some part of that love was for each other.

"It's a kind of dagger the Gaaminii tribe in Kiloth use for ritual sacrifice. They call it the *divine tongue*! Apparently, they sacrifice other humans and consume their organs to gain the strength of their gods."

"Positively chilling," Jauhar said, appalled, then her features softened. "He will *adore it*. Is it only the dagger? It would be so much better if there was a tale to go along with it. He loves a disgusting story." She chuckled a bit.

"I know. But this trader was very dull. I'd heard already about the tribe from Okal, so I asked for a story. And all he said was they'd traded the dagger for some of his dried meats and hadn't expressed any interest in eating him. He thought it was all a gruesome tale put about to keep people from going there as Kiloth is apparently a bountiful place."

Jauhar nodded along, with regret apparent in her face. Then a light sparked at the edges of her gaze, and she leaned in closer, by no means in the fun way one might a cohort, but conspiratorially nonetheless. Asha leaned in as well, eating up this moment of affinity.

"Zuberi needn't know the trader was so dull."

"No," Asha agreed brightly. "He could have seen the whole thing. Watched them eat someone else alive."

"Perhaps he escaped with only one of his legs."

"No." Asha rolled her eyes. "How would he possibly have gotten away? It must be an arm."

"Yes, an arm is much better." Jauhar laughed. "Perhaps an ear as well.

For a moment, they grinned together, and their harmony was soft and soothing. Then Jauhar remembered her hatred. She straightened. "Well, that is a good honoring for his return. See you prepare it properly."

She swept away, her desire to make Asha into one of the servants forgotten. Asha didn't bother knocking on Sabra's door again. Sabra had certainly heard their entire conversation and not attempted to come out, nor join in discussing gifts for Baba's return. She must truly be ill. Asha walked away disappointed, but still cheerfully imagining Baba's smile over dinner. He loved it when she made up stories for him, and this would be her best yet.

But he didn't hear the tale that night, nor even return home as expected. When a body was finally found on the South road, picked apart by predators, the only reason anyone knew it was him was because of the knife he still held in his hands.

And everything, absolutely everything in the world, changed.

CAST OFF THE SHADOW

Sabra woke before dawn, as Lin cried out to be fed. As quietly as she could, she lifted her fussy son and allowed him to nurse. She lay back against her wall, rubbing the sleep from her eyes and trying to wake herself as much as he would need. Lin tended to wake early and remain active and noisy for hours. She knew Asha and Nuru had not gotten much sleep and she didn't want to steal more of their rest with her playful son. So she dressed slowly, holding him with one arm and pulling a wrap around herself.

By the time she was fully dressed, he was done feeding and was gurgling loudly in an imitation of speech. She smiled brightly, taking a soft, loose swath of cloth and wrapping her son to her chest, soft and secure so they could look into each other's eyes, but she could have her hands free.

"Who is my bright boy, up with the sun?" Sabra cooed at him as she tied off the sling. "You are, yes you are."

As quietly as she was able, she slipped out of the hut. Asha was asleep in the main room with her sewing still in her hands. Sabra had watched her last night as the news of the new ball and the stranger was shared. She felt certain she would have known even if she had not seen her friend slip out of an explosion of magic and race to hide in the brush. Asha was the stranger.

Sabra felt like she should be more curious as to how such a thing could happen. Asha had always believed in the magic of mortal beings, but Sabra never had. Sabra's parents had told her the same stories of gods and goddesses that the rest of the children in Maltuba were raised on, and she'd believed. Sabra was a faithful worshiper of Ether, but she never believed in magic in this world and Asha was just the opposite. She'd not believed in any of the gods. But if someone told Asha there were monkeys living in the jungle who could sing and talk, she wouldn't doubt it for a moment. Sabra had always pretended to go along because she loved the excitement she felt when she was with Asha. But she had never believed.

Now it seemed Sabra was wrong. Just as she had been wrong about so many things. She shuddered inside, as she remembered her husband boasting over his evil accomplishments.

"Do not cross me, Sabra. You are mine. I have killed men and beasts. I have bested beings of magic. You are nothing compared to me. You have no family nor any friend now. Anyone you see, you see at my side."

Sabra shook, having to cast the ghost of him from her skin. He was gone. She was free. It didn't seem possible. Even as she'd watched his body burn on the altar at the mouth of Ether, she'd known, but she hadn't truly believed. But he was gone. And no one seemed to want to control her. She wished she knew what she wanted any longer. She used to have desires. But the only things she knew now were that she wanted her son safe and loved, and that she never wanted to be owned again.

Sabra stopped at the sand alter behind their home. She knelt, laying a hand on her son's back though she knew him to be safe. It was nearly dawn, and it felt so peaceful to be able to pray with the sunrise again as she had as a child. She'd had to learn more flexibility in her religious practice since she was married. She wondered what Ether thought of that. Sabra had been raised with a way of dressing and a specific hour for prayers, a *practice* of faith built into so many aspects of life that when Zuberi denied her the chiian wrap for her head, and the alter for her prayers, or even the right to visit her parents on the Day of Balance, Sabra hadn't known who she was.

Sabra was grateful every day to Jauhar for protecting her and teaching her to believe even when her practice of faith was constrained. She only hoped Ether saw it the same way. The Qi'on called her the sister goddess, the only deity who had chosen to live in this world with humans so she might protect and truly understand their souls. Sabra believed Ether would understand.

She believed Ether would honor the faith that continued to live in Sabra no matter how Zuberi sought to kill it. She knew Ether to be a loving goddess, but she wondered how it affected her opinion of Sabra.

Sabra breathed in slowly, shutting her eyes. The alter was a round basin of sacred stones filled with an even layer of sand from the desert. Sabra knelt, so she faced east towards the desert. She dipped one finger into the sand; Lin giggled and stretched out his hand, imitating her.

"That's right, one day you will do this yourself." Sabra dragged her finger around the rim of the alter and slowly inward, creating a spiral. "We stir the sands that guard us. We ask our sister Ether to see our faith, and feel our love, and to keep our spirits with her when they leave our bodies. So we might be forever as the sand. Forever present. Forever changing. Forever infinite. One among legion for all days." Sabra alternated days, praying one day in Fairy, and the next in Maltuban, so Lin would be exposed to both from childhood.

Lin giggled and clapped, gurgling along, and Sabra felt her heart burn with peace.

With her prayers complete, Sabra decided to get some bathing water. The river was loud, and Lin loved playing in the water; they could be alone for a bit and pretend it was only them.

"If you could go anywhere in the entire world, where would you go?" Asha asked as they lay under the stars making wishes as children.

Sabra rolled her head on the ground to watch her friend. "Why would I want to go anywhere? You're here, our families are here."

"Not forever. Just for an adventure! Don't you want to see the world? See mountains so high you cannot reach the top of them. Or magical lands where dragons and fairies roam. Or places so cold that the water freezes!"

Sabra had laughed and laid back to look up at the stars. "Would I have to go alone?" Sabra asked.

"Of course not!" Asha propped up on her elbows to look at Sabra incredulously. "We'll go together. I'm just letting you choose one of our destinations."

"So generous." Sabra giggled hard. "But you don't need to be. I'll go anywhere with you."

"Promise." Asha insisted, leaning in close.

"Promise." Sabra agreed.

Sabra kissed the top of her son's head, navigating down a little rocky ditch with the buckets balanced across her shoulders. She'd meant every word at the time. Thought sure nothing could make her break her promises. But someone had. Now that Sabra was finally free, she realized that part of what was keeping her from befriending Asha again was fear of the power

Asha had over her. Sabra's desire had always been to be next to Asha, to do things that made *Asha* happy. When she was young and innocent, that had been fine. But Sabra had spent years belonging to someone else. She didn't know that she could go back. Asha's desires might feel like being owned again.

The river was deserted; most people chose parts of the river closer to the city. She set aside the buckets and took Lin out of the sling, letting him play at the edge of the water. She sat on the bank, with one hand by Lin, keeping him from falling into the water or crawling away, but letting him splash and scream to his heart's content. Sabra leaned back on her free hand and shut her eyes, allowing herself to just feel the air, and the solitude and the freedom.

"He is a beautiful boy." A stranger's voice startled Sabra.

She sat forward and yanked Lin against her chest, glancing around.

"Oh, I am so sorry," the woman above them at the ledge of the ditch shook her head in apology.

She was dressed in heavy dark fabric shot through with silver threads that looked like flowers bursting to life. She was plump and a good deal older than Sabra. She had old eyes, grey and tired. Sabra didn't recognize her, but Jaccada was not so small that she should know all its citizens. Still, the woman felt...sinister perhaps. She looked in all ways like someone who ought to be trusted, but she felt... out of place.

Lin began to cry and struggle, reaching for the water. The stranger looked at him, and a fond smile played at her lips.

"I did not mean to startle you," the woman said softly. "I just came for my water."

The woman lifted a bucket that Sabra hadn't noticed a moment ago, and looked shyly down. As if asking permission to take water from the river everyone used.

Sabra calmed her rushing heart and smiled up at the woman.

"Navish szou." Sabra shook her head. "He is far more alert than myself; you merely woke me up."

The woman chuckled, lumbering down the little path. "There is nothing to forgive. I well recall those days. Half asleep I cleaned and cooked and ate.

I do not think I have been as awake as my children were since the day they were born."

Sabra laughed and allowed Lin a bit more freedom. He splashed in the water, spraying his own face, and his tears quickly turned to laughter.

"Shall I never stop being tired then?" Sabra asked with a chuckle.

"I cannot say," the woman crouched by the river. Laying aside her bucket, she dipped both her hands in the water and brought it to her face, splashing it over herself in a more restrained version of Lin's game. "I had far and away more children than I was prepared for. Do you mean to have more?"

"No," Sabra said at once, shaking off a shudder.

"So certain?" She asked provocatively. The air began to sing with cicada music for no reason. Sabra touched Lin's back with a hand stretched out like a guide for him and searched the banks.

When she glanced back to the stranger, she was watching Sabra in a deep probing fashion that slightly unnerved her. She wasn't sure from where she plucked the knowledge, but Sabra knew the woman was waiting for more explanation.

"My husband is dead, and I've no desire for another. Lin shall be my only love."

The woman tipped the bucket upside down in an impressive little flip that spoke of years of practice. She sat on its upturned bottom and leaned her arms on her legs to observe Sabra gently.

"You are a wounded bird, afraid of every brush of air or shifting shadow."

"Some shadows wither everything they fall upon. Stealing every light," Sabra said, her tone sharpening without intent. "So nothing can grow beneath them without being warped."

The woman looked far older seated next to Sabra; her face was wrinkled with lines of pain and of joy. And her eyes, though they had seemed grey before, were now glowing with a near silver light. Her head was wrapped in a scarf that was flattened on top and stretched wide. It reminded Sabra of how her grandmother wore her chiian. *Honor me*, that scarf said, *for I have endured a long life*. Sabra felt like she might cry. It was almost as though the woman's features were becoming those of her grandmother as they spoke. When she reached out a hand, Sabra instinctively took it.

She gripped Sabra's hand softly. And infused her voice with gentle power. "You were one of Zuberi's wives, yes?"

Sabra nodded tightly.

"But not by choice?" She asked.

Sabra shook her head, tensing even further and casting a look sidelong at her son.

The woman chuckled at that look. "Mean you to keep that from him? Mean you to hide ugly truths and keep him pure and free, and —*foolish?*" The woman asked disdainfully. She was speaking in a voice of wisdom, so like Sabra's grandmother's that she would think it was her, but that she'd never learned the Fairy tongue.

"There is a difference between protecting your child from the bad in the world and hiding them from it. One gives them strength; the other weakens them. Haven't you seen that yet? You cannot give all your love to your son and expect that he will know how to love. Children learn by example." She softened, leaning nearer. The world began to smell like day, warmth seeped off of the water and grasses, and sand, lilies sweetened the air. "Zuberi is gone. Cast off his shadow, wounded bird. Live in the sunlight."

She released Sabra's hand and stood in the same motion, sweeping up the bucket from beneath her; she brushed it through the river, filling it perhaps halfway, and turned to walk back up the hill. It was all done so swiftly Sabra had to catch her breath to focus at all.

"Mind you heed my advice," the woman said, struggling back up the little lip of the ditch. "Lest that shadow be cast over your, *only love.*" She chuckled. "So young. I was once foolishly sure of life."

"You..." Sabra called out and hesitated, but the woman stopped and looked back, her eyes expectant. "You think like Jauhar, that I should marry again and give Lin a father?" Sabra asked, as though she was asking her grandmother. Desperate for her guidance.

The woman shook her head. "You needn't give love to another husband to show your child the way. Only to more than him. Give love to a dream. To a friend. To yourself. Show him all the beautiful forms love can take. Show yourself. What do you want?" The woman echoed Sabra's earlier thoughts. "What would you wish for if you could have anything? Do you even know? You are free now to find the answer."

The woman climbed over the ditch and walked away. She was out of sight in moments, and Sabra was oddly sure she would have vanished completely if she climbed the little crest to look. But she didn't try. She'd felt like she was speaking to her grandmother, and chasing down a dead woman was foolish.

Sabra wondered if Ether, hearing Sabra's prayer, had bid her grandmother's spirit to pick up her sands and follow Sabra to help her understand what freedom was. To show her that her faith had indeed been seen and honored. For surely the sister goddess wanted freedom for all her devotees.

Sabra lifted the buckets one at a time and filled them, pressing them deep into the river. She watched Lin out of the corner of her eye, but did not need to be right on top of him to keep him safe. She gave him a few more minutes to play before she lifted her son back into his sling, strapped the buckets over a rod and stretched it across her shoulders, starting back home. The sun was in the sky, and the world was new. She could be new as well.

IN THE HUT OF THE PRESENT

Hadhi woke early. She lay in bed knowing she should go get water from the river, or prepare breakfast for her family; most of them had not slept last night. She used to help prepare breakfast when she lived in this hut as a small child. Once they moved into the mansion, there were servants to do most of the work. Hadhi might hunt for their food, or trade for vegetables, even occasionally help to clean, but she had not had to do much in years. Not really.

She should get up now, but in the past year, whenever she moved to help with anything, she heard a bellow so loud inside her that it overpowered her will to move. She felt ugly and hated, and she saw no point to any of it. She had not actively wanted to die, but nor had she seen a point to living, so she did nothing. She let her mother force Asha to work because she resented her sister so much that even as it ate at her, she rejoiced to see Asha brought low. Hadhi knew she was vile. Knew she was as ugly as her father had ever wanted her to be, but without him here to rail against or to try to please, she had no idea what to do. So she sat around this hut, watching and waiting. Dead inside, but living.

But today, as she lay in bed, there was something different inside her, something that was not holding her down. She had never felt like this. It was so...lovely.

She woke from a dream of dancing. Noam had led her through the steps of the cozy with his arm around her waist and her body pressed up against his side. He was so warm, and she had felt their breaths moving in time with one another. Everyone around them faded away. He told her things about his home, and she told him that there was a similar sounding word in Maltuban, *coozie,* that meant to whisper. So he had leaned his head next to her ear and whispered that he wanted the dance to go on forever. She felt the words resonating inside her. He spun her out onto the capitol terrace, but there was no one around in her dream, and there, all alone in the evening, he kissed her.

Hadhi lay abed now, reliving not the dream, but the reality, the look on Noam's face as he pulled her fingers away from her lips. She felt the tingle from head to toe, the warmth spreading through her, and the urge to move closer to him, to *feel* him, to be felt by him.

Hadhi had never experienced *desire*. She had never thought herself capable of such feeling. She could not explain why she was not repelled by his touch as she usually was with just looks from other men. Hadhi's feelings had always seemed confined to fear, anger, jealousy—and a fierce love for her family. Nothing about her had ever felt...soft, or magical, or...exciting. But something was now.

She wanted to see Noam again. She wanted that kiss his eyes had promised. She wanted him to make her feel desirable and beautiful, even though she knew it was not true. It could not be true. Even if it were, he was surely only interested in her because...

Hadhi could not think of a single reason.

Hadhi rose from bed and wrapped herself in an old fading brown silk. Nuru was asleep on the bed across from her, but she was a heavy sleeper. She would likely sleep through being mauled if an animal were fool enough to sneak in here. Asha was sleeping against the wall of the main room, with a gown still in her hands. Hadhi stood still a moment ,watching her half-sister.

There had been a time when Asha was little when they had not felt like half-sisters, but sisters in truth. When they had been friends. And Hadhi knew it was not Asha becoming more beautiful than her sister or developing outside friendships that had changed it. Hadhi would likely never have made as many friends as Asha; she was not that comfortable with others, even Nuru made so many more friends than Hadhi, and they were still close. And Nuru was lovely like Asha and Mzaa, but Hadhi was never envious of that.

The distance between Asha and Hadhi had been sewn, one stitch at a time, by a master of rage and manipulation. By their father. *Hadhi, you are my own image. A monster of rage and destruction. You will decimate all before you.*

Maybe Hadhi could still fix things between her and Asha. Maybe she could live as though she had escaped him, not just survived him. Maybe she could be something her father could not have imagined. Maybe she could be happy.

Hadhi slipped out the back of the hut, yanking her spear off the wall almost habitually. She did not want her father's voice to be chasing her around. She wanted to be like Noam. She wanted to love her siblings despite the fact that Baba loved Asha better, despite the fact that Nuru could be happy anywhere and that Lin already had more of Mzaa's love than Hadhi could ever remember having. She just had no idea how to do it, how to be happy with others, when half the time she hated herself.

Hadhi was unsure if she was ready for a proper hunt, but she slipped the spear end under the handle of a bucket and lifted it. Perhaps she would get some fish; they were plentiful in the rivers in the morning. She walked away from the hut, with her mind busily trying to explain Noam's behavior.

Perhaps he just had not thought he could tempt the other women. A ludicrous notion. He had to know how attractive he was. He was a bit taller than Hadhi and had the lithe figure of a man who kept quite active. But it was his spirit that made him most attractive. His eyes were so warm and inviting, and his smile very nearly tickled the air. He was charming. Everyone must want to be with him. So why would he want her? She was not sweet. She was not beautiful, nor even pretty. She was scared and cold, and not nearly as intelligent as other women. She was a bad dancer and had been rude to him.

Maybe he was another of Baba's spies. Maybe they were playing games with her. Maybe—

Hadhi saw his eyes again, staring at her lips as if entranced, his head lowering. She felt the whisper of his breath on her face: *there is a smile you should not conceal. It is very becoming.*

A tingle raced up her spine, making her smile as breath deserted her.

She could think of no reason for him to like her—but he did. She had felt it. She felt it, and for the first time in her life, she wanted to feel it more. It did not intimidate or anger her; it did not put her on edge. It woke her up!

For the first time since Baba died, she was awake.

Hadhi caught sight of Sabra walking up from the direction of the river, with Lin wrapped against her chest and two buckets of water stretched out on a pole across her shoulders.

189

She had yet to notice Hadhi. She was laughing and giggling with her son. Singing. She was awake as well. Hadhi watched them a moment, comforted by their peace. Hadhi was never sure if the rest of her family were better or worse off with Baba dead, but Sabra was better off for it. Sabra was allowed to be a girl again.

Hadhi thought about moving forward to take the water from her, but Sabra looked quite capable of the chore she had chosen for herself. And Hadhi was never sure how to speak to this woman. Hadhi ran around the other side of the hut and made her way to the river, being sure not to cross Sabra's path.

Asha heard a commotion outside and woke with excitement tingling under her skin. But aches rolling through her as well. It could just be the way she'd slept, but she didn't think so. She felt tired and heavy, and empty. She wanted something. She wanted to be filled. To be brought to life.

She wanted magic.

But she stretched and rolled, carefully checking over the gown she'd prepared for herself in the night. It was nothing compared to the one she'd made with magic, but it was beautiful. Golden threads and brown ones woven together, giving her a look almost like a cheetah, and the intricately carved and painted beads she'd strung together to hang from one shoulder were provocative and bright.

Asha shook out the gown, checking over her stitches, then lay it over a stool to rise before Mzaa Jauhar could kick her awake. For a moment, she feared Jauhar, or Hadhi destroying this gown as they had her mother's, but her chest hardened with the thought. There would be no stopping her today. If she had to attend the ball entirely nude, she would still be there. She'd given Azize a challenge, and he was meeting it, *come find me.* He would know her, even if her face was not the same as the night before, and her dress not as fine. He would know her. He had to. And if he needed a little nudge, she still had the second slipper hidden with Jauhar's things. She could be loved again. She could be filled up again.

Asha was going to bring in water to wash, but she saw Sabra outside, warming the tub. So Asha raced out the front of the hut to the kitchen to prepare breakfast; Mzaa Jauhar would not find anything to fault Asha for today. When the smell of breakfast was filling the air, Sabra came around the outside of the hut, to where Asha worked.

She stood next to the wind wall that protected the fire pit and stared at Asha with an odd smile. It wasn't her old smile that was soft and innocent; this one was...knowing.

"How is my sweet brother this morning?" Asha called out. Lin was generally the only thing Sabra allowed them to talk about.

Sabra pulled her head back and looked down, with bright eyes to her son, gurgling and humming against her chest. "How are you?" She asked him in a bright, sweet voice. "How is my love? Are you well? Tell your onja, Asha. Say *well,* can you say well?" She nudged him with her nose and tickled him softly.

Asha felt a painful swelling in her chest as she watched. She wondered if her own mother had ever held her so. Her mother had died when Asha was too young to remember much. And for so long Asha would call Jauhar Mzaa and rush to her, throw her arms around her, look to her for guidance and approval, and love. But not once had Jauhar looked at Asha that way.

Asha turned aside. She pulled the meat out of the fire and laid it out on a tray for her family, adding vegetables and fruits to the spread.

"Are you hungry?" Asha held out the tray.

"Thank you." Sabra selected some fruit. She bit off a tiny amount and chewed it to soften it before pulling it from her lips to feed to the baby, before she ate her own bite. She watched Asha again over the baby's head. "The stranger at the ball last night was beautiful and vibrant, and...if it were not for the fact that I would know your face anywhere, I would have sworn she was you."

Asha startled. Last night she'd so badly wanted Sabra to recognize her, but she hadn't seemed to. Asha opened her mouth, wanting to blurt out that it was her, that Sabra had missed an epic adventure. But Sabra was speaking again.

"She asked me to join her in an adventure like you used to. And I wanted to join her but—"

"You were too busy doing what Jauhar makes you." Asha shook her head at her old friend. "Just because she was Baba's first wife doesn't mean she has power over you."

Sabra drew back and her shoulders tightened. "I will never approve of how Jauhar treats you, Asha," Sabra said in a heavy, disappointed tone. "But of her treatment of me, I have no complaints. She is a hard woman and a very unhappy one. No one ever invited her on any adventures. I didn't join the stranger, because since I joined this family, I have seen another person who was never offered adventures, and I wanted to help her to see...her family wants adventure for her." Sabra repeated Asha's words from the night before, infusing them with meaning. Asha was utterly struck still. "But I do not think it was I that Hadhi needed to hear that from."

She didn't say anything else. Selecting a bit more food, she took it in her hand and walked away, back to the house. Asha stared after her angrily. What was that about? What exactly had happened that stopped them being friends? Asha had never understood it. One day they were sitting up all night discussing village boys and the trade ships from foreign lands that Asha wanted to sneak onto. And the next night, Baba brought Sabra home and announced that they had wed. Asha was overjoyed. They need never be apart again! She was sure that was half the reason Baba had chosen to marry her, that and that Sabra was so beautiful and good, no one could help but love her. But Sabra had not said more than five words to Asha.

She'd kept to her room nearly every hour of the day unless Baba required her. She'd lost weight and...light. And Asha was all alone again, with no one but Baba to love her. He'd said Sabra was just adjusting to being a woman married and consoled Asha by taking her with him to the docks all the time, introducing her to more foreigners, made her one of the most honored girls in the kingdom by having her nurse the dying queen. Baba kept her so busy she should not have been able to miss her friend, but she had missed her. She missed her still. For the life of her, Asha couldn't think what she'd done in that one night to lose her friend's love.

Now Sabra was trying to make Asha feel sorry for Hadhi. Hadhi! Who had done nothing but try to spoil their fun all her life.

It made no sense. Asha clenched her hand around the platter. She needed out of this hut. Out of this family. She needed to be loved again.

That was what the aching empty was inside. She needed to be someone's beloved again. And she would never have that here.

Nuru arranged stools outside between the hut and the bathing tent. In the mansion, there had been an entire chamber set aside for bathing. The floors were closely fitted stone and there was a low pool that cool water could be pumped into and also had a spout that led from the fires where a cauldron sat for warming water.

No one but the king had such luxury. But Baba was a great man, the king's dearest friend, and most useful aide. Many families, even those in the most central parts of the city, bathed at the river. Though more and more of the king's friends were trying to replicate his level of luxury. But here, there was just the tent, and even that had been added by uncle Kafil to appease Mzaa. Inside there was a standing tub for deep bathing and bowls of water and rags for daily needs.

Nuru thought that of all of them, she should most resent their reversal of fortunes. She had only ever lived in the mansion, and when he'd left on his last trip, Baba had promised to find something special to offer to Eshe so Nuru could join the Spirit Dancers. She should hate this home the way Mzaa did, but Nuru didn't mind the bathing tent or the smaller chambers.

What Nuru minded was the feeling that they were outside of life. Outside of Jaccada. Outside of the entire world they'd known. Outside of even being a family. They were just...five women and one baby boy living together at the edge of the desert, waiting to fade out of the world completely.

She wanted to change that so badly. So Nuru woke up far earlier than her body wanted and set out stools and gathered the remnants of embellishments for dresses and a basket of beads and rings. They could all dress together, like other families did for special occasions. It would make them closer, make them see how much they really did love each other. Make Hadhi and Asha see it; they were the ones who needed it most. They were sisters, and they loved each other; Nuru knew they did. They just didn't know how to tell each other.

She was just sneaking into her mother's room for the paints when Mzaa grabbed her wrist. "What are you doing? You should be dressed already."

"I thought we could all dress together. We can help each other with paint and—

"Nuru, this isn't a party for your entertainment. This is a competition. One woman will win, and every other will lose. And if we are the losers, you and your sisters will die inside these walls together."

Nuru swallowed and firmed her shoulders, trying again. "I know Mzaa. But...don't you think Hadhi will be more comfortable, more herself if we—"

"We don't want her to be herself. Tonight she needs to be someone desirable."

"She is! She just...needs you to say it!" Nuru shouted angrily. "You and Asha and Sa—"

Mzaa laughed cold and sharp. The sound shattered the air, so shards of Nuru's hope fell to the ground, scratching and slicing her open so she bled though her skin was left entirely unmarred.

"Is that what this is? You want that girl to play your sweet sister. She isn't your family. And she most certainly isn't Hadhi's. That girl who taunted your sister since before you were born. You didn't know your sister before Asha came along. She had a smile then; she was sweet. But your father's *most beloved* stole his love and your sister's joy and her confidence. Even her dowry. That cheetah that ripped your sister open and left her ugly—*delighted* Asha. She laughed over it and loved it, so it was given to her, though she did nothing to earn it.

"That thing isn't a sister. It is an enemy. Be clear about that before you help her sparkle for the ball, because if she wins the prince instead of Hadhi the only one who will benefit is Asha. Just as she has always benefited while Hadhi suffered." Mzaa ground Nuru down with every word. Her body felt exhausted, and her heart felt dry. She wanted to just lay down and give up.

"If you want to help this family, help Hadhi win so she can finally escape Asha's shadow."

Mzaa swept away and left Nuru crushed behind her. Was she right? Was there no way for them to be family?

Nuru started back outside without the paints and with her imagination forming images of Asha wrapped up in the cheetah pelt, laughing while

Hadhi lay bloody and sewn together. And of Hadhi standing by silent and cold as Asha wept over the ruins of her mother's gown.

There wasn't any way for the two of them to love the other, was there? And if not, did that mean Nuru had to choose only one sister to love?

UGLY WORDS

Zawadi perched in the brush partway up the hill behind the home of her enemy's family. It wasn't much, two domes of mud and sticks and small entrances blocked with silk hangings. Not the mansion Zuberi had spoken of. No, this was the place he feared. How she wished she could have seen him here, forced him here as she picked apart the life he was so proud of. If she'd only found him living, she would have brought him here, then she would have brought him lower and lower until he was begging her for death.

If only he could have felt the extent of her vengeance.

His eldest child made her way out of the hut now, headed towards the river wearing the smile of a softer woman. Who did she think she was fooling? She was nothing that was soft.

Her feet were bare, but her steps were quick and silent. She followed a circuitous path which took her through the strong scent of the looma blossoms and by way of a cluster of stink beetles, intentionally muddying her scent. No. Not intentionally— *habitually*. Her mind was far too far away to know exactly what her body was doing. But even distracted, she moved like Zuberi: confident, powerful, deadly. A killer. Just like her father.

Zawadi had hated the girl on sight last night. Today, with her hair wrapped up off her face leaving those scars, which ought to evoke an empathetic kinship, visible, Zawadi was only more angered. It was as if the girl, aware that she had not her father's magnetism, nor her half-sister's endearing innocence, had given herself a scar to earn sympathy. To evoke pain. But she hadn't suffered. Zawadi knew that trick for what it was, and she would not be drawn into feeling for the child of her enemy. If she wanted the world to think she'd suffered, Zawadi would be happy to assist her.

Zawadi watched her as a bird, trying to decide what form to use with her. Her half-sister had been easy. Asha was too open and thrill seeking to turn away from anyone foreign, and Wren's forceful voice and loving spirit were perfect to set her at ease. And though Zuberi's third wife was naturally suspicious, she still held onto enough belief to trust the face of her own grandmother. But this girl...

Without being near enough to delve into her mind, Zawadi could tell she trusted no one she did not know already. A foreign body would never do. And if she came to the girl in the body of a dead relative, she would know she was unsafe. Perhaps she should borrow the body of one of her living family members, but Zawadi doubted they would be so giving. Perhaps her best option would be to speak to the girl through her own reflection. Many were those comforted by speaking to themselves.

The girl paused a way yet from the ravine that led down to the river. Smoothly she sunk into the long grass around her, barely disturbing its sway as she scanned the area. One hand slipped the bucket noiselessly from her spear. Had she sensed Zawadi? Again. As a bird? Last night those eyes had followed her, and the anger that girl carried within had burned at Zawadi's skin. Yet, Zawadi would not have expected to be sensed now.

Too late, Zawadi heard the footsteps and laughter behind her. She took to the air in swallows bird form, darting away from the group of men heading down the hill. She noticed Hadhi's eyes follow her for a moment before returning to the men. Five men of Azize's party. Zawadi circled them a moment before perching in a nearby tree.

She had hoped to catch Zuberi's eldest alone, as she had not last night. But though she clearly hated company, she was rarely alone. While her sister, who thrived on activity and attention was alone most hours of the day.

One of the men paused in a manner similar to Zuberi's eldest. His name was Kane. Zawadi knew them all from her months of following Azize's ship and urging the prince home. Most of their group, Daniel, Omar, Masahiro, and Noam were making their way across the hill, towards a little cliff that overlooked the sand dunes of Ether. An endless view, and a bit of a dreary one, if you asked Zawadi. But Kane locked his eyes on the hut in the distance, and he tilted his nose into the air, studying its scent.

Crouched in the tall grass Zuberi's eldest seemed torn between watching Kane and watching his retreating friends. Kane took a step forward.

"Kane," Omar called out. "It is this way."

"I'll be right along," Kane said, and his voice lowered. "There is something ugly following us. I'm going to scare it off."

Zawadi wasn't sure if the girl was near enough to hear, but her muscles coiled, and her breathing slowed. For a moment, Zawadi saw, not that girl but the monster who had trained her.

Zawadi fought the urge to send the men away. To protect them. She didn't want any of them slaughtered because she had needed Azize to stir up this land. But if she interfered, she would miss the chance to see more of the beast Zuberi had created. Did she kill like her father? Was she as swift? As merciless? Was she everything he boasted over?

Zawadi had used words she knew would make Asha open herself to a stranger, but even as she had, she'd known only half of them were about Asha. Asha was her father's *best beloved*. But himself reborn, and his legacy, those words referred to the hunter crouched in the grass, awaiting her moment to strike.

Zawadi had originally intended to avenge herself against Zuberi alone, but before she recovered enough to chase Zuberi down, she had felt him die. It had been—*glorious!* Richly deserved. Exhilarating. Resplendent!

But time passed. And it was not enough. She knew there were others in the world, killers he'd trained, men he'd served, women who'd loved and benefited from his evil. It wasn't enough that he was gone. His entire legacy had to be destroyed, or one of them might grow into his place and destroy another family like Zawadi's. That girl, who moved like her father, so calm as she killed, she would take his place if Zawadi allowed it.

She would never allow it.

The rest of the men had walked on without their companion. Kane stepped forward again, scanning the area. He knew the girl was out there, but he did not seem to know where.

"Out hunting?" He asked lightly, clearly not expecting an answer. "Your father said it was your only talent."

Zawadi watched the girl, waiting to see her reaction. There must be one surprise that this man had known her father? Zawadi was surprised!

Flinching or tears from the slight? But Hadhi appeared entirely unmoved. Zawadi hadn't studied the insides of these men's minds and souls. They weren't useful to her plan. But perhaps she should have delved.

"You do understand, don't you? That Azize is not like your father? You cannot go to him with your kill between your teeth and expect praise like a good pet. You do not possess the gifts to tempt Azize."

Zawadi was—shocked. She wasn't sure entirely what she was feeling. She'd come to offer this girl a wish. She'd come to trick her into harming herself with her own desires, but now—she was angry with the man taunting her.

He winked into the distance and reminded Zawadi of her enemy. Not as powerful, not as clever, but entirely as cold. Zawadi needed to examine these men much closer, it seemed. Kane was...unsettling. He turned away casually and rejoined his friends.

It wasn't until he was a ways away that the girl stood. Slow and smooth, one continuous motion, a deadly flower blooming before Zawadi's eyes. Her hands were clenched, her eyes were hard, and there was a heaviness about her that unnerved Zawadi for the empathy it wanted to stir.

The girl stared at the hill for several moments before turning away, her bucket forgotten and her spear hanging softly at her side as she walked back towards her home. Her head fell as she walked, traitor to her inner pain.

Zawadi glanced after Kane. Who was he in truth? Zawadi saw another man turn this way. Noam lifted his arm to wave, trying to get the girl's attention, but he was too late. Together Noam and Zawadi watched Zuberi's eldest walk away. She was a dark cave: dangerous, unknowable, and compelling. But doomed. Still doomed.

Zawadi was not leaving without her vengeance. And even great hunter that the girl was reputed to be, she didn't feel the real threat. Not taunting boys with ugly words. But desires bright and beautiful. Burning desires that Zawadi would use to destroy her.

SMILE THIEF

"**J**auhar." Hadhi froze at the sound of his voice, *Noam*. Her heart pounded so loud she had trouble hearing him over it.

She had seen him on the hill with the other men. *You can't go to him with your kill between your teeth and expect praise like a good pet.* Hadhi shook off Kane's voice. Noam had not been looking the way of the hut when his friend taunted Hadhi. He was off with the other men, looking at Ether. So he had not seen her or heard his friend. How had he even come to be here? Was he here to see her?

She should not hope for any such things, but...she wanted to see him again, and she wanted him to want it too. What was wrong with her? She was never like this. But—she did not care. His friend was right, Hadhi had neither the looks nor the talent to attract Azize. She had never intended to take Azize a kill, but that was Hadhi's only talent, and it would not impress Azize, or Noam, most likely. No one was impressed by her but butchers and tanners. Hadhi could not win Azize, so what should stop her from enjoying Noam?

"Can't you reach?" Nuru came up behind her sister, taking the long ribbons from Hadhi's hand to tie the dress up.

Hadhi leaned away from her sister to listen.

"It's a group of the prince's friends," Nuru explained, misinterpreting Hadhi's interest. "The man who took you to the king, and Masahiro, and Daniel, and two others I haven't met yet."

"Did...they say why they are here?"

"To see Sabra." Nuru finished tying off the gown. "Daniel said they wanted to meet Lin since they had not last night. Most of them are outside with her and Asha, but the one you danced with said he came to see Mzaa; he is upstairs talking with her."

"Of course," Hadhi whispered, still straining to hear.

"Asha would not stop asking questions about the prince and the girl he danced with. All night long, it was, 'Is Azize handsome now? Do you think he's in love with this girl? Did anyone know who she was? She wouldn't shut up."

Hadhi was only half listening. Noam was in the other room, and just the sound of his light, friendly voice made her feel freer. She did not care if he was here to see Mzaa, and anyway, he might not be. Of course he would say that. One had to flatter Mzaa to get anything from her. Hadhi could never have him. He was bound to reject her eventually or leave when Azize did, but she could have a few moments, maybe even a few hours with him.

Absent-mindedly Hadhi helped her sister into her own gown from the night before. Adjusting the sash so it hung a little longer. Nuru seemed a bit morose, but Hadhi's mind was far away. Nuru's hair was still in the braids with the threads and beads adorning it, but now it all hung loose down her back. Hadhi gathered the braids around her face, twisting to pull the underneath ones up and make little rolls on either side of her sister's face. Then she pulled it all together at the back of Nuru's head, making a little bursting twist, enjoying the variation she could give Nuru's hair, unlike her own, which was styled exactly the same as last night. As she worked, Hadhi trained her ears on the other room; every once in a while she caught a few words.

"I couldn't risk missing you in the circus of this ball," Noam said, and Hadhi smiled. *What on earth was a circus?*

"Why are you smiling?" Nuru asked, and Hadhi could not answer, embarrassed to have been caught. "Mzaa says if Asha marries the prince instead of you, we'll have to live here, forever."

Oh. What had Nuru been saying about Asha? "This is not such a terrible place, Nuru."

"We'll never be married." Nuru sounded confused, maybe probing.

"Since when do you even care?" Hadhi rolled her eyes. She was not used to her sister listening to much their mother said, but if there was one thing you could count on from Nuru, it was melodrama. "All you want to do is dance."

"I want to marry." Nuru shrugged, looking at her feet. "Just not yet. And not to the prince."

"And you think I want to marry him?" Hadhi demanded, so quickly were her ugly insides set ablaze with resentment. Nuru could brush aside duty so easily, just like Asha. A trait they inherited from their father.

And what have you inherited, monster?

Hadhi fought a shiver as her father's voice raced across her nerve endings. Fought the urge to glance around for his ghost. Somedays, his voice just seemed so real. And that man, Kane, he unnerved her. He spoke with her father's words. He felt like another of Baba's tests—or his punishments.

He was an axe, hovering over her head, waiting to fall until she was at her happiest. That was always when Baba struck.

"I don't think you care one way or another who you marry," Nuru said at last, gazing at Hadhi as though it had never occurred to her that her sister possessed feelings. "You look on all men the same."

Hadhi flinched. She could no longer hear voices in the other room. She spun around and marched up the stairs and out the back of the empty house. She walked towards the bathing hut; Mzaa would never allow strange men near there. Hadhi could hear them all around the front of the house, where the kitchen was, facing Jaccada. So she walked away from the voices moving behind the bathing hut where she would be blocked from them and staring off into Ether.

You look at all men the same.

What way was that? Hadhi never had a boy care about her or one that she cared for over all others. Did that mean she never could? Hadhi was being unfair to her sister. Until yesterday Hadhi *had not* wanted any man. How was Nuru supposed to know what had changed inside her sister if Hadhi did not share it. Before yesterday just the idea of a man touching her made Hadhi ill and angry. So she had looked at them all the same. She looked at them with contempt, or maybe...fear.

But why was that not reason enough to exempt Hadhi from marrying the prince? Like Nuru was exempted by age and Asha—

"Here you are?"

Every nerve, every thread of air, every bit of Hadhi softened and swayed at the sound of his voice. Her rage shuddered into pleasure, and she smiled in spite of herself as tears gathered in her eyes. She looked at him differently.

"What is a circus?" She asked, with her back to him. Noam's hand came down slowly onto her left shoulder.

Her breath caught; she loved the feel of his hand on her bare shoulder. It was the strangest thing. As long as she could remember, she had hated being touched, most especially being touched without seeing it coming. But her body curled up in the feeling of him and wanted to go on feeling it. She *wanted*— and it was glorious torture.

She turned and found a wide smile on his face, his eyes crinkling at the corners. He had such a lovely face, so kind.

Not like hers.

"There's that look again," he whispered. "I kept seeing it last night, every time you were on the verge of that surrender we discussed." His free hand rose to rub the spot between her eyes softly. "It's as though you go somewhere else whenever you're about to be happy."

"To be happy would be to go somewhere else," Hadhi said honestly. She would never be happy; she had known it since Baba died. He had died and left all of them just as ugly as ever, and Hadhi hated herself even more than she had before.

"So sad, Hadhi?" His finger traced the bones of Hadhi's face until her eyes drifted shut. "It won't do, not for someone so beautiful."

At this Hadhi's eyes popped open as she was overcome with laughter.

"There's the smile I was after." Noam's voice was light and playful as his hand left her face, but there was something else in his eyes, something like anger or frustration. He blinked and it was gone. "A circus is something spectacular," he said. But Hadhi was not listening; she was looking for that expression again. "We never had them in Glen Harrow; they were considered dangerous. I saw one for the first time on Gods Parted. It's a spectacle with music and dancing, impressive feats, and exotic animals, and all sorts of magic."

Hadhi smirked, goading him, trying to see another flash of his hidden self. "Exotic like here?"

Noam laughed, and his hand slipped away. Her shoulder met the air and she shivered for the loss of his warmth. "I suppose so. What do you find spectacular?"

You.

She could not say that, so she blurted out the first thing that popped into her head. "Ether."

"The vast desert that swallows up all who enter it?" He asked with a brow in the air.

Hadhi walked by him towards the dunes, moving close enough to brush his arm and feel the rush of power between them. "No one has ever returned from it." Her voice tickled her throat with excitement from being this near to Noam. "They could be dead. Or in the next life. Or," she looked over her shoulder, her eyes alight with excitement. "Maybe she freed them. Maybe they are happy."

Noam held her eyes and Hadhi felt the warmth of it rushing through her, as though he was holding her in his arms. She froze, waiting, hoping. But neither of them moved, their gazes alone touching each other.

"Hadhi!" Mzaa's impatient voice sounded from the kitchen area, snapping Hadhi free from the spell of his eyes and sucking the excitement right out of her. Hadhi nodded and made to walk around him, but he caught her arm as she passed.

"It's working," He didn't meet her eyes as he spoke, but that easy smile was back on his face. His false smile, she realized with a tingle of joy. "Azize and his father are mystified by you."

"Yes," Hadhi laughed. "By my gall. But it is the mystery woman whose foot he seeks."

"Hadhi, come on, we need to leave," Nuru called out. "The men have offered us their camels." She added like an enticement.

Hadhi smiled, raising a brow at Noam. It was surely his idea. He shrugged, releasing her elbow and redirecting the conversation. "Azize has sworn to consider every woman who fits the shoe, not a specific one. All we need to do is be sure your foot fits and keep you very much in his mind. You can still have your prince."

Hadhi said nothing because she wanted to ask the way to win him instead of his friend.

She did not want a prince, or an adventure, or anything but these quiet, far away moments with Noam. Where she could just look at him and feel entirely new. Where she could stand next to him and pretend she was in a different world.

He was wearing what must be his own clothes today, in place of long silk robes that reached the calves and soft, loose leg coverings beneath; he wore a short tunic, loose and barely adorned, with holes and cord tying the neck area closed. It barely reached past his waist, leaving the whole of his legs visible with closely worn leg coverings. Nothing about it was decorative in the least, the colors were dull shades of brown, yet Hadhi could not decide in which attire she liked him better. In the silks he looked fine, and important, and the vibrant purple threads had highlighted the depth in his brown eyes. In these plain clothes he looked like a man of labor, and...he alone was the decoration. It was *intriguing* to see so much of his physique so plainly. Her eyes kept drifting to his legs without intent.

"When they try the shoe on you allow it, grudgingly, as though you are not interested in marrying Azize. Later, when he has to dance with you, talk about something other than him."

"You cannot know my foot will fit." Hadhi pointed out quietly. Forcing her eyes back to his face, as they'd drifted again. He did not want this to work, did he? But he was helping her. It was wonderful. And it was torture.

"I have seen it; your foot is near enough in size." He bent his head to examine her feet. Hadhi smiled at the crown of his head. He was lovely. "If the slipper is a bit small, curl your toes. If it is loose stretch them out." Noam straightened, still smiling.

Before Hadhi could think any better of it she stood on her toes and pressed her lips against his smile. It was over in seconds, the meeting of their lips. Hadhi settled back onto her heels, having stolen his smile, his expression blank where hers beamed. She tingled all over, feeling light enough to float off the ground like a bird.

"Do not smile so much," Hadhi said, unable to banish his stolen smile from her own lips. "You are beautiful, even when you do not smile." *Szo quri.* Her mind added, but her tongue was too shy to voice what she felt for him: desire. This was desire. *He* was her desire.

His eyes widened, and his lips jerked to speak.

"Hadhi, your mzaa is getting..." Asha's voice trailed away.

Hadhi startled, tearing her eyes away from Noam. She wanted to hide him before he could lay eyes on Asha and love her. Everyone loved Asha. She would turn his head, and this would all be over.

"Oh, hello. What a pleasant surprise," Asha greeted him cheerfully, as though they knew one another. Hadhi wanted to shove Asha back into the hut, or into the dirt or anywhere to keep her away from Noam, but she didn't move. Frozen between them, waiting for the axe to fall. "I didn't realize we had more guests. But that makes sense of the five camels we were offered."

Noam smiled easily with his head cocked to the side. "I could swear we have never met. Yet you seem familiar."

"Oh," Asha had the decency to glance away shyly at her overly forward greeting. Hadhi ground her teeth. "Yes, I do have that effect on one. I'm a bit too familiar with everyone."

Noam raised an eyebrow and looked ready to laugh. "Do I have the right of it? Am I at last in the presence of the infamous Asha?"

"Infamous?" Asha looked at Hadhi smugly. "What bad have *you* to say of me, Hadhi?"

Hadhi bit her tongue to hold back the rage and the tears. Plenty, she had plenty of bad to speak of her half-sister, and she had not told Noam half of it. Her head began to pound with rage.

"I am hardly the cause of your sour face," Asha said it so lightly, as though it was an endearment fondly used. Hadhi felt Noam's mouth open, felt him stretching out to...what? Defend her? Laugh? She could not stand to see.

"Sorry to disappoint you, *sister*." Hadhi bit out the word like it was a curse, because when she spoke of Asha, it was. No matter how she tried to change that. "But your...infamy comes from the prince. And is all of your own making."

Hadhi was so angry she could barely see straight, she swept past Asha and around the house without glancing back.

To be happy— would be to go somewhere else.

FAMILIAR

"**D**o that often, do you?" Noam asked the callous girl in front of him as he watched Hadhi go. He was suddenly amazed at his ability to mask the rage boiling within. One second Hadhi, had been happy, and alive, and startlingly beautiful— then her sister spoke, and she was dull and defeated.

"Don't worry about her," Asha said lightly. "Hadhi simply does not know how to be happy."

"Then perhaps someone as happy as you should teach her," Noam countered.

Last night it had disturbed him that Hadhi had not defended her sister from her mother. It reminded him of his older brother, Ethan. But watching them together, Noam could see that there were layers of resentment to this relationship, far beyond those that had been a part of his own with his brother. Ethan loved Noam; he just didn't know what to do with their father's resentment. But here...Noam saw from Hadhi's sister the same sorts of resentments that Hadhi carried, though perhaps none of the anguish.

There was something familiar about the girl, the way she spoke, her ease with him. He knew her; he simply could not place how. Which made no sense. They could only have met last night, and she had not been present at the ball. But though he wanted to throttle her for the way she was treating her sister, his smile was in place, his tone was light, he was...like Hadhi's mother.

How did Hadhi know him so well, so quickly, and not know him at all? She laughed when he called her beautiful, like it was all a part he played. Did she honestly not see he was different with her? If she didn't, why the kiss?

He still felt the warmth of her lips brushing his. It could hardly be called a kiss that, too innocent, too quick, and too *tame*. Especially from Hadhi.

She was quiet, and she was less than joyful, but she was anything but tame. He'd bet his life on it.

"It's so odd," Asha spoke again, examining him closely. "I have to know, how it happened?"

"What?" Noam asked at a loss.

"How did the most sour-faced girl in Maltuba find a friend in such a light-hearted man?"

"You've known me all of one minute."

"I'm an excellent judge of character," she dismissed, flirtatiously wiggling her brows at him.

"Your assessment of your sister says otherwise."

"*Ooo.*" She said pityingly, like one would to an injured child. "You really like her. You must tell me now. Or I will think she has put a hex on you."

"Your sister is a kind, welcoming young lady. I simply do not understand your treatment of her."

Asha shrugged, "she isn't your half-sister. Come, share the story. I need to leave before Mzaa Jauhar sends Nuru after me, but I really must know how she tricked you into thinking she's kind?"

"By being so."

"Asha, hurry," Sabra called out.

"Ugh. You really are the worst storyteller I've ever met." Asha grumbled.

"I..." Noam opened his mouth to respond, but the girl was already rushing around the house without so much as a goodbye, and Noam was struck again by that feeling of familiarity.

Where did he know her from? There was something about her that tickled the back of his mind, but he could not put a finger on what.

He was glad he had recommended to Daniel that Sabra ought to have a camel since she was carrying a baby. Otherwise, he would have rushed out to follow them. He would have left his camel with the others just for a few minutes more with Hadhi. For the chance to make her smile again.

Last night he'd decided not to pursue her. It was the most unnerving moment of his life. He'd pulled her hand gently from her lips so he could truly see her real, full smile. And he'd felt the most intense hunger overtake him. Not just desire. *Need.* A sudden, painful feeling that standing before him was the sort of woman who could fill his life. Someone he could love, who could love him back. Someone who would take his side and share the quiet with him. It was utterly terrifying. He'd only known her a few hours. Not even that! They'd barely spoken, and he felt a hunger for love and attention like he hadn't felt since he left home. He wanted her to want him, to know him. And he knew the sort of pain and loss of self that came from devoting all your time to trying to win someone's love...so it was better just to be friendly with her. Better to help her fail to catch his friend, who most certainly didn't intend to stay here. At least that way, he could be near her, and he could make her unwanted task a bit less of a chore.

That was what he'd decided. And he should stick to that decision. But there she'd been, again, looking forlorn and all alone, and he'd wanted to be near her. It needed to stop because the more he was with her, the less he cared about her family and their need of a prince, and the more he wanted Hadhi. He wanted to be the one to make her smile. He wanted to be the only one to discover just how wild she was. He wanted to be the place she went to that made her happy.

Noam glanced back at her home, two conjoined conical domes with a pattern that reminded him of woven baskets embossing the walls. It was so different from everything he'd known, but Hadhi, her feelings that he understood entirely. *To be happy would be to go somewhere else.* He used to feel that. Before he met Azize, before he found a way to leave that place and most of its pains behind him.

Noam had only been allowed into the main room of Hadhi's home, with its lamps tucked into nooks on the walls and rugs and cushions on the floor for seating. He'd stood inside and been charmed by the closeness of the space, the warmth of the lights and the homy rugs. He'd thought of his own home in Glen Harrow with its stiff walls, the same bench sat in his living room as graced every home in the city. The walls were built the same, the curtains, the beds—everything was the same. Noam was the only thing that was different. The only thing that stood out.

Noam saw a flash of his sister, with her chin notch up defiantly as she was marched into the town square for public discipline and sighed. He had not been the only one that stood out. But Noam felt, and his father had made similar feelings plain as well, that Shiraz would have been able to fit in, had Noam not been her brother. She would not have it any other way, as she was proud to say repeatedly, the only thing that should change was the place. But Noam wondered if things would have been any different for them here. It was saddening to realize that every land, no matter how diverse and colorful, held some soul who did not feel welcome.

Noam walked around the house to join the other men. They had several hours to kill with the amount of time it would take Azize to get through the line. They had not, as they said, come out here specifically to see this family. They'd examined the exterior of the palace this morning and were heading out to a cliff one local suggested as a good place to observe the vast dunes of Ether. It was beautiful, lonely and entirely compelling. Then Noam had seen Hadhi.

"What kept you?" Kane asked lightly.

"Just looking around." Noam lied. By all accounts, Kane was Azize's earliest traveling companion and *friend,* but since arriving in Maltuba Kane's entire attitude had altered.

Noam didn't like the way Kane spoke to Hadhi at dinner last night. Hadhi had seemed shy and a bit uncomfortable with Azize. Hesitant and awkward when she spoke, and that smile looked like she had to carve it on. Then Kane whispered to her. Noam couldn't hear his words, but he felt Hadhi growing tight, and angry and Kane kept laughing. It bothered Noam even before he knew her.

"What now? Should we start walking back or head into the desert and let it take us," Omar joked.

"I'm not quite ready to give up on this life," Daniel remarked. "Anyway, it is meant to be an honor to suffer for ladies."

They all laughed, but Kane also shook his head. "Only if you mean to have a reward from her."

"What, none of them suit you?" Daniel asked, his tone light.

"The little one is too young, her mother too old," Kane listed their defaults. "The second wife too shy, and Asha entirely too loud. What say you Noam, should I take pity on the scarred one?"

"I doubt Hadhi needs anyone's pity," Noam said, striving for playful.

He supposed if his friends had asked last night, Noam would have given pity as his reason for dancing with Hadhi. But it would have been a lie. He'd gone to her to satisfy his curiosity about those intense eyes and that toothy smile. He loved unsettling her. Loved the way the lights that looked like anger in her eyes transformed when he caught her in a lie, and he could see that there really was depth to her. He'd examined those telling eyes of hers as they spoke, she could say two words and open up corridors to her soul, and every open corridor was lined with...sorrow.

Then Hadhi, the girl who did not know how to smile, and hated a lie, took up Noam's side, without even an hours worth of acquaintance. She was enraged on his behalf, wanted to comfort him. It was the sweetest thing he'd ever experienced. It touched him so much that for the first time since his mother died Noam felt truly himself. Free to love his father, or to hate him, free to let go of his past or resent it, it didn't matter what he did, this near stranger would take his side. He wanted her to feel the same. Better even, he wanted her to know she was loved in her own home, as he rarely had been.

He wanted to show her how to kiss. Noam recalled the expression on her face after her lips touched his. As though she was so proud of herself, so impressed. He wanted to see that look again.

As they started back towards the palace, Omar and Masahiro launched into a discussion about architecture, but Kane was still smiling at Noam, knowingly. Noam should be careful. Not just for himself, but for Hadhi. He didn't know these people, but it was clear Kane did. And what he knew he was keeping to himself, except to taunt Hadhi. What had he been saying to her earlier? How did he know her?

Noam should *just be friendly*. He didn't know what deeper pains waited for Hadhi here if she followed him into some misstep, he would not see. He couldn't let his presence be what caused her harm. He should...help Hadhi try to snare his best friend. Azize was a good man; he would take care of her. If indeed he stayed. Of course there was a very good chance Hadhi would not win, whether the mystery woman showed up or not. But if Noam had helped her, done his best to see she married her prince, then Hadhi was bound to be grateful. Wasn't she? Bound to smile at least once more, only for him.

Zawadi waited until the women left on their borrowed camels and walked out from the road to the river carrying buckets of water and dressed up in Emu's skin. Well, Emu's skin with a bit more height. She fit in better here, having been born on the continent of Ether, someway to the south in the grassy plains. A fairy of the earth, she had hated heights. Was the only fey among the flock whose bird form could not take to the air, but it never slowed her path to those in need. Such a good soul she was—had been.

Zawadi made to pass the men, pretending to bend slightly from the weight of the water on her shoulders and keeping her head down as though not to disturb the strangers. They were talking about their friend as she approached them.

"It seems a mistake to agree to his father's plan to try the shoe on all the women if he doesn't mean to stay," Omar remarked.

"It seems a mistake to seek the woman at all if he doesn't mean to stay," Noam replied in a nearly dark tone. Zawadi had never felt a thing but light from him as they traveled. She shifted nearer to Noam first, as he was at the back of the party walking towards the city.

The closer she drew, the more she could feel. Magic rolled off of him in waves, not his own. He didn't seem to be magical. Curse magic and blessed magic swirling together in his makeup, trying to balance themselves. How intriguing. Magic owed him a debt and it meant to repay it. Zawadi felt around its edges and her magic paid less and less attention to the other men as she tried to understand this one, but before she could complete her study of him a violent shout of flames tore her attention away.

"What makes any of you think he means ever to leave?" Kane said in a bright, amused voice. But there was fire inside him that belied his tone. Rage and anger and resentment. Zawadi was pulled nearer like a moth to a flame. He lived and breathed vengeance, this man. "This is his home. Here he can be powerful and fawned after. Everything he wants, he can have."

So much of him was painted in the angry brushstrokes of the man who'd trained him. Just like Hadhi. Was this another of Zuberi's children? Did he have a secret family? Why? He could easily have brought home another wife.

No. No. He was not the man's blood, but he was—

"Madam," Noam's soft voice invaded Zawadi's consciousness. She opened her eyes and found that all of the men had stopped walking to close in around her.

She dropped the buckets in false fear and stumbled backwards. Daniel caught her. She could feel his life through the sudden contact. Listless and heartbroken and empty now. He clung to Azize like a purpose in life. Satisfied that he was no threat, Zawadi jumped out of his arms.

"We won't harm you. Here." Noam stepped forward, easily lifting the branch and restringing the buckets on either end. Zawadi pretended fear, looking away, and her eyes fell on the man she'd come to investigate.

He smirked. Some might think that lovely tilt of those perfectly shaped lips and the expanding of his sparkling irises was a smile, but it was a smirk. A smirk Zawadi was well familiar with. If it were not for the fact that she didn't believe in ghosts, she would think she saw Zuberi before her. An actual shiver raced down her spine.

"Jobah iziqi, tiou, kup jatomara ur nong onguddi pathull." Kane spoke in a soft voice using the Maltuban tongue. *Run home, mouse, the lions are not hungry today.*

Zawadi's focus on the man sharpened. *Mouse.*

Zawadi was unnerved, not by the man's taunt, but his recognition of the people Emu had been born to. The Teazou, were a group of ground fairy, small by most fairy standards, they maintained a pacifistic lifestyle, living in the grasslands south of Ether. The Bor, who lived near them, had called them Tiou, *mouse*, because it sounded similar to their name and because they were so small. When Emu came to the order, she'd been fleeing her home, under attack by humans who knew how to kill the fey. She was trying to protect her daughter, *Kiwi,* and found them a new family in the process.

For all the good that flight had done them. Zawadi stared into this man's eyes a moment longer. Wondering if Emu and Kiwi had escaped one attack by Zuberi only to be brutally destroyed in another, two years later. This man had most certainly been a student of Zuberi. What all had he done for him? Did he recognize only the type of fairy she was? Or had he seen Emu's face before? Just how long had Zuberi spent planning his attack?

"What does that mean?" Noam asked tightly, watching Kane suspiciously.

"That she is perfectly safe." Kane lied with a lovely grin.

"I'd no idea you spoke Maltuban so well," Daniel said brightly. "You should teach us all some."

Kane laughed. "I thought you didn't expect to be here for long."

Zawadi ignored the byplay as the others began to respond. Latching onto the branch, she stretched the buckets across her shoulders and made to run by the men, brushing Kane's arm as she did.

From within him, she heard a chorus of pained screams. His, as well as other's. She felt such heat. Smelled the stench of death. Then she felt a soothing flap of wings and a peaceful coo. *Dove*.

Zawadi ran from the men before they could try to stop her. She ran to the outskirts of Jaccada and left the buckets of water by the side of a home. Slipping behind it, she ran out again in a new body. Kiwi's body. She couldn't let those men find her again, but she needed to know more.

Something was very wrong with Kane. He was touched by magic. By Dove's magic. And there was as much punishment in that touch as there was blessing. Something was very wrong with him indeed.

COMPETITION

Asha couldn't help watching her half-sister as they *rode* to the capitol palace. Sabra was becoming quite the useful family member. Twice now, they'd been lent camels because she was a new mother. Asha hadn't noticed motherhood affecting Sabra's ability to walk, but it was useful, so she felt no need to comment. What really puzzled her was how Hadhi attracted such a friendly man. It made no sense. It made even less sense than realizing the man Asha had danced with, tempted, and played with had been *Azize*. Had he changed so much? Perhaps all it took was seeing the world.

Asha was anxious to see him again, anxious to know if she had been right about him last night or as a girl. He was looking for her, had set up an entire ball, simply to find her. That said something.

But what?

Asha had planned to take the second slipper out of its hiding place with Baba's things, but when she snuck into Jauhar's room this morning, it was missing. If Jauhar had found it and knew it was Asha who had come to the ball, Asha surely would have heard about it. Asha was terrified that it being missing meant that the magic had faded away, and Azize would not have his slipper either. She had been calling and calling, every moment she got alone, she called for Zawadi, but the nymph had not come. Now Asha would not be going to the ball as the woman Azize had known. Nor would she have her other slipper to prove herself. What if he didn't like the ordinary Asha?

Her eyes darted to Hadhi again. Hadhi's stiff, unyielding back, to be more specific. She said Noam had heard bad things of Asha from the prince. It wasn't precisely surprising. Asha hadn't liked him either, but it was a bit scary.

It shouldn't be. She had no great desire to marry a prince. But he wasn't just a prince, was he? He had seen the world. He was not content with Maltuba alone. He had stories that took her with him. He made Asha hungry, like Zawadi's magic. And he loved her.

She needed him to...give her a chance. She needed his love.

"What bad stories?" Asha burst out, into the near-silent traveling party, startling Lin awake. He screeched, and four angry pairs of eyes swung Asha's way. She shrugged, just barely catching the pleasure that darted across Hadhi's face.

Sabra lay her lips right next to his ear as she urged her mount on ahead of the group.

Nuru looked like she was falling asleep on her camel.

Jauhar glared at Asha as though ready to kill her for the tiny offense. "Do try to act as though you were taught a little decorum when you are in the king's presence." She snapped and urged her camel ahead as well.

Hadhi kept her pace, waiting. She knew what Asha was asking, and the malicious smile at the corner of her lips said she meant to have fun with it.

"Well," Asha prompted.

Hadhi only smiled. "Well what?"

"What did the prince have to say to make me infamous?" Asha ground out.

Hadhi shrugged. "I do not know exactly. Something about you being a pest. Seemed pleased that you were not at the ball."

"Oh." Asha wasn't sure how to take this. A pest? Well, she was a child, and he was hardly sweet. Surely the past was something they could forget. "Did he speak of me often?" Asha asked, oddly hopeful. Even if it had not been well, leaving a lasting impression on a man was a good thing.

"Now you want a prince?" Hadhi demanded coldly.

"It is not as though you will catch his attention," Asha fired back, perhaps unkindly.

Usually saying such things would not disturb Asha. Hadhi had no love for her. Why should Asha put an effort into loving her half-sister. But Noam's words and Sabra's played at the back of her mind and made her notice things she rarely did, like the glisten of tears in Hadhi's glaring eyes before she looked away.

"I already have his attention," Hadhi remarked.

Asha laughed. "Now you are the mystery woman? Try to impress me with better lies."

"That woman left at midnight," Hadhi snarled. "I did not. I am not the only one with his attention. But *you*." Hadhi looked her half-sister up and down critically. "Have only his...dislike."

Hadhi stuck her nose in the air and continued on, she made no effort to pass Asha, but it was clear she would speak no more. Asha was struck again by how odd it was that Noam, a very nice man, if a poor storyteller, should like Hadhi at all.

Asha *had tried* to befriend her when they were young. Several times. But Hadhi never wanted a thing to do with Asha.

"You cannot sneak into the palace. It is guarded. You will be punished," Hadhi had informed Asha coldly. Asha was about ten, making Hadhi fifteen, and already well on her way to being the most sour woman in Maltuba, yet still, Asha tried to make them sisters in truth.

"I know the way around them," Asha explained. "Baba showed me. Let's go see the menagerie. They have a foreign beast!"

"Have Baba show you, when he comes home. It is not safe." That was her favorite thing to say. Nothing was safe if Hadhi was to be believed.

"Come on, it will be fun," Asha begged.

"You are not going, Asha. If you try, I will tell Mzaa, and you will be cleaning with the servants for a month."

It always ended the same. Threats and tattling and Asha's joy ruined. Sabra was wrong; Hadhi had been offered adventure; she just preferred to be unhappy and to make everyone around her unhappy too.

Asha and Hadhi did not speak for the remainder of the journey. When they reached the capitol building, Asha was unsurprised to see many a woman had the same plan as Mzaa Jauhar. There was a line at the doors of the palace at least twenty women long. They dismounted and Hadhi led all five camels to one of the servants at the side of the palace. Jauhar nodded to the line, glaring at Asha as though it had been she and not her own daughter who held them up.

Asha planted her hands on her hips and looked away, waiting for the doors to open. Waiting for the sight of him. Perhaps it had all been the work of the magic. Perhaps she had not even liked him as much as she thought. But the fluttering wings in her stomach at only the thought of seeing him said otherwise.

Hadn't she loved making him chase her down the halls? Hadn't she been charmed by how pampered he was? Delighted by the bright wildness of his eyes? And near desperate for his lips on her own?

Azize had grown up. She liked him as a man, in ways she would never have imagined liking him as a boy. He was adventure. And Asha meant to have him.

But she was not the only one. Who would have thought Hadhi would be interested?

Behind them, the line began to stretch. If they did not open the doors soon, it might reach into Ether before long. They had been standing in line for near twenty minutes, women, silent, chattering, young old, fat, thin, with child....it was endless the types and the looks, they emerged from all around to take their place in the line. All for Azize. The more she saw, the more Asha's stomach churned. She would have no chance would she? He would see only the girl of her childhood and hate her. And one of these... greedy, ugly women, like Hadhi, would claim Azize in the absence of Zawadi's magic.

Silently Asha begged whatever power existed in the universe to send the woman to her, to give her magic, so she could claim her prince. And rescue him from all these vultures.

There was a little girl, perhaps seven, hanging by her knees from a branch of an old tree across from Asha. She swung back and forth, smiling knowingly, her eyes all for Asha. With a giggle, she let her hands trail the ground and hummed to herself as she swung, Asha had never heard the song before, but it was familiar.

Asha started forward curious and hopeful.

"Where do you think you're going?" Jauhar snapped, yanking hard on Asha's elbow.

"Over to the tree for a moment." Asha yanked her arm back.

"All of us would like the shade; you are not special. You will wait."

"I am not going for shade. I want to speak to the little girl," Asha protested.

"Your father is no longer here to spoil you. You will stand with your sisters as he should have made you since birth. And be grateful I allow your presence here."

"I am going to speak to the girl. Not because my father thought I was special, but because you cannot stop me," Asha said with calm superiority. "You do not allow my presence here, the king demands it."

Asha stomped off through the dust, feeling Jauhar's glare drilling into her. More even, she thought she felt Hadhi's and Nuru's glares as well. Their jealously would not stop her; she was special. Baba knew it; that was why he sent Zawadi to her. Only to her. Sabra's words wouldn't stop her either. She knew nothing of how this family had tortured Asha. She owed them nothing.

The girl did not stop swinging when Asha reached her, but she stopped humming. "Ready to rule are you?" She asked playfully, and Asha knew at once she was right. This was Zawadi, in a new form again.

"Please, you must help me."

"I said one wish," Zawadi said in a playfully tempting voice.

"I know." Asha nodded vigorously as she prepared to beg. "I do, but he will not know me as I look."

"I cannot help you forever. It will wear on you. Make you hunger," she spoke in a joyful sing-song voice that sent a chill racing up Asha's spine. "Make you crave. And then, when it all but fills you up with power and knowledge and life—then it will *rip* life from you. Pulling you apart in all directions."

"I don't care." Asha shook off the chill; she needed the magic. "If I am not in there, he may marry one of them."

"The women who come as they are?" She teased and swung back towards the tree quickly. Grabbing on with her hands, she swung around the branch, freeing her knees, and landed on her feet in the dust. Just watching it made Asha dizzy, but the girl just smiled, revealing the gap of her two front teeth.

"I...I am not lying to him. I promise I will tell him. But he will not give me a chance as I am now. He hated me as a girl."

Zawadi bobbed her head this way and that. "He was a boy then. Now he is a man, and you are lovely. Generally, all a man needs to forgive is a glance at loveliness. You knew this last night."

Asha did know that. But her stomach churned with fear that Zawadi meant to refuse her. An ordinary man would forgive almost anything for a bit of beauty, and Asha knew she was beautiful. But, her gaze found the line, there was a great deal of ugliness among them, but there was plenty of beauty as well.

He had no reason to forgive her when the world was full of lovely women who had done nothing to alienate him. Hadhi thought she already had his attention. What if she was right?

"I cannot risk it. What if he likes one of them better? Is there nothing to be done?"

"I don't know," child Zawadi tilted her head back and forth as though this were a game she was playing. "The king has ordered you there, and I cannot transform you where so many can see? What do you propose?"

Asha looked again at the line of glaring women. Jauhar watched her with enraged eyes, and her half-sisters looked resentful. Even the other women looked angry at Asha, for the moment at least free from the heat. They were only jealous that they had not thought of it first. But even for something so small most of them would enjoy finding revenge. "Could you not meet me inside? After I have gone through the line, I will slip away so the king can have nothing to say."

"I might be able to," Zawadi said slowly, like she were one of Baba's friends, waiting for payment before promising help.

"Please, Zawadi," Asha begged. "Hadhi has already caught his attention, and she will be—"

"She has certainly caught someone's attention." Zawadi interrupted with a giggle. Asha spun to face her half-sister just in time to see the group of men who'd lent them the camels walking by. Noam was at the back of the group, and as he passed Hadhi, he reached out casually and squeezed Hadhi's fingers. It was only for a moment, but Hadhi's eyes grew wide, and her features softened into a sweet smile, and Asha would swear her half-sister's fingers climbed through the air after Noam's.

"But... she said—"

"I will meet you inside. This all looks too fun to resist." Zawadi smirked, climbing back into the tree. Just before she would start swinging, she paused. "Have you ever seen your sister before this day, daughter of Zuberi?

I think not. It is often the way with sisters. But I wonder, did you ever care to meet her?" She waited a long moment for a response, but Asha had no idea what to say. "Perhaps you should use the magic for more than just capturing a prince."

The Song of the Nymph
I am midnight and laughter and adventure.
I am a life embraced.
I am the darkness banished.
I am daybreak and music and wonder.
I am a love claimed.
I am desire—manifest.
You who dwell in the twilight
Longing ever to be whole,
Look upon me and marvel
I am the answer to your eager soul.
I am drought and desolation and hunger.
I am your greed chased.
I am the quiet defeated.
I am storm and rage and danger.
I am a hope abandoned.
I am desire, void of thought.

THE TRICK AND THE TRICKSTER

THE LURE OF MAGIC

Noam found Azize staring out his window, on the top floor of the capitol palace, looking at the line of women awaiting him. Noam stood back and watched his friend a minute.

Azize hadn't slept much last night. Noam was not surprised; Azize tended to have nightmares when he was on dry land. And here, in the place where the nightmares were born, it would be so much worse.

Why were they here? Since his mother's death, Azize had spoken of this place as though he would only return after his father had died. Noam supposed it could be that Azize felt safer with Hadhi's father dead. Zuberi was one of the monsters that haunted the prince's dreams. But his own father was the other. And Enzi was very much alive. Noam wondered if perhaps they'd come because, as much as Azize denied it, he wanted his father's love and approval. Noam understood that confusing aspect of love very well. But fortunately, he had left that behind to travel with Azize and found such wonders to take its place.

Two days ago, they'd been on the deck of a ship, with this nation coming into view, and Noam had felt intrigued and excited. It was the same sort of bubbling interest he'd felt at each new land they encountered. Perhaps it was a bit special, because this was Azize's home, but overall he'd just felt the same *certainty* that this was a new world for him to love. Noam had yet to encounter a land where he could not find something to love, or to inspire him. But two days ago, he hadn't expected it to be any different than any other land they'd visited. And Noam had been wrong.

This place was special. It was making Noam reconsider himself and the things he'd always known to be true. Azize used to tell Noam stories of his Maltuba, stories full of anger and fear. He knew Azize had spent his whole life feeling guilty for terrible things his father did and fearing that when he became king, he would have to do equally terrible things. Azize wished he'd never been born a prince. He believed any circumstance was better. And Noam had always felt sorry for him, never fully understanding the fears perhaps, but sympathizing with the pain.

Noam looked over his friend's shoulder now, to the array of women lining up one at a time in the sun, waiting for Azize to look at them. How many of them knew, as Hadhi seemed to, that this was pointless and Azize never meant to come home permanently? Noam wondered if Azize would even go outside.

As Noam wondered that, Azize pulled out the slipper and held it before him.

He would stay to find her. But what then? A woman like the one who'd led Azize and half the men at the ball around all night, just because she wanted to be entertained, if she really was the nymph she claimed to be, she might not even come. She'd had plenty of entertainment last night. What would he do if he didn't find her?

"Admiring the banquet your father has laid for you?" Noam teased from behind his friend, surprised he'd been able to stand behind him so long without Azize noticing.

Azize spun around wide-eyed. "No," he said in shock. "Thinking of running away actually."

Noam smirked but didn't say a thing to that as he walked forward.

"Why did I agree to this? Any one of them may fit this." Azize cradled the shoe before him.

Noam looked at it out of the corner of his eye uncomfortably. He knew the woman was most likely just some clever girl sneaking into a party in disguise. She had made a point of not going near any of the other citizens of Maltuba. But Noam didn't like the idea of his friend being manipulated by magic.

"Even if I find her," Azize went on, squeezing the slipper tighter and tighter, unaware that Noam was a bit distracted himself. "My father made me swear to try it on every single one of them."

"I should think they deserve at least that for having waited all day in the sun," Noam said with a slightly appalled laugh. Azize could not seriously believe it was alright to force all of these women here, just so he could find one woman, and then expect them to turn happily around and go home once he found her. Could he? Well...he thought every circumstance better than his own.

"I might not even see her for more than a moment," Azize said low, and perhaps afraid.

Noam sighed sympathetically. Azize was always afraid of something, and now that Noam had seen him in his home, he thought he might have been wrong all these years, assuming Azize was most afraid of his father. Azize was afraid of doing the wrong thing. He didn't trust his own instincts. And the girl he'd spent the night obsessed with, the whirlwind of excitement and power and confidence, she was the sort of girl Azize would be more than willing to follow. He was following her already. She had left the slipper, and now Azize was bringing the world to him, in order to find her.

It was clever of Enzi to force Azize to try the shoe on every woman. It would force Azize to see them all. His people. It would force him to speak to each one of them and have a chance to see if any of them had an equally magnetic power. It made Noam wonder anew if the woman wasn't some fantasy employed by the king to trick his son into staying. Many kings made alliances with sorcerers to help them keep their thrones.

What was it Hadhi had said? That they viewed any power *not their own* as a threat. Maybe he had forced some magical being to serve him.

"Do you see your siren among them?" Noam asked carefully, trying to nudge Azize into seeing the possibility all on his own.

"Not yet, but the line stretches so far who could say." Azize growled the words. His hand tightened again around the slipper.

Noam reached out and lay a hand over his friends. "How often do you touch it? Once a minute? More?" Noam asked intensely, and Azize truly took notice of him for the first time since Noam entered the room. "The magic will crawl inside you, brother. Take a bit of space from it."

"Why do you distrust magic?" Azize yanked his hand back suspiciously.

Noam smiled a bit bitterly, seeing his friend's expression. Whatever magic the shoe had was working already, wasn't it? Azize had never mistrusted Noam before.

"What do you really know of me, brother?" Noam asked. "I know your mother and father from your stories. I know what foods you have a taste for.

I know you sleep best on the water. I know your darkest nightmares and your brightest wishes. I have called you brother and treated you as such for years, but to the world, it seems that you are a prince, and I am the clown you allow near."

"Noam, I do not..." Azize began, looking contrite.

Noam laughed. "Do not worry. I have no concerns over my treatment. I ask because you have known me nearly four years and have not once asked what drove *me* from home."

"I assumed you would speak of it if you had need." Azize stiffened, offended.

"And you were right. Had I a need, I would speak." Noam looked off out the window. No, not off, down.

His eyes fell through the air and landed on a particular swath of purple and orange silk, wrapped loosely around a head and shoulders to keep off the sun. Hadhi. As if she could feel him watching, she lifted her head and looked up at the palace. She wasn't smiling; her eyes were so serious, so impatient. It made Noam smile. But his mind drifted over what he wanted to say to Azize, and he realized he had perhaps needed to speak of it for years, but hadn't known how. Hadhi showed him how. Noam could speak of it now, because his past, and his pain had taught him things that others needed to hear.

"My father never loved me," Noam said softly, his eyes still trained on Hadhi's lovely impatient face. "He *could not* love me, because I was the result of a magic spell put upon him by a former lover. As she and her child died, she cursed him that his wife would bear a child not his own and that he must raise him and keep his wife, but never escape the shame."

"I...I am sorry." Azize said, sounding vaguely disgusted, though if it was about the curse itself or his father's reaction to it, Noam couldn't say.

"It was long ago, and nothing can alter it now. I do not speak now because I need comforting, but because you are right, I do not trust magic. It is manipulation, cold and destructive." Noam waved out the window with a smile of utter disbelief on his face.

"Look at them. Hundreds of women, sweltering in the sun, waiting for you to look upon them. Yes, many are doing this happily for the chance to marry a prince. But many were forced by your father. And all of them, wait there, angrily or happily, but honestly, and all as the result of the one *dishonest* woman you want. They have all already lost, and for what reason? Because they did not pretend to be other than they are and tease you into the night?"

"I have never seen you so serious," Azize said at a loss. "Are you alright?"

Noam smiled, fighting the urge to look for Hadhi again. "I am well, brother. Thank you for your concern. I only worry for you. I would not have you manipulated by magic. Perhaps she is everything you say; I truly hope so. But—be sure—before you give your heart away and are trapped with her forever."

"I will," Azize promised.

Noam nodded once and backed from the room. But from the way Azize watched him go, Noam would wager that he didn't have as much of his friend's trust as he used to. Had Azize only trusted Noam because he took his part in all things? It hadn't seemed so before.

Noam waited nearby until he saw his friend draw in a deep breath and march out towards the line, then Noam moved out of the shadow beneath the stairs and walked to the window. His eyes found Hadhi immediately. All around her, the other women had abandoned their orderly line and were standing in groups chatting, laughing, fanning themselves. Hadhi stood, a boulder bisecting a river, unmoved, gazing straight at the castle, like her gaze alone could bring out the prince. His hand tingled from where their fingers had brushed as they passed. There was something about her. He couldn't explain it for the life of him. It was desire and compulsion and so much he couldn't explain. The more he saw of her, the more he needed to. The more he knew of her, the more he admired her. She *consumed* his world.

The other women jumped apart, lining up in front, or behind Hadhi, and her gaze shifted slowly to the ground floor where Azize must be. Perhaps Noam had been too harsh with Azize about the slipper. Noam was beginning to understand what a powerful lure magic was.

Hadhi had surely wrapped a spell around him.

THE SLIPPER TEST

Jauhar ground her teeth watching her husband's favorite daughter playing in the shade with a child Jauhar did not recognize. She reached a hand into her pocket and squeezed the infernal shoe Asha had hidden among her things.

Jauhar had a feeling the girl Asha was playing with was some sort of magical creature. And the looks she kept casting Jauhar's way seemed to confirm it. Jauhar was uncertain what to do. The king had ordered that Asha be at the ball. And if Jauhar were to expose her for the fraud she was, there was a great chance that Azize would forgive all and ask for her hand.

Jauhar would not allow that. She twisted the shoe, its beads crunching against one another in her hidden palm. Asha, unlike Jauhar's own daughters, was skilled in handling men.

But she didn't think Asha understood women. Look at her now, probably begging that creature for more magical assistance. It was a mistake. If she had known Zuberi, she was not here to offer kindnesses.

Zuberi and Enzi both hated beings of magic for very different reasons. Enzi because their existence threatened his belief in his own divinity. And Zuberi because he had no respect for beings who possessed power without earning it.

"Have you not learned enough about them yet?" Jauhar asked from outside of her husband's bedroom, as he prepared to leave. He didn't like anyone inside his room without invitation. Even when they'd lived in the hut, he kept his own space that none could touch.

"Nearly. I just need to know how much they feel. How fast I shall have to move."

Jauhar nodded. "And she has not guessed your intent yet?"

Zuberi laughed. Crossing to the doorway, he took Jauhar's face in his hands, pressing his lips to hers for a hungry kiss. "No one is as clever as you, ethuri. No one else has ever known me so well." He laughed and turned away so quickly Jauhar nearly fell forward at the loss of his passions. But years of such shifts in mood had trained her to keep her footing, to hide any feeling he did not want to see. "Be careful you don't make any wishes of strangers though." He tossed a causal smile over his shoulder. "They'll kill you with your own desire."

Jauhar should let Asha go on wishing. If that creature was here for vengeance over something Zuberi had done, she would surely kill Asha.

But what if Asha, so magnetic like her father, had simply found the magic she'd always wanted?

"It's alright," Sabra was assuring her son, with a bit of desperation in her voice. Lin had been fussing for several minutes. She'd tried to feed him, but he wanted none of it. He was bored, like the rest of them, and he was hot.

Jauhar cast one last withering glare at Asha, the cause of all this nonsense, then turned to Sabra.

"Come, my dear, let me hold him a moment. Go rest in the shade with Asha."

"Oh, I couldn't." Sabra said at once, her eyes darted around her, shyly. Nuru rolled her eyes.

"Go, Sabra," Oni called from in front of them. "We shall go in shifts."

Behind them, little Arya laughed. "It makes no difference how neatly we wait. None of us is the woman the prince is seeking."

Several women laughed, some groaned. And Jauhar saw enough mothers casting their laughing daughters dark glares to know that like her own daughters, none of these girls would be allowed to abandon their quest to win the prince.

"Who do you think she was?" Nuru asked Arya.

Nuru's friend shrugged. "I've never seen her before."

"Me neither," Koffi, Arya's mother, joined the conversation, stepping out of line.

"Where is Ayinde?" Nuru whispered to her friend.

Jauhar and Koffi exchanged amused looks. How many more years would Nuru be with Jauhar before she married and started a family of her own? It seemed likely that Ayinde would be her spouse. He was very fond of Nuru. Jauhar had only been two years older than Nuru was now when she married. But Nuru seemed too young, even if Ayinde was a sweet boy.

Zuberi would not have allowed Ayinde and Nuru to marry. The boy was destined to take religious orders, and Zuberi had not respected men who allowed higher powers any say in their lives. He made his own destiny, and only respected men who did the same. But Kafil would like that Ayinde was sweet. Jauhar did not mind that herself. Hadhi would protect her sister, Nuru did not need a husband to do so.

"Men don't have to try on the slipper," Arya rolled her eyes.

"Lucky," Nuru muttered and the girls giggled together.

"He'll join us later if I fit the slipper," Arya went on. "He is in the palace already. Whenever Baba doesn't need him, Ayinde goes to the palace to apprentice for the vaashta."

"He's already made an offering and been accepted?" Nuru demanded in shock.

"He's only been accepted as an apprentice," Koffi said soothingly. "It will be years before one of the gods accepts him into service."

"He is well-favored," Jauhar said kindly. "Few young men are even accepted to apprentice."

Jauhar watched Nuru nod along, pleased on her friend's behalf. She was very young. Too young to realize what Koffi was saying: that if Nuru were to be his wife, there would be many years when she was alone as he studied. Years when she would have to provide for the family, and well enough to make more offerings for her husband. Jauhar doubted it even occurred to Nuru to imagine such a thing might have anything to do with her. She was still innocent enough to think of him only as her friend. Soon all of that would change. Too soon.

Sabra hadn't taken Jauhar's advice, but as the other women moved out of line, she took her son out of his sling and let him play on the ground. All around, the women began to relax, but not Hadhi. She stood precisely where she had been. Jauhar wanted to criticize her for never being able to bend, but she restrained any comment; there was always reason to criticize Hadhi. Nuru's insistence that Hadhi needed her mother to tell her she was desirable played at the back of Jauhar's mind and made her sorry she'd forgotten to give her the silk Lolia had made her.

Koffi interrupted Jauhar's thoughts. "I've asked every neighbor; none of us knows her. Salama thinks she might be one of the women from Imara's tribe, trying and to trick Azize into overthrowing his father and allowing all the tribes to separate again."

"One supposes with Zuberi gone, he at least has a chance," Abiola whispered from three women ahead, but managed still to be heard.

Jauhar had heard many a similar theory circulated last night. That the Tikoo and the Bor had killed her husband and were now after Enzi through the mystery woman. That the woman was fey, and the king was afraid of her. That she had killed Zuberi. All these women hissed and whispered and pretended Jauhar and her daughters could not hear. But they heard. And they would not forget. When Hadhi was their queen, all of them would be made to pay.

Koffi, though, was only theorizing about the mystery woman; if she had something to say of Zuberi, she wisely kept it to herself. And her theory was almost true. As the daughter of one of Imara's strongest fighters, Asha could easily be considered part of the Tikoo. Her mother had been Zuberi's favorite wife, not because she was beautiful, nor because she loved him. She was his favorite, because he'd *conquered* her and the army she led. Jauhar wondered what Asha would think of that story. Her father had certainly never shared the truth with her. That he and Enzi had set out to conquer more of the continent and unite them under his rule and along the way had stolen and broken and destroyed. Zuberi had fed her on his ambition, but hid its destructive power. It would shock Asha. Destroy her. Jauhar's hand tightened on the shoe. Why hadn't she told her?

"Does Zuberi's spy know who she is?" Oni asked, almost tauntingly.

Jauhar's muscles tightened at that tone. Did Oni truly think Jauhar did not know the woman had been intimate with Zuberi? He had never kept such things from Jauhar. But Jauhar pretended not to notice Oni's provocative tone. She never let the woman see the effect she had. In truth, though Jauhar knew her husband had kept spies among Azize's companions, she never knew which men they were. But she was not going to let this woman know that either.

"If Mzaa doesn't know her, no one does." Nuru dismissed casually, but Jauhar could hear the grief in her voice and anger.

Jauhar had forgotten Nuru was there a moment. She twitched, intending to pull Nuru near and comfort her, but the doors at the northern entrance to the palace were thrown open and the king emerged with his son. Jauhar shoved her feelings deep, focusing solely on the moment at hand.

"Greetings, women of Maltuba," The king intoned from the top of the capitol stairs smiling like a man before a feast. "One among you is our future queen."

A cheer went up among the women, as the king wanted. They formed back into their line without any bickering. Hadhi wasn't cheering, *of course*, Jauhar nearly slapped her on the shoulder, but she saw Azize noticing her dismissal and smiling at it.

Jauhar was completely flabbergasted. How was Hadhi being herself and attracting attention? Had Hadhi been given a wish? Jauhar's gaze darted to the grinning gap-toothed girl.

The king believed the mystery woman was fey. *The king* believed she had killed Zuberi. Other people's gossip swung through Jauhar's mind as that girl had swung from the branches of the tree. Impossible. That *thing* could not be her husband's killer. No mere woman, fey or not, could best him! Zuberi was the strongest, fiercest man in the world. The girl winked like she knew Jauhar's thoughts.

"Today, each of you will present yourself to the prince and allow him to test this slipper upon your foot. Any who fit, and your family, may join us in the capitol for a banquet," the king announced. Jauhar yanked her gaze back to the king. That woman might be fey, but she was not Zuberi's killer; she was merely trying to rile Jauhar. But like Oni before her she would fail. Jauhar would not be distracted; she would get what she deserved and deal with that woman later.

"Any who do not fit will leave by way of the garden where refreshments have been prepared. All are worthy and welcome. But I must weed such bountiful crop somehow."

Enzi spoke as though joking and, well used to their role, laughter rose up among the women, but few and far between were the faces that showed true pleasure. Jauhar wasn't sure this king knew how deeply he was hated. Zuberi always knew when he was hated. He reveled in the hatred, but Enzi seemed oblivious to the revulsion and fear cast towards him. Even his own son looked disgusted.

The king clapped his hands, and Azize stepped forward, holding out a hand for the first lady. He led her to the queen's throne, which had been brought to the top of the stairs for the occasion. Jauhar rolled her eyes. Enzi had been a student of Zuberi's manipulative talents, and bringing the queen's throne smacked of such tricks: give all the women the thrill of the queen's seat and they would happily overlook little things like being forced to wed the prince whether they wanted to or not, and that the prince didn't want any of them. Nor care enough about his dance partner to know anything, but that her foot fit a particular slipper. Jauhar had lived with that sort of manipulation for years. She was immune.

The stairs were raised high enough above the masses that even twenty women back Jauhar could see all. Every woman in line watched and strained to hear, eager for their chances or for this to be over. Every woman but Hadhi.

The first girl in line was Nuru's age, thirteen. Shivering and giggling, she sunk into the throne and closed her eyes for a moment as though praying. When she opened her eyes, Azize was kneeling on the bright green pillow before her and reaching out for her foot.

She stretched her foot forward, and Azize removed the girls shoe. His left hand reached out for the slipper displayed on a green pillow like he kneeled on, Jauhar, gripping the shoe's mate, felt the moment his hand touched the slipper. *Wasn't that interesting?*

She felt Azize's desperation that this girl not fit. The beads stretched wide on their strings as the shoe grew in her hand, and likely in Azize's hand as well.

Jauhar smiled, glad now that they were not the first in line. This was worth exploring. Could she manipulate it too?

The girl on the throne nearly kicked Azize in her haste to have the shoe on. Her tiny foot slipped into it, swallowed whole. She lifted her leg to show all it fit, but the slipper fell from her foot. Azize yanked it from the air and placed it on the pillow, failing to hide his pleasure that it had not fit.

"Ah, too bad, my dear." The king led the young girl away before she could be overcome with sadness at her failure, her eyes lingering on the throne.

It went on like this for a while. For every woman who ascended the steps, Jauhar focused all her energy into that slipper, squeezing the beads so tight that no foot could pass its entrance, or so wide a foot might swim in it like a duckling in an empty lake. And it was working! Jauhar felt her determination change the shoe—in most instances. Now and again, a beautiful woman would smile at Azize, and his attraction would warm the beads of the slipper until it fit.

The second time it happened Jauhar had to avert her gaze, so no one saw her rage. But someone had. The little girl, still swinging from the shady tree, grinned at Jauhar, displaying the wide gap in her front teeth and winked. Jauhar repressed an angry shudder. She was nothing. *Nothing!* That girl might have magic, but Jauhar had something more powerful, something she'd learned from Zuberi. She had a single-minded focus. Her daughter would be queen. Jauhar was owed.

Three women out of twenty-four had fit the slipper when Sabra climbed the steps. She carried her son in her arms with her head high, refusing to pretend to be other than she was. Jauhar was so proud of her. It would be easier to get Azize for a husband were she to hide her son, but Jauhar was proud of Sabra for presenting herself confidently.

At the sight of his boyhood love, Azize hopped to his feet and held out an arm for Sabra, smiling gently, condescendingly. Azize was no longer attracted to Sabra—another man had had her. It annoyed Jauhar that he treated Sabra like she would break, like she was an object of pity. She had been wife to the greatest man in Maltuba. She had borne his son! Sabra was a woman to be honored and desired, and cherished, never pitied.

"You look well, Sabra," Azize said gently.

Sabra smirked, recognizing his lack of desire. "You look well also. If a bit like a frog for all this up-down, up-down."

Azize laughed. Sabra leaned back, relieved after hours of standing. She took her time allowing him her foot, as a queen should, only lifting it when she was ready.

Jauhar focused all her attention on the slipper hidden in the folds of her dress. She tightened its beads as Azize slid its match over Sabra's foot, until it was a perfect fit.

Azize startled. And Sabra laughed.

"Now if only we did not both know I was not your dance partner." She teased as the king stepped forward.

"My dear, that means not a thing. He may yet marry you." The king remarked.

Sabra allowed the king to lead her away with a hand beneath her elbow. Nuru raced up the steps and was sitting on the throne before Azize even turned around. Jauhar rolled her eyes. *Nuru.* Her daughter eyed the shoe like a viper. Jauhar didn't bother to help her one way or another. Azize would never marry her.

Azize lifted her foot to slip the shoe over it, "It doesn't fit!" Nuru exclaimed, jumping up before he even had her foot halfway in. Jauhar tapped her foot a bit impatiently. But Azize and his father only laughed. Everyone laughed. Even Hadhi unbent enough to smile.

Then the king leaned in to lead Nuru away, Jauhar stiffened, and she felt Hadhi stiffening as well. Sabra had not entered the palace; she turned back to latch onto Nuru's arm.

"Oh well, no prince for you." Enzi teased Nuru. "Best wait with your Mzaa Sabra."

"Of course." Nuru agreed brightly.

Jauhar looked between Hadhi and Asha. She had intended to wait until they had both gone in to take her turn, but Hadhi couldn't go forward as stiff and edgy as she was. Jauhar sighed; she could make sure the shoe didn't fit Asha from within the palace. Hadhi's distaste for Enzi would not spoil Jauhar's plans.

Jauhar stepped up. Azize rose to help her into the throne. Jauhar gracefully slipped her foot free of her own slipper and raised it for Azize. Just a glance at the slipper showed it to be the wrong size for her foot, and she had no reason to change that. When her foot failed to pass the entrance, she did not try to shove as some had. She smiled and laid her hand on Azize's wrist in a mothering fashion.

"I was there to see you born. You are more suited to one of an age," she tilted her head gently Hadhi's way and felt her daughter sigh. It was a frustrated sigh, and she wasn't smiling, which grated at Jauhar's nerves. But there was nothing to do about it now.

Then Hadhi went a step further. When Azize's eyes touched her, she rolled her own. Azize, hid a grin. How? How was her sour attitude attracting the prince?

Enzi came forward and took Jauhar's free arm, leading her back to observe her daughter.

"You have raised the most interesting women in Maltuba, Jauhar," Enzi whispered. "I had worried about you all, in that hut, so far from the city, but you have made the most of it."

"One does what one must," Jauhar said softly, her eyes intent on Hadhi and Azize. The king, equally interested, allowed her to watch quietly.

"My turn?" Hadhi remarked without enthusiasm.

She did not wait to be seated. Showed no hesitance, nor fear, taking the seat the way Zuberi might because it was there. Jauhar could barely keep her countenance. Hadhi was nothing that was gentle or soft, nothing that was desirable. *You've been taught!* Jauhar wanted to bellow.

Hadhi removed her own shoe and held out her foot, all with a slight impatience. At the base of the steps, Asha shook her head at Jauhar to despair of Hadhi with her.

"You left abruptly last night, Hadhi. I hadn't a chance to say goodnight." Azize said as he raised the slipper.

Jauhar focused her attention on the slipper in her own pocket. Stretching it as wide as she could and infusing her determination into it, so it would fit her daughter's large foot.

Hadhi cocked up a brow at the prince. "Would you like to do so now?"

Azize chuckled and reached out for her ankle. And Jauhar felt, along with her own will, Azize's laughter warming the beads, altering the shoe. The slipper fit.

"She is coming into her own in a most impressive fashion," Enzi whispered so close to Jauhar's ear that a shudder raced down her spine. "Very *spirited.*"

Jauhar tilted her face towards the king, but could only manage a slight smile before she tore her eyes back to her daughter. Hadhi stared at the slipper disappointedly, allowing Azize to remove it. Enzi stepped forward, taking Hadhi's arm, though she looked ready to refuse.

"I shall see you at the banquet." Prince Azize looked utterly confused by Hadhi's reaction.

With her arm held by his father, Hadhi's gaze returned to Azize and she nodded briskly.

But when she spoke, her tone was light with humor. "Do you think you will be done before tomorrow?"

Azize laughed again, and before he could respond, Hadhi removed her arm from the king's and crossed into the palace.

Jauhar pretended to follow her, but ducked behind a column to wait for one last *daughter*.

"She is nothing like I remembered," Azize said aloud. Lost and intrigued —by Hadhi.

"No," Asha agreed, sounding suspicious.

Jauhar smiled to see her jealousy. She was about to be even more jealous.

Azize, clearly unaware of who he was speaking to, offered Asha his hand. She snapped out of her reverie and flashed Azize a blindingly sweet smile.

Jauhar watched the prince examine that lovely face and ground her teeth. Jauhar had no illusions; Asha was a lovely young woman. Her eyes drew one in; her soft round features spoke of innocence and friendliness. She was lively and eager, and she knew well how to smile at a man as though he was the whole world. The slipper in Jauhar's hand was already warming in preparation to change its shape. Altering from Azize's interest, and he was not even holding it yet.

"No one seems to be quite what I remembered." Asha lay her hand gently on Azize's and allowed him to lead her forward.

Jauhar was fighting with the shoe in her hand; the longer Azize and Asha lingered together, the stronger its will to mold itself on Asha's foot became. And Jauhar, who had been as shocked as anyone to see Hadhi capturing the prince's attention, Jauhar who had been wondering if Hadhi perhaps didn't need her mother's help, remembered why she had to take Hadhi in hand every minute.

Asha existed.

No matter how much notice Hadhi might get, Asha was a bright sun beside her, blinding the world to any minor light Hadhi could cast.

Azize led Asha gently to the throne, holding her gaze. When she was seated, he knelt before her. She stretched out her foot, still covered in a slipper waiting for him to do the work. Like a servant Azize did as her gaze instructed, removing the slipper with delicate care.

He reached for the magic slipper and slid it over Asha's foot, never taking his eyes from hers.

It was loose, Jauhar could feel it; her power was working, the shoe would slide off Asha's foot at any moment.

Azize smiled up at Asha. "It's a perfect fit," he said entranced.

Jauhar crushed the slipper in her hand, the beads grinding against each other with an unpleasant crackling noise. But it was nothing to the bellow sounding in her head.

Enzi came forward chuckling. "I should have known it would fit you, Asha. Where were you last night? We missed you."

"Asha?" Azize demanded, yanking the shoe to his chest angrily.

Jauhar felt a moment's vindication. At least he was regretting his foolish mouth. But it wasn't enough. She needed him to be certain she was not the woman he danced with. She needed him to want nothing to do with her. She needed Asha to know he would choose any woman but her.

"Did you not recognize her?" Enzi mocked his son.

Asha looked between the pair with innocent contrition displayed on her face. But Azize jerked away to call up the next lady, ignoring Asha completely.

Jauhar waited a few moments until she would not be noticed, then slipped into the palace.

MOST ENTERTAINING COMPETITOR OF THE DAY

ost people crammed along the veranda when they first entered to watch Azize's progress through the line. But that quickly became dull and everyone broke into groups to talk. Nuru was with a few of Azize's friends and two Spirit Dancers, Faizah and her brother Yenge. Nuru *strongly* disliked Yenge. He was nowhere near as talented as his younger sister, or really any of the other dancers, and he was rude. But he wasn't leaving Faizah's side tonight, so Nuru had to put up with him if she wanted to be near Faizah, which she did. Faizah was amazing!

There should have been entertainment. Were it not for the fact that she got to listen to Faizah talking about her favorite parts of dance Nuru would be bored out of her mind.

The vaashta were walking through the hall speaking to different mothers, as the three representatives of the great spirits. Nuru assumed they were hoping to make a bride selection among the lot to recommend to the prince. She wondered about that; were young men afforded any more choice than young women? By and large, it was parents who negotiated a marriage. At least a first marriage. Ayinde caught her eye and smiled.

He was in his apprentice robes. They were plain brown, no adornments or symbols of any kind, and covered from neck to ankle. It made him look quite a bit more grown. Nuru never thought of herself as being almost a woman, but just now, looking at him seeming very much a young man, she was struck by what an odd age she was. What odd ages they both were, and what odd beings they were among their generation. Young women of Nuru's age tended to only be thinking about marriage, and the young men of Ayinde's age thought only of building a home so they could marry. But both she and her friend were drawn instead to vocations, neither would prevent them marrying, but it was not their focus.

Ayinde spoke quietly to Vaasht Bakari. The man glanced Nuru's way and nodded. Ayinde broke away from the vaashta and came over. Nuru backed out of her little group.

"Why didn't you tell me you were apprenticing with the vaashta?" Nuru asked as Ayinde stopped before her.

He looked down shyly. "I didn't think it was likely to come to pass. The voices of the gods rarely take apprentices."

"But you are rare among the other men of Jaccada, so they have chosen well," Nuru said brightly, proud of her friend.

Ayinde's eyes flared and he seemed momentarily at a loss for words. He had to clear his throat twice before he could get words out. "Where is Arya?"

"The slipper didn't fit her or your mother, lucky." Nuru rolled her eyes. She wished her friend were in here with her. Even Neema was much further back in line and might take hours to get in.

Ayinde's eyes darted to Nuru's feet and back to the vaashta. "It fit you then? When does the prince propose?" He said it like it was a joke, but his voice was a little too serious to be playful.

"That isn't funny," Nuru said. Her eyes drifted across the room to where Hadhi and Mzaa were speaking with the three vaashta now.

And you think I want to marry him?

Why hadn't she thought about that? Hadhi just...never seemed to mind what she was doing.

"Nuru," Ayinde tried to get her attention. But Nuru was absorbed.

What if Hadhi was as opposed to marrying the prince as Nuru was? What if she felt trapped?

"Nuru," Ayinde said again. "Did the prince say anything to you when the shoe fit?"

"She never gave him a chance." Masahiro stepped out of the group to join Nuru and Ayinde. He didn't touch Nuru, but he had a charged personality that pulled Nuru back into the moment. "She barely gave him time to try the slipper on her foot before declaring it did not fit."

Ayinde laughed, as did Omar and Faizah behind them, drawing the whole group to them.

"Most entertaining competitor of the day by far," Omar saluted her.

"Then why are you inside?" Ayinde asked sounding...happy. Nuru was slightly unnerved by that. Had he been pressing her for answers because he was interested in her? Was she not entirely right about them being the same?

"Hadhi fit. And Mzaa Sabra, and Asha, so I wait." Nuru answered, exasperated.

"Hadhi is the talk of the evening," Faizah said with a pleasant smile and soft voice. Everything she did was graceful. Nuru could watch her all day, dancing or no. One day she hoped to be half as captivating. "Prince Azize seemed quite taken with her."

"For a moment," Yenge scoffed. He either missed Nuru's glare or was unimpressed with it, as he kept right on saying stupid things. "As soon as he saw Asha, he forgot Hadhi existed."

Faizah gave her brother a look, then smiled at Nuru. "He does try to focus on one woman at a time."

"It has been known to be a more effective courtship practice," Omar commented dryly.

"It was a different sort of attention entirely," Yenge pressed. "Hadhi entertained him, but he was attracted to Asha."

"I wouldn't underestimate being entertained," Masahiro remarked. Then as with the night before, he redirected conversation away from the uncomfortable. "I had a chance to examine the reliefs as you suggested. They are truly amazing, such passion! But I was told about a god or spirit you did not mention; Zifva, I believe they said. I am told the palace was built to honor him."

"Her." Faizah corrected with a little smile. "Gzifa, is the creator spirit."

"She appears in our creation story, but never again, so she is not worshiped like the others," Ayinde informed them.

"Ohhhh, I would not express it so," Faizah argued. "She is marked in every story, chairs are left vacant for her at every feast, our calendars and temples were all built around her fazes. She simply has not interfered again —yet."

Nuru liked that and smiled broadly. The idea that Gzifa would return was more a part of the Ga'ogo tradition than any other, but all felt her presence.

"Gzifa and Nur battling over the heavens is one of my favorite stories to dance," Nuru said brightly. "I love the mingling of opposites within it and that each dancer has a moment when they are the driving focus of the dance."

Faizah smiled softly. "Which is your favorite character to dance?"

Nuru's cheeks heated and her breathing grew erratic. Was Faizah offering to dance *with* Nuru? Nuru had wanted that for years. Ever since the first time she saw her dance. It was at the festival of balance two years ago and Faizah was merely one among many swaying around the alter at Ether, but Faizah was magnetic; the light of the moon was drawn only to her. The music spoke through her. Nuru could barely breathe watching her.

Nuru stumbled over her words. "Both are lovely...but when I saw you dance as Gzifa I...thought I saw the great spirit herself."

Faizah took Nuru's hand and bowed over it. "You honor me, my friend. Please, dance your namesake."

"But she—" Yenge began, but Faizah took charge.

"Thank you for dancing Maltuba for us, Yenge. Ayinde, would you speak the story for our guests? If you would like to see, of course?" She smiled up at the foreigners.

"Oh yes!" Masahiro exclaimed.

"Please," Omar agreed.

Faizah had that effect. The men backed away to give the dancers room. Nuru's heart was racing; she couldn't believe this was happening. She'd danced with her family and with her neighbors and friends. She'd danced with everyone at the festivals, but this was different. She was being invited to perform by the best dancer in the world.

This was everything!

A WOMAN'S HONOR

Hadhi had expected Noam would be waiting inside with them. She had hoped. But he was not there to hear how well she had done, making Azize laugh in the receiving line. Or to simply see, for a few moments of happiness.

When her family was waiting in the line, before Azize came out, Noam had walked by and caught her fingers in his. Tangled them together for just a moment as though he *had* to touch her.

Hadhi's fingers tingled and she had to catch her breath as it tried to race after him.

She felt alive, and beautiful, and desired. Struck with that same warmth as when her lips were pressed against his.

She wished he was here. Even if he did not come near her. If she had to gaze at him from across the room, she was sure it would be enough. But she should not want that. And she should not have taken the kiss. She was forgetting herself, forgetting her sour face and smiles were crawling over her lips without her having to force them.

He just made her so happy, so daring. With him, she was not sour-faced-Hadhi. With him, it felt like she never had been that girl, never was her father's monster, or her mother's disappointment, or anything but beautiful. When she was with him, she could forget everything but him.

She longed to keep him forever. But that seemed impossible. He might stay to be near his friend if Azize stayed. But that would mean Azize marrying someone here. Which was not terribly likely. And if he did, from the looks cast Hadhi's way by the mothers of her contemporaries, it seemed many people thought Hadhi was likely that person.

If only Azize would pick someone else. It had not seemed unlikely hours ago. But she could still feel the tingle of recognition from when the slipper settled around her foot. It should not have fit. She had been so sure it was too small. She had wanted it not to fit, so she could be free to flirt with Noam. But the shoe hugged her foot like it belonged to her. That bewildered her. But it also— *excited* her. She never thought of herself as being a thing like the mystery woman!

The woman who twinkled with excitement and power and allure. Everyone in the room noticed someone like her; everyone wanted to be near her. No one ever noticed Hadhi that way.

She was certain she was nothing like her until Noam noticed her. Until he saw her angry sour face, and still wanted to be near her. She was certain there was nothing alluring about her until that slipper slid across her skin and prodded Hadhi to claim her power.

She could be captivating too; she could be alluring, and desirable.

It was exciting. Terrifying. She had never been the object of such attention, not pleasantly at any rate. And Noam had started it all, with four words, *don't smile so much*. He saw her. He made her see herself. Hadhi wanted to revel in it. For once, she was competition for someone's attention. But when she felt the excitement from Azize's attention, a slow melt of betrayal followed. Noam was the one who really saw her.

Still, she was having her first taste of power and attention, and she did not want it to end. She had too much of her father in her. Not just the monster, but the hunger as well. She wanted to be desirable. She wanted to —*finally*— feel what other people felt. No matter where that feeling came from.

But Hadhi barely got a moment to enjoy the attention or the pride before reality forced its way in on her. In the form of her mother and the voices of the desert, the jungle, and the sun.

Mzaa had her arm wrapped through that of Vaasht Bakari, the voice of the desert. He looked intrigued and superior, and Mzaa looked ecstatic as she led him and two other men Hadhi's way. Hadhi glanced around her, not precisely for escape, she knew there was none, but she did not want to watch them closing in on her like a pack of hyenas over someone else's kill.

That's what Hadhi felt like: a kill left to carrion animals as all-around other animals watched in delight—or envy. Sade and her mother were whispering excitedly to one another, or perhaps angrily. Sade was joining with an important man, but if Hadhi married Azize, Sade would not be the most important woman in their family any longer, Hadhi would.

Hadhi hated thinking that way. Thinking like her father. Thinking everyone was out to get something, that everyone was competing. It had been easier not to when she was not a part of the competition. But she was now, and there was no escaping that voice in her mind.

Mzaa and the vaashta were nearly upon her. As Hadhi's gaze swept back towards them, she took in many a speculative gaze. Oni with her narrowed, jealous eyes. Eshe with hungry anticipation. Salama intently interested. Bayo buoyant with curiosity. Then Hadhi's view was blocked.

She hadn't been looking for an escape. But she had been looking for comfort, a friendly face to calm her unease. For Noam. But he was not here. Hadhi must see to her own racing heart, as she always had.

Hadhi drew in a deep breath and bowed her head for the vaashta as her mother's glare and tradition dictated. The men fanned out around her, their gazes taking her in from head, to scar, to toe. To scars again. Without once meeting her eyes.

"I believe your daughter is older than the prince, Jauhar," Vaasht Oba said without greeting Hadhi or acknowledging her bow. The voice of the sun was examined her like she were a cut of meat in the market, possessing no voice, no will, no purpose but to provide sustenance to others.

"Indeed," Mzaa acknowledged softly confident. "Three years. All twenty-three of her years have been spent learning to honor her nation and king by respecting the will of her betters. Her maturity and silent dignity make her an excellent first wife for a young man with much to learn yet from his own father. She would never seek to draw attention to herself and away from her husband." Clearly, Mzaa had anticipated this concern.

The vaashta made noises not quite in agreement and continued to study Hadhi. She held still and silent with her stomach tied in a heavy knot and her tongue caught in her teeth. But her heartbeat was slow, her breaths were even, and her mind was clear. She behaved as if she were lying in the long grasses, downwind of her prey, waiting. It was best to hunt silently. Best to focus only on the moment. Thinking beyond the moment led fear to fill the air and give you away.

"Do you know the oath of marriage?" Mwara, the voice of the jungle asked, dismissively.

"I do," Hadhi answered.

The vaashta of the sun and desert glared at her, but Hadhi thought she saw a small grin come and go on Mwara's face. "Then speak it," he prompted.

Hadhi ground her teeth, despite her mother's wide-eyed smile, meant to remind Hadhi to smile as she performed for these men.

"I pledge my hand in service and obedience to thine. I bind mine honor to thine own. My tongue to thine will. Mine body to thine service. And my life to thine cause," Hadhi bit out rapidly. Of course she knew the oath; in Maltuban and in Fairy. There wasn't a girl in Maltuba who did not know it. Though if there were five among the thousands who spoke it who truly meant the words, Hadhi would be thoroughly shocked. Particularly when all a husband need say to each oath was *I accept your pledge.*

Vaasht Bakari stretched closer, loosening his arm from Mzaa's. "One role of a queen is to exalt the nation through her beauty. And scars— prominent scars might make a prince look weak."

"Perhaps," Vaasht Oba sounded only partially to agree. "But the prince may have many wives, each with her own function. This styling is a most effective way of concealing those scars," he said, reaching forward for Hadhi's hair. "And it would suit the links of the queen well."

Hadhi's heart leapt against her will and she took a quick step back before he could lift her hair. Her skin was shuddering in revulsion and rage. All three of the vaashta and Mzaa as well cast killing glares at her. Hadhi forgot her hunter self, and like the prey she was, cast about for a way to escape them. Perhaps she should just offend them more, so they would never approve of her.

Past Mzaa Hadhi caught sight of Nuru, surrounded by onlookers— dancing. Dancing with Faizah and her brother— Spirit Dancers. Where she belonged.

Hadhi thought of that hungry, speculative gaze she had seen from Eshe, the leader of the Spirit Dancers. She had been wondering what treasures she might extract from the family should Hadhi marry the prince. She had been making plans to welcome Nuru among them. Hadhi sighed and calmed her wildly racing heart. She wasn't being hunted. She was the hunter. This was part of the plan, the vaashta had to approve of her if she was to marry the prince as Mzaa wanted.

"Navish szou," Hadhi begged forgiveness as softly as she could manage, bowing low. "My sister is performing and...a woman's honor is in the accomplishments of her family, not the glory of herself." Hadhi bit out a common admonishment used by vaashta at joining services.

She saw Mwara's half-smile again, and Oba's eyes narrow in consideration, but did not wait on their approval. She darted around them and rushed off to a corner to watch her sister perform.

THE BATTLE FOR THE SKY

Faizah and Nuru stood opposite each other with Yenge between them, bent at the waist as Ayinde began the story.

"In the time before life, there was only darkness, then slowly the universe filled with a soft glow as Gzifa took form." Ayinde spoke the legend in a voice made weighty by the long history of his subject. "Her light fell gently through the darkness illuminating a lonely barren rock floating nearby." Faizah stretched out in fluid steps, orbiting her crouched brother. "Gzifa floated around the rock to see what else there was in the darkness. As she did, a bright light exploded into existence, casting illumination to the very edges of the galaxy as Nur awoke."

Nuru leapt up, throwing her arms and legs wide as she danced in a circular perimeter around Yenge. Faizah followed the same perimeter with small steps, soft twirls and sways. A gentle presence in contrast to Nuru's wild intensity. Hadhi smiled watching her sister perform as Nur, bold and bright she commanded the room. She was marvelous.

"Nur shouted over that empty rock between them, proclaiming his might and his power, proclaiming himself the strongest being. His light could brighten half of the world at a time." Ayinde continued. "He could scorch its ground with his power. But Gzifa was gentler than her brother; she insisted it was not necessary to scorch the ground to be powerful and drifted by the world, presiding over the night with her soothing presence. Nur railed—"

Nuru raced at Yenge, throwing her body against his back and reaching out around him for Faizah.

"He demanded his sister concede that he was mightier and worship him as her ruler."

Faizah spun on, calm and unmoved. So Nuru leapt higher and higher. Throwing her legs wide, bright and distracting. Nothing altered Faizah's orbit.

Hadhi grinned, but from the corner of her eye, she caught sight of Asha watching and began to relate her life to the legend of the battling siblings. All their lives it seemed Hadhi and Asha had been pitted against one another.

Every time Hadhi thought she could find a way to put an end to their struggles, Asha just had to shout out how much better she was than Hadhi. Had to call her sour-face or crow over her superior knowledge, and Hadhi would want to grind her into nothingness, so that she could shine for one moment. She longed to shine with even a quarter of the light Asha cast. But...Could they not *both* shine?

If Hadhi did what Mzaa wanted, if she won the approval of the vaashta and captured Azize for a husband...what would Asha do to outshine her? Would she marry him as well? Only she would be the wife tasked with standing beside him, displaying her beauty to the world, while Hadhi would be the hidden wife, running his home and hiding in shadows lest she bring shame on him. Even if she won Azize for a moment, Hadhi would never win in truth, would she?

There was utter silence as Nuru danced. Hadhi pulled her eyes away from Asha and let herself be caught up in Nuru's gift. She commanded the attention of every eye. Dictated the beat of every heart. Nuru, in her element, was a bright shining goddess of dance. Hadhi watched entranced. Nuru eclipsed sound and emotion and thought.

Never but when she watched Nuru dance did Hadhi believe so completely in the existence of the great spirits. Nuru belonged among the Spirit Dancers. She belonged among them more than Hadhi had ever belonged anywhere.

It should not be so difficult to sacrifice a little to see her sister's purpose fulfilled. Hadhi had always known she would eventually marry someone, and she never expected to love them. Why not Azize? Just because she had felt *desire* for the first time in her life, and it was for a different man? Just because she did not want to spend the rest of her days in shadows feeling ugly? Those were not good enough reasons. And...*a woman's honor was in the accomplishments of her family.*

"Nur raged and scorched," Ayinde intoned, calling over more and more observers. "Shouting of his might and his sisters weakness. Until faced with Nur's relentless magnitude, Gzifa began to shrink."

Asha's heart pounded as she watched Nuru dance, breathing with the room. She was fabulous! Baba would have been so proud. As Faizah's twirls became smaller and her steps slower, Nuru continued her broad wild movements.

"When the siblings passed one another in the sky, Nur took up a dominant post, blocking the barren rock from his sister's sight. Gzifa drifted quietly by and with each day less. Shrinking before her brother's light. Until came the darkest night, when Nur could not find his sister in the heavens." Ayinde spoke on unnecessarily; his words were not conveying the story nearly as poignantly as the dance.

A gasp went up among the audience as Faizah dove between the legs of a few observers. Nuru spun around, wild, violent movements, tugging Yenge this way and that, searching for Faizah.

"Nur had won the sky."

Nuru danced around Yenge joyfully, leaping and spinning.

Nuru was so like Baba in that moment! He was always so bright. So entirely full of life!

Asha had never cared for this story. She preferred stories of real beings or far-off tales of adventure. And this story, in particular, had always annoyed her because of the way people treated Gzifa as pitiable one moment and as a heroine the next.

She just...gave in. She hadn't light enough in herself to protect the earth, but wanted to deny her brother the accolades he was due for bringing the light that fed the earth. Had she not been fighting him Nur's light would never have scorched the earth. Just look how much better the earth was in Gzifa's absence.

It annoyed Asha, knowing what was to come. It was all the same old thing: jealousy. Gzifa was jealous of her brother's light, so she had to steal it to make herself happy.

"The sky, the rock, the day, the night all were Nur's to rule by his superior strength," Ayinde continued. "But with no Gzifa to rail against, Nur grew despondent. His light mellowed and his heat gentled."

Nuru's movements began to shrink. She leapt, but plopped heavily on the ground when she landed. And when she reached out towards Yenge her arms extended only a short way. Yenge began to jerk and rumble.

Asha's eyes were drawn away from the dance to another sister, and she realized suddenly that the story was reminding her of Hadhi. Of her quiet, pity-me, exterior that hid her ugly jealousy. No one good would have unspooled the gold from Asha's gown.

And yet here she was, rewarded for it. Everyone whispering about how taken Azize was with her. The vaashta speaking with her. Azize staring after her. Hadhi *stole* and was rewarded. It was unfair.

Hadhi always tried to steal any joy Asha found.

Nuru noticed both of her sisters as she moved. Hadhi was beaming with pride. And Asha leaning in, intent and pleased. Eshe was among the audience too, smiling softly. Mzaa was against a wall, with her head high. And even Faizah was crouched awaiting her triumphant return, and watching Nuru with pleasure.

This was...*indescribable*! Even while they were dancing together, when Nuru's heart had been breaking for the dying goddess, still she'd felt such exhilaration. At last, she was dancing with Faizah! As much as she longed to be one more spirit dancer, she knew nothing would ever eclipse this moment for pure wonder and joy.

"Nur grew lonely in the sky," Ayinde said. "When he passed over the very top of the world and what would become Maltuba he saw a softer light in the sky. *Gzifa*."

Faizah slid out to join Nuru and Yenge, twirling up to her full height, remaining where she was to twirl around and around.

"Gzifa had returned to the sky, larger than ever before. She waited until her brother met her in the sky, large, confident and protective *Gzifa* blocked his light from scorching the earth."

Nuru's leaps brought her to Faizah, so they faced one another, Faizah's body blocking Yenge. They danced the perimeter together. Nuru leaping and throwing her body wide. But no matter how broadly she moved, Faizah softly swayed to block her motions, protecting the earth. It was as though Nuru could feel Faizah's heart beat before it happened. As though their beings were connected though they'd never danced together before. Their passion was so matched their souls must commune.

"Gzifa matched Nur's path through the sky, allowing only the tiniest ring of light to touch the earth. Gathering his light into herself, Gzifa glowed brighter. For one day and one night, she blocked Nur's path through the sky and soothed the earth. She called the oceans forth to spill across the land, and the ground shook, letting in air for new life to breathe. All of the world soothed by their first defender.

"When she moved out of Nur's path, allowing his light to touch the earth once more, the world bloomed to life."

Now was Yenge's turn. He leapt stretched wide, spun around shaking to life.

"Gzifa returned to her old orbit, twice as large as before, waxing and waning in her time. Each cycle rousing more great spirits to protect the earth. When Nur saw the blooming earth he rejoiced, he need never be lonely again. He circled the heavens at peace with his sister, one sibling ruling the day."

Nuru leapt and spun arms wide, smile large.

"And the other the night."

Faizah spun softly, swaying around the earth.

Ayinde stopped speaking and bowed his head. Nuru, Faizah, and Yenge stopped as well, but with heads high, each taking a stance that embodied their character. There was a seemingly endless moment of silence— The crowd around them began to cheer. Nuru couldn't contain her smile. She'd never felt such joy, such power surging through her! Overcome, she threw her arms around Faizah and tried to thank her, but her words sounded garbled and nonsensical to her own ears.

"You danced that beautifully, Nuru." Faizah hugged her back.

Nuru heard Masahiro and Omar asking Ayinde questions about the story. Nuru preferred her grandmother's telling, full of emphasis on Gzifa's power, but she would never forget Ayinde's version because this one she had lived. Her eyes scanned the crowd for her sister. Either sister. This was the best feeling in the world, and she wanted to run to her sisters and share it with them. But Asha had darted back to the window to watch Azize and Hadhi was turning away down a hall.

While she was dancing Nuru stood between her sisters like Maltuba between the battling spirits, and she'd realized Mzaa was wrong. She had to be wrong. Couldn't they feel it in the air? In the story? It was a call to come together. The greatness of the story was in each character having a chance to see their own power and share it with the universe. It required them *all*.

THE KILLER IN THEIR MIDST

Hadhi walked down the silent halls of the palace, away from the ballroom. She had spent enough time here when caring for Queen Imara to know where she was going, but she had never been in the room that had so fascinated Asha. When Hadhi heard the whistle of strange birds and the low mewls and yawns of other animals, she glanced around to see if anyone was watching and slipped into the menagerie.

She could not get comfortable. Her stomach roiled with unease and her mind darted from one subject to the next, one sister to the next. One unlikely future to the next.

Asha had seen the menagerie several times now, so Hadhi should not feel bad, but it felt a bit like betraying her sister. She knew how much Asha had wanted to see this place. She just could not help her. Asha had been such a bright, trusting child. It was too dangerous.

Hadhi walked slowly through the room. It was fairly dark, the sun was setting outside, and the lamps had yet to be lit. Monkeys were curled up around the trunks of small trees asleep, and at the far end of the room, a cheetah on a chain was up and prowling the length of his tether. She shuddered to see that great creature chained so. It reminded her of Queen Imara. Of the scars at her ankles from where she had been chained for the first years of her marriage to King Enzi.

Her scars had never fully healed, but they were so much easier to conceal from the world with jeweled cuffs. What so many thought were beautiful gifts to adorn a queen, were more cruel reminders that she was never free, as Imara had known and eventually Hadhi too, when she cared for her. No part of Imara's body was her own once Enzi claimed her. Even its wounds.

Hadhi shook off the thoughts. She had to; all of her muscles were coiling with fear and disgust. So she focused on the animals; several remained awake and were tensing up as she wandered among them. They sensed a killer in their midst. Hadhi stopped before an unfamiliar animal. Was this Asha's foreign beast?

Its pelt was a fluffy, dirty white color, and at first glance, it looked harmless. Then Hadhi saw its head. Thick round horns protruded from it, all but daring one to get closer and take those horns in the gut. It tensed, staring Hadhi down and pawing at the ground with its hard hooves. Hadhi stayed well back and observed this strange creature.

"Have you never seen a sheep before?"

Hadhi spun around and caught her breath. Noam. He walked towards her, smiling gently.

"They are perfectly safe."

"You have seen them before?" Hadhi asked, really just to say something.

Noam passed right by her and knelt on the ground before the animal, running a hand gently along its back. The sheep allowed it, relaxing in Noam's touch. He was so gentle.

"My family raises these exotic creatures." Noam laughed. Hadhi noticed he held onto one of the horns as he pet it and wondered if he was not quite as confident as he seemed.

"Did you leave home because of your father?" Hadhi asked softly. As Noam focused on calming the animal.

"I was thinking about that today. Why I left. There was a part of me, there still is perhaps, that wanted his love. But he didn't know how to give it; I was too painful a reminder. We were a very small community. Everyone knew everything, about everyone."

He said nothing more for a long while. Hadhi started to move closer to him, but the animal tensed. Noam laughed. But Hadhi felt the animal's recognition. Noam was safe, but Hadhi was a killer. This creature knew the difference. Why did Noam not see it?

"They knew he did not love you the same as your siblings?" Hadhi asked, stepping back. Before she made it very far, though he was not looking, Noam reached back and caught her hand. They both froze a moment as a charge danced between them. Noam drew her nearer.

"Crouch down slowly. All of these animals," Noam glanced around. "They are used to more space; they think you're here to hurt them."

Hadhi followed Noam's instructions. She let him take her hand and run it down the sheep's back. It was the oddest thing; its coat was fluffy and coarse at once, it scratched softly against the inside of her palm, but she barely felt it, barely breathed. Noam's hand guided hers and she was curled up in that feeling.

Hadhi could feel him thinking through his words though he remained quiet. She liked that he was quiet with her. He always seemed to be entertaining other people, but he was quiet with her because he knew...she would wait. She wanted all of his words.

"They knew I was not my father's son," Noam said at last. "My mother had *strayed* from her marriage. My father had as well, but that my mother had was the only thing that concerned our neighbors."

"I am sorry," Hadhi said softly. A corner of her mind wandered over that oath the vaashta made her recite. Why were things sins for women that were not for men? It had always concerned her, but she never felt there was anything to be done about it. There should be something to be done. "What your parents did was not your doing. They should have...held you...proudly. They should have *loved you!*"

Noam faced her fully for the first time since entering the room, wearing a soft smile.

"You sound like you want to charge into the world and make everyone love me," his voice laughed, but his eyes looked nearly sad.

Hadhi shrugged a little. "They should."

Noam's eyes crinkled and his hand around her's tightened briefly. There was such intensity in his grip, she felt it throughout her body, as though they were wrapped together in a powerful embrace. He was quiet for several long moments, embracing her with his eyes and his hand.

"Some of them did," he said, at last, his voice low and a little hoarse. "Certainly people my age. And when they didn't, Shiraz would loop her arm through mine and Ethan would step up on my side, and we would face the world together. And...that was enough. I knew they loved me, and my mother adored me, and sometimes even my father cared for me. But more than anything, knowing my siblings loved me was what made me strongest."

Hadhi swallowed the burning sadness in her throat and tried to simply smile at Noam and hear him, not relate his words back to her own life and feel the less for them.

"I am glad. You should be loved."

Noam's lip lifted at the corner a moment before he went on with his story. "I left because I wanted to find a place where it was okay that I was my mother's child and not my father's. I left because I wanted to see if the rest of the world was full of small people unable to see beyond what they expected. All of my siblings left."

"Even your sister? Or do you mean...to marry?" Hadhi asked in shock. Women did not tend to go off alone in Jaccada. They didn't start their own lives, make their own ways. She knew it was allowed in some tribes, but not the way it sounded when he said it. Women of the Bor might live without men, but it was in a community of other women. They all cared for the children together, worked together, ate together. But going off on ones own, that was...radical.

"Shiraz left alone. All she took was her staff, a bag of men's clothing," Noam smirked sideways. "A wool fleece, a bit of gold and seven books. She said she was going to find the singing hills written about in the book of Anolani. Ethan joined an expedition...seeking witches. We each wanted different things from the world. But most of all, none of us could live among people who had shunned and condemned the mother we loved. I was the last to leave. I kept waiting to be accepted, I think. When I left," he laughed. "It was because Azize's ship had come to my home. They had lost several men and were looking for more hands. I heard them talking about a prince who'd left home to see the world, and I felt this...overpowering certainty that I needed to do the same. So I took a job working in the ship's kitchen, serving the prince, but very quickly I became Azize's friend."

Hadhi smiled. There was so much in his story she wanted to know more about: the book his sister spoke of. Why anyone would want to seek out witches? What happened in the time Noam spent alone with his father? So much, but she smiled for the things that were clear to her. She could easily see him charming his way from servant to best friend of a prince. He was so much more open than other people. He would help anyone. Look at him, trying to help her win a prince, though he knew next to nothing about her. And though, in some moments, he seemed to want her for himself.

But perhaps she had made that up. He had not said a thing about their kiss. Perhaps taking her hand outside was only meant to be friendly. Perhaps this stirring need Hadhi felt to be near him was one-sided.

It did not seem to matter to her desire, whether or not he wanted her; she wanted to be with him either way. She wanted to open her mouth and speak her desire. She wanted to curl up in his touch and pretend the world was beautiful and safe. She wanted to be who she was in the quiet moments alone with him. No matter what.

Hadhi opened her mouth to ask about his travels, to exist a while longer in his beautiful world. But sweat dripped down her back, and her own reality shuddered through her. Hadhi shivered, remembering Vaasht Oba reaching for her hair. *This styling is a most effective way of concealing those scars. And it would suit the links of the queen well.*

Hadhi hated wearing her hair like this, combed out to its most voluminous expanse, with a crown of chain pressing down the front, so the sides pushed forward around her cheeks. It was a striking style. Mzaa knew her art well. But it was so hot, and it felt dishonest trying to hide her scars. She wished she could wear braids like Nuru or wear it up off her neck in a scarf like Sabra. Or shave it off altogether and show off her scars to the world, at least then people could look at them outright, rather than feeling they had a right to touch her, to see her ugliness.

She was so different from Noam. He had been sad and rejected, but he still managed to be such a beautiful being. What she would not give to keep him near her forever, and hope that eventually, his beauty fell on her and brushed away her ugliness.

As the sweat dripped down her back, Hadhi envisioned her future. A more realistic future. Wearing her hair so forever. Hiding her scars as best she could so as not to shame her royal husband, doing everything she could to earn the approval of those around her. She saw herself lying to the world and hating every moment.

Then she felt Noam's hand lifting hers slowly from the sheep and just... holding it, and Hadhi...envisioned herself sneaking into this room in the dark, with her hair wrapped up in a scarf for sleep, cool for the first time all day. She would sit on the bench under the trio of colored glass panels and shut her eyes. Waiting. Noam would slip out of the shadows and come to her. He would tell her about his home or take up her hand. Kiss it. She could feel the imagined kiss dancing across her skin so softly it was lighter than a breeze. He would kiss his way up her arm, pull her to him. And she could hide in the dark with her secret love and be the beautiful being he made of her.

As long as it was a secret.

Being with Noam, touching him, feeling this power, seemed to be all she could think about today. Her mind bending around trying to find her ways to have it all. If she married Azize, she could give her family the care she owed them. Make her mother happy. Give her sisters more freedom, and keep Lin with Sabra. Noam could stay in the palace with his friend, but secretly, with her. Hadhi would be lying, which she hated, but at least this lie would be sweet.

Noam was helping her already; surely she could convince him to stay. She could be happy in stolen moments with the gentlest man in the world. And curl up in his touch like a tamer creature than she had ever been allowed to be. It would not be perfect, but it might be enough.

Noam was watching her, still crouched. He was slowly raising her hand towards his lips, like he was seeing the vision with her, like he was offering to give her exactly that. He was so...willing to bend for others. But he *deserved more*.

Hadhi drew her hand away and shifted back.

"Hadhi?" He asked softly. "Are you alright?" He began to rise, looking confused and contrite. "I won't hurt you."

Hadhi smiled, nearly laughed. She was not a gentle creature in need of his protection. She would be the one who did the hurting. She would destroy him.

He was too beautiful a creature to be touched by someone like her.

"I'm sorry—"

"Hadhi, are you in here?" Nuru's hesitant voice interrupted Hadhi's attempted confession.

Hadhi cast Noam one last look and crossed quickly for the door of the menagerie. She felt the cheetah and the jackals perking up as she ran, sensing a hunt to be had. But they could no more escape their tethers than Hadhi could escape the ugly within. They were all predators, and they had no business with gentle creatures.

PEST

Asha grew anxious as the hours passed. She had momentary distractions like watching Nuru perform. She must be thrilled. Nuru talked about Faizah constantly. Asha was happy for her; she'd finally achieved her dream of dancing with her. And even that was not the distraction it should have been, reminding Asha too much of her life. But when the dance was over, and one after another, beautiful women kept entering the room Asha grew anxious again. It was not a feeling she had much experience with.

They should have stayed to the end of the line, been the last to see Azize. At least that way Asha would not have to watch all the beautiful women enter, wondering if he'd laughed with them, smiled at them, thought them beautiful. All the while hating Asha.

Asha had never thought of herself as a liar. Even when she went out of her way to lie. But the longer she spent alone, with her eyes trained on the door, as the other women relaxed, awaiting their fate, the longer she had to think and the more she saw his perspective.

And it wasn't good.

The first time they'd interacted, she'd fought with him, ruined his chance to sail away from home, distracting him until he crashed his father's boat. It wasn't intentional! She hadn't realized he was running away while his father and hers were away putting down a revolt. She'd just snuck on the ship to find something exciting and exotic. But Azize had caught her and tried to threaten her. That was his mistake. Baba had taught her never to be anyone's victim.

"What are you doing here?" A hand yanked Asha off the stairs into the ship's hold and dragged her into the light. She stumbled over the last step and fell. Looking up, Asha recognized the young prince and his shock.

Asha narrowed her eyes and looked around, this ship was meant to be empty, but here he was, alone. "What are you doing here?" She countered.

"This is my father's vessel. The king's vessel. Do you know the punishment for stealing from the king?"

"Do you know the punishment for stealing from the king?" Asha taunted right back. That got him.

His hands fisted, his eyes narrowed and his nostrils flared wildly. "If you don't shut up and get off this ship now, I will have yo—Aaaaaaa!"

He'd broken off to scream in shock as the ship knocked into the dock and sent them both rolling. In retrospect, it was likely not very much of a bump; the ship was merely unmoored at one end and beginning to respond to the current. But it was the shock of their young lives. Screams came from the docks, and by the time anyone got on board, Asha was shouting at Azize and calling him a fool for unmooring the ship.

Asha blamed Azize for everything when a group of soldiers took them to his mother. And Queen Imara had believed Asha.

Their second interaction hadn't been much better. He'd been pining after Sabra. Sabra, who he laughed with today, jumped to his feet to care for. When Asha was eleven Azize pining after Sabra only seemed silly and— useful.

She had been a pest, hadn't she?

Asha only wanted to see the palace menagerie. She had tried twice, and both times been caught by Hadhi and punished by Jauhar. Baba had promised her a trip, but then he had to leave Jaccada on a mission for the king. Mzaa Jauhar always turned on Asha when Baba was gone. But Asha had a plan. Baba always said, "You have to count on yourself to get what you want, Asha. Other people fail you. Be your own greatest ally."

All she needed to do was get rid of the guards for a little while. Sabra was always game for one of Asha's adventures. She was two years older than Asha, but she wasn't as savvy, so Asha was their leader. The trouble was Sabra would want to see the menagerie too, so she couldn't be the distraction. They needed someone truly frightening. Hadhi would be best. Her sour face would scare the guards away. But she was no fun. She only did as Mzaa Jauhar said unless Nuru was in trouble. That's when she got really scary.

So that's what Asha needed, Nuru to get caught and Hadhi to come rescue her. In the chaos, Asha and Sabra would sneak into the menagerie. Hadhi would know what had happened and tell her mother, and Asha would be making breakfast with the servants until Baba came home, but it would be worth it.

Asha was sneaking through the long grasses; it was the quickest way to Sabra's home. She was almost there when she saw him hiding.

Asha crept closer. Baba taught her it was better to know as much as possible about a situation before others know you were there. So she snuck, quietly as she was able to see what captivated the prince.

When she was directly behind him, Asha stood on her toes and stared over at her friend. Sabra was humming as she washed laundry. Asha tried to examine Sabra neutrally. She knew her friend was pretty; she also knew men talked about how she had matured. But it was odd to see the prince hiding in the grass to stare at her.

Asha felt him sensing her presence and ducked in to the grass; it rustled a bit, and his head shot up, looking her way, for a moment. He must have thought she was an animal because he went back to his staring.

Asha smiled to herself. It would all be so easy now. The prince could simply walk her and Sabra into the menagerie. There would be no risk of getting in trouble, either with the guards or Mzaa Jauhar.

Asha walked confidently out of the grass. "I can convince her to talk to you."

He jerked around, glaring already. "Go away," he hissed.

"I'm her greatest friend," Asha said, with a superior smirk on her lips. "If you want her favor, you need my help."

He should have told her he didn't need her help, that he was the prince. It was what Asha would have done in his place. But he didn't understand his power.

"Would you just leave," he begged. "I want nothing to do with you."

"I only want one favor."

"I'm not doing anything for you."

"You'll get to be with Sabra."

"What?" He acted as though he was not listening. But Asha knew she had his whole attention.

"Sabra wants to see the menagerie," Asha lied. Sabra would want to see it, once Asha explained why she should. But Sabra was naturally contented.

"But she can't go alone," Asha rushed out when she saw him considering.

He rolled his eyes. "Does she even want to go?"

"Of course. Go ask her," Asha waved boldly. If he were willing to talk to Sabra, he wouldn't be hiding.

"Fine," he snapped. "Go get her. We have to go before my father returns."

That alone would not have been so bad. He wouldn't like her better, but he might have forgiven the blatant manipulation. If she hadn't decided to embarrass him on top of everything. But once he snuck them into the menagerie, it turned out Sabra quite liked the prince. She walked around sweetly with him while he explained everything, let him hold her hand. And Asha was left all alone, like she always was at home.

She hated being alone. She hated feeling like the only person everyone could do without. Sabra never treated her so, until Asha had introduced her to the prince. And the prince suddenly realized his power, whenever Asha started to say something, he chastised her, as though he had a right to, saying things like:

"Please remember you are my guest. I can eject you at any time."

Or:

"This is not your menagerie. Please refrain from trying to touch the animals."

It was the first sign of backbone he'd shown, but Asha hadn't seen it like that. She didn't take criticism half as well as she met it out.

Sabra kept looking away shyly, embarrassed by Asha. It was too much!

Asha could have gotten in without his help. This was exactly the sort of thing Baba warned her about. But he had also taught Asha how to make sure no one ever saw her as their victim. So when they came across an enclosure of monkeys, and one was sitting off by itself watching the others play, Asha brightened up considerably.

"Oh look, Azize, it's you." She pointed excitedly to the lonely monkey. "Hiding all alone and sad, watching Sabra. I wonder where the Asha monkey is, to come and rescue him."

He turned on her then, wide-eyed, looking ready to cry. Really he had been such a sensitive boy.

Yes, she had definitely been a brat. The way Azize looked at her today, when his father said her name, he definitely remembered. He saw today as Asha trying to show him up—again.

She hadn't been. She was only enjoying the moment, looking into his eyes and hoping. But there wasn't any hope, was there? She deserved his derision.

And the way he'd looked at Hadhi was repulsive. It was terrifying. Hadhi was right; she *did* have his attention. How had that happened? When did sour-faced-Hadhi learn to flirt?

This was a nightmare.

Asha needed the power back. The longer she stretched on without it, the longer she spent in corners, with her insides aching and her mind whirring and her heart pounding. Baba always told her to rely only on herself. Why hadn't she listened? She should have found a way to sneak into last night's ball on her own. She might still have met Azize, might still have captured his attention. But now, Asha was terrified. She was like Azize in the past, entirely unsure of herself. She needed the power. She could fix this with the power.

Zawadi had promised to meet her inside, but Asha could not find her anywhere. When she peeked out at Azize every now and again, she saw him growing slowly more defeated and angry. Before long he would hate both Asha and his mystery woman. It was such an utter mess.

If only she had the other slipper, then she could make him understand.

LOVE IN SECRET

Noam stood slowly, following behind Hadhi towards the open arch to the hallway. She'd done it again, gone from being her quiet, compelling, whirlpool self one moment to jumping up the next with a manic energy like a wildfire. He wanted to laugh aloud at the change, but he resisted, following as quietly as he could. He knew she didn't change so drastically for no reason.

He had been avoiding the ballroom earlier for similar reasons, because he knew he shouldn't be with her. He wasn't as skilled as she at hiding himself, so he had intended not to go into the ball before Azize. He had hidden in the corridor and watched Azize make his way through the line of women. From his spot in the stairway, he could see both Azize kneeling before all the women of his kingdom and cross to the opposite side of the stairway and look down into the ballroom where the women the shoe fit waited.

The later into the day it grew, the more he worried for Azize. His mystery woman might be a nymph or a siren, or a girl who'd bought a potion to steal into a ball. But the shoe was magic. Noam had watched, appalled as the thing shrunk or stretched to fit the feet of the women to whom Azize was attracted. Somehow, his friend did not seem to notice.

But that was not as shocking as the level of Noam's anger when the shoe stretched to fit Hadhi's foot. He didn't know what he expected, but not that, not this seething feeling inside that the shoe stretching had something to do with Azize being attracted to Hadhi or Hadhi being attracted to him. Not this rage that his friend was trespassing on something special, something that belonged to Noam. Azize would never even have noticed Hadhi were it not for him. He didn't understand her. But he was coming to like her, and Hadhi meant to marry the prince.

Meant to, not wanted to. The difference did not matter much to Azize or her own family. Perhaps it shouldn't matter to Noam either, but it did. That tiny distinction kept him from abandoning this longing he had for her. This longing just to be near the woman, who with less than a day's acquaintance with him had offered him comfort for old pains that even his closest friends did not know. Hadhi was special. And Noam had shoved that special under the nose of his closest friend.

Noam had slowly found himself looking down into the ballroom more and worrying over his friend less. He'd watched Hadhi enjoy her little success, as her mother fawned over her for a few moments. He watched her search the crowd, over and over again, her eyes scanning the same spaces. For him?

He hoped so. But he didn't go down.

Not until he'd seen her tension as she spoke with those priests. Not until he watched her slip away after her sister danced. He couldn't resist following her then. Couldn't resist telling her his life story when she asked the simplest of questions. Couldn't resist taking her hand in his just to feel closer to her. He couldn't resist her. But it seemed he should.

Hadhi raced out of the menagerie and latched onto her sister's hands, speaking brightly. "I saw you dancing! You were *spectacular!*"

Her sister looked around curiously, but didn't spot Noam against the wall. "It was the most exciting thing in the entire world! I want to do it again and again," Nuru said brightly.

Hadhi laughed. "Then you will. I promise." Hadhi urged her sister back towards the party.

"Hadhi, are you alright?" Nuru asked softly. "I...what did the vaashta say to you?"

"They mostly spoke to Mzaa," Hadhi answered flatly. "Wanted to know if I knew what a wife owes a husband, that sort of thing."

Nuru stopped in the middle of the empty hall. Her mouth opened and closed several times, then she met her sister's eyes and found a way to say what she wanted. "Everyone is talking about you! How lovely you look. How you impressed the prince. Mzaa is saying how proud she is."

Hadhi seemed to cringe, her jaw clenched angrily as she answered. "I will do my best to marry Azize," she bit out. "But even if I fail, we will find a way for you to join the Spirit Dancers."

Noam felt his muscles clenching up with the words and fought the feelings down. *I will do my best to marry Azize.* It wasn't as though she'd pretended differently, and there was nothing in her tone that expressed any pleasure. How did her sister not hear that? Every syllable of Hadhi's tight words was one of pain, but her sister just stood there, no assurances that she wanted no such thing, no arms closed around her. Noam hated this. The secret of him. Because he knew, if he walked out and tried to close Hadhi in his arms, she would not allow it. Couldn't, whether she wanted him or not, not if she meant to marry the prince and save her sisters.

Hadhi shuddered and fought off the urge to cry. Her heart was breaking, and for what? She had not won the prince. Nor had Noam offered to stay and be her love in secret. All her turmoil was for fantasies built in her own mind. But she felt trapped in her own ugliness. She had tried to imagine a happy future and seen herself hurting someone she had begun to care for. All her solutions in life led to ugly places. She wanted to just surrender, like Noam did, like Nuru did. To follow the music and see where it led, but she could not. Her being was at war.

Dormant parts of her soul had shuddered to life, making her realize that she could *feel.* That she could do more than what her father had taught her. But as soon as her heart woke, the part of Hadhi that had ruled for years reared up to explain she was not like other people. There had always been something less deserving about her. And in came Nuru—to explain the same thing.

Hadhi knew what she owed her family. No one needed to remind her. They lived in a hut at the edge of the nation—outcasts. Punished for Hadhi's sins, though none of them knew it. Nuru was denied her place among other dancers. Asha was forced to serve the rest of her family. Mzaa was a queen displaced and railing at the entire world. Hadhi saw it every day.

Did they think there was anything but what she owed her family that would compel her to try to win Azize? There was nothing else—and they *did not even care* that she felt this burning rage within. Felt caged like the cheetah in the menagerie and wanted to strike out, to sink her teeth into something, longing to feel free. Surely Nuru could hear it in her voice; Hadhi could not lie, everyone said so. But the seconds stretched and Nuru said not a thing. Waiting on something else from Hadhi, but she had no idea what. What more did they need of her?

"That wasn't what I..." Nuru began, but it was too late. Hadhi wouldn't hear it.

"I will marry the prince no matter what it costs! Is that what you want to hear? Mzaa shall have something to boast over. Asha can afford her adventures, and you will be a Spirit Dancer. And I will be dressed by other hands and told where to sit and when to smile and marry a little boy who wants to run away, but somehow I must do what no one else can and keep him here."

"No!" Nuru shook her head wildly. "I was just...trying to cheer you up. I know Mzaa says things that...hurt you. But you can confide in me. You don't need to trust strangers. I am here."

"Trust strangers?" Hadhi bit out like a question, but she knew to whom Nuru was referring.

Nuru rolled her shoulders, looking vulnerable. Like the sheep, she tensed in Hadhi's presence, sensing the monster.

"Azize's friend, who...took your hand in line."

Hadhi raised a brow rather than asking what Nuru's problem with that was. She knew. She knew. Hadhi could not marry a prince while flirting with his friends.

"I am here," Nuru repeated. "There are many people who would care for you if you gave them a chance. They are happy for you already."

"They are happy for themselves, Nuru. Like you are." Hadhi spit out. Nuru gasped. "Happy that I might marry the prince instead of them. None of them know me or even care to."

"Why are you angry with me?" Nuru burst out, with tears gathering in her eyes. "I haven't done anything. I only want you to talk to me. Tell *me* how this is different from any other thing Mzaa makes you do. You always do whatever Mzaa tells you, and you are never happy about it. What's different? It is unfair to be angry with me for fighting for what I want, just because you have never wanted anything!"

Hadhi burned. Angry and resentful. She did not want anything. That was what Nuru thought. She thought that Hadhi had never wanted friends. Or to be held and supported—desired.

There's no such thing as love, monster, not for creatures like us.

She was not good enough to be loved. That's what Nuru meant. Hadhi was not allowed to want anything for herself. Hadhi had long since accepted that her mother thought so, and her father. Long since accepted that Asha thought Hadhi too ignorant to have desires. But that Nuru, who Hadhi had loved and cared for and protected, thought so little of her was...*enraging*!

"I might never have wanted anything, Nuru, but at least I do not expect everyone else to provide me what I want. Why not offer services to Eshe yourself? Or collect silk to make an offering? You want everything prepared for you, and when that does not happen, you pout."

Nuru's eyes flared wide, and her tears slipped out, but it seemed she had nothing left to say. Hadhi spun around alone and walked calmly back to the ballroom, burning with rage, and ugliness, and sorrow. She wanted to be alone with her sour-face and her angry heart. She wanted to wallow in her pain as she had been since Baba died. But she had a prince to win. How had she let herself forget? She could never be like the mystery woman. Maybe the woman truly was a nymph. Maybe this was her plan. Making Hadhi want, making her forget, so it would only hurt more when she realized she could not keep Noam. Even if he wanted her. Even if Azize picked another woman.

It would be over as soon as he met the real her. She was not the girl she pretended to be with him, the girl who had other things inside of her but rage and ugliness. She had been that girl once, but—Hadhi had murdered her long ago. She was only the monster now.

Noam leaned against the archway between the menagerie and the hall and watched Hadhi's younger sister brush aside tears over their argument. This was the girl Hadhi boasted over. The girl Hadhi was willing to give up her own desires to protect. *If he looked after Nuru, saw to her happiness, I could love a*

man for that. But her sister had come to pressure Hadhi to make the very sacrifice she was already trying to make.

Noam's muscles were clenched from his anger with this girl, and from resisting going after Hadhi. He'd known he shouldn't spend so much time near her. He didn't know these people. His soul knew Hadhi; she had a good heart, and she wanted to protect others and she was so lonely. He knew her. But he didn't know her daily life. He didn't know what his association would cost her.

He couldn't be like the man who had given him life and nothing more. He couldn't...lead to Hadhi being further shunned. He'd always had such anger for that man. But he was beginning to understand how the affair might have happened. How someone could consume you beyond reason. He knew Hadhi deserved more than the way she was treated. He wanted to show her how much she deserved. He wanted to charge into the world and make them love her. But in this foreign land, he had no idea how to go about it.

Her sister looked up suddenly, choking back a sob. She glanced over her shoulder towards the menagerie and spotted Noam. Her eyes narrowed, full of fire and suspicion. Two things struck Noam at once, how young she looked and how like Hadhi all of the sudden. He hadn't thought them all that similar before.

The girl crossed the empty space to stand before Noam.

"What game are you playing with my sister?" She demanded. He wouldn't have thought her that bold yesterday. But then, he hadn't thought Hadhi as bold as he knew her to be until he'd spoken with her alone.

"I am playing no games with her. I am her friend. I took her hand in line to encourage her."

Her eyes widened slightly when she realized he'd overheard the argument. But she recovered quickly. She lifted her chin. "And I suppose you snuck in here to see her alone just to be friendly? And kissed her behind our home, to be friendly?"

Now it was Noam's turn to be shocked. He hadn't realized anyone saw that. It was not he who had done the kissing. That ought to mean something, but it didn't. And he couldn't honestly say he hadn't gone to their home imagining more time with Hadhi, imagining her lips.

"I like your sister," Noam said, forcing himself to maintain his outward calm, breathing out as he spoke and clinging with his teeth to his pleasant veneer. "But she has made it quite clear that she...intends to marry Azize and *rescue* you and your sister from your uncle's control. So—"

"She said that to you? Those words?" The girl gasped and she turned her entire body to stare after Hadhi.

"Yes. And since I care for her feelings, I will not get in the way of that."

The girl faced him again and her eyes were threatening. "I won't let you hurt her."

Noam raised a brow at that. "*I* wouldn't. Unlike the people she loves."

"I didn't come to fight with her! She didn't even let me speak." The girl clenched her fists and looked ready to launch herself at Noam. "And whose fault is that? She wasn't angry when she left the ballroom."

Noam had nothing to say to that. He didn't know what had happened. One moment she'd been gazing at him like she wanted to be kissed again, inching closer, gripping his hand, breathing in time with him. Then all at once, her eyes shut down and he saw that sadness that came over her whenever she was about to be happy. She looked angry and sad and guilty. She even began to apologize, and that was before her sister showed up.

"I wasn't coming to talk to her about Azize." Nuru shook her head. Looking deep into the empty hall. "Not that way. I just wanted to ask if..." She shook her head, unwilling to finish. Her head rose with sharp eyes and more weight than he would have expected. "No boy has ever liked Hadhi. A few have pretended to, but it is only ever a game." Nuru's tone was deadly, like she would find those men and slaughter them. "She pretends it doesn't hurt, but I cannot see how that can be true."

"I would never hurt your sister," Noam said with quiet sincerity.

"Yes, you would," Nuru remarked sadly confident. "Maybe not like that, but you will ruin her chances—"

"Do you honestly think she wants to marry him?" Noam interrupted, angry with the selfishness of her entire family. "Or do you care so little for Hadhi's feelings?"

Nuru's eyes raked across him in a way that was all her mother, knowing, jaded. "Not her chances with Azize." The girl bit out. "Hadhi has been so different since Baba died, sad and angry and withdrawn. She is even angry with me when she never was before. But last night...she has *never* pleased our mother as much as she did last night. For a few moments, she looked so proud, so happy. Like her true self." The girl broke off, choking on tears again. "She doesn't seem to like herself with Baba gone. But she liked herself last night. And being with you will cost her Mzaa's approval."

Noam was stunned. He had completely misjudged this girl. This wasn't just about herself. Would his attention really hurt Hadhi so much?

"I am playing no game." He repeated. "I want Hadhi to be happy."

Her little girl's face did a little twist like she would cry, but instead, she looked through him, heavy and thoughtful. For a long while, there was nothing but silence between them. She walked around him, towards the menagerie and he could see from her expression she was thinking over where her sister had been and the things she'd said in the hall.

She walked back to Noam her steps light despite the fiery intensity about her.

"You say you want her to be happy. What does that mean?" She asked.

"It *means* I have been trying to help her win Azize," Noam bit out. "Because she wouldn't be happy if she wasn't providing for your family."

"So, you mean to help her win him. And then once she has what? Stay and help her keep his attention? Or leave her?"

Noam was struck again. What would it look like if Hadhi married Azize? Would he be able to remain anywhere near them? Impossible.

He couldn't watch that. Nuru, a child still, who should not understand any of this, watched him with a knowing expression, as though she could read his mind. Noam had nearly wanted to attack his friend earlier, just because the shoe fit Hadhi. Just because he was looking at her and laughing with her and was allowed to touch her. If she was married to him; if Noam's closest friend touched Hadhi every day. Held the woman Noam loved in his arms—Noam felt his chest tightening so far he couldn't breathe, so angry just from the thought. And so utterly shocked.

The woman he *loved*. Was this love? He knew he cared. Knew she consumed his every thought, but they'd known each other only a day. It was impossible to feel so much so fast.

"If she fails to marry Azize, what then?" Nuru continued to press. "Do you mean to live in Maltuba? Do you know?" Her words fell over him like an angry parent protecting her child.

"If Hadhi married you, where would you live? Do you even want to marry her? Or is this just a moment?" The girl kept on forcefully, but perhaps also hopeful. "Baba loved *many* women. There are women out in that room who he loved for only a few days or hours. They talk about it behind Mzaa's back, but she knows. It made her the angry woman everyone sees." Nuru shook her head, revealing the sadness she concealed well with her childish exuberance. "It is true I want Uncle Kafil to release our dowries. And I do not want to marry the prince. But I want my sister to at least be content. And she would not be, if she gave her love, and love was not given back."

"That wouldn't happen," Noam whispered. Hadhi had his love already. But Noam hadn't contemplated the future at all. He would happily spend the rest of his days with Hadhi. But what would that look like? He didn't imagine a woman as devoted to her family as Hadhi would be happy leaving them behind. Nor would she be happy if she stayed but failed to provide for them by being with Noam.

Nuru's eyes fell away, she passed him, speaking in a low whisper, "People will talk if you continue favoring her so specifically. Come, join our family while you think beyond the moment."

Noam wasn't sure he should accept her invitation, the *instruction* as it really seemed. He'd known it was dangerous grabbing Hadhi's hand as he passed her. Right there, for all the world to see. But he wanted to do much more for all the world to see. He wanted her to be his unequivocally. But at what cost? Would she hate herself forever with him?

ANYONE COULD SEE IT WAS A MAGIC SLIPPER

Zawadi waited until the very end of the line. Until the king, with his magic repelling sword, had escorted in an unfortunate young lady and left Azize to the last few women. She had watched women of all ages, sizes, and personalities approach the king and his son, and either pass their test or fail. Wasn't it intriguing what magic did when its creators did not pay enough heed to guide it? She'd given Asha magic for five hours, but that girl hungered so wildly for the power that she managed to keep her magical creations past their hour of expiration. Those slippers should be steadily fading in power and leaving this world, but every skin they touched fed power into the pair, so they remained.

She'd watched Zuberi's first wife play tug-o-war with the young prince trying to control the slippers. Neither of them aware that while they were urging the shoes, their's were not the only wills affecting it. Every woman whose foot touched the shoe left a bit of their own desire behind.

And the one that had most intrigued Zawadi was Zuberi's eldest. Everything about that girl felt like her father in ways that Asha did not. Though Asha surely had his callousness and wonder, which looked so lovely, but cut so deep. But his eldest—her foot had fit in the slipper despite her being shouting out that it wanted nothing to do with the shoe, that she wanted to shatter the beads apart and be free—the slipper ignored her.

True, her mother was one of an iron will and was fighting to see it fit. And the prince's momentary desire had effected the shoe as well. But it was as though the magic couldn't touch her. And it was something Zawadi had already been feeling from her.

She was so angry and self-loathing that even Zawadi couldn't find a punishment that would take from her what she already denied herself.

It was a challenge. But there was nothing keeping Zawadi alive but this quest. They would all be punished. And his eldest would be stopped before she as well decimated an entire people.

The prince was ready to turn inside by half past six. Tired and sweaty and so self-pitying that he felt his day of judging his female citizens was a torture. He had no idea. Zawadi approached the young man, in child form, *in sweet Kiwi's form.* Zawadi tugged at his tunic.

"You forgot me."

Azize faced her and laughed, full of amusement and pity. Too often, Zawadi saw men who thought themselves superior because they did not see another's worth. Size, gender, age, nation, they found so many reasons to look on another being and hold themselves higher. He would be his father's son if he didn't learn better soon. Enzi's sort of power had a twisted appeal for frightened little boys.

"You may come in," Azize said in a tone he thought generous.

"I have to try it on first. The king said," Zawadi persisted. She didn't break rules lightly. Already she was bending her quest, granting Asha the power for a second time. It wasn't how Zawadi had envisioned that girl suffering. She'd expected to watch her hunger for that magic for the rest of her days, slowly unraveling as it ate up any control she had with passions far stronger than her human form could contain.

Each time Asha took in the magic, she shortened her life. And Zawadi was giving it, because the moment seemed to call for it, because the magic seemed to want it, and because— Zawadi wanted her to figure it out! She wanted Asha to *know* she was being punished. And that girl was still too consumingly confident to see the threat.

"Well I am the prince and I say—"

"You don't think I can fit it, do you?" Zawadi asked disdainfully.

Zawadi walked around him and hopped lightly onto the throne. She held out her already bare foot. "I don't cheat. Either you want me inside or you do not. Slipper please."

Azize laughed and knelt before her. She could feel his amusement softening the beads of the shoe, pulling them tighter. He raised the slipper to her foot and watched in open-mouthed wonder as it glowed bright and shifted, shrinking until it was the perfect size for her tiny foot.

"Anyone could see it was a magic slipper," Zawadi said smugly. "It lets in the people you like."

Zawadi removed the slipper with her own hands. The prince was too flabbergasted to do anything but watch. She hopped from the throne and stared at him expectantly.

"You shall save me two dances," Zawadi informed him pertly. "Once you've bathed." She turned on heel and marched away regally, instructing over her shoulder, "come find me, soon."

She could feel him startle and smiled to herself as she walked into the palace.

TENDER

Hadhi was at the back of the line for refreshments. She was a bit too nauseous to eat yet, but the line already stretched out of the dining hall towards the ballroom, so she entered it before it stretched as long as the line outside had.

After fighting with Nuru, Hadhi had walked right in and approached the vaashta. She answered every question they had, lifted her own hair out of the way so they could see her scars better. She was so angry already she barely felt the resentment they caused her. And Nuru's friend Ayinde kept trying to help, mentioning ways Hadhi had looked after her sister or her cousins and relating each statement back to the old tales. It was sweet, if strange. Now she just needed to find a way to stand out to Azize personally.

Hadhi noticed Asha behaving strangely. She was just...waiting against the wall, not talking to any of the foreigners. Perhaps Nuru was right and she really was determined to win Azize. Odd. Hadhi would never have believed it if she were not seeing it. But she supposed in Asha's place any husband would be better than being stuck with Mzaa. Perhaps that really was what they all needed to be comfortable, space from each other.

The longer Hadhi waited, the more she thought about things that had nothing to do with winning a prince. She thought of Noam being the last of his siblings to leave the community they resented, because he was still seeking approval. Was that what Hadhi was doing?

You do everything Mzaa says, and you're never happy.

Hadhi knew she had done that with her father. Right up to the end of his life, though she hated him for years, still she begged for his approval. Was she doing the same with her mother? Was there a way to do differently? Was there a way to be different?

Surely Hadhi could find a way to make Nuru a spirit dancer or earn money to send Asha on her adventures the way Noam's sister had gone on hers. She could keep Sabra and Lin together. The only person Hadhi would truly fail by not marrying Azize was her mother. And Hadhi knew —she *knew* even if she married him, Mzaa would never truly be proud. Any success would be Mzaa's, and she would berate Hadhi for any misstep. Looming over her forever.

There was no pleasing Mzaa.

Hadhi had seen Noam with her family before she entered the line. She wanted to go over, but could not. Noam had seen her too, but the moment her eyes touched him, he looked away. She was not entirely certain what had changed since the menagerie, but something had.

It hurt. Especially with the way her mind was spinning, and her heart was fluctuating between rage and longing and sorrow. It hurt in a new way that made her stomach ache with the emptiness. Something had changed, and he did not care for her any longer. Perhaps it was hearing her argue with Nuru. She had expected a change after he met Asha, but that was not when it happened. He had taken her hand after that. It must just be her.

It was always her. She never knew exactly what about her was unlovable, but the ugly power inside her always found a way to take away any fleck of love she experienced. Of course it would take him too. Monsters did not deserve to be with people so...lovely.

She felt someone behind her. She felt eyes on her scars and fought her mother's voice in her mind telling her to tilt her head aside or pull up her gown to hide them. Hadhi never hid them, but she often wanted to. He moved closer, and a delicious tingle raced from her scars down her neck, and her spine, and she knew who it was—Noam.

"How did you get the scars?" He whispered.

She had not noticed him looking at them much up to now, she always noticed when people looked. Now he was. Hadhi drew in a deep breath steeling herself and glanced back. She expected to see the same look she saw on most faces of those observing her scars: disgust, sometimes fear, or pity. But his eyes were soft, and though he was unsmiling, his regard felt warm and safe.

Hadhi glanced down and away, releasing her breath. She hated talking about that day. But Noam was here! She did not want him to leave, and he did not feel like he wanted to either. He felt magnetic and intent on her. Had someone said something to him about being near her? It must have been Mzaa. She hated anything that disturbed her plans, just as Baba had.

But standing in the line for refreshments, talking about Hadhi's most prominent physical trait, that no one would think strange. She just had to force herself to speak.

"Hunting," she said. It was the absolute truth but entirely incomplete.

Noam chuckled quietly. "So enlightening. A truly gripping tale."

Hadhi tingled from embarrassment and chewed on a bit of a grin that wanted to bloom over her lips. His voice was so light and enticing, and his regard warm. It whispered that anything she said would be alright. But he only sounded so because he was unaware of how close he skirted to a monster. His voice said it knew no fear nor any darkness. Until he spoke again.

"I am sorry if I have made you uncomfortable," he said more seriously. "When I see the scars, impractical as it is, for I can see by their healing that you suffered them long ago. Yet, I feel for the girl who was torn open. I worry for her life." There was a smile in his voice and such sincere concern. She felt valued as she had never been before.

Hadhi curled her fingers into her palms to keep from reaching for him. He had been avoiding her for a reason, and it was not as she had suspected at first, that he was done with her. She could *feel* their bond in the air between them, pulling them together. He might be protecting himself, or he might be protecting her, but he was not avoiding her out of any newfound distaste.

The line moved forward, and so did they, but just a bit slower than the people before them. They stood at the corner of the wall, blocked on one side by the column and on the other by the corner the line had turned.

"You must have been terrified." Noam's fingers rose slowly, hovered in the air above her scars, tickling the air between them. Hadhi bit down on her tongue to keep herself from rising on her toes to feel his touch in truth. She had never wanted anyone to touch her scars, but she did now. Surely his touch was all she needed to be healed. Even tracing them through the air Hadhi felt his tenderness and yearned for more.

Such a word that, *tenderness;* she was sure she had never used it. Certainly not in connection to herself or her treatment.

"I want to know her story," Noam said, drawing Hadhi's gaze back to his face. "Though I know she came through alive. I want to know it so that I know someone was there protecting you," he laughed at himself quietly. "Even if only now. It's silly, isn't it?"

Hadhi shook her head slowly. Not silly— *tender*.

She was on the verge of speaking and reliving the story as she had not done in years, but he nodded towards the line, and Hadhi shook herself out of the cushion of his eyes and moved forward before the gap grew too large. She kept a little space between her and the women before her though. A shield between her and the pain that was so much a part of her world.

Their space.

A world of tenderness.

STALKING

Nuru noticed her cousin in the crowd as Noam left to get refreshments for the family. Mzaa was trying to help Sabra with the baby; he was much fussier tonight. He wanted down, anyone could see that. He was learning to walk and he liked it. He liked the freedom. Nuru winked at her baby brother; she began to think she might understand him better than anyone.

She would have said it was Hadhi she understood best before. Not related to. No. Nuru was not really like any of them. They all seemed to hate their lives in some way, but Nuru didn't. She wanted to join the Spirit Dancers, and she had preferred the mansion in the city, to the hut at its outskirts. And she really could do without her mother's tongue more often than not. But she loved her life. Mzaa wasn't soft, but she was fierce, and she loved Nuru. And Baba had loved her bright spirit. And Lin loved playing with her best. Even Asha admired Nuru's dancing, and they had friends in common. And Hadhi loved Nuru like she loved nothing else. Nuru loved them all.

Even beyond her family, there was so much to love. Nuru loved to go from one grandmother to the next in town and ask them to tell about their lives, and she would dance the stories they told. She loved to play with her cousins, who were nearer her age than her siblings. She loved to explore every year a little bit further into the jungle, pretending that she didn't know Hadhi was following somewhere behind her, protecting her secretly. Nuru loved the services of the sand and the sun and the Festival of Balance. She loved watching the golden fabrics being sewn and sent far away to share the beauty of Maltuba. She loved it when traders came from the southern provinces and told her about their celebrations and their animals and their stories.

Nuru loved the old stories. The traditions. She had been thrilled when she was finally old enough to have her skin painted with symbols of their nation for the solstice nights. In the sun, or under the moon, there was always something to love. But she didn't think the rest of her family knew that. Particularly not Hadhi.

Nuru felt terrible about their fight. She'd wanted to talk with Hadhi about how it felt to dance, to share what she loved with her. But...Nuru began to suspect the trouble was that Hadhi had finally found something beyond her family to love and didn't know how to embrace it. She must feel like if she did, she would be hurting her family.

Nuru would not allow her own desires to be the impediment to Hadhi's happiness. Hadhi always made sure Nuru was happy. Maybe she was right. Nuru did wait for Hadhi, or Mzaa, or Baba to solve everything for her. But now that she knew that, she could do things differently. She could find a way to become a spirit dancer on her own. Or —even if she didn't— she could still find opportunities to dance with them as she had tonight.

She'd brought Noam to be with her family, partially to show Hadhi she wasn't trying to push her at Azize. And also so he could prove his devotion. If he did, then Nuru would make sure her sister got what she wanted for once.

Mzaa, however, was not so easy. She'd been flagrantly rude to Noam when he joined them.

"Another Maltuban silk, have you no clothes of your own?" Mzaa asked with a little titter like it was a joke, but no one was fooled.

Nuru had noticed that he wore a long tunic in the brown, black and gold, rippling bows and diamonds of the Bor, but she had thought it simply a nice gesture to the nation he was visiting. It even had buttons with the runes for each of the five tribes. It must be a very expensive silk.

"Not very many," Noam admitted with a small smile. "And none fine enough for such an event. The prince kindly gifted me a few of the silks he took with him in his travels."

"The silks that take months to make and were prepared as gifts for dignitaries and foreign royalty? Generous indeed of the prince to bestow them on his favorite servant."

Nuru gasped. Suddenly embarrassed of her mother's manners. Mzaa never spoke so to men.

"I am sure *the prince* chose well who to bestow his gifts upon," Sabra said, sounding a little desperate and eyeing Mzaa with shock.

"Of course." Mzaa agreed, her smile friendly but her tone still cold. "Tell me what did you do in your home nation?"

Noam met Mzaa's smile with a bright one of his own, as if unaware of the insults she'd been paying him. "I was a shepherd, I suppose. My family kept many kinds of livestock; I was generally responsible for the sheep."

"So you hadn't much experience with royalty?"

"None at all. My nation is ruled by a council of elders," he said in a friendly, informative tone. But Nuru could see in her mother's eyes that look she got before she devoured one.

"I am getting hungry," Nuru blurted out to change the subject. "What about you, Mzaa. We should probably join the line."

"Please ladies, allow me to attend you." Noam bowed like the servant Mzaa wanted him to feel. "What can I gather to refresh you?"

Nuru, who had hoped to provide him an escape from Mzaa's tongue was appalled to hear her mother begin to list an assortment of items in Maltuban, which he likely didn't know, and dismiss him without so much as thanks. Nuru sighed as he walked away, preparing to try again to convince her mother to just be kind to Hadhi and the man she liked by extension. But it was then she spotted her cousin. Shafira's presence was both odd and far pleasanter to take than Mzaa's, so Nuru slipped away from her mother, following Shafira through the crowd.

Three years younger than Nuru, Shafira was only ten and should not have been forced to try on the shoe. Nuru followed her until she ducked between two columns and did not come out. Was she sneaking around? What fun was to be had *here,* from sneaking?

Nuru looked around to be sure she was not observed and ducked between the columns as well. Shafira jumped. Realizing it was Nuru, she lay a hand against her heart and shook her head.

"You scared me," she whispered.

"Why are you hiding?" Nuru asked, equally soft. She couldn't think what reason her cousin would have to hide, but she had no reason to expose her either.

"Baba sent me in secret. To see how you were."

"Why?"

Shafira shrugged. "He said to stay hidden. Not to let the king see me and to watch Hadhi."

"Just Hadhi?"

Shafira nodded, and her voice grew even smaller. "He asked if it was her who fed us after he fell from the mountain. When I said it was, he grew quiet. He said to watch her. He wants to know how people treat her and what she does."

Nuru didn't say anything for a moment. That was very odd. In the silence, Nuru saw her sister moving along the wall, with the line for the refreshments. Noam was behind her, whispering.

"What will you tell your father?" Nuru asked with her eyes on Hadhi.

"They treat her like they always did. They ignore her, or they tease her. Except that one." Shafira jerked her head in the direction of one of Azize's friends, not Noam, another man. Kane, one of the men who offered their camels.

He was a ways behind Hadhi and Noam, but he was watching them closely. "What does he do?"

Shafira bobbed her head from side to side. "He asks questions about all of you. He's very cold to Hadhi, like your father was. He watches her." Shafira squeezed Nuru's hand. "I will also tell Baba everyone says the prince might marry Hadhi. Don't tell anyone you saw me."

She hissed the last and took off into the crowd, following Hadhi more closely. Nuru watched her go and wondered if she was a hunter, like Hadhi. Not just knew how to hunt, but *was* a hunter, as Nuru was a dancer, in the way that defined you, even if it was not acknowledged. She moved like Hadhi, slipping into shadows and between people, but never observed.

Nuru's gut twisted up as she watched. She always thought Hadhi told her the absolute truth; everyone remarked on what a poor liar she was.

There is never any doubting how Hadhi feels about you that sour face of hers shows it all.

Nuru had heard people say such things and laugh at her sister's expense. She'd heard Baba say it. And when Hadhi heard it too she would look at Nuru, roll her eyes, and ignore. It used to bother Nuru. She used to fight with people about it, but somewhere over time, she had begun to ignore it, to the point where she didn't even notice it anymore.

Nuru watched Hadhi speaking to Noam without looking his way, her face cool and detached. She never unbent. Her shoulders were always straight, her head was always back. Except to sleep, Nuru didn't think she'd ever seen her sister shut her eyes. Not the way one did when the music called to them or the air caressed their skin, consuming them in a different world.

Hadhi didn't unbend. Nuru used to think it was indifference, but watching her with Noam, Nuru wondered if it wasn't fear. Maybe, long ago, before Nuru could remember, Hadhi had bent, and all those words had hurt her so badly she hid from them now. What frightened Nuru most was the thought that Noam might be like Baba, smiling and sweet and loving, but only for a moment. Wouldn't it hurt Hadhi even more if she unbent for Noam, and he didn't stay?

Zawadi followed Zuberi's eldest, slipping between skirts and into shadows, far more easily concealed than the girl's other stalker. It amused her to be in the body of a child, following her prey, and to see another child doing the same. But it was clear their intentions were not the same.

Zawadi watched Zuberi's eldest, with her dark mind and even darker soul twisting her every thought into one of pain. Such an interesting creature. How had she attracted a man like Noam?

Zawadi had felt his soul. It was bright and soft, loving though it had not always been loved. His soul was stretching out to this angry creature who put one to mind of her father.

Well. Not exactly.

The longer Zawadi watched her, the more she saw the differences. The girl held herself separate from her neighbors, but not above as Zuberi might have; she simply did not allow herself to...attach to them. And she was heavy for one with such a soft tread. Zuberi was an enthusiastic, social, magnetic man in all outward appearances. He'd seemed content with his life and curious about the world. He'd seemed good. But inside, he was frightened, ugly, angry, and hungry. And all of that painted his eldest's face. She could be his soul rendered visible. While Asha showed all the characteristics, Zuberi revealed to the world. So why did Zawadi almost feel bad for hurting Asha? She knew she would not feel sorry when the time came to punish his eldest.

Noam would get in the way of that if she wasn't careful. And it would break all the rules. He could not be touched by the magic; already magic owed him a great debt.

Zawadi let Noam and the girl walk through a crowded room speaking secrets. Hadhi's time would come. Zawadi would let her enjoy her moments of peace with Noam. It would only make the punishment sweeter.

As she was slipping away, she caught sight of Kane following the couple, his intense eyes trailing their every step and his ears trained on their voices. Zawadi needed a better look at his soul; she had a feeling he too would need stopping. Like his mentor before him, this man kept his soul well concealed. But Zawadi refused to approach him in Kiwi's body. This child had faced evils enough.

SOMETHING MAGICAL

"My father taught me to hunt when I was ten." The words slipped out of Hadhi, quiet and calm nearly emotionless. "The first animal I killed was a gazelle. I was so hesitant I hurt it far more than was needed." Hadhi heard herself echoing her father's reproach, as she told Noam the story, but she could not seem to stop her tongue. "I killed it, as he wanted. And I waited for praise that was not coming." *As I still am,* she thought but kept on with the story. "So I made myself become better..." Hadhi bit her lip, searching for the word, frustrated and itchy from how near her neighbors were. Near enough to hear her fumbling foolish tongue. "Knowing firmly." She bit out.

"Certain," Noam suggested so softly none, but Hadhi could hear. The word brushed over her neck and warmth enveloped her entire being.

Hadhi sighed. Longing to turn into his arms and feel his lips again. Longing to feel his arms close around her. It was the strangest thing; she should have been offended or embarrassed by the help, but not from him. Everything he did made her want him more. She nodded, softly moving her head only enough for him to see.

"Certain that when I was a great hunter, he would..." she stopped herself saying the word *love;* it had no place in a conversation of her father. "*Approve* of me. He gave me greater challenges, and I met each. Hungry for his approval." Hadhi wanted to be able to conceal the rage in her voice and the self-disgust, but she could not.

She could tell from the quiet of the women before her that they were listening. Could see her cousin hiding behind a table and her father's spy trailing them quietly. But Noam wanted to rewrite this story so that she was safe, and more than anything, she wanted that as well. So she had to keep speaking.

"When I was eighteen, I was known as a great hunter; butchers, traders, my uncle, all sang my praises. But never Baba. So when he took me to a ridge near a lake, with little brush, two trees, and a short way between me and a lone gazelle and he told me to kill the gazelle, I knew it was a test. It was too easy a kill. But I did not question; I brought the animal down in one throw of my spear. And I waited, again.

"And so did he," Hadhi said and felt her tone darken. She was speaking truly quietly now. The women around them no longer even tried to hide their interest, staring outright. But she continued the story. "When we heard the mewl of a young cheetah, Baba smiled. He held out his own knife, 'go get it,' he said."

Noam stiffened beside her. "He sent you to get the meat, knowing there was a predator nearby?" He demanded, appalled.

The women ahead of them looked at Noam like he was a fool. Everyone in Maltuba knew her father. They knew he was the monster in this story. Though its details had been unknown to them moments ago, it must seem commonplace. Noam did not know her father.

"It was a test," Hadhi lifted her chin, revealing her scars in all their gruesome glory so that his gaze followed the line. She felt his eyes on the scars again. Felt his pulse pound and his tightly held rage. She loved that he felt so strongly for her, but she also felt shy —unworthy of his care.

The women before them crossed under the arch into the dining room; there was still a growing gap between those eves-droppers and the line and a gap between Hadhi and the eavesdroppers as well. As they entered the room, the noise of others talking gave Hadhi a bit of comfort; her words might be lost in the jumble.

"Everything was a test. But I was not scared. I was...*hungry*. This would be my moment." Hadhi actually laughed at her younger self. Her mouth opened. She thought she would tell all. This was the moment, and Noam's ears the safe place where she could relive the whole sordid tale. He would not mind if she stumbled over the right words in his language.

She could see it all. Staying downwind of the cheetah, so as not to be smelled. Rushing, but not so fast as to draw its attention, trying to keep her heart from pounding and heating her blood as that would surely give her away.

She even reached her prize safely. Then she looked up and found herself staring straight into the eyes of her soon to be mauler. Her soon to be victim.

She saw it, but not everything came out when she spoke. Here—and not in that moment of true peril—Hadhi felt her heart pound, and her body begin to sweat. Here she was vulnerable. Then she had faced only death.

"I was not scared," Hadhi repeated. "Not when the cheetah snarled over my kill. Nor when he—bent, to attack." Hadhi's body hunched a bit to show what she meant. "Nor when I saw it was a cub, learning to hunt from its parent. Not even when he did this really." Hadhi's fingers trailed lightly down the long healed scars from her right cheek to chin and down to the edge of her right shoulder. She saw the claws racing at her again. Her own fault, then and now. She had been so eager then, glancing up to see if Baba was impressed, and the animal took advantage, swiping out at her with a force that could have killed her had she not fallen away as quickly as she had. She had only gotten scarred as a result of her faults then, but if she revealed all now...

Hadhi knew Noam was not here to stay. If he were, he would have said it. He was not here for her. He was here for his friend. But if she told him all she might lose that tender way he looked at her. Here she was again, so hungry. Always so hungry.

"If anything it made me want more to win. It was a fight for my life. So I...won." Hadhi spoke truth again, and again it was entirely incomplete. Won was not the right word. She did not know the right word in Fairy. That moment had not been a contest or a source of pride. She survived, and she had done everything her father asked, but it was no triumph.

"I took home a gazelle, two cheetahs, and these scars. I believe my father had a few offers of marriage from butchers after. He bought Mzaa fine jewelry off the paws and one of the pelts. The other pelt came home. It is part of Asha's dowry."

"Asha's?" Noam demanded, sounding truly offended for her.

And though she felt nothing that was good or happy inside, Hadhi smiled at the tone. "When it was cleaned and brought home Asha was fond of it, so Baba gave it to her."

"You killed it."

Hadhi shrugged. It was long since decided, and honestly, she never wanted it. Though it had wounded her anew to see it given to Asha. Hadhi loved that Noam took her side immediately. "Everyone was impressed, if disgusted to see me, covered in blood and ugly scars."

"Not ugly." Noam interrupted. "No part of you is ugly, ethuri."

Hadhi released a breath of wonder and amusement. He could not be real. He must not mean it. There was nothing beautiful about her. But her heart burned and she lost the ability to speak for a moment. When she could speak, she hid inside the story again. Tucking that startling and tender endearment inside.

"I...my father was not impressed. I should have won without getting scarred. But I do believe he liked the scars. They marked me as..." *a monster,* her mind whispered, "powerful," she finished aloud.

Hadhi wondered at herself and the ugly she hid with her omissions. Maybe they were worse than outright lies. Noam would never really know about the blood of so many animals that had drenched her, dripping off her and mingling with her own blood. The smell of her, like death, like meat. He would never understand about the hours of shaking and tears as she was bathed and sewn, as she pretended to sleep. It was impossible to explain what she had felt hearing the mewl of the anguished mother as Hadhi threw the dead cub off herself, and before the mother had time to attack, launched herself at it as well. It had been such an anguished, heartbroken sob that mewl. It haunted Hadhi for months; it still did. Every time she heard it, though it was an animal sound, it slashed into her shouting *monster.*

Why hide it?

It would be better to scare him away now than to wait until the loss would score her soul? Was she so hungry, even for praise she knew to be false?

She felt a lovely dancing tingle in her fingertips and glanced down to see Noam's fingers gently tangling with hers. It was so softly and so subtly done that no one could have noticed. Hadhi had never felt so cherished. Noam saw the girl the monster had killed, and somehow he was—reviving her.

Hadhi shuddered, more afraid than she had been in years. Because he was waking that hungry little girl and she was so desperate not to lose his tenderness. What would she do to keep him? Who would she destroy? She knew no tender ways.

"And—" Noam spoke softly, releasing her hand as he glanced around the room. "Had you done it all yourself? Or had he stepped in to protect you?"

Hadhi's tongue stopped working. She had no idea how to tell the truth without revealing the whole of the monster that lived inside of her. That she had killed three animals in as many minutes and barely felt a thing. The gap in the line grew as she searched for the words, but she could not think what to do about it.

"No," Noam answered his own question heavily. "It was a test. And you rose to the challenge. You saved yourself. Alone."

Hadhi wanted to cry, wanted to beg him not to ask her to explain it. Wanted him not to look at the story too closely and know she had killed a mother and her child. For nothing but her father's sport. Not to see how truly monstrous her father made her. She felt tears crowding her eyes, in fear of losing him. But Noam did the most foreign thing in the world.

He shook his head softly, and his lips moved. "I am so sorry." She had to strain to hear him, but his words slid through her like a peaceful balm. "You're safe now, Hadhi."

So quickly she wondered if it was magic, he brushed his lips across his own fingers and touched them to the scars. He pretended to be brushing something off of her, but Hadhi was too busy curling up in the gentle intimacy of the feeling to care if anyone saw.

His hand drifted to his side, and they walked forward once more, as if nothing had transpired, but something had. Something profound. Something magical. With a tiny touch and four gentle words, Noam did exactly what he said he wanted. He went back in time and stood beside the girl, too foolish to realize that fighting for her life should be more important than earning someone's approval. He stood beside the girl so hungry she barely felt the pain of her face ripped open. He stood beside the girl who had been feeling like a pit of death that must eventually consume the world, a girl becoming a monster. Noam stood beside her and made her feel just a little bit human again.

FIVE HOURS TO MIDNIGHT

It was already seven, yet Azize had not finished the receiving line. Or perhaps he had. The king had returned to the hall. Where was Azize?

A hand tugged lightly on Asha's arm; she glanced down at the little girl Zawadi and nearly cried with relief.

"You're here!"

"I said I would be. Come along," the little girl said impatiently. "We should go where no one will see."

"Zawadi, I do not think this will work?" Asha whispered desperately. She was vaguely appalled at herself. She was never so easily defeated, but she couldn't stop worrying.

"You would prefer to remain as you are?" Zawadi asked, walking ahead of Asha.

"Maybe I should."

"Alright," the child stopped in the middle of the hall and turned to Asha. "The truth is better, I'm sure."

"But," Asha grabbed for the little girl's arm, stopping her where she stood. "Will you give me magic again?"

She stared Asha down a moment, her silvery eyes swirling. "If you wish."

"What if I just wish for him?" Asha said and was thoroughly appalled with herself. Before Zawadi could open her mouth to answer Asha waved her hand in the child's face and pulled her shoulders back.

Be your own greatest ally.

"No." Asha shook her head. "He either wants me as I am, or he is not worthy."

"Good for you, dear." The nymph patted her hand soothingly, her child body doing nothing to conceal the condescension of her tone. "I will come to you some other time."

"No," Asha shook her head. The thought of losing both Azize and the magic left her aching and hungry. She *must* have the magic. It brought her to life as nothing else ever had. "I want the magic. Five hours just like last night."

The child grinned, gapped toothed and incredulous. "I thought you wanted him to take you as you are."

"I do. And part of me is that power. It might not be mine for always. But while I can have it *I must*. Don't you understand?"

The little girl wobbled her head this way and that, and her eyes narrowed with an odd sort of dislike. "Yes, I understand. You are Zuberi's daughter. Bend down child, let me kiss your head. I will give you the power you desire."

The moment the child's lips brushed her head Asha felt every cell tingling and dancing. She came to life! The world around them, only a moment ago bright and alive, looked vague and indistinct and somehow... larger?

"Wait!" Asha cried out, looking down, horrified at her tiny arms and hands. She was not in her body any longer, but in a child's, as Zawadi had been.

"Would you look at that," Zawadi's voice chuckled out of Asha's body.

"No!"

They'd switched forms! Impossible.

"You tricked me." Asha sobbed, felt the power of her fear and sorrow and shock overwhelm her being as the magic had.

The nymph gave her a superior look that was all too familiar, but for the silver beginning to devour her irises. "I told you magic skins never appear the same way twice."

"But—you looked like this," Asha wailed.

"Yes but," she chuckled harder, "you didn't. Five hours, as promised, the magic knows best. Ha!" The nymph all but danced away in Asha's body, leaving the real Asha alone, sobbing in the hall.

Asha felt the power coursing through her and tried to latch onto it and change herself as she had the night before. Tried to change her gown, her bare feet, her body! But nothing worked. She could feel the power offering her wonders, but every bit of her was too frantic to latch onto it. Fear and anguish and shock, rolling over the magic like tidal waves and brushing it away before Asha could grip it.

Asha shoved her face into a corner, her body wracked with sobs. The power coursing through her, strengthening even her emotions; her body could barely contain them. Oh she understood now how too many hours of this would kill an ordinary human. Every sensation, every emotion was so large, how could they help but alter the world? Was this what magic truly was?

"What is the matter, dear?" Hadhi's oddly soft voice so startled Asha that she forgot herself. She spun around, throwing herself into her half-sister's arms.

"Oh, Hadhi, she tricked me." Asha buried her head in Hadhi's neck and cried.

Hadhi was clearly startled, her arms remained stiffly outstretched around Asha for a long frozen moment. Then with an almost grateful sigh, Hadhi closed her arms around the child's body and rubbed a soothing hand down her back.

"Who tricked you?" Hadhi asked kindly, but there was a core of steel in her voice, as Hadhi only used when she was defending Nuru. "What did they do?"

"Just look at me," Asha pulled out of her sister's arms and waved at her childish body. "Azize will never give me a chance to win him, looking like this."

Hadhi struggled not to smile. Asha couldn't understand why, of everyone here, she was turning to Hadhi for comfort. Or why Hadhi was listening. Or how she'd never noticed that Hadhi was quite pretty when no one was watching her. But Hadhi had an oddly comforting presence. It reminded Asha of being seven, when she had fallen ill and Hadhi was her nurse.

Baba couldn't come near for fear of catching ill himself. And Mzaa Jauhar refused for fear of infecting baby Nuru. But Hadhi sat by Asha's side constantly, soothed her restlessness, fed her broth, warmed her chills, told her stories. She was a good nurse.

Odd, Asha had not recalled that until just this moment.

"Well," Hadhi shook her head. "Are you very sure you want to marry the prince?"

Asha was taken aback. Hadhi should be crowing over her sister's defeat, rejoicing that Asha did not have a chance now. Even if she did not recognize her, what was Hadhi doing comforting a rival? Asha would never do so. It so startled her that she had to stop and consider. Why was she reacting so wildly to the threat of losing Azize's attention? Did she want to marry him? After only one night. Or was the magic strengthening even those feelings?

"I don't know," Asha admitted. "He seems wonderful. I think he could love me. I need so badly to be loved again. But I do not know him very well."

"No one does," Hadhi agreed softly.

"I only know that I need him to give me a chance. I don't understand why Zawadi tricked me. She promised me help."

"It seems to me, if you have been welcomed into the ball, the prince must give you a chance," Hadhi offered cheerfully. "At least you want him for himself. Let me have a look at you," Hadhi lifted Asha's arms, examining the thin, fraying fabric she was wrapped in. "This must have been very lovely in its day, but what do you say to borrowing some of my dress?"

Asha released a breath. She stared at Hadhi, disbelieving. "You are kinder than I expected."

"Of Sour-faced-Hadhi?" She asked with a bitter smile. She looked away, shifting her hands through the different layers of cloth that made up her gown. Most of it was too well sewn to come apart, but her hands reached for the bloom at the shoulder, the touch of green Asha had suggested Nuru add to conceal some of her sister's scars. There she found a seam to tug.

"The name my sister Asha gifted to me." Hadhi kept her eyes on her task. "It is all I am known for."

Not once before when Asha called her sister by that name had she felt bad for Hadhi. It was only teasing; surely Hadhi knew that. But Asha felt bad now. Zawadi was right; she did not know her sister well.

"Why?" Asha asked.

"It suits well enough. I am sour-faced," Hadhi said flatly. "I think it must be easier to be sweet-faced when one is happy."

"But—why shouldn't you be happy? You are sisters." Asha asked with a frightening pinch in her chest.

Hadhi shook her head incredulously. She managed to tug the fabric free and snapped it out before Asha. Her own gown looked rather plain now. The extent of her scars from jaw to shoulder were boldly displayed, and the golden threads of the gown made Hadhi's eyes a bit dull. But Asha was surprised to realize her sister was still *lovely*, in a quiet, lonely sort of way.

"My gown is my sister Nuru's work. She has no patience for sewing. Asha does beautiful work," Hadhi said softly and Asha was struck, watching her half-sister's face come alive, and transform into something truly beautiful as she spoke of Asha, not realizing she was before her. Was she not hated by Hadhi?

"Even were we not poor, Mzaa would want Asha's hands alone at the needle. She has a talent for making the world as beautiful as her. All of the world but me." Hadhi laughed. She worked free the little knot at Asha's shoulder, holding her wrap in place, shielding her from the room with her own body as it fell to the ground. Efficiently she set to work wrapping her sash around Asha's small body one and a half times, just under her arms and trying the ends tightly together at one corner.

"There, you see," Hadhi smiled genuinely. "I may not have my sister's beauty or her gift, but I can find ways to show off already beautiful things. All you need now are a few beads."

"Why shouldn't you be happy?" Asha asked again, in a whisper. She felt lonely for this stranger that was her sister. Why had she never wondered before what it was that made her such a sour-faced girl? Hadhi would not meet her gaze.

"I was no one's best beloved." Hadhi's words punched the air right out of Asha, startling a few more silent tears from her eyes in shock. No ones? But...Hadhi had a mother and sister. It was Asha who was alone but for Baba. It was Asha who had been unloved by her own family. Wasn't it?

"Asha is beautiful and intelligent and lively. Everyone loves her." Hadhi chuckled. "I did not want her to come. Not because I wanted the prince, or because I wanted her to suffer, but—" Hadhi breathed in long and deep. Asha worried she wouldn't finish. "She speaks with such confidence and grace. While I stammer like a fool. No one sees me when Asha is near. Azize does not even like her, but the slipper will have fit. She will get away from my mother and be free." Hadhi laughed, but there were tears visible at the corners of her eyes. Asha gripped one of her sister's hands tightly.

"When I woke this morning, I thought I would go to her and embrace her and tell her I am glad she is my sister. But when I am near her, I feel his ghost rise up between us. So much anger and resentment fills my being. So we fight and she feels my...sourness as hatred when it is only...sadness. And nothing changes. Perhaps it is best that the slipper fit." Hadhi sighed heavily, and her expression shifted, so a bit of resentment showed through. "Azize will forgive his dislike; she will make him forget even the mystery woman and marry her. That is always the way with Asha."

Asha had to bite herself to keep from telling Hadhi who she was, telling her of Zawadi's trick. Telling her she wanted her for a sister too. She felt sorry for Hadhi. Asha had never wanted her to feel unloved. There was a long while when Nuru was very little when Asha had been so jealous, wondering why she was not good enough to have a sister's love. And it felt like now was a chance to have that love. But if she told Hadhi, who she was, Hadhi might ruin this adventure like she ruined so many others. She might find a way to stop Azize from noticing Asha. Asha wasn't sure, even with her pity for Hadhi, that she could let her win.

"Do you want to marry the prince?" Asha held her breath, awaiting Hadhi's answer. Awaiting just a little more understanding of the woman with the sour face and the apparently kind heart. Who would have known?

RIPPLES OF MAGIC

BIRD OF PREY

Zawadi watched Asha throw herself into her sister's arms, overcome by the power and the change of form. The magic was taking a heavy toll on her. Zawadi was thrilled to see the child of her destroyer, acting like her father and being pulled apart bit by bit with her insatiable hunger for power.

Or she should be.

She lingered a moment in the shadows watching as her prey turned to the sister she knew so little. Zawadi remembered a time when she had arms to turn to. She watched Zuberi's eldest, though she could not know the girl before her was her sister, crouch down and try to comfort her. It made no sense. She had a dark soul. Perhaps not evil, Zawadi hadn't spoken to her yet, hadn't offered her a wish. But it was dark, uncharted territory that even Zawadi's magic was afraid to traverse.

Yet Zawadi watched her and felt awakened to memories she'd thought long dead. Memories of taking joy in her power. Memories of when the magic was new and she'd turned to other arms in excitement, in wonder—to show off. For some fairy, the change of skin was as simple as blinking an eye, skin slippers; they were known as among the fey. Only as many as three were born in each generation with the natural gift. Zawadi had not been a natural. She was born a fairy of the light, her power tended towards guiding others, but it was not until she was eleven and saw the death flock for the first time that she was drawn to this power.

She had been playing in the Whispering Wood, chasing a bit of a riddle between the branches of trees, back when she had a name given her by her parents, back when she thought the world lovely and uncomplicated. She had raced up the trunk of a tree, and out across its branches, she saw a group of fairy, surround and attack another. She felt the man scream out in pain. Felt it in her soul. She'd rushed towards him, intent on saving him, but he was dead already when she reached him, and his attackers had fled, hearing the high screech Zawadi had not realized was her own at the time.

She'd sat with him crying, then she felt the birds above her; a flock of dark birds, their wings and tails so thick they looked like robes of death billowing in the air. They swooped down beside the dead man and their feathers split apart, creating a whirlwind around them before reforming into dark gowns and shawls over their heads as they became women. Mother Bird was the first to move, she looked down at them and glanced behind her.

"Wren, bless this victim's wish." At her words, a young woman in the back of the gathering rushed forward and lay her head against the dead man's whispering and the air about him glowed.

Mother Bird watched Zawadi silently observe the process. When it was done, Mother Bird crouched before her. "That was quite the cry you let out, Oriole," she said, a soft smile tilting her wrinkled lips.

"That isn't my name," Zawadi had said, and it hadn't been.

"Not yet," she agreed, her voice a scratchy chuckle. "But it could be. Our flock has been longing to grow, and then I heard your cry."

"But...I am not a skin slipper."

Mother Bird shrugged one tiny shoulder. "This magic is merely a skill to be learned. But to cry out like that, to pull the entire flock back into the Fairy Realm from which we were banished, only to bless one dying man. To have in your soul such a desire to right wrongs— These are qualities that cannot be learned. These are powers unseen in the flock for generations. The flock will welcome you, should you choose to join. Should you not, we still will watch you grow with great interest."

It had been the most startling, exciting thing she'd ever heard. And for years after she joined, she'd met each new challenge with enthusiasm and joy, and the same excitement she'd had when Mother Bird asked her to join. It was beautiful, the other women were her sisters and her friends. They traveled the world offering wishes to the dying so that their wills might live on past their lives.

It had been beautiful.

Zuberi's eldest turned, revealing the scars on her neck. Zawadi shuddered, feeling her own scars hidden by this borrowed skin, but forever marring her being. Zawadi wasn't here for new members of the flock.

She should not look back on those years with pleasure and nostalgia. She should never have joined. The old Mother Bird was wrong to welcome Zawadi among them, and even more a fool for making Zawadi mother of the flock when she united with eternity. She had been mistaken about Zawadi; her power wasn't to right wrongs. Her power was to guide a soul—to its doom.

Now she would use that power on the family of her enemy since using it on her enemy was impossible, though she was not finding this as satisfying as she'd expected.

Zawadi spun around and set her eyes on her next quarry: Jauhar. She crossed the ballroom straight for the woman. This skin was the perfect form with which to torture her. Zawadi used to feel the magic choose a skin and know it was one that would bring the most comfort to the dying. Not so now. She'd come to Zuberi's beloved in the skin of the women he'd slain. Selecting them herself, so they might take part in the vengeance. But this— Asha's skin—Zawadi couldn't tell for certain if it was the magic that selected it or her own will. And it made little difference. It was serving her purposes well. She began to feel the moments that formed Asha, the moments that connected her to Jauhar. She didn't care what force had selected the skin, as long as it served her purposes.

Zawadi was no longer the girl she'd been born, nor the young woman she chose to be, nor even the mother bird she had been for a time. She was a new creature, created of suffering and rage. She was Zawadi. A bird of prey, cloaked in magic to appear harmless as she dove in for the kill.

INSATIABLE HUNGER

Jauhar watched Asha approaching and let her hand slip over the shoe hidden in the folds of her dress. A shock struck her. Jauhar yanked her hand away, narrowing her eyes on Asha. Asha knew, didn't she? She knew Jauhar had the slipper. She was attached to the magic somehow.

"Sabra," Jauhar said without taking her eyes off her husband's favorite. "Would you see if you can find Hadhi? She shouldn't be sulking in corners."

"I am sure she isn't sulking," Sabra said gently. "But I will be happy to check on her."

Sabra walked away just as Asha came to a stop before her.

"Wanted her out of the way so you can chastise me in secret?" Asha taunted cocking her head to the side in a perfect imitation of her father.

Jauhar carefully drew in a breath. Asha wouldn't see how her games effected Jauhar. She despised this child. She existed only to torture her. Asha's every movement was reminiscent of one of her parents.

"What should I have to chastise you for? Have you been disrespectful to our hosts?"

"Of course not, *Mzaa*." Asha expelled the word like a dart, her eyes tearing into Jauhar's flesh. "But you've never needed reason before."

Jauhar's soul laughed bitterly, but her face gave nothing away. "Have I not? Tell me Asha, do you think I should not defended my daughters from you?"

Asha smiled smugly. "They need more defense from you, *Mzaa*. Do you remember when I was little, Nuru wasn't born yet, so I must have been four, making Hadhi nine. We were preparing for the Service of the Sands, you had pulled Hadhi to you, to adorn her for the festivities. You painted her eyes for the desert, her cheeks for the jungle and her lips for the sea. She looked *so* happy."

Jauhar caught her breath audibly; her body felt as though it was being sucked back into that moment. Her hand fought to reach into her pocket, fought to crush the beads of the slipper, hoping it would take Asha's power away. But Asha spoke on, as though it were merely a conversation, as though she knew nothing of the magic forcing Jauhar to relive the moment.

Hadhi was a chubby warm bundle on her lap, sitting in the light outside the hut. Already Hadhi was a bit dourer than her age should have made one, but still sweet. Still hopeful enough to try time and again to please her parents. She sat still as Jauhar painted golden sweeps around her eyes, and a cluster of green dots on her cheeks, and the single strip of blue right in the center of her lips from the top to the bottom. Didn't fuss or fidget when the beads got caught in her curls and pulled a bit. She made a twisted little face, but she didn't complain.

And Jauhar was soaking in the sweet moment as mother and daughter. Then out of the corner of her eye, Jauhar saw Asha poke her head out of the hut to watch with her bright, hungry eyes. Rama's eyes.

"I watched as quietly as I could," Asha said. "I didn't make a noise or a mess. I wasn't in your way. I hadn't insulted Hadhi, nor stolen Baba's attention. But when you were all finished and I asked if you would dress me, do you remember what you said?"

Jauhar set Hadhi away, ripping her eyes away from Zuberi's other child and focused on her own.

"You look lovely, Hadhi. You must dance the desert dance tonight and not be too shy, alright."

Hadhi began to bite her lip, rather than answer, and Jauhar's hand flew out of the air, slapping her daughter on the shoulder. "Do not spoil your paint." She'd snapped. Tense all over and angry for no reason she could explain. She glanced out the corner of her eye and saw Asha waiting silently at the entrance to the hut.

She was usually such an obnoxious, loud thing. Always underfoot. Always eating up everyone's attention. But when she was at her neediest, she was quiet. Then she came to you and sucked you dry, stealing every bit of your energy. Just like her mother. It wasn't right. It wasn't fair that she have to look after that woman's child.

Jauhar barely even heard Hadhi promising to stay clean and neat. Hardly heard her own words as she dismissed her. But she could remember quite clearly the redness in Hadhi's eyes and the downcast look, when only moments ago she'd looked happy. They'd been alone and happy together. Then Asha stuck her head outside and ate up every joy.

"Mzaa," Asha said sweetly as Hadhi crossed to the hut. "Will you dress me too?"

Jauhar remembered Hadhi smiling at her sister, urging her towards Jauhar as though they were real sisters. And even that had enraged her.

"I haven't time. It takes an age to make Hadhi look presentable. Have her help you." Jauhar snapped. Hadhi flinched at those words, though she'd not flinched at the slapped shoulder. Hadhi took her half-sister's hand and led her away. Jauhar wanted to scream, and rant, and sob. She wanted to rush over and pull that little girl into her arms and kiss her and tell her how sorry she was. She wanted to tell her she was safe and loved and protected, that nothing would ever harm her. And what had made Jauhar the angriest was that the child she wanted to comfort was not her own.

Asha smiled at her now, as if she knew the truth of the story. The truth Jauhar would never say. That as much as she hated how well Zuberi loved Asha, what built the most distance between them had very little to do with him. Jauhar looked at this girl and she saw her mother. She saw the sweet woman she'd hated for four long years. The woman she'd wished dead every day until she died. She looked at Asha and Jauhar saw only her own ugliness, and she hated this girl for that.

"Do you know what I wished all—" Asha broke off as Bayo interrupted.

"What are you two discussing so intently," Bayo interrupted the pair cheerfully.

"Hadhi's *wild* success of course," Asha said sarcastically, and at once, the other woman chuckled. Jauhar said nothing. She was able to move again and her hand shot into the folds of her dress to squeeze the slipper with all her might. It stung still, but Jauhar did not let go. She waited until both women stopped laughing to look Bayo in the eye.

"We were discussing a family matter." Jauhar nodded away, not even addressing Asha's quip. Bayo raised a brow, but departed quickly, offended or afraid; Jauhar didn't care which.

"What I remember," Jauhar snapped. "Was you, from the time you were born trying to eat up all the energy and attention of anyone around you. You wear a being out, Asha. Try to win the prince; I challenge you. You might even manage it. Though it would be easier if you still had the second slipper." Jauhar waited for her quiet taunt to strike. Asha showed only vague interest. And Jauhar rushed on. "Even if you manage it, it will make no difference to you. His love will never be enough for you. No one's love is. Your hunger will wear him out, just like it did your mother."

Asha should have flinched, should have been cowed and broken and weak. But she smirked, and Jauhar felt old and dried up and ugly. The only thing that kept her standing was how brittle her bones had become, stiff from years in this same angry pose.

"What I remember," Asha said, leaning in next to Jauhar's ear, as they both saw Sabra approaching. "Is that I loved you once. But love just slides right off of you. I don't think there is anyone who loves you now. Don't you wish there were?"

Jauhar wanted to lash out and strike Asha across the face, but the shoe she gripped wouldn't let her, and Asha kept right on talking.

"I used to wish I could change things between us. But I make better use of my wishes now. Tell me, *Mzaa,* what do you wish for?"

Sabra stopped beside them, speaking without even waiting to see that she was interrupting a conversation. Jauhar barely heard her, shaken within. She hated Asha so much. Would she never be free of her?

◆⟡◆⟡◆⟡◆⟡◆⟡◆⟡◆

A CHILD OF MAGIC

Noam returned to Hadhi's family, bringing the plate of refreshments he'd promised. Her mother looked to the plate and back to Noam, her eyes full of suspicion.

"I thought certain you would never come back, as long as that took you," Jauhar remarked.

"I was somewhat afraid of that myself." Noam agreed brightly pretending not to notice the cold suspicion.

He wondered if Jauhar had seen him take Hadhi's hand outside. She had been nothing but polite yesterday, nearly cloying, but today she clearly wanted him gone. Noam had asked Hadhi to return with him, but she'd said she needed to be alone for a moment, and he understood. He'd needed an extra moment himself.

That story—Noam could happily find her father and murder him if he weren't already dead. He'd never appreciated his own father more. Bad enough the things Hadhi knew her father had done to other people, but who did that to their own child? No matter how good a hunter, no matter how much you wanted them to learn.

This family's dynamic was very complicated; Noam couldn't quite wrap his head around it, not for the least reason being that Hadhi's mother seemed far kinder to her husband's other wife than she was to her own children. He wondered if it had been the same while he lived. Nothing Noam had heard of the man implied that anyone should miss him, but Noam knew love wasn't that simple. You could love someone and hate them at the same time. This entire family seemed delicately poised to strike out at one another. Having brought the food, he felt like maybe he should take his leave and mingle more, perhaps just keep to Azize's friends.

Sabra smiled at Noam in a way that made him think she knew every uncomfortable thought going through his mind and was amused by them. At least that's what he thought her smile meant.

"I saw Hadhi down the hall, if you would like another dance," Sabra said.

"I would be very pleased to dance with you if you will have me. Or any of the lovely ladies surrounding me now," Noam said easily.

Asha raised a skeptical brow. "Really, we thought you had a preference," she teased.

She seemed different from when he'd met her earlier. For one thing, he had not expected to find her with her family. Azize's foreign friends were mingling amongst the guests, but she had not approached one of them, though Azize's description of the girl made her out to be extremely curious. There was something off about her, but Noam couldn't quite put his finger on what.

"Come to know me so quickly, have you?" Noam probed.

"You are not so hard to puzzle out," she commented.

Sabra rolled her eyes, resigned, and Jauhar looked away with a tight expression. Perhaps this was how Asha always spoke, but Noam was certain this was not the same girl he met this morning.

"Enlighten me," he said it lightly, watching her. What felt familiar and so...sinister about her?

"You are a lie."

"A liar," Noam corrected.

She shook her head slowly, her eyes full of mischief and her smile eerily familiar. Her family was watching her strangely now too. Sabra's eyes widened, darting from Asha to the hall she'd said Hadhi had ducked down. And Jauhar's gaze was narrow and suspicious. Noam had a sinking feeling that the conversation was putting Hadhi's family in danger. It shouldn't matter; he'd found very little to recommend this family. But Hadhi loved them and perhaps he was just too angry right now. He knew Nuru loved her sister, and Sabra seemed to care a bit. But her mother and her sister Asha— Noam didn't know that he cared for them at all, but this was definitely not the Asha he met this morning. If she hurt Hadhi's family, Hadhi would be hurt as well.

She had her face and her self-confidence. But this was the nymph. Why, he wondered was she honing in on him now? But even as he was realizing it, he saw Jauhar looking her over with sharp eyes. Did she suspect who the woman was?

Noam smiled playfully, glancing at the other women to release some of the tension in the air. "There is a rather popular phrase in my home that applies here, I think, *like recognizes like*."

Sabra forced laughter, but her eyes darted uncomfortably between Asha and Noam. Jauhar was breathing heavily and staring with an intensity better suited to her eldest daughter; she was *very* suspicious of this girl. Not just suspicious, enraged.

"Will you dance with a lie, Asha?" Noam challenged.

She smiled knowingly, nodding her agreement. Noam hesitantly reached out for her arm; the second their skin touched, he felt the charge of magic rushing beneath her skin. He was right. They walked calmly out to join the dancers, neither saying a word.

Once they were on the floor, Asha dropped her pretense. "It is sweet the way you protect these women. Strangers, that you do not even like," she laughed. "Would they do the same for you?"

"Would it be as sweet if I were certain they would?" Noam's muscles tightened.

"Ah, nobility. Your father would be so proud." She chuckled.

"Which one?" Noam muttered and regretted it at once. Her eyes glowed with amusement and her smile spread. He didn't trust that smile. "You are not the same woman you were this morning."

"So perceptive. But then I find all children of magic are fascinating beings," she said, sounding truly intrigued by him. She sounded far older than the girl whose body she was inhabiting.

"I am not a child of magic." Noam glanced around, lowing his voice.

"Don't worry," the nymph leaned close to whisper. "No one cares what you say or do. You are no one."

Noam stiffened and she patted his hand soothingly. "Don't offend so easily. There are benefits to being invisible. Invisible people always know their true friends, and they tend to know their power."

"I am not *magical*," Noam bit out, wanting more than believing it to be true. He had no idea who his real father was, no idea what strangeness coursed through his veins. He only knew that whatever it was kept him from his father's love, from his home, from being...visible.

"Magical? No, you are not. But you are *the result* of magic. All spells leave remnants behind." Her voice became vaguely more sympathetic and she gazed down the hall to Hadhi crouched comforting a child. "One cannot only curse; there is a balance to magic that exists nowhere else. Wielder's of magic are forced to make up for the pain caused by association with our victims."

"What does that mean?" Noam demanded.

Her eyes returned to his sparkling. "It means your father was cursed for his treachery; as your mother was the curses tool, the magic had to give her some joy. Which she had of your true father, *trust me*. Mayflies are wildly talented lovers." She tittered.

Noam ground his teeth across one another, hearing in the back of his mind that infernal song the village children used to taunt his mother with whenever she walked through town. To taunt Noam with.

> *Stayed the mayfly for a spell,*
> *In springtime, when the evening fell.*
> *He sought a woman's company*
> *And built for her a fantasy...*

The woman before him smirked like she knew every thought in his head. She probably did. Many fey creatures could read minds.

"And of course there was the joy she took in you." She winked. "And *you*, as the byproduct of the curse, suffered from your father's lack of love and had to be blessed with a bit of," she tilted her head back and forth, deciding on the right word. "Luck."

"You mean like the luck of having my father hate me? Or perhaps you mean the luck of befriending a man who would lead me to the sort of woman I could love, and then having that woman need my help to win my friend?"

She chuckled like this was the most diverting thing she'd ever heard. "You can sense magic, so it hasn't the hold on you it did on your parents. You sense the greatness within other beings. The things people did not sense in you. And look at you, even as you want her for yours, helping your love get what she wants. A child of magic, such oddly powerful and loving beings you are. So unlike both humans and the fey."

Noam bit his tongue, not sure what he wanted to say. Magic might not have as great a hold on him as it did on others, but that didn't mean it couldn't be made to hurt him. And though she seemed to have nothing against him, Noam was certain this woman was here for some mischief.

"How long have you had Asha's body? How long do you intend to keep it?" Noam asked.

The woman shrugged. "I have had it, and will keep it for as long as it was lent to me."

Noam began to seriously doubt she was a nymph. They were said to be playful, adventurous spirits, well known for tricking men, but rarely for harming them. She was some sort of fey, but nothing so innocuous as a nymph. From this being, he felt a much more malevolent spirit.

"What is your plan here?" Noam asked.

"None of your concern." She ran her hand up his arm in a way that made Noam cringe.

"I will not let you hurt them."

"Hurt who?" She asked. "Or don't you know? My kind never hurt without cause."

"No?" He snarled the question. "Not without making it up, with a few nights of passion or a bit of luck."

She threw her head back and giggled like a tickled vixen, but it was all a show. For what purpose he couldn't say, but when she lifted her head and stared at him, there was only calm certainty and a warning.

"I have no cause to harm you, Noam, son of a magic spell. But I will if you interfere. I have a debt to settle."

"I know Azize; he has done nothing to cross you."

"Indeed, he has not," she agreed easily. "Yet."

"You cannot punish a man for what he might do," Noam bit out.

"My quarrel is not with him. He has not been harmed."

"No? Are you not driving him mad with that slipper?" Noam demanded.

"In fact, no." She preened superiorly. "That is no spell of mine. And you have warned him to stop touching it."

"What do you want?" Noam demanded, just as the music came to an end. The woman only smiled and removed her hand from his arm.

"Heed my warning, the way your friend, even now, fails to heed you." She walked away to rejoin Hadhi's family before Noam could stop her, but what would he do if he did? He had no magic and no certainty of what she wanted. Perhaps she didn't mean to harm Hadhi's family at all; perhaps Asha's was only a convenient body. But he did not think so.

He needed to figure out what she wanted. He had to protect Hadhi, as no one else ever had.

WHY SHOULDN'T YOU BE HAPPY

Hadhi could not understand why she was so comfortable talking to this child. Lifelong secrets were just spilling out of her. And she could barely move, not from the girl's most recent question, but from again and again, *why shouldn't you be happy?* As if it were so simple. As if it were merely a choice she had made. As if the monster within would let her be anything as precious as happy. Well, maybe it would. It let Zuberi be happy, but he had reveled in the darkness, and Hadhi would not.

When Noam had asked her to return with him to her family, Hadhi told him she could not and slipped away. The truth was she felt so different inside, so much better. She did not want to go near Mzaa and Asha and have them peck away at anything lovely inside of her. She had walked down this hall thinking exactly the same question this girl kept asking her: *why shouldn't* she *be happy?*

What truly should stop her from embracing, not what was most efficient for her family, but what would make her the happiest? They might never be rich nor powerful enough to force Uncle Kafil to release their dowries. But they could be happy. She could live with Noam; they could have a tiny hut, just one room to share for sleeping, with all their cooking and bathing done out of doors. Perhaps Noam was used to nicer things, but Hadhi could provide for them. She had not been able to hunt since they got word of Baba's death. But she could now. It need not feel ugly or like a show of her power. It would just be a necessity, providing for those she loved. She might even make them rich at it. And Azize was his friend; he might convince Uncle Kafil to be kind to the other girls simply because he cared for Noam's happiness.

Why was she allowing Mzaa's plans to rule her the same way she had Baba's?

But Hadhi was getting ahead of herself. Far ahead. Racing into fantasy, which was nothing like her. Noam liked her, perhaps even desired her, but that did not mean he wanted to share his life with her. He barely knew her; he knew nothing of the monster. She had only hinted at the tiniest of her sins. He was too fine for her. Yet she wanted to—surrender to all that was beautiful in the world and dance into his arms, follow where he went, because every turn he made was so lovely. Every turn Noam made, made Hadhi feel safer.

Hadhi could be happy—with Noam. But could he be happy with her? It seemed like even when she wanted to surrender some part of her could not let go. She had been on the verge of going to him, having the time with him, even if it was not alone, then this little girl appeared, and something in Hadhi just had to help her.

She always had a soft spot for scared little girls, but there was something different about her. Something that felt like, if Hadhi helped her, she could salvage a bit of her soul from the monster's clutches.

Perhaps it was because she remembered sobbing in a corner after Asha had made her think she wanted her along to play, when all she wanted was someone to blame for her mischief. Or perhaps she reminded her of Nuru— or Kiho.

Hadhi shuddered, biting her tongue, the pain reminding her she was in the here and now. She heard Asha's laughter from the ballroom and glanced over her shoulder. With the rest of the room, Hadhi watched her half-sister dancing with Noam. Running her hand up his arm like he were hers. Gazing into his eyes flirtatiously. Why? Hadhi cringed, wanting to bellow, wanting to rush into the ballroom and physically shove her sister away. Why did Asha always feel the need to best Hadhi? It was so easily done there could not be much joy in it. Here Hadhi had been talking about her regrets over their strained relationship and Asha was off in another room trying to remind Hadhi and the rest of the world with her that no one was as desirable as her, that there was nothing and no one she couldn't have.

"Want is for girls like Asha," Hadhi snapped. She turned back to the girl, yanking two strings of beads from her own throat. Forcing calm Hadhi wound the beads together around the girl's bald head. Tying it firmly at the base of her skull Hadhi leaned back and admired her work. "You look like the princess you long to be."

"But..." The girl's face dropped, looking down at her finery and back up at Hadhi with wide wet eyes. "I am only a child. He will ignore me."

"If the slipper fit, he owes you a dance. Be like Asha," Hadhi said bitterly. "She would never stand for being ignored. Go to the prince and demand your due."

"She wouldn't, would she?" Slowly the child's lips grew into a dazzling gap-toothed smile.

Hadhi had no idea why this child thought she needed to win Azize, but she knew enough of the prince to know the girl was safe with him. So Hadhi played along, trying to help her feel special. The girl tilted her head to the side, examining Hadhi.

"Why shouldn't you be happy?" She asked for a third time. "If you want to be."

Hadhi shook her head; this was the oddest conversation. "Go find the prince and demand a dance."

"Don't you want to dance with him?"

"I can wait."

"And she will not wait alone." A deep jovial voice startled Hadhi and had her stomach dropping so far, so fast she thought she might vomit the bit of food she'd only just consumed.

How had she failed to feel him approaching? To feel him watching?

"Your Majesty." The little girl sunk at the knees, smiling sweetly for the king as he emerged from behind a column at Hadhi's back.

Hadhi stood slowly, forcing her rage down. She faced the king, pushing the girl behind her as subtly as she could. When he only stared at her, Hadhi remembered herself and curtseyed, grinding her teeth.

There were two men in the world she held in absolute hatred—well, only one now, and he stood before her. It was easier to think of him only as the king when there were others around him. But alone, with that knowing smile on his lips, Hadhi saw her father's friend. Another who took delight in evil.

"Run along and find the prince, child. I will keep Hadhi company." King Enzi said his words laden with interest.

The child, apparently oblivious to the evil before her, nodded happily and ran away. Hadhi wanted the king far away from this little girl but...she did not want him near herself either. She curled her fingers into fists to keep from reaching out to stop the child, just so she would not have to be alone with this man.

"Your father would be truly surprised to see the woman you've grown into, Hadhi," the king smiled, and his eyes roved over her leaving a wake of slime.

"Good," Hadhi snapped impolitely. The king's gaze shot back to her with wide amused eyes.

"I have not said if it would be a pleasant surprise," he commented.

"I do not care." Hadhi snarled, wanting to offend him. Wanting to be away. He might cast her entire family out over her rudeness. But it was all she could do to resist grabbing the ornamental sword at his waist and cutting him open, leaving him bleeding on the ground, so the only evil thing left in Maltuba was her. She could do it too, with Kiho so fresh in her mind. It would be an easy kill; the king was so sure of his own importance, his own safety.

You have to know your moment.

Hadhi hated agreeing with her father's echo, but here, in the palace, she would be caught. She could not walk away hollowly, with his blood on her hands, and bring home a dead animal to cover the sin. Here she would die for her evil. And her family must suffer as well.

So Hadhi struck out with her words, "I never earned his approval while he lived. Why should I care to when he is dead? I am only pleased that not all his goals will be met."

King Enzi threw back his head and laughed. He was not a quiet man, had no reason to be. All conversation in the ballroom fell away as people strained to see who had amused their king.

His laughter slowly receded and he reached out a hand, sliding it from Hadhi's scarred shoulder to her wrist. Her body wanted to shiver in revulsion wanted to flee, but Hadhi held herself stiff by force of will. He enjoyed fear.

"Come, Hadhi, dance with your king. I will tell you all the ways you have disappointed Zuberi's hopes."

A scream of absolute hatred shredded Hadhi's insides and the monster within fought to lunge for that sword. But every eye was on her. She could no more kill him than she could refuse him. She felt the stares, some of hatred, some of jealousy, but out there in the midst of everything, she felt warmth and concern.

She felt Noam.

Hadhi let her eyes find Noam; he stood with her family, Asha, Nuru, Sabra, and Mzaa all watched her. *Everyone* was watching. Mzaa looked excited beyond her wildest dreams.

But as Hadhi took the king's hand and walked stiffly into the ballroom, her eyes were all for Noam. She wanted to run to him, and flee this place, forever. But the monster wanted to pounce on Noam and rip him apart. This was all his fault.

For as long as she had known what King Enzi was, Hadhi had rejoiced that she never caught his notice. Now she was on his arm, with her skin crawling and her entire being clambering to hide or to kill. And it was all Noam's fault. For making her forget, for making her want to be noticed. For making her, for however brief a time, desirable to the world.

She could see Noam was realizing what he had done and regretting it.

"Your father expected you to be married by now, Hadhi. Is that sour face tripping you up?" The king wanted to draw blood; clearly he knew that name bothered her. He wanted her angry, and what made Hadhi angrier than she could control was that he was getting what he wanted. "Some men do not mind a sour-face."

"Some prefer a cowering one," Hadhi whispered darkly.

The king examined Hadhi in a way that made her want to rip off her own skin. Why had she said that? There was one edict her father had made that she followed without question, to never let the king know what she had seen, to never even hint at it. And now he might guess. She wanted to kill him. As she had wanted to on that day. If only Baba had not stopped her, everything would be different.

When she was about ten, Hadhi followed Baba when he left the house one morning without Asha. He rarely left Asha at home anymore. Hadhi thought this must be her chance, to be loved as her sister was, to share a bond with her father.

Hadhi had tried so hard over the years to forget that day, to put it behind her. She felt so sure if she could only forget, then she would be happy, and beautiful, and anything other than what she was. But there was no forgetting.

She had followed. Wanted to be loved, like Asha, wanted her father to want her company as he did his best beloved. *That day should have put an end to such desires. Maybe it had for a while, but the monster was growing within, and the monster always wanted love.*

"Just what did you mean by that, Hadhi?" the king asked, drawing her back into the present.

Hadhi tried to find someone in the crowd to latch onto. But Noam had his back to her and Hadhi refused to look at Nuru while she was in this man's arms. If she did, she would have to kill him, no matter the consequences. She would not let him touch her sister.

That day— She could not get it out of her head!

Father had gone to Ahon's house; everyone knew who he was, the man who spoke out against the king. Hadhi followed at a distance, but half way there she knew where they were going. She had not fully understood why, but she knew it was for trouble. As soon as the king and his guards joined father, she knew.

Still, some part of her had been shocked, horrified to see her father shove Ahon's wife into their home, kicking her aside so he and the guard could enter. Hadhi knew she did not want to be there, but she could not move. She crouched on the ground and waited, silently begging her father to come out of the house for everyone to be well.

Then she heard the screams. Cries for help, for someone to stop. It was a child's voice. A little girl's. Hadhi was up and racing for the house before she even realized—

"Hadhi," King Enzi shook her a little. Hadhi was so tangled in her memories and her revulsion at this man, she could not help the small jerk to get out of his arms. He chuckled and tightened his hold, drawing Hadhi closer. "Sour-faced-Hadhi, your father's girl after all, are you?" Hadhi cringed internally, too lost in her memories to be her stoic self.

"Sticking your nose in where it doesn't belong."

"I would like to return to my mother," Hadhi said in a small voice and hated herself. Why should she, the monster, escape this man when Kiho had not?

"Show more spine, Hadhi," the king instructed, dismissive of her fears. "That's what earned you the attention of your king."

"I do not want your attention." Hadhi was shaking inside, from the guilt, from fear, from holding back the monster. She would give anything to kill this man.

"Not yet." Baba chuckled.

Hadhi did not remember how she had gotten into the house, or how Baba came to catch her before she reached the king with her rock in hand. All she remembered was that evil man, hurting that tiny girl. She wanted to kill him; she wanted to strike him as hard as she could, over and over. But her father had lifted her into the air, carried her away, before the king even realized she was there. He dragged her outside, yanking the rock from her hands as she began to beat her father with it, trying to be free. She still heard the screaming.

Her father just chuckled. "You're a little monster, aren't you? Baba's monster." He carried her away from the house to a clump of trees and put her on the ground, holding her in place by the shoulders when she made to run around him.

"You have to stop him!" Hadhi shouted, trying to shake free.

"He'll only do the same to you, Hadhi. Is that what you want?" That stopped her. Froze her inside and out. How she wished that had not stopped her. *"You'll be my monster, Hadhi. And you'll have your chance at vengeance. But not yet. You have to know your moment. Now run home, and never speak of this again."*

He just turned around and walked back into Ahon's house, trusting she would do as he said. But she could not. Could not move. Not to run away, not to help. She just stood there, hearing the screams and hating her father and the king, and most of all herself.

He was right. She was a monster. Only a monster would just stand there, crying and wanting to die, or to kill, but doing nothing.

Whatever she got now was no less than she deserved.

"Do you know, Hadhi." The king's breath threatened her neck. "I wonder now if he wasn't hiding you from me. Zuberi would know the pull of a woman like you."

Hadhi cringed, and in her mind, she saw her father again, telling her to run home, telling her never to speak of it. Yes, he had been hiding her. Hiding them all. And how did she thank him?

"Come, Hadhi, where's that voice? You have my attention; that is power. Use it."

"I only want Azize," Hadhi lied. She did not want anyone ever who reminded her of her father, or the king, or the monster. Did not even want Noam. She did not want to be touched or looked at. Or to exist. Right now, all she wanted was death. Death for all the evil things in Maltuba.

The king scoffed, "he's for Asha. You know that. You're a bit of a distraction, and his notice of you will goad her to work for his attention. Their marriage has long been a plan of mine and your father's. You must know Zuberi never wanted power for you. If disappointing him is what you are after," he whispered through a twisted smile. "I am your only hope."

SECOND ACQUAINTANCE

Asha waited on the back stairs that led to the ballroom. She knew the palace fairly well, from her time caring for Queen Imara. Even before that, she'd been here often enough. She could remember coming to the palace with her father. When she was little, he held her high on his shoulders. When she grew a bit older, she was racing ahead of him and giggling the whole way. Or holding his hand, swinging it forward and back, competing to see who could swing it the hardest.

"Will I be queen, Baba?" Asha had asked once, swinging Baba's arm so hard it hurt her own shoulder, but she barely noticed too happy just playing the game. "Is that why you take me to the palace so often?"

Baba laughed. "You can be queen if you like, beloved. Is that what you want?"

Asha hadn't wanted to disappoint him; she swung his hand a little harder as she shrugged. "Maybe."

Baba stopped suddenly, dropping Asha's hand; she was afraid for a moment and nearly assured her father that of course she wanted to be queen and sit around all the time, with nothing to do. But Baba grabbed her around the waist, lifting her high he began to spin, faster and faster, so Asha's legs hung out behind and felt like they were being tugged at by invisible beings.

"Is that what you want?" Baba laughed as he spun, his eyes so bright and loving Asha had to giggle with him. "Do you want to be a queen, little one? Do you want to marry a prince and rule Maltuba? Do you?"

"No!" Asha squealed.

"No?" He demanded, seeming to spin even faster. "Then what do you want?"

He gave one last giant chuckle and set her on the ground, kissing the crown of her head. He braced himself on his knees, panting and grinning, and staring expectantly into her eyes.

"Adventure," Asha whispered. As he grinned wider, she grew bolder. "I want to see the world. I don't ever want to be still and quiet and respectful!" Baba chuckled as Asha listed off Mzaa Jauhar's most frequent admonishments of Asha. "I want to know everything and be just like you Baba."

Baba stood with a proud smile. He nodded to her like she wasn't a child, but a peer. "That's my Asha," he said. Taking her hand up again, he led her forward. "I take you with me to the palace, because you are my best beloved, and I want the whole world to know it. And because within those walls, Asha, is the means to have all those adventures you want."

Asha leaned against the wall in the body of a child and felt tears slipping down her cheeks. She missed him so much. Missed being loved. Missed feeling alive. But as she looked up the staircase, waiting for Azize to come down and feed her the love she'd been missing, Asha wondered about things she hadn't before.

I was no one's best beloved.

Asha was so used to Hadhi's disapproving gaze following her. For as long as Asha could remember, she'd been jealous of Hadhi. Hadhi, who had a mother and father and a whole sister. She had everything. Baba taught her to hunt, though he taught no one else. He'd even given her his own knife when she was first learning. Hadhi had so much, even aunt Lolia had preferred Hadhi. How could anyone with so much love be so angry?

Asha felt a bit bad about those feelings now. Maybe Hadhi didn't feel as well-loved as Asha thought she did. Jauhar had never been gifted at sharing her feelings.

The oddest thing had happened as she was talking with Hadhi, she'd heard her half-sister's words, and she'd seen her past in a way she hadn't in years. She'd felt it, like she was living it again. But—so differently this time. She'd remembered watching Jauhar and Hadhi together. Jauhar was dressing Hadhi for a celebration, holding her close, smiling. Asha remembered wishing she could feel something like that, wishing she could remember her mother's arms around her. She had even wanted it from Jauhar, though she went out of her way to let Asha know she was not her mother, though she was cold to her more often than not. Asha had been so desperate to be loved by a mother that she'd even asked. Begged really.

And Jauhar, in usual cold fashion, had dismissed Asha, told her to go, refused her anything she asked for. But tonight, as Asha was remembering it, she recalled the pain that had attacked her, and she also remembered Hadhi. Hadhi had looked almost hopeful when Asha asked. She'd wanted her sister to be happy, and when Jauhar had refused, Hadhi had been sad—for Asha, leading her away by the hand gently.

I haven't the time; it takes an age to make Hadhi look presentable.

Asha hadn't really remembered that until now. Perhaps she was so used to Jauhar treating Hadhi terribly that it made no impact. No. Hadhi had never been Jauhar's favorite child. But Asha hadn't had a mother's love at all. And no, Hadhi wasn't Baba's favorite either, but he had a special relationship with each of his girls. He bragged about her hunting skills.

Sometimes.

"She can't sew, she can't do beadwork, and she's such an ugly thing." Baba laughed. "She had to make herself useful somehow."

Asha wasn't meant to have heard that. She and Baba teased Hadhi playfully at home, but this was different; it felt mean.

She rushed to the butcher's hut, hissing low, "Baba, you can't say such things where people will hear you."

He'd even looked a bit ashamed for a moment. Then he'd narrowed his eyes. "Your sister doesn't need your defense, Asha. Does she protect you from your Mzaa Jauhar?"

She didn't. He was right. And even though it had made her a bit uncomfortable, she'd taken the lesson to heart. Now it was all confusing. She felt bad for her sister; she didn't want Hadhi to feel unloved. But she couldn't escape the feeling that most of Hadhi's problem wasn't other people; it was her. She wanted love to look a certain way, so she didn't know that she had been loved by Baba. Hadhi could be happy if she would stop being so angry. She had more love than Asha ever had; why was Hadhi the angrier of the two of them? She wasn't forced into doing all the work to care for her family; she wasn't used and mistreated.

Asha's mind was shouting it, while her heart was...crying. Crying for her sister's pain. She felt jittery just waiting here. She hated waiting for Azize. But she couldn't leave. She needed him to love her; she needed him to feed her need for adventure.

Asha heard footsteps on the stairs and glanced up, pushing off the wall to block the bottom of the stairs. "Azize!"

Azize nearly tumbled backwards in shock. He caught himself on the wall and stared opened mouthed at Asha, in the body of a child. She began to grow self-conscious, scuffing her bare feet along the palace floor.

Azize nodded his greeting. Straightening, he walked towards her. "Was I not fast enough for you? You did demand I bathe."

Asha shook her head; she had done no such thing. But perhaps Zawadi had. He was never going to believe her, was he? He was never going to accept that she hadn't done all of this for the purpose of shaming him.

"Azize, I have to explain," Asha said softly, "but I do not think you will believe me."

"Believe what?"

"That I never meant to trick you. I have always *longed*," Asha stretched the word out, needing him to understand. Needing him to forgive her and accept her. "To see the world. To have an adventure!"

"Ah," Azize looked away heavily. "You never wanted me to seek you out?"

"Of course I did," Asha answered, utterly lost. "I left the slipper... *Wait*! You know who I am?"

"Who else would demand two dances?" Azize asked with a broad grin, holding up the second slipper. "And demand that I bathe first to be rid of the smell?"

Asha didn't know what to say. She could find Zawadi and kiss her! Why hadn't she trusted her when she said the magic knew best? He knew her, even without the shoe. He knew her. Well, he knew she was the woman he'd danced with last night; he didn't know the real her. But she could explain. She could make him understand.

She giggled. "I thought you would never know me."

"I would know you anywhere." Azize ran his hands along the slipper.

Asha liked the words at first. But they weren't true. She tilted her head sideways, narrowing her eyes. "You did not know me earlier."

Azize fumbled, shaking his head. "I wasn't sure. I won't make that mistake again." He examined her for a quiet moment before asking hesitantly. "Will you always look...so?"

Asha giggled slightly; she notched up her head with an arrogant smile. "Magic skins never appear the same way twice."

"And you are magic," Azize said with a bit of awe.

"For as long as I can be," she nodded excitedly.

He laughed briefly. "I traveled nearly the whole world and never once saw a magical being, and here you are, in the last place I ever would have looked."

Asha grinned. She'd felt nearly the same thing when Zawadi showed up. That she never would have looked for magic here, that it was so odd that she didn't even have to leave home to find it. "Isn't it wondrous! Only think what you could do with such power, Azize!"

"Leave my slipper for you to follow," he teased.

Asha let out an indelicate little snort of laughter. "I never knew you were funny."

"What did you know?"

Asha looked heavily away.

Have you ever seen your sister before this day?

I was no one's best beloved.

"Not so much, I'm afraid," Asha admitted, more to herself than to him. There was a great deal she had never seen. But it wasn't too late, the magic could do such wondrous things. Asha raised her eyes to Azize excitably. "But I want to know. I want to know you. What would you do, if you had magic for only a few hours? If you could do anything, what would it be?"

Azize shook his head, "If I'd had the magic, looking out on that line this morning, I would have wished to find you." He tilted his head a bit sheepishly. "And perhaps to run away."

She laughed, "you always did want to run away."

Her remark seemed to unnerve him a bit. Azize examined her more closely.

"Tell me your name," he commanded, walking down the last few steps so he stood only one higher than her, but towered above her. She had to step back and tilt up her head just to see him.

Asha hadn't planned to just blurt it out, it would take a bit of explaining, but the longer she delayed the more it would seem she'd intended to fool him. "Is that what you would do with the magic now? Learn my name?"

"Tell me your name," he repeated. Saying nothing more

"Zawadi says the magic knows best. I thought she tricked me, but...I should have asked for an adventure. I should have asked to see the world." Asha said, growing itchy again. For a moment, just having him here to talk to had sated the hunger, or...it had obscured it. But the longer they spoke, the more the hunger built.

"What did you ask of the magic?" Azize asked slowly.

"To feel its power, to wield it as long as I can," Asha answered honestly. "And again and again, for a way to come here— to you."

He laughed. "Coming here is easy; just walk in the door. My father would welcome any woman in the hopes of keeping me."

"Yes," Asha said with a jealous snarl, her eyes scraping across him. "And you would welcome only the pretty ones. I should have had more imagination. My father would be ashamed of me, using a wish to come to a ball."

"It was your wish." Azize pointed out. "I let other women in seeking you. Please, tell me your name. To my soul, I am certain if you do not tell me tonight, tomorrow we will both suffer."

She shook her head slowly. "You will not want to see me."

"I do not care who you are. I only want a way to find you when the magic changes you once more."

Asha felt her lips spreading wide, felt air rush in-between this child's missing teeth. "What would you do with the magic now? I want..." Asha broke off. Her fingers traced the bit of gown and beads Hadhi had given her. And all she could think of were all the things she hadn't seen before Zawadi came. "I was not a bad person before, but I have been a bit of a brat. People have reason to resent me."

"At your age," Azize teased.

Asha didn't laugh. "This body is not mine."

"I know." Azize crouched before her, like she was a child, even as he denied thinking any such thing. "The woman I danced with last night had no malice in her. Only passion, and life and wonder. There can be no cause to resent someone like that."

Asha felt a tear or two sting the corner of her eye and smiled at him gratefully. "If only that were true. Let me show you I am not the girl I used to be. Tell me what you would do with the power, Azize."

Azize rose, shrugging as he went. "I would be my own man. Not bound by my father's edicts, or duty or Maltuba. I would run into the night and escape the sea of women. I'd..."

The more he spoke, the more Asha smiled. He wasn't so different from the boy she remembered after all. He had never liked attention. He still wanted to run away.

Asha grinned to herself a little, though his desire to leave Maltuba was one of the things she had most disliked as a child. Maybe it was Asha who had changed, because she didn't mind his desire to flee so much anymore. She was happy to give him what he wanted.

The hall grew light, as she sent out her power. She nurtured the light, shaped it. The power flowing through her as though it had always been a part of her, and she was just now learning to reach it. She moved them with it. Until the walls and the stairs vanished, everything vanished but her, and Azize, and the light.

The world rocked gently to and fro, as the light faded from around them, settling back behind Asha's eyes. They stood on the deck of the same boat he'd tried to run away on eight years ago. Asha grinned up at him smugly.

"Well, are we going to run away then?"

THE HERO

"She shouldn't be dancing with him," Noam said under his breath. He hadn't meant to speak, but he watched Hadhi with her hand on the king's arm, looking stiff, and shattered and he couldn't stop the words.

"She is Zuberi's eldest. Who else should grace the arm of a king?" Jauhar all but drooled.

Jauhar was too cunning a woman to be fooled by a man like King Enzi, so how could she possibly tolerate watching him touch her daughter? But she was not just tolerating it; she looked overjoyed, almost fanatical in her glee.

Noam had followed the fey woman to Hadhi's family, hoping to prevent trouble and figure out what she was after. Nuru had returned and was glancing between Noam, her mother, and Hadhi, her expression a mess of confusion. Sabra seemed to agree with Noam, but there was a look of resigned fear about her. And about the nymph, there was a mix of glee and intrigue. Noam didn't think this was entirely her doing, but she was enjoying the show. She was eager for some outcome Noam didn't understand yet.

"Why shouldn't she dance with him?" Nuru asked softly. Her mother swatted her in the shoulder.

"Ignore him, Nuru. Hadhi is where she belongs."

"He is not a good man," Noam insisted. He didn't know why he kept trying with her, but...he couldn't stand the idea that there was no one, no one in Hadhi's life who would protect her and put her first. Her sister might love her, but she was trying to protect Hadhi from the wrong things, and in secret, when what Hadhi needed more than anything was to *see* she was loved. And Sabra was too cautious to protect anyone. So Hadhi stood alone and defenseless.

"Go rescue her," the nymph said playfully and gained the eye of everyone in the group. Jauhar gasped. The nymph wearing Asha's skin smiled at Noam and goaded him, ignoring the others. "Imagine how grateful she'll be. You love to be the hero, don't you?"

"Don't you dare." Jauhar latched onto Noam's arm needlessly, as she turned on the girl she thought was Asha. "Keep your tongue behind your teeth, or you will never leave that hut you despise."

The false Asha chuckled softly. "It's you who hates it, I think."

"I am not going to interrupt the dance." Noam attempted to draw Jauhar's attention away from the threat she didn't recognize. "The king hates me already; anything I do would only make it worse for Hadhi."

"I see your interest in her." Jauhar turned her biting eyes back on him. "Everyone sees it. Enzi and Azize would never have seen her without your attention." She smiled with twisted glee, punishing Noam with the truth. "She hasn't the looks nor the personality to tempt men."

"You underestimate your daughter." Noam yanked his arm from the woman's hold, barely resisting the urge to shout his censure.

"On the contrary. Hadhi is a good girl: obedient, selfless even. And more importantly, *strong!*" The word vibrated from the woman, and where at any other time she would melt and flirt, Jauhar drew up her shoulders and stared Noam down. "There is *no breaking her*. Trust me, I watched her father try, time and again." Nuru let out a little gasp, but Jauhar ignored it. "But none of those qualities could win her the attention of men at whose feet women are strewn. But give an unremarkable girl the attention of a desirable man, and suddenly the world desires her." Jauhar beamed as though this had been her scheme and not an accident of Noam's interest in Hadhi.

Noam was sick; his eyes longed to trace Hadhi, to offer her any comfort he could. If even half the things Azize said of his father were true, Hadhi should be nowhere near him. And from the expression she wore, Hadhi knew it. This was all his fault. He'd wanted to see the real Hadhi, to show the world the real Hadhi, and look what he brought about. How was this luck?

"You will not have my daughter." Jauhar continued to beat at him with her words. "Why would she take a bastard when she could have a king?"

Noam drew back, surprised. From the corner of his eye, he noticed the nymph leaning closer with flashing eyes. Was Jauhar her prey?

"Jauhar," Sabra hissed. "This is not the time."

Jauhar laughed. "You are surprised that I know." She ignored Sabra and pressed her advantage with Noam. "Did you think the king would not know everything about his son's traveling companions? And my husband was his closest advisor. There is nothing I cannot know."

"Then you know what sort of man has your daughter in his arms," Noam snarled, disgusted. "Do you care nothing for her?"

Jauhar shrugged, looking past Noam. "A woman of Maltuba can be married to a cheetah or a gazelle. With a gazelle, Hadhi would spend her life slaving to keep him safe. With a cheetah, she will *rule* in comfort."

"And see to your comfort as well." Noam hissed.

"Mzaa," Nuru whispered. "What do you mean a cheetah?"

"Hush, Nuru, you are no use here. Go dance with your neighbors and be happy."

Nuru jerked away and ran from her mother. Jauhar held Noam's eyes coldly until he could stand it no longer.

Noam swept past the woman and out onto the terrace, into the night. He kicked the stone column before him, not seeing a thing.

There is no breaking her. Trust me, I watched her father try, time and again.

Why hadn't he just left her alone? Let her have her secrets; let her fail to catch Azize. She just looked so lonely, so certain of her own worthlessness. He'd watched her sink one little bit after another, with that ridiculous toothy smile, as her mother flirted with him and left Hadhi in her shadow. He couldn't stand it.

You love to be the hero, don't you?

Well he was failing miserably at it.

◈❈◈❈◈❈◈❈◈❈◈

I AM...MAGIC

Asha was shaking from the magic. She hadn't really used it last night. Only for a little trick, a gown, a new face. But when she'd stopped fighting to change her form and stretched out her mind to feel Azize's desires, when she'd let the magic rush forward to fulfill them...

Ohhhhhhhhh. It was *marvelous*. She'd never felt so alert, so alive, so... There were no words!

She wanted to do it again; the *magic* wanted it. Azize was wandering around the deck of the ship, examining it. Any moment he'd recognize it as the one he'd crashed, and some part of Asha was tickled and longed to see that moment. But more of her was awakened by the magic. Out in the night, she felt other creatures, animals, people, bits of life she might never have known existed, just floating by in the air. There was so much and her being stretched towards it all.

She rose from the deck where she'd been laying and let the magic pull her to the rim of the ship, let the night and the creatures in the dark depths of water call her near.

"This is my father's ship," Azize whispered, but Asha wasn't paying attention. "How did you know?"

Asha stared down into the water. There was something beneath the surface, something large and alive.

"Do you think it's a sea monster?" She whispered gleefully; she couldn't say who she was asking. Azize surely could not sense this. Only she could. "Wouldn't it be too ridiculously wonderful if Mzaa Jauhar and Zawadi were right all along?"

"What?" But she didn't hear Azize's startled exclamation.

"If I had my eyes trained too far into the horizon to see what was in front of my face." Asha stood with her toes curled around the edge of the deck and leaned out over the water. She needed to get closer. To see. To feel. And the magic let her. She bent, and though she could feel she was still in a child's body, a body far too short to ever reach, she grew closer and closer to the water. The magic didn't stop stretching her until she hung straight down from the ship, with the small swath of silk Hadhi had given her for a dress wrapped around her again and again as though it was three times as long, it hooked itself around the side of the ship, and let Asha hang safely, with her nose touching the water.

"Wait!" Azize shouted, grabbing hold of her dress trying to pull her back onto the ship. Asha wanted none of that. She was alive for the first time. Her magic rushed out to stop him from yanking her aboard.

"Let go," she giggled. Asha stretched out one of her hands, and danced it along the water, watched the water shift, and light with her magic. "Azize..." she sighed. "I've never felt so. It's indescribable. Do you think this is what nymphs feel like all the time? Do you think they feel the world passing through them, moving around them, welcoming them?" She giggled once more as the dark creature pushed its bulbous nose out of the water to nudge her hand.

"I can't move. Help!" Azize shouted, yanking hard. "Don't let it hurt you. Get back up here, now!"

"I don't think I can." Asha ran her nose along the nose of the creature, and it let out a little cry. A puff of water and air flew into the night, startling a giggle from Asha. "Azize, look! It likes me. Do you want to see?"

She glanced back up at the deck. In this darkness, all she could make out was Azize, with his hands wrapped in the fabric of her gown, his face desperate and confused.

"You want to be your own man, but how can you, if you will not see the world around you?" Asha challenged gently.

"I...I can't let you fall," the words were torn from him with ragged breaths. "I can't lose you."

"I am midnight, and laughter, and adventure," she effervesced. He did not look comforted, only more confused. "And I can swim." She smirked.

The comment startled a small laugh from Azize. "What is your name?" He asked so quietly Asha barely heard it; the creature was rubbing its face along hers, shoving her higher into the air as it rose further and further from the water.

"Does it matter?" She shut her eyes, rubbing noses with the sea monster. "You would know me anywhere."

Slowly, as if terrified with each loosening finger that she would fall to her death, Azize released the fabric. Asha hovered where she was, upside down with her face beside the sea, and her feet in the air, and a long tail of fabric waving in the breeze. Azize shuddered and stepped up to the edge of the ship. He took a heavy breath, watching the whale rub its face on Asha's.

"Alright. Show me the world, Asha."

Asha burned brighter than the sun. Burned from her heart out of her skin, lighting the night. *He knew her!* She spun around, stretching out a hand for Azize. The magic rushed from her fingertips into the air, and pulled Azize from the ship, pulled his hand into her own, so they hung together, hand in hand above the sea.

"You know me," she whispered, and her tears rushed out to join the sea. So much was rushing through her, joy, excitement, wonder, life. She couldn't catch hold of a bit of it. But most of all, where every emotion passed, where every nerve tingled, *magic.*

"Who else?" Azize spoke on a laugh, his free hand reaching out for the whale. "You were always just a bit more than I could handle."

Asha giggled, and her eyes drifted shyly back to the whale. "Do you suppose he was here all along like you were?"

"No." Azize shook his head. "He had to leave home before he could see it."

Asha laughed. "What do you want to see next?" The words rushed out of her. She was too excited to be contained with such a little display of power. "Do you want to go wander in the jungle? Meet the jaguars and the snakes. Or wander the capitol invisibly? Go hear what all those men whose women you've stolen have to say about you? Would you like to taste the *THUNDER?*"

At her shout, a cacophony split the night, shaking the world with its power.

"Ethee oxtia! Asha where did you get this power?" Azize trembled, nearly pulling away from her. "Is it even safe?"

Asha released Azize's hand, and he continued hovering upside-down as she let her laughter spin her around in the air. The whale slowly sunk into the water, as though he were also afraid of her.

"What fun would there be in adventure if it were safe?"

"Asha...shouldn't it be better to live than to have an adventure?"

"Oh, plllllgh!" Asha stuck out her tongue and wiggled it at him, like the little girl in whose body she was clothed. "I'll live. But never like this again! Come along, don't waste our hours. What do you want to see?" She demanded, screaming the words joyously into the night. "I will show you anything."

"Alright," his eyes were round and intense, and beautiful. She shouldn't scoff at his worry. It was sweet; no one had ever worried for her before. But she couldn't waste precious seconds on worry or sweetness. It would be tomorrow in less than three hours. She had a lifetime to live with him before then.

"Show me your favorite spot, Asha."

Asha grabbed his hand once more and let the magic race and roll beneath them like a chariot of wind, dragging them into the night.

SHELTERED BY THE MONSTER

Nuru ran off to the side of the room. Everything inside of her was swirling with worry and fear and doubt. From the time she was very little Hadhi had always made Nuru avoid the king. When Queen Imara fell ill and Hadhi and Asha were tending to her. Nuru begged to go with them and Asha was willing. Even Baba was willing, but Hadhi wouldn't take her along. She'd said she would refuse to go if Nuru was sent; it was the only time she'd openly defied Baba and she was punished for it, going three days without food, sitting in the center of the courtyard day and night. Asha tended the queen alone until *Baba* relented.

Nuru remembered Baba early on the morning of what would have been the fourth day of Hadhi's punishment, walking out to the courtyard where Hadhi was forced to sit. Nuru had been sneaking out to give her sister food since she knew no one else had and she was looking weak. Nuru was annoyed with Hadhi for taking the stance, but she didn't want her ill. Then she saw Baba coming and hid. He'd crouched in front of Hadhi. She jerked upright, for she'd been slouching and swaying a bit. He smiled at her.

"I thought at first you were afraid for yourself, monster, but that isn't it, is it?" Baba asked, sounding amused. Hadhi didn't move a muscle, staring straight ahead. "You've got your Baba's will, don't let anyone tell you different. It is past time you started setting limits." He stood, throwing his last words over his shoulder as he walked towards the wall around the house. "Fine, Nuru stays safe at home. Get cleaned up and go nurse the queen. Your sour-face is safe enough."

At the time Nuru, had been so annoyed that she would be denied a chance to go to the palace that she hadn't really thought about his words or how odd it was that he relented. But now.

A woman of Maltuba can be married to a cheetah or a gazelle.

Nuru watched her sister being pulled around the floor with the king. Hadhi didn't like this dance, the escálaa; you were too close to your partner for her, and Hadhi hated being touched. She was stiff and awkward even when Nuru had taken over teaching her from Sabra. But watching her now, she looked even worse. Her eyes were burning and she kept jerking as if to get away when the king leaned in and whispered.

Nuru shuddered as her sister jumped in his arms. Hadhi was never afraid. Never. She'd been mauled, but she just went back into the jungle to hunt with some of her wounds still stitched shut and her jaw not strong enough to chew meat. She wasn't afraid of anything, but she looked afraid now.

Nuru kept reliving all of the fights she and Hadhi had had today. They never really fought. But when she'd told Hadhi she looked at all men the same...Hadhi had looked at her the way she looked at Asha. Like she resented her. Like she almost hated her. Nuru watched her sister now and realized she had been wrong. That look she'd taken for indifference to men was, in fact, a quiet distrust. Right now, there was nothing quiet about it. She hated the king. She was afraid of him, and...Baba had known the reasons she might be afraid but sent her into his sphere anyway. Why would he do that?

Nuru spotted Shafira again, slipping out onto the balcony. Uncle Kafil's question came back to Nuru: would Baba have consulted them before accepting an offer of marriage? She knew he hadn't given Sabra a choice. Did any fathers give you a choice? Nuru moved towards her cousin. Maybe Uncle Kafil had listened to Nuru; maybe that was why Shafira was here.

Nuru crossed the room, hugging walls and caught bits of conversation between people watching Hadhi or Mzaa.

"I wouldn't be salivating if it were my daughter he was holding that way," Tabia said.

"No, but then Hadhi isn't like other girls, is she?" Oni asked lightly.

"*No one* deserves to be treated to his sort of attention," Neema hissed. Nuru had not even seen her enter the ballroom. When had she come in? Nuru appreciated her defense of Hadhi, but felt a strange shudder at the tone and the expressions the other women exchanged.

Nuru's heart was pounding hard as she moved by them.

"Abiola overheard her in line. She says Hadhi claimed that not only did Zuberi want her scarred, but he didn't even kill the second cheetah like he claimed," Isoke whispered to a pair of women, none of them taking their eyes off of Hadhi long enough to see Nuru behind them.

"That sounds like Zuberi," Nia, Sade's mother remarked, her daughter stood beside her silently, with wide eyes and clenched fists. "Hadhi and Sade used to play together. She was a sweet girl, if not that bright. Then overnight, she refused to leave her mother's or her sister's sides and wouldn't speak to anyone. I asked after her, and Zuberi said she was finally learning her place. And look at Jauhar just grinning as Enzi drags her child around like the newest addition to his menagerie. Poor girl."

Nuru bit her tongue and felt tears stinging her eyes as she finally reached the veranda. She wished she could just run away, run home. She didn't want to hear these things anymore. Nuru ducked out and saw her cousin climbing over the veranda wall to shimmy down a tree.

"Wait," Nuru called out. Swallowing her tears, she rushed forward. "Are you leaving?"

Shafira hugged the tree with her arms and legs. "Baba will want to know this."

"Did he tell you why you must avoid the king?" Nuru asked quietly, leaning out of the railing so no one could hear her.

Shafira's eyes darted over Nuru's shoulder, back towards the palace, then she looked up and down the veranda. "He said...he likes hurting people, and if I was caught, he would hurt me too."

"Then..." Nuru swallowed, touched and also a bit saddened by the thought of her cousin risking injury for them. "Why did you come?"

"Hadhi would have come to watch over me. Remember when we ran away into the jungle?" She grinned. "We thought we were so brave, until it was dark and we didn't know which way was home. And something took our food, and there were snakes—"

"And Hadhi rescued us," Nuru said flatly. Hadhi had come; she'd probably been following them the whole time, even though Nuru had shouted at her about not being any fun. Even though Mzaa and Baba and everyone had said no to Nuru going into the jungle, but it was Hadhi saying no that made Nuru angry.

"I have to go," Shafira said. She shimmied lower slowly. "Don't let the king find you alone." She advised as her feet hit the ground ten feet below Nuru. Shafira spun around and raced off in the direction of the mansion.

Nuru watched her go a moment, then turned around to see the king leading Hadhi to Mzaa. Something had happened to Hadhi's gown; the sash at her shoulder was missing. Had the king done that? Nuru's stomach dropped, she thought she might be ill. *A cheetah or a gazelle.* Nuru shuddered, biting down on one of her fingers to keep from crying. The sash had been shaped into a flower, right where Hadhi's scars were. Now they were left in the open, and all Nuru could think of when she heard her mother's words in her mind was her sister mauled—over and over again.

UNTOUCHABLE

The king led Hadhi to her mother, Asha and Sabra. Luckily Nuru had escaped somewhere. Hadhi did not want the king anywhere near her sister. Noam was gone as well, not that it mattered. Five minutes with the king and Hadhi's skin crawled, her soul shuddered, and her sour face was stuck in an eternal scowl.

The king kept her hand trapped on his arm as they stood together, showing her his power. She had no choice. The best she could do was clamp her lips shut. If he enjoyed her insults, her silence was best. She might still escape. Not that she deserved to.

I wonder now if he wasn't hiding you from me. Zuberi would know the pull of a woman like you.

"Where is the prince we were promised?" Asha teased the king so easily, nudging his arm with the back of her hand, batting her eyes. Was she truly so oblivious? So completely innocent that she did not know evil when it stood before her? Hadhi had never liked the king. Long before she became her father's monster, the king had made Hadhi uneasy. Perhaps evil could only be seen by its own kind. Perhaps Hadhi was evil even then.

"Does he mean to drag us all here only to abandon us?" Asha asked with a pout.

King Enzi laughed. He freed Hadhi's hand only long enough to pat Asha's shoulder. Then latched onto Hadhi again before she could slip away and squeezed tight, making plain her captivity.

Hadhi saw Mzaa noticing the action, but her smile never faltered.

"Do not worry, Asha," the king comforted. "The slipper fit; you will have your chance to lead my son on a merry chase." He laughed. "If I didn't know better, I would think it was you in disguise playing tricks with him last night."

"Sadly no." She laughed. "I am jealous. It would have been fun."

The king chuckled with her, as though the idea of this girl making a fool of his son was a pleasure. Perhaps it was. Hadhi's father only wanted her to be his monster; perhaps this father only wanted his son for amusement.

"Where is little Nuru?" The king asked, making Hadhi stiffen further. Her being transmuted into razor-sharp diamonds; ready to slice the king to bits if his eyes so much as touched on Nuru. "She has such spirit that one. You've raised your daughters well, Jauhar."

Hadhi felt his eyes go sliding across her but refused to look, training her own eyes out the open arch to the veranda. She tasted her own blood, but could not force her teeth to release her tongue. The monster was hungry.

"Thank you, Your Majesty," Mzaa sunk at her knees, but her head remained tilted to the side, smiling up at the king. "I am so pleased you have noticed."

Hadhi observed her mother from some far-off separate self. Her eyelids were half-closed, but her eyes peeked out from her lashes, asking permission to see the king. She always tilted her head so that the long column of her neck displayed the well-worn path straight to her lips. Hadhi could not call up a moment from her memory when her mother had looked at a man eye to eye. She was always contorting herself into some pleasingly harmless shape.

It should not be such a difficult thing to emulate. Mzaa had always said as much, but Hadhi could not do it. Could not bend. Or flirt, or flatter—or surrender. She looked men solidly in the eyes. She could be truthful, or she could be silent. She must always appear strong.

And for what? What had it gotten her?

"How could I not notice such beauty?" The king chuckled. "I must go fetch my errant son, but promise to send Nuru my way when she returns. I so enjoyed her company earlier," he raised Hadhi's hand to his lips, his eyes boring into her with flagrant challenge. "I hope to dance with her before the evening is out."

"Hadhi!" Sabra blurted out so suddenly it startled everyone. Hadhi's narrowed eyes shot to Sabra, only then realizing that her free hand was drifting towards the king's sword. Her hand hesitated. The king stared at Sabra curiously. "Would...would you hold Lin a moment," Sabra held out the baby. Mzaa and the king relaxed, but Asha watched Sabra in amused surprise. And Hadhi could not move.

The king released Hadhi and walked away without another word. Still, Sabra held out her son. "Please, Hadhi," she said more gently this time, her eyes full of understanding and entreaty. She understood what no one else seemed to: that Hadhi would kill the king given half a chance. She was begging her not to, begging her to spare the family the punishment they too would suffer from such an offense. "My back is tired."

Hadhi did not move. Everything in her screaming with suppressed rage. That man was evil, and he was just allowed to live. Allowed to commit all manner of sins unchecked.

"My soul is tired," Hadhi hissed and made to leave them, but Mzaa was not so easily put off.

She grabbed her daughter by the wrist, pulling her to a stop. Mzaa ran a hand along Hadhi's chin. "Smile, my darling. You have just been honored by your king. This sour look does not suit."

Feeling tears run from the corners of her eyes, Hadhi hissed, "he seems to prefer it."

She yanked her chin from her mother's hold and swept away, catching Asha's tiny smirk out of the corner of her eye as she fled. People jumped from her path. Apparently, her sour-face was good for something; it frightened all before her.

Or perhaps that was an effect of the king staking his claim. He had made her untouchable.

Zawadi was utterly delighted as she watched Zuberi's eldest march away. She marveled at the power of magic. Just one wish, well two, but the same wish each time, and look what ripples, what waves, what fractals the magic created.

Who knew shy Sabra was observant enough to see that monster preparing to strike, or bold enough to *stop her!* And Hadhi...she had not even been gifted a wish and look how the magic played with her. Attracting her the attention of two such opposite men, Noam with his blessed heart and Enzi with the festering putrid, mire of evil that lived where a heart should be. The magic even brought that girl to the point of killing another of Zawadi's enemies! Fascinating!

Zawadi would have let her do it too. It would have settled her debt with the two of them quite neatly. Enzi, her next prey, would be dead, and Hadhi would be put to death for the offense and Zawadi would barely have lifted a finger.

Magic! It was so exciting watching it work in a world like this, a world where magic was shunned. It was the most diverting thing she'd felt this age. But now that the girl had not killed the king, he needed to be dealt with. Zawadi had hoped Asha's skin might be distracting enough to get her past the fey bleeders on Enzi's sword, and she knew now that it was! When he'd approached, when he'd *patted her arm,* the fey bleeders had neither repelled her magic nor drained it. In this skin, those stones didn't recognize her as a threat! It was perfect.

Zawadi slipped away while Jauhar was preening to her neighbors over her daughter's *success.* Before she'd reached Enzi Zawadi spotted Kane trailing Hadhi towards the veranda. Silently Zawadi sidled up on his right and leaned out the arch watching Hadhi with this man.

Noam slipped out of the shadows on the veranda to comfort Hadhi, as if that blazing mess of rage and fear could ever be extinguished. Ha!

"What is it about her that attracts you all?" Zawadi asked in a playful whisper, startling Kane.

He grinned slightly and shook his head. Asha's form was easily the most effective one Zawadi had taken. It set so many at ease and so many others on edge; she was a magnificent catalyst.

"Attracts isn't the right word on my part." He remarked. "I am pleased to see your father taught you something other than just playing coy."

Zawadi grinned, playing coy indeed. "I had heard rumors you were my father's man, but I began to doubt when I watched you pining after Hadhi."

Kane shook his head. "What *interests* me about her is how little she makes sense. She moves like a predator; nothing touches her if she doesn't want it to, not light, not bodies, nothing."

Zawadi found that an intriguingly apt observation. Hadhi was... untouchable. Even the magic though it shaped the world around her, seemed unable to truly alter that creature.

"Zuberi's perfect killer." Kane scoffed. "Your father offered her to me. Did he tell you that?"

Zawadi nodded to keep him talking. But... *no*. She had not known that. She still found this man's mind difficult to penetrate. As Zuberi's had been.

"He said I should have the greatest weapon he'd created at my side. Look at her, crying and useless. Does she look like a killer to you? Didn't it frustrate you, how much better he loved her than you? How he admired her? Or didn't he tell you? Zuberi loved his games."

Zawadi said not a word, letting the man rant, letting his chaotic energy paint the screaming, envious thing that should be his soul.

"*I* proved myself. I killed and schemed and planted his seeds of destruction all over the world. But *she* is his legacy? Why? She may move like a killer, but then she just lays down and lets the world trample her. If she hates Enzi, why doesn't she do something more than cry about it? She should kill him. Zuberi would."

For a moment there, this man had seemed observant, but now Zawadi had to shake her head at his foolishness. Everything Zuberi had ever done, every people he decimated, every child he warped, every nation he destroyed was done with the blessing of his king. She doubted Zuberi was afraid of Enzi, but he was afraid of something, the consequences perhaps, that hut he'd grown up in. Something had held him back from killing his king, and it wasn't friendship. Were the consequences what were stopping Zuberi's perfect weapon from killing Enzi now?

Were they what stopped this hysterical, envious, desperate boy from destroying the girl whose place he wanted?

"How could he admire someone so...powerless?"

"We're all powerless." Zawadi prodded playfully.

"I am not." He turned on her then with fiercely defiant eyes. "I make my own destiny."

Zawadi shuddered inside at the echo of Zuberi's last words to her. And her power coiled preparing to simply kill this man, without ever granting him a wish. He was like Zuberi, but he was almost more dangerous, so erratic and volatile. Zuberi had been evil, lacking empathy, and so ravenous for power, but he was always a calm, calculating man. But this one was hysterical. Who knew what might fire off his destructive nature, and if he'd been trained by Zuberi he was very dangerous indeed.

"I *will be Zuberi's legacy*. Once I prove myself to the king, I will be the most powerful man in Maltuba," Kane insisted quietly zealous.

"Is that what you wish for? To prove yourself to the king?" Zawadi asked, reaching out a hand for one of his.

"Yes." The word growled between them, shaking the air.

"Then it must be so." Zawadi kissed the back of his hand with its burn shriveled skin. As soon as her lips touched it, sending out her power to grant his wish, she felt a jolt of agony. Screams ripped through her mind. She dropped his hand and backed away with Asha's smile in place, though her own form was far from comfortable.

She couldn't shake the feeling that she should not have done that.

NO SUCH THING

Hadhi stomped out to the veranda and around the right of the palace, where even the light from within could not touch her. She leaned against the railing, squeezing the stone fixture until she thought it might shatter beneath her hold.

I wonder now if he wasn't hiding you from me.

A hiccup escaped Hadhi, and with it, a sob. There should be nothing in the world capable of making her miss her father. But the words stabbed at her, each jab chipping at the stone Hadhi within who guarded her secrets, her monstrous heart.

"Hadhi." Noam's hand fell on her shoulder. She jerked away, pulled herself further into the darkness. "Don't cry."

"Go away," Hadhi hissed, looking around to make sure no one else was out here. "You should not be here."

"I'm not leaving you like this."

"You should. It is working!" Hadhi laughed bitterly and felt her face growing wet. Why could she not make herself wipe the tears away or make them stop? "Your instructions got me the attention my mother wanted. *Better*!" Her voice screeched, breaking as she tried to force joy into it. "Who would have known Sour-Faced-Hadhi could attract a king?"

"Don't call yourself that," Noam ordered, his voice vibrating with anger.

"Why not? You—do not know me, Noam." Hadhi laughed bitterly, coming undone with the fear and the sorrow. "You think you do because you make me smile or because you saw that there was more to me than one expression. Because I shared a piece of my past with you. But you do not know me. I *am* Sour-Faced-Hadhi— my father's monster."

"Hadhi, I'm so sorry." Noam rubbed a hand over his face, and he walked to the railing, limping a bit, as Hadhi backed further and further away. "I never meant for this to happen."

"Oh, I believe that." She spoke with growing agitation. "Who could have foreseen it? An *unremarkable* catching the eye of the king. No one!"

"You aren't un—"

"No! Not no one," Hadhi screeched. If Noam said anything kind, said she was beautiful or interesting, or anything but sour and angry and ugly, she might just split the heavens with her rage.

Why shouldn't you be happy?

She knew better than to let herself want such things. She knew better, but she let her guard down, and now Baba would be proven right. He was dead, but still, his words and his lessons loomed over her darkening her every moment.

There is no such thing as love, monster.

Why did he always have to be right? Why could his voice not have *died* with him? Why could his evil not have *burned* out of their lives, along with his body. Why could she never be happy? Why could she never be loved? Why could she not love her sisters and have them love her? What had he known that she did not? What—was—*wrong*—with—her?

"My father knew!" Hadhi laughed. She leaned against the wall of the palace as the twisted, painful hilarity overtook her. "My father," she felt the rage untangling her tongue as nothing else ever had. "Who laughed as Asha named me sour-faced-Hadhi. Who called me ugly and stupid and berated my every word when I could not learn his precious Fairy well enough. My father, who smiled as he watched me nearly die and then took credit for a rescue I *had not needed!*" Hadhi snarled, wanting Noam gone. Wanting him to see the evil and leave now so she could fester alone in her rage. "My father who said I was useless when he spoke with other men and told me I would be his monster when there was no one else to hear. *My father* knew the..." she broke off, searching for the words as her stomach roiled in disgust, and anguished tears sprayed the air. "He knew... *the pull of such a woman.* What is that?"

Hadhi marched forward, right up to Noam. His arms were braced on the railing, but as she approached, he reached a hand out. She side-stepped him, and his expression shut down. She wished she could regret it, but she was too consumed. Her being was an angry swirling mass of pain and sorrow and disgust. Her skin was crawling and her soul screaming. She could not bear to be touched. Not now. Not ever.

"What is the appeal of a sour-faced, unremarkable monster?" She begged the answer with a tiny hysterical laugh. "I do not understand. Too stupid, I suppose."

Hadhi waited. It seemed that Noam would just stare at her forever, his eyes seeming as anguished as her own. At least he made no attempt to correct her. She could not have borne that. After a moment, his eyes fell away, and he swallowed.

"You are strong." The words came out hoarse, and he had to cough to clear his throat. "What would appeal to King Enzi is the challenge—of breaking your spirit."

Hadhi giggled and caught her breath, her hand rushing to cover her mouth as she fought the sobs that wanted to escape. But she could not hold back the laughter or the tears racing freely from her eyes.

"Oh, I hate him. I hate him so much." She laughed.

"Hadhi." Noam caught onto her shoulders; she did not shake him free this time. What was the point? She had no control over anything. She never had. Any moment she had felt in control was an illusion. And it was not as though Noam's warmth could reach past her skin. She was all, and only cold—hard. "Run away with me. I will take you anywhere. He can never have you."

Hadhi laughed even harder, unsurprised when Noam's hands fell away. "I did not mean the king." She shook her head; this should be obvious. "I meant *my father*. Zuberi. A great man! Right hand of the king. *Weapon* of the king. I hate him," the words came out as a sob, wanted to be a scream, but she did not have the breath.

"I thought it would go away when he died. I thought I might like him better in death, come to love him perhaps, like you love yours." She chuckled through her tears, watching Noam's eyes grow round and nearly frightened. And she had not even told him the half of it. "You do not know me. But he did." Hadhi's hand climbed into her hair, shoving the hot mass up off her face and gripping it so tight she was nearly pulling it out of her skull. "I was his monster. He was hiding me, biding his time." She bent at her waist with laughter, but that was not far enough.

The hilarity dragged her down into a crouch. She released her hair to hold onto her ankles with crossed hands and panted as if she had run for miles. How she longed to be someone else. To be *anyone* else.

"I hate him so much. But he was hiding me. I should be grateful. I should love him for hiding me, right?" Hadhi asked, her gaze searching the stone walkway for answers.

"No!" Hadhi shouted, answering herself. "It was not for me! Not because he loved me," she shook her head, could not see the world before her, only her father's eyes the last time she saw him, that look of betrayal and...pride. "He *did not* love me! I was just his monster, that's why he hid me," she whispered.

"Hadhi." Noam said only her name. He knelt in front of her and closed her into his arms. It should be comforting, warm, and beautiful. He cared for her. But Hadhi could not feel it. Could not feel anything but the rage, and the fear and the horror—Baba was right. He was always right.

"I am glad he is dead, do you understand?" Hadhi insisted. "I *celebrate* that. The world is better for it. I am glad he is dead. I am glad. I am glad." She repeated it over and over, lost track of how many times she said it, the words lost meaning. She just lay there, with her head against Noam's shoulder and tears streaming down her face, repeating the words. "I am glad he is dead."

"It's alright," Noam whispered every time she said it. "It's alright." Then, at last, when she was too tired to speak any longer, he said it again. "It's alright, Hadhi. I love you."

And something broke within her. Came completely undone. Her sobs returned, powerful and aloud, shaking her to her core. She felt it all rising within, loneliness, anger, resentment, hatred, self-loathing, but over it all, fiery and bright and at last— *love*.

It was beautiful, and she wanted to reach out and pull it into her heart. But her heart was an ugly thing. There was no place for such beauty in her.

There is no such thing as love, monster. Not for creatures like us.

Hadhi fought with everything in her, shoving out of Noam's arms so suddenly he tumbled back, striking his head on the railing. His eyes popped open, wide and wounded. She backed away, shaking her head, and pushed to her feet.

"You do not know me," Hadhi whispered once more and took off running around the veranda. She did not stop running. Did not look back. She just ran. And ran. And ran. Perhaps she would never stop.

AUTHOR'S NOTE

Dear Reader,

When I began the first draft of *The Battle for the Sky* I had no idea what important roles language and the ability to express oneself with confidence, would play in the story. I had originally envisioned a very different heroine. I expected this to be Asha's story, just a light adventure with something sinister lurking in the background. But Hadhi wanted to be heard. She *fought* to be heard, no matter how hard it was for her to express herself, changing the story in my head and shifting around the skies until her voice eclipsed every other.

Once that happened I needed to give her a unique inner voice, so I created a language. It should have been a much smaller project than what I made of it. I planed to make up a few essential words, gzufiga, ethuri, and of course kuffik, because I desperately wanted to have curse words only I understood. So I would write a few key words and a few connectors, no big deal. But the more I wrote the more I needed. Until I had a collection of no less than five-hundred words in my fake language, and only six of them are curse words, I swear. I had a few common phrases, and even the beginnings of a small guide to my entirely useless language.

It was at once a frustrating and ridiculously fun experience. I particularly enjoyed coming up with the curse words, finding the phonetic combinations that best expressed the feelings I wanted to convey! It made me smile every time. The entire language writing process was very enlightening. It made me think deeper about the society, how they were put together, what is essential to them, how they emote. I invented many more words, customs, and legends for this story than have made it into the novel, but I needed to, and I didn't even realize it until I began.

Now I know the bedtime stories that Rama shared with her daughter, and Hadhi. I know the stories Nuru would collect from neighbors. I know

Sabra's prayers, and what once inspired Jauhar. I know their world and their love for it.

The whole process reminded me of something I tend to take for granted, my ability to communicate. It is so rare that I have to stop and filter my thoughts through a sieve of *what words I know*, rather than what I truly mean. But Hadhi feels that constantly and it feeds into a number of her insecurities. I hope you will be as patient with her as my dear Noam and wait to hear all she has to say, the ugly and the beautiful.

While the rest of the language is of my own invention, the words for father and mother: baba, and mzaa, are in fact Swahili. Baba and mzaa are remnants of my original draft when I still saw the book as Asha's and I had gone looking for another word for father, because I didn't think papa, or daddy, or any of their variations suited a little scene I had written. Baba is used as father in many languages, but *mzaa* is the word that led me to Swahili. I love that word, the feel of it when spoken, its appearance on the page, and now that I've used it for Jauhar, the beautiful tension it creates. So I couldn't be parted from those two words and built up the rest of the language.

I hope to share more of the language, and the legends of Maltuba with you in the remaining volumes of the *In the Shadow of a Monster* trilogy, but for now I shall part with you leaving behind a common Maltuban phrase or two, and my favorite invented curse word for your enjoyment (but I won't tell you what curse I'm using. Guess!)

Daku uli. Thank you.

Uzaok!

Nin kup uvaasha thioon uli.

May the spirits preserve you.

Dalila Caryn